WHITE CARGO

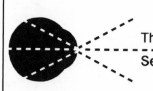

This Large Print Book carries the Seal of Approval of N.A.V.H.

WHITE CARGO

STUART WOODS

THORNDIKE PRESS

An imprint of Thomson Gale, a part of The Thomson Corporation

Detroit • New York • San Francisco • New Haven, Conn. • Waterville, Maine • London

THOMSON

━━━━✦━━━━ ™

GALE

LIBRARY OF CONGRESS CATALOGING-IN-PUBLICATION DATA

Woods, Stuart.
    White cargo / by Stuart Woods.
        p. cm. — (Thorndike Press large print famous authors)
    ISBN-13: 978-0-7862-9388-9 (alk. paper)
    ISBN-10: 0-7862-9388-8 (alk. paper)
    1. Large type books. I. Title.
PS3573.O642W49 2007
813'.54—dc22   2006101634

Published in 2007 by arrangement with Simon & Schuster, Inc.

Printed in the United States of America on permanent paper
10 9 8 7 6 5 4 3 2 1

This book is for
Pitts Carr
who made it necessary
for me to learn to fly.

1

Wendell Catledge sat up and squinted at the smudge on the horizon. It should not have been a surprise, he thought, but it was. The boat slid smoothly along in the light wind, and even the slight movement made it hard to focus on the shape, but it wasn't a ship or an oil rig, and in the early morning light, it seemed to be pink. He pulled at his beard and ran a hand through his hair, which was a good six months overdue for cutting. Hell, it just might be, it just might be what he guessed it was.

He glanced at the sails, left the autopilot in charge, and climbed down the companionway ladder to the navigation station. As he slid into the chart table seat he allowed himself yet another look at his instrument array. It was all there — full Brookes & Gatehouse electronics, VHF and SSB radios, loran, Satnav, Weatherfax, a compact personal computer, and his own brainchild and namesake, the Cat One printer. That little machine had brought him all this — the yacht, the gear, and the time to sail. Cat had waked up one morning and realized that, after nearly thirty years in electronics, he was an overnight success. He gave the printer a fatherly pat and turned to his chart of the southern Caribbean.

He pushed a button on the loran and got a readout of longitude and latitude, then plotted the coordinates on his chart and confirmed his suspicion. They were south of their course from Antigua to Panama and the Canal, and the smudge on the horizon wasn't all that far off the rhumb line. A tiny thrill ran through him. This is what it's all about, he thought, that little thrill of discovery, pushing back the boundaries, punching through the envelope. He laughed aloud to himself, then he banged his flat palm onto the chart table.

"All hands on deck!" he shouted, grabbing the binoculars and starting for the companionway ladder. "All hands on deck!" he yelled again, pausing in the hatchway, "Come on, everybody, shake it!" There was a rustling noise from the after cabin and a loud thump from the forepeak. He raised the glasses and focused on the distant, pink smudge. It was. It was, indeed.

Katie was the first into the cockpit, rubbing her eyes. Jinx was a step or two behind, having paused long enough to find a life jacket. "What is it, Cat? What's wrong?" his wife demanded.

"What's going on, Daddy?" Jinx yelled, wide-eyed.

He was pleased that, in her excitement, Jinx had forgotten to call him Cat. When she addressed him as an equal, it reminded him she was growing up — had grown up. "Right over there," he said, pointing at the smudge.

Both women squinted at the horizon, shielding their eyes from the sun, which was now just above the horizon, big and hot.

"What is it?" Jinx demanded. "I can only see sort of a smudge."

"That's South America, kid," he replied. "Never let it be said your old man didn't show you South America."

She turned to him, a look of astonished disgust spreading over her face. "You mean you got me out of the sack for *that?*" She turned to her mother and shrugged, spreading her hands.

"For Christ's sake, Cat," his wife said, "I thought we were sinking." Both women turned back toward the companionway.

"Hey, wait a minute, guys," Cat said,

thrusting the chart toward them, "that smudge is the Sierra Nevada de Santa Marta, a little mountain range that goes up to nearly nineteen thousand feet; that's the La Guajira Peninsula of Colombia out there; just south of it is the fabled Venezuelan port of Maracaibo. Doesn't that name send a chill right through you?"

"It sends a yawn right through me," Jinx said, yawning.

"No, wait a minute, kitten," Katie said to her daughter. "Look at it through the glasses. Your father didn't bring us all this way to miss this sort of thing."

Jinx took the binoculars and looked through them at the smudge. "Gee," she said, flatly, "you're right, it's a mountain. I've never seen a mountain before." She handed the glasses back to her mother.

Katie raised the glasses to her eyes. "You're right, it's a mountain. I've never seen a mountain before, either. Wow." She handed the binoculars back to Cat. "Can we go back to bed now?"

"Aw, listen, I know it's early, but you've got to get into the spirit. How would you like to have lunch in Colombia? How about that for a little unscheduled adventure?"

"I thought you were anxious to get through the Canal," Katie replied.

"Well, what the hell? It's not much out of the way, and we need to get that alternator fixed, you know. No more showers or microwave or hair dryer until we can charge the batteries again, and all that stuff in the freezer is going to go, too." The alternator had been down for two days, and they didn't have a spare. "Take a look here, both of you," Cat said, spreading the chart on a cockpit seat. "Here's Santa Marta, just down here. It's a commercial port, and they're bound to have some sort of electrical repair place there."

"Listen, I don't like what I hear about Colombia," Katie said. "All I hear is pickpockets and drugs and stuff. Sounds like a pretty rough place to me."

"Don't believe everything you read in the papers," Cat replied. "Hell, lots of people go there all the time. It's just like any other place; a few of them get ripped off, sure. We've been in neighborhoods in Atlanta that were probably as dangerous as anything in Santa Marta."

"I don't know, Cat."

"Listen, Mom," Jinx broke in, "I don't mind getting ripped off if I can use the shower pump again. My hair is terminally dirty."

"Come on, Katie," Cat cajoled, "we'll be

11

there in time for lunch, we'll get the alternator fixed, and we'll be back at sea again by
dinnertime. What do you say?"

Katie shrugged. "Well, okay," she said,
reluctantly, "I guess I could use a shower,
myself."

"You're on," Cat said, switching off the
autopilot. "Showers for everybody. Stand by
to come about." He put the helm over,
tacked the boat, sheeted in the headsail,
and, using his palm across the compass rose
on the chart, set a rough course for Santa
Marta. The women started below.

"You want some breakfast?" Katie called
back.

"Well, as long as you're up," Cat grinned.

"Oh, I'm up, all right."

"So am I," Jinx echoed. "I'll give you a
hand with the pancakes. You do want pancakes, don't you, Cat?"

"Need you ask?" Katie said. "He really
needs to put on some weight." They disappeared below.

Cat placed an exploratory hand on his
belly. Well, maybe he was getting a little
thick about the middle, but hell, he was
hungry. He wasn't sure what he weighed at
the moment, but he reckoned it must be at
least twenty pounds over his usual two
hundred and twenty. He was a tall man,

though, six-three in his bare feet; he could carry a few more pounds.

He sat back, steered the boat by hand, and tried to think if he had ever been happier. He had not. He had thought he was too old to be this happy. He'd had the boat built in Finland by Nautor and shipped to Fort Lauderdale, where he had supervised the installation of the electronics himself. Katie and Jinx had joined him, and they'd shaken the boat down, cruising down the islands as far as Antigua before reprovisioning and starting for the Canal. Once through, they would take a few days to haul the boat out, scrub the bottom, and make any last-minute repairs before pointing toward the South Pacific. After that they would have another eighteen months of his two-year leave of absence from the business to circumnavigate the world.

Jinx came up the companionway ladder with orange juice and coffee on a tray and sat beside him, bracing her feet on the cockpit seat opposite. She seemed to be wearing only a T-shirt; the girl rarely bothered with underwear, and it made Cat nervous. Never mind that he had powdered her bottom and changed her a thousand times; at eighteen, she was tall, slender, and full-breasted, just like her mother, and even more beautiful — heart-stoppingly beautiful. Cat was afraid that some movie agent was going to capture her out of a university theater production and whisk her off to be a starlet. Cat had a theory that beautiful women were at a disadvantage in the world, that once their looks opened a few doors, they would be exploited and used up while they were young and left with no better alternative than marriage to the richest and least unattractive man available. He had seen these women in bars and around hotel swimming pools, worrying about the sag of their breasts and the wrinkles at the corners of their eyes, contemplating the latest cosmetic surgery. Jinx was a smart kid, and he wanted her to have a career that would give her some independence and self-esteem. When she had graduated from high school, he'd taken her aside. She had laughed aloud at his concerns.

"*Me* a cheerleader, entering beauty contests? Come on, Cat, you know me better than that!"

He was glad to postpone her college for a couple of years and show her some of the world. More than that, he was glad to have her close to him for a little while longer before she flew the coop entirely. Cat didn't know whether she was still a virgin, and he wasn't about to ask her, but he thought the chances were good that she was. They'd always kept a tight rein on her, and she had usually accepted their judgment with good grace. Not that she had been unduly sheltered; she'd had a full social life in high school, but none of the weekend house parties with fraternity boys three and four years older, none of the drinking and drug use. She expressed contempt for all that. There was a quiet wisdom about Jinx that contrasted sharply with her line of bright patter and her extraordinary, dark beauty. There was also a naïveté — Cat thought she was still not fully aware of the effect her bun-revealing shorts and tiny bikinis had on the opposite sex, not excluding himself. For all her native intelligence, she was still very much the child-woman. These two years of sailing were going to be precious to him — the rare gift of an extension of what had always been a remarkably close father-daughter relationship.

They sailed along quietly for a couple of minutes, then, without any warning, she said, "Daddy, what about Dell?"

Cat's stomach knotted at the sound of his son's name. "What about him?"

"Why don't you call him from Santa Marta and ask him to meet us in Panama?

15

You know what a great crew he is."

"I don't think Dell is interested in sailing these days. Besides, he'd probably get arrested going through customs."

"Cat, you need to patch it up with him," she said, gravely.

"Wrong, Jinx," Cat replied, quickly, "Dell needs to patch it up with the world. How can I possibly patch it up with him while he's doing what he's doing? Are we going to have big, family Sunday dinners and worry about the cops busting in on us? Am I going to take him sailing through a dozen foreign ports and have to sweat getting busted in customs every time?"

"He needs your help."

"I'll give him my help when he's ready to ask me for it. It's been rejected too many times." God knew that was true; he had given up thinking about the number of scrapes he'd gotten the boy out of, the number of new schools and fresh starts he'd financed. In marked contrast to Jinx, Dell had always been rebellious, lazy, and surly.

Katie appeared in the companionway with two plates of pancakes and they both shut up.

Cat grinned at her. "Now I remember why I married you."

"You want these in your lap, buster?"

16

Katie grinned back.

Jinx patted his belly. "Yeah, you might just as well apply them directly to the paunch. Why go to the trouble of eating them?"

Three hours later, the entrance to the harbor at Santa Marta loomed ahead. The three of them stood in the cockpit and gazed at the land. To their right, a group of high-rise buildings stood behind a fringe of palms. "That's the beach area," Cat said. "The port is over there to the left, behind that little island. The main town is at the port." An older, more Spanish group of buildings could be seen beyond the beach.

Suddenly Katie said, "Cat, let's don't go in here. I've got a bad feeling about this place."

Cat didn't speak for a moment. Katie had had bad feelings about things before, and she was usually right. "Oh, hell, Katie," he said, finally. "We're half an hour away from getting the alternator fixed. Showers for everybody!"

Katie said nothing.

Glancing frequently at the chart, Cat held his course for the harbor entrance.

2

Cat had expected a marina of some sort, however primitive, but he was disappointed. There was an area to his left that berthed half a dozen modern ships, loading and unloading; there was a mixture of smaller craft around the harbor — a small coaster or two, some fishing boats, and the odd sportfisherman — and tied next to a concrete wharf were four or five sailboats, ranging from roughly twenty-five to fifty feet in length.

With Jinx and Katie standing by with lines at bow and stern, their regular drill, Cat eased the yacht into a vacant spot at the wharf. Jinx had changed into a bikini, and he could almost hear the eyeballs click on the boats around them and on the quay as she hopped ashore and secured her line.

Cat slipped the binoculars from around his neck, deposited them on a cockpit seat, and stepped onto the deck. "Get some clothes on, kid," he said as he brushed past Jinx. "We're in a strange place; there might be some strange people." She rolled her eyes, sighed, and jumped back aboard. Cat climbed a rusty steel ladder and came onto an area containing some buildings that appeared to be warehouses. Nothing like any small-boat repair facility. A couple of hundred yards away, traffic bustled through downtown Santa Marta, an orderly collection of white stucco buildings dotted with palms and other tropical vegetation. He could see the spires of a small cathedral over the red-tiled roofs. He turned to see a soldier approaching, bearing an old American .30-caliber carbine, the sort he himself had carried as a Marine officer.

"Hasta la vista," Cat said to the soldier, exhausting his Spanish.

The soldier asked something in Spanish.

"Speak English?" Cat asked, hopefully. It was going to be tough if nobody spoke English.

"No, señor," the soldier said, shrugging.

Over the man's shoulder, Cat saw somebody less Latin-looking coming toward them.

"American?" the fellow asked.

Cat looked at him hopefully. Small, deeply tanned, tousled sun-bleached hair, a little

19

on the long side — faded cutoff jeans, worn Topsiders, and a tennis shirt that had seen better days. Somewhere in his twenties. Cat knew in a moment he had found his man. The kid had Boat Bum written all over him.

"Sure am," Cat smiled.

"Where from?"

"Atlanta."

The kid stuck out his hand. "My name's Denny. San Diego."

Cat took the hand; it was rough and hard. The boy had hauled a few ropes in his time. "Cat Catledge, Denny. Glad to meet you. You don't know how glad, in fact. My Spanish is nonexistent. Could you say to the soldier, here, that I just want to get my alternator fixed, then shove off?"

Denny spoke in rapid Spanish to the soldier, who replied more briefly. "He says you'll have to come to the port captain's office and check in, then you'll have to clear customs, but the port captain and the customs officer are both at lunch, so it might be awhile before you're legal."

Jinx joined them. She had slipped a T-shirt over the bikini, but it wasn't long enough. Her creamy buns protruded from the bottom. "What's happening, Cat?"

Cat raised a hand to quiet her. "Just getting some information from our friend, the soldier, here. This is Denny, he's an American."

"Hi, Denny, I'm Jinx." She fixed him with a dazzling smile.

Denny looked vaguely stunned. It wasn't the first time Cat had seen this sort of reaction to Jinx. The young man looked around him. "Listen, you're just here to fix your alternator, right?"

"Right," Cat replied.

"Well, if you don't want to hang around any longer than that takes, I can probably fix it with this guy for a few bucks, and you can avoid the formalities."

"How much?"

"Ten bucks American, maybe twenty."

"You're on, Denny," he said to the kid.

Denny spoke to the soldier again and got a sly look and a nod. "Give him ten," he said to Cat.

Jinx spoke up. "Cat, are you bribing somebody? You want to get us all arrested?"

"Jinx, clam up," Cat said. "We're going to get out of here as quickly as possible."

Cat handed the money to the soldier, who turned away without another word.

"Thanks," Cat said to the kid. "I really do just want to get our repairs done. I'm off a Swan 43 back there, name of *Catbird*. You know anybody around here can lay hands on a sick alternator?"

"Sure," the boy replied. "There's a guy up in the town. Let's pull it off and I'll run it up there for you. You'll have to stay inside the fenced compound here, unless you want to start messing with customs."

"You work here?" Cat asked as they climbed down the ladder to the yacht.

Denny grinned, exposing a set of good teeth. "Nobody works much around here," he replied. "I work the sport boats, hire out when somebody hauls a boat, clean a bottom now and then." They were walking toward the boat, Jinx ahead of them. Denny couldn't take his eyes off her. Cat felt almost sorry for him.

They reached the boat, and Katie stuck her head through the hatch. "Katie, this is Denny; he's going to give us a hand with the alternator. Denny, this is my wife, Katie."

"Hello, Denny," Katie said.

"Hi, Mrs. Catledge," Denny said, shooting her an infectious grin. Katie waved and went back below.

They climbed aboard, and Cat led the way down the companionway. He lifted the ladder and unlatched the engine cover.

"Beautiful boat," Denny said, admiringly, looking around the saloon. "I haven't seen a

Swan around here for a long time. She looks new."

"Brand-new, nearly," Cat replied. "We shook her down from Lauderdale to Antigua, now we're headed for the Canal and the South Pacific. Gonna take a couple of years. Right after we get this alternator up and running."

"Bet it's the diode," Denny said, kneeling to the engine. "Got a wrench?"

Cat handed him a wrench set rolled in canvas and watched as Denny quickly unbolted the alternator. He seemed to know his way around engines, something Cat admired. He, himself, was something of a genius in electronics, but unlike most other technical types, he didn't much like mechanical things.

Denny stood up. "Give me an hour or so," he said, "if it's the diode and my guy has the part. If he doesn't, I'll have to scrounge around some. Suppose he has to order it from Bogotá? That would take a couple of days, even if it's airfreighted."

"Cat . . ." Katie said, worriedly.

Cat shook his head. "In that case, just bring it back. I don't want to hang around here. We'll get it fixed in Panama."

"Right," Denny said.

Jinx spoke up. "Say, Mom and I want to

get cleaned up. Is there a shower around here?"

"Yep, over behind that building there. No hot water, but around here the water doesn't get very cold. Lock the door, it's coed."

"Maybe I'd better go with you," Cat said. "What do you think, Denny?"

"It's okay," Denny replied. "Safe enough; I wouldn't worry." He climbed into the cockpit with the alternator.

Cat followed him up and glanced around the cockpit. "Katie," he called below, "did you take the binoculars down with you?"

"Nope," she called back. "They were in the cockpit a few minutes ago."

Cat looked around the cockpit and on deck in vain.

Denny stood by, nodding slowly. "Welcome to Colombia, Mr. Catledge," he said sorrowfully. "First thing you have to learn is never leave *anything* lying around. Tell me, did you used to have a spinnaker pole?"

Cat looked at the foredeck and was greeted by the sight of empty chocks. "I don't believe it," he said. "I wasn't gone five minutes and Katie was on the boat the whole time."

"You'll be lucky if you've still got an anchor and warp," Denny said.

Cat ran forward and opened the anchor

well. "It's still here," he said with relief.

"Just one guy then, and he had his hands full," Denny said. "I'd take it below now, and your winch handles, too. Make sure your cockpit lockers are secured, or you won't have any sails, either."

Cat nodded dumbly and started getting the anchor out.

"Be back in an hour or so," Denny said, hopping onto the catwalk and starting for the ladder. "Depending."

Cat waved him off and struggled aft with the heavy anchor and chain. Then he stopped. Jesus, he'd had his binoculars and spinnaker pole stolen, and now he'd just let a perfect stranger walk off with his alternator. He'd been a little slow in adjusting to the local climate.

The women were leaving the boat with soap, shampoo, and towels. "We'll be back after a while," Katie said.

"You're not taking any money or anything valuable with you, are you?" Cat called to them.

Katie took off her wristwatch and handed it to him with her wallet. "You're right, and believe me, we won't linger in the shower."

"Maybe I'd better come with you," Cat said. Having a thief on board in broad daylight had rattled him.

"No," Jinx said, "if you do, when we get back the boat might not be here. Don't worry, we'll take care of ourselves, and we can scream real loud if we have to."

"I guess you're right," Cat said. "Somebody had better stay here with the boat." They left and he went below to the chart table. He grabbed the chart, a pencil, and a plotter and headed back for the cockpit, checking to make sure his shotgun was still secured in its hidden cupboard behind the clever flap that concealed it. He'd had that done in Fort Lauderdale, and he felt better knowing they had some sort of protection aboard in this part of the world. He'd heard the horror stories, and he meant to be careful. He climbed into the cockpit and started planning his passage to the Canal. Ordinarily, he would have done it at the chart table, but now he wanted to be where he could see who came and went.

Four hours later he looked at his watch and then at Katie. They had all showered and had lunch. He had done his passage planning and a couple of odd jobs on the boat. The kid, Denny, was nowhere to be seen. "Well, I guess I did the wrong thing," he said.

"Cat, let's get out of here," Katie said.

"This place gives me the willies."

Cat nodded; he didn't like it much, either. "There's probably enough juice left in the engine battery, but I want to save it for when we get to Panama, and I don't think I want to try to sail her out of here," he said, glancing around the area. "Too confined. We'll inflate the dinghy and tow us out with the outboard. When we get to the Canal, we can radio for a tow. I can make a radiotelephone call to the builders on the way, and we can probably have a new alternator and spinnaker pole waiting for us in Panama."

"That seems like the sensible thing," Jinx chimed in. "I'm really surprised about Denny, though; I liked him."

"So did I, until now," Cat replied. "Let's get moving. I'll get the anchor back in the well; you two get the dinghy out of the aft locker and connect it to the pump. We'll be gone in five minutes."

As they spilled into the cockpit, there was a shout from above. "Hey, give me a hand, will you?"

They looked up to find Denny standing on the key, a cardboard box under one arm and *Catbird's* spinnaker pole under the other.

Three broad smiles greeted him. "Where'd you find the pole?" Cat called.

"You wouldn't believe me if I told you," Denny yelled, tossing down the pole, then carefully handing down the cardboard box. He hopped down onto the deck. "Sorry about the binoculars, but I had an idea about the pole and thought I ought to pursue it; it just took me longer than I figured."

"What luck with the alternator?" Cat asked.

"Good news and bad news," Denny replied. "There isn't a diode anywhere in Santa Marta, but I found a new, identical alternator. The guy wanted a hundred and fifty bucks for the exchange. I know that sounds steep, but around here, it's not bad, and I knew you wanted to get out of here."

"That's just great, Denny," Cat grinned. "I'd have paid more."

Shortly, Denny had the new alternator in place. Cat switched to the engine battery he'd been saving, started the engine, and they checked the ammeter. "Charging just fine," Denny proclaimed. "You're in business."

Cat followed him into the cockpit. "You've been just great, Denny, I can't thank you enough." He pulled some bills from Katie's wallet. "That was a hundred and fifty for the alternator, and here's another hundred for your help. Is that okay?"

Denny held up a hand. "Listen, Mr. Catledge, I was glad to help, but instead of the money, there's something that would be a lot more important to me."

"If I've got it, you can have it," Cat said.

"Look, I'm a good hand. I grew up on boats. I've done two races from San Diego to Hawaii on a Class One boat; I've sailed a Southern Ocean Racing Conference series on a maxi-rater; I've spent a year as mate on a ninety-foot gaffer — that's how I got to Colombia. I know engines, and I can even cook. There's hardly anything I can't do on a boat."

Cat nodded. "Yeah, go on."

"Mr. Catledge, I want to get out of Colombia. This is a crazy place, full of thieves and drugs and people who'd just as soon cut your throat as look at you. My folks sent me the money, once, but I blew it, I was stupid. If you'll give me a ride as far as the Canal, well, from there I should be able to hitch a ride up the west coast of Mexico and home to California. I know you don't know me or anything, but I come from good people, my dad's a dentist at home. I just sort of got off track down here, and I'd like to get back on again. I don't have much gear, and I don't take up much room. I promise you I'll work my tail off for you. You won't regret taking me."

Cat looked at the boy; he seemed practically in tears. He thought about the young man at home he hadn't been able to help, who wouldn't take his help. He glanced over Denny's shoulder at Katie and Jinx. They both nodded. He turned back, took the boy by the wrist, and slapped the money into his palm. "You'll need the money when you get to Panama, Denny, and you've got yourself a berth."

Denny let out a shout. "I'll send the money up to the alternator guy — my gear's up in the shed. I won't be thirty seconds!" He leapt from the boat and ran down the catwalk.

"Stand by to cast off," Cat called out, and the women stood by their warps. Denny was back on board almost immediately, clutching a single duffel. Cat put the engine in gear. When they were clear of the wharf, he started a tight turn to bring the yacht back into open water. "Toss your gear in the starboard pilot berth in the saloon," he said to Denny, and the boy dived below with his duffel bag.

As they came out of the turn, they passed close by a boat of about their size moored at the other end of the quay. Cat heard a muffled shout from below on the other boat, and a man's head popped up through the companionway. They were no more than twenty feet away. "Christ," the man called to his wife, who was sunning herself in the cockpit, "now they've stolen our goddamned spare alternator. What next, the mast?"

Cat winced. Katie and Jinx, untying the mainsail, burst into helpless laughter. Denny was still below. Cat hesitated for just a moment, then kept going. "Hoist the mainsail!" he laughed.

3

By the time they had been an hour under sail, to Cat's relief, Denny had integrated himself smoothly into the running of the boat. Cat had enjoyed giving him an extensive tour of *Catbird,* showing off the details of his careful planning and superior electronics layout. Denny had been particularly interested in the small touches Cat had installed, like the large chart cabinet and the "gun deck" — the stainless steel, light shotgun in its hidden compartment. Denny had proved his worth with his expert handling of sail, sheet, winch, and helm, and Cat was already feeling relaxed and confident with his presence on the boat. Katie and Jinx had grown highly competent with the yacht, but it was good to have another man's strength and expertise available in the event of some emergency.

Denny seemed to have grown somewhat more reticent, less ebullient, since their sail-

ing, and Cat attributed this to the young man's realization that he was, at last, on his way home. Cat wondered whether Denny's reunion with his family, who, no doubt, disapproved of him, would be accomplished with more success than his own attempts to achieve some reconciliation with his own son, Dell. A scab never seemed to fully form over that wound, and Cat wondered, wearily, if it ever would.

Denny insisted on taking the eight-to-midnight watch so that the family could dine together. Cat would always remember that dinner — rare, because before Denny, the three of them could never sit down at the saloon table for dinner together. Their talk at that dinner seemed a summary of all the good things in their relationship. Over a bottle of a good California cabernet, they had fallen to reminiscing, Cat and Katie about their early married years, when Dell was small and Jinx tiny, and Cat was a struggling young engineer; Jinx about her memories of them in those days. They had laughed about the time when Jinx, three, had climbed high into a tree, then fallen asleep in the crotch of two limbs. They had been afraid to wake her for fear she would fall, and it had only been with some difficulty that Cat had finally managed to

reach her. They had never been able to figure out how a three-year-old could have made such a climb. Cat thought of the incident as an early sign of the determination Jinx had always shown. He felt a pride and pleasure in her intelligence, beauty, and good sense that helped to make up for his disappointment in his son.

By midnight Katie was asleep and Jinx was nodding. "You'd better hit the sack, kid," he said, reaching across the table and placing a hand on her warm cheek.

She crawled over next to him, ducked under his arm, and laid her head on his shoulder. "I think I'll sleep right here," she said, snuggling close.

"You used to go to sleep there all the time," he said, stroking her thick, luxuriant hair. "I'd put you to bed when my arm got numb."

"I remember," she replied. "I wasn't always asleep, you know."

"I didn't know."

"I just liked it when you carried me to my bedroom and tucked me in."

"I liked it, too."

"I'm glad I didn't go to college yet," she murmured. "I'm glad I came with you and Mother on *Catbird*. I didn't want to leave you, not yet."

Cat wanted to reply, but his throat had tightened. Her head rolled a bit, and she was asleep. He gathered her in his arms and took her to the forecabin, tucking a sheet around her.

"Mmm," she said as he brushed her hair away from her face. Cat kissed her on both eyes, the way he had done when she was a little girl, then he walked aft and started to shut the door to her cabin.

"G'night, Cat," she said.

He laughed, then got into a safety harness, poured himself a cup of coffee to fortify himself against the wine, then climbed into the cockpit to relieve Denny at the helm. The wind was holding nicely, and the boat seemed to race through the waves. The sensation of speed was greatly increased at night, Cat reflected, especially on a dark night like this one.

"No thanks, Mr. Catledge," Denny said in the darkness. "I'm happy to go all night, if that's all right with you."

"I don't believe in all-nighters," Cat said. "No need to wear yourself out your first twenty-four hours at sea by pulling two watches. Save your strength; you might need it later." He slid behind the wheel and took it from the younger man. "Besides, this is my favorite watch, midnight to four. I'm too stingy to let you have it."

"Well, if you insist," Denny replied, rising reluctantly from the helmsman's seat.

"I insist," Cat laughed.

Denny climbed onto the deck from the cockpit. "I'll just have a look forward, make sure everything's ship-shape."

"Good idea," Cat said, tossing him a safety harness from a cockpit locker and retrieving one for himself. "Ship's law is nobody goes on deck at night without a harness. I'd prefer it if you wore one even at the helm. It's a nuisance to have to come about and recover bodies from the sea."

Denny got into the harness, clipped onto a jackstay, and worked his way forward. He spent a good ten minutes there, most of it behind the headsail, where he couldn't be seen. Just enjoying the night, Cat thought.

When Denny had gone below, Cat experienced a tiny moment of regret. It seemed, with the warm Caribbean breeze blowing across his face, that he had reached some sort of peak, that things couldn't get better than this, so they would have to get worse. Then, he remembered that, after the Panama Canal, the South Pacific lay before them, that there would be many more nights as lovely, many more days of tropical sunshine with his wife and daughter as crew and friends. He passed his watch in a haze of bliss.

At a quarter to four the galley light went on, and Cat knew that Katie was awake and brewing her tea. But shortly before four, Denny appeared in the companionway, holding a mug. "I was awake," he said, "so I thought I'd let Mrs. Catledge sleep. I'd like the watch, if that's okay."

Cat shrugged. "If you're sure you don't need the rest." He slid from behind the wheel and relinquished the helm.

"I'd rather pull the watch," Denny replied. "Sleep well."

Below, Cat got out of his harness, shucked off his jeans and T-shirt, and crawled into the double berth with Katie. She stirred as he snuggled close. "My watch?" she asked, sleepily.

"Denny's taking it," Cat said, cupping a breast in his hand.

"Oh, good," she said, turning toward him. "I get you in the middle of the night, for a change."

He kissed her, then they made love, gently, slowly, lying facing each other, coming quietly after a few minutes, together, as they usually did. Years of practice, Cat thought. Then he fell asleep.

■ ■ ■ ■

A change in the motion of the yacht woke him. There was light against the curtains in the after cabin. Cat glanced at the gold-and-steel Rolex wristwatch Katie and Jinx had given him as a launching present: not quite 6 a.m. Why had the motion changed? Then the yacht, which had been heeled to port, rolled to starboard and seemed to settle. They were hove to; stopped. Then came a muffled, slithering sound and the thumps of footsteps on deck. The mainsail was coming down. Why? Had something broken? A halyard, maybe. The actions on deck seemed to fit that scenario. The main halyard had broken, and Denny had, quite properly, put the boat on the opposite tack, with the headsail backed while he got the mainsail in hand.

Cat rolled out of the berth, naked, got into his jeans, and felt for his Topsiders with his feet. He didn't like to go on deck bare-footed; he had once nearly broken a toe, tripping on a deck fitting. He moved slowly, sleepily into the saloon; there didn't seem to be any great urgency; Denny was not calling for him. He climbed halfway up the companionway ladder and stopped, puzzled.

The wheel was locked; Denny was standing on the stern of the boat, looking aft, shielding his eyes from a rising, red ball of a sun.

"What's up, Denny?" Cat called out. "We got a problem?"

Denny turned and looked at him, silhouetted against the rising sun; Cat could not see his face.

"No, no problem," Denny called back, then turned and looked astern again.

Cat climbed into the cockpit, raising a hand to shade his eyes. "Why are we stopped? What's going on?"

Denny did not reply but continued to stare astern.

Now Cat heard an engine. He started aft toward Denny, staggering a bit with sleep and the gentle rolling of the yacht. He made the stern and climbed up beside Denny, holding on to the backstay for support as the hove-to boat rolled with the swell. "What is it?" he asked again.

"I don't know," Denny said, dully.

The young man seemed to be breathing rapidly, Cat thought. He looked out astern, the sun hurting his eyes, and, for the first time, saw a white shape that had to be a boat a few hundred yards out, coming toward them. The sound of an engine was distinct now, borne on the light breeze. Cat looked around the cockpit for the binoculars, then remembered that they had been stolen in Santa Marta. He squinted at the boat, trying to judge its shape and size. It seemed to be a sportfisherman, he thought, something on the order of thirty feet. It came on, steadily, toward *Catbird.*

"Why did you stop the boat, Denny?" Cat asked again.

The younger man stepped down from the stern and stood in the cockpit, still watching the approaching boat, now only a hundred yards away.

"Nothing's wrong, Mr. Catledge," Denny said. "Everything's okay."

Cat was wide awake now, and becoming irritated at the lack of an answer to his question.

"Denny, I asked you why you stopped the boat. Answer me."

"Uh, there was a problem with the mainsail. I thought it ought to come down."

It was as Cat had suspected, then. But what about the approaching boat? It was less than fifty yards away, and Cat could clearly make out a man and a woman on the flying bridge. There was a name visible on her bows, too: *Santa Maria.* The boat had slowed markedly, and her skipper was clearly bent on coming alongside. Cat could make out her crew's features now. The woman, who seemed quite young, disappeared below. The man was in his mid-thirties, bearded, and rough-looking. Cat thought that all he needed was an eyepatch, and he'd look like a storybook pirate. Pirate. The word echoed in his head. He turned. "Denny," he called back, evenly and distinctly, "please go below and hand me up the shotgun. Do it right now."

"Yessir," Denny said, immediately, and turned for the companionway ladder.

Cat turned back to the approaching boat, which had stopped perhaps ten yards off his port quarter. "What do you want?" he called to her skipper, who was leaning on the helm staring at Cat, keeping the throttle at idle. The man grinned broadly, exposing some gold teeth, but did not reply. Cat thought he must not speak English. He was trying to think of something else to say when he heard Denny's footfall behind him. He turned to see the young man approaching, the shotgun in his hands. Katie was right behind him, coming up the ladder.

"What's happening, Cat?" she was calling.

Cat reached out for the shotgun, and to his astonishment saw Denny step back and raise the weapon, pointing it directly at him.

"No fooling around, Denny," Cat barked,

alarmed. "I need that right now."

Denny did not reply, nor did his expression change.

Cat stepped down from the stern and started toward Denny. He heard Katie call his name, and then a flat, heavy object seemed to strike his chest, propelling him backward. As his head struck the yacht's wheel, a terrible roar filled his head, and he had just time to know that he had been shot before the noise spilled over into his vision, turning everything red, pressing him down, down into a dark place from which he knew he would never rise again. He tried to call out to those above him — Katie! Jinx! But he could only make a rattling noise as his breath left him and he sank into the darkness.

4

Cat dreamed. He dreamed heavy feet on deck, dreamed shouts, struggle, screams, strange laughter. Gunshots. In his dream there was light, but he could see nothing. Finally, the sounds went away. He retreated again into dark silence.

There was something cool, then he coughed, strangled, and came awake with the pain. He tried not to breathe; breathing hurt terribly. Then the strangling and coughing came again. There was a salty taste. Was he strangling on his own blood? Then he could see something, a word, sideways. Fuses. He knew that word, had written that word. Sideways. He hadn't written it sideways.

His chest was a garden of pain, and he was swimming in and out of sharp consciousness. The bottom drawer under the chart table was marked "Fuses." Salt water ran into his mouth, and he spat it out. He could not bear to cough again. Gingerly, he pulled an arm under him and lifted his head up and away from the water. A wave of nausea swept over him, but he kept pushing until his head and shoulder were propped against something and he could rest. He fought to remain conscious and orient himself. If he could see the drawers under the chart table, he was in the galley, his cheek pressed against the cupboard that supported the sink. There was an inch of water lapping at the bottom of the cupboard. That offended Cat. This boat had never had water over the floorboards, had never leaked a drop.

Where was Katie? Where was Jinx? The boat rocked gently, was silent; he felt absolutely alone. There was something he must do, he knew, if he could only remember. His eyes wandered over the navigation station a few feet away; their focus softened, then came back. Something orange. That was what he wanted. He struggled to think, then the orange thing came into his vision. Fastened to the cockpit bulkhead, just next to the companionway ladder. EPIRB. That was the word. What did those letters mean? He could never rattle them off, he always had to try hard to remember them.

Never mind. Don't remember. Just get hold of the goddamned thing. He experimented with moving in ways that might not hurt. There weren't any, as it turned out. He would have to move and hurt, too. He struggled until his back was against the cupboard, his knees pulled up. The trouble with moving was that it made him want to breathe, and breathing hurt.

Directly in front of him was the oilskin locker, and a yellow slicker dangled toward him. Why did it dangle toward him? It should hang straight down. The boat was listing forward, down by her bows, that was why. He got hold of the slicker with both hands. He would be able to do this only once, he was sure of that. Slowly, biting off groans, he pulled himself until his feet were under him, legs straight, knees locked. Then, for the first time, he saw the blood on his body. His chest was bright red, and his jeans soaked dark. Don't think about that. Not now. First, EPIRB. What did those letters mean?

He could nearly reach out and touch it, two, three feet away, uphill. He would have to pull again. He didn't want to pull anymore. He pulled on the slicker until he could rest against the oilskin locker, knees still locked, keeping him erect. He got an arm over the top rung of the companionway ladder and dragged himself sideways. He couldn't hold on with his hands, couldn't make a fist.

Now he could reach the EPIRB. He got a hand on it, but it was fastened into place by a steel band with a quick release clip. His fingers didn't want to undo it. First, the switch. On. He could do that. He did. Now the clip. He pushed a finger under it. Like the pop top on a soft-drink can, he thought. He always had trouble with those. He pushed harder. God, it hurt, but it was almost a relief to have pain somewhere besides his chest. The clip moved, then suddenly released, letting the orange thing fall.

He was astonished that he caught it. He brought it close to his mouth, got the end of the tube thing in his mouth. What was the word? Didn't matter. Pull, or it was all over. He couldn't last much longer, he knew that. He bit the metal and straightened his arm. The chrome tube extended easily. Switch on, tube thing out. That was it. Very carefully, he reached up, over the companionway threshold, and set the EPIRB on the cockpit floor. There, done.

Katie and Jinx. They must be on deck. Oh, God, he could never make it into the cockpit; no strength left. Still, he must. Just like pulling on the slicker, he had to do it all at once. He did it, and his body vomited, to show its disapproval. He lay on the cockpit floor, in the thick puddle of his last night's dinner, and tried not to pant, because panting hurt so much.

Soon, to his surprise, he was able to push himself into a sitting position. Something hurt his back, and he moved it. The EPIRB. He placed it on a cockpit seat and watched the little red light flash on and off for a while. He had to look on deck for Katie and Jinx, so he managed to get to his knees, facing the companionway. They were not on deck. Gone. Those people had taken them. Why? He sagged back on his heels and gazed stupidly into the cabin.

First, he saw the water, and there was more than an inch of it. *Catbird* was sinking by the bows, and the forepeak was already flooded.

What he saw next he saw only for an instant, less than a second, before he clamped his eyes shut, willing the sight to leave his memory. He turned away and curled into a fetal ball on the cockpit sole, making whimpering noises, trying to erase just that one, brief glimpse of a scene that would haunt him forever. He could not forget. His brain projected the image onto the inside of his eyelids, burned it permanently into place where he could not ignore it. Katie, lying on her back on the port settee, her nightshirt pushed up around her shoulders, her breasts bared. Her head jammed against the forward bulkhead at an odd angle, and her mouth open. Her face streaked with blood from her mouth that streamed in dried clots down the bulkhead until it met the rising water. There was not the slightest hope in his heart that she was not dead.

Jinx, facedown, naked, on the saloon table, her feet toward him, her face, thank God, turned away. The back of her head pulp. Her legs open, blood in her crotch and on the backs of her thighs. On her left buttock, clearly imprinted on skin kept white by bikinis, a large handprint. Not hers, the angle was wrong. Handprint of someone standing behind' her. Handprint in her blood.

He stared up at the sky, wanting unconsciousness, but it would not come, not yet. His mind groped for something else to think about, something to blot out what he had seen.

EPIRB. What did those goddamned letters mean? Let's see, yes, almost; got it!

Emergency Position Indicator Radio Beacon!

But what did the words mean? He could not think anymore. He gave himself, gratefully, to the rising red and blackness.

5

Cat woke gently, as from a deep sleep. It was amazingly cool, he thought, for such a hot climate. There was a lot of whiteness around him. Everything was white.

He felt a rush of panic and tried to sit up but could not. He was too weak. What was happening? He tried to calm himself; he looked around the room, wanting a clue to his whereabouts. A hospital, obviously. There were three other beds in the room, all empty and unmade. A stand beside his bed held a container of clear liquid, which was attached to a needle in his arm. Had he hallucinated? Had all of it been a horrible dream? He placed a hand on his chest and found thick bandages. He pressed slightly, and was greeted with a stab of pain. No dream. It had happened, and to his great sorrow, he was having no trouble remembering all of it.

He found a buzzer hanging near his head

and pressed it. A moment later a Latin woman in a nurse's uniform rushed into the room. "You are awake," she said, rather stupidly, Cat thought.

He tried to speak, but his throat and tongue were as dry as paper. Nothing would work. The nurse seemed to understand and poured him a glass of water from a bedside thermos, stuck a glass straw in it, and offered it to him. He drank some cool water, then flushed his mouth until the paper feeling went away.

"Where?" he managed to say.

"You are in Cuba," the woman replied. Her accent was only slight.

"My family," he said. He had to know if it had been real.

Her face twitched. "I'll get somebody," she said, and left the room.

A couple of minutes passed, then the nurse returned with a young man in a white jacket over what looked like naval uniform trousers. "I'm Dr. Caldwell," he said to Cat, reaching for his pulse. "How are you feeling?"

Cat merely nodded. "My wife and daughter are dead," Cat said. He stated it as a fact; he didn't want to give the man an opportunity to lie to him.

The young man nodded. "I'm afraid so,"

he said. "You remember, then."

Cat nodded. "Are you Cuban?"

The doctor looked puzzled for a moment. "Oh, no," he said, finally. "You're at Guantánamo Naval Base, not on Cuban soil. A Coast Guard search and rescue chopper brought you in here two days ago."

"How badly am I hurt?"

"Well, you weren't in very good shape when you arrived. We spent a couple of hours picking birdshot out of you. What was it, a .410-gauge?"

Cat nodded. "My own."

"Be glad it wasn't a twelve-gauge and buckshot. You're in no danger, as far as I can tell. In fact, I'm surprised it took you so long to come around. It was almost as if you didn't want to wake up."

"The boat?"

"There's an investigating officer here; I've sent for him. He'll fill you in."

As if on cue, another officer, a lieutenant, entered the room. "Hello, Mr. Catledge," he said. "Welcome back."

Cat nodded. "Thanks."

"You feel up to a chat?"

"Okay." He pointed at the bed. "Can you crank this thing up?"

The officer raised the bed until Cat was nearly sitting.

"The boat?" Cat asked again. He wanted to ask about bodies.

"My name is Lieutenant Frank Adams, call me Frank. I'm a military police officer. Is your name Wendell Catledge?"

Cat nodded.

Adams looked relieved. "I ran your fingerprints," he said, "and we got the registration on your boat. You didn't have any identification."

Cat lifted his left arm and looked at the wrist. "My name is engraved on the inside of my watch." There was a white stripe against his yellowing tan.

"You weren't wearing a watch."

"I'm sure I had it on when they came," Cat said. "It was a little before six in the morning. What about the boat and my wife and daughter."

Adams pulled up a chair and sat down. "A little after eight in the morning, Thursday, that's two days ago, a Lufthansa flight from Bogotá to San Juan picked up the signal from your EPIRB. Less than an hour later, a Coast Guard helicopter found the boat and put two frogmen in the water. She was well down by the bows. You were in the cockpit. Your . . . the women were in the main cabin, both dead. Before the two men could even get you into the chopper, the boat stood on her nose and went straight down. You were in the water for a couple of minutes before they got you up. The bodies went down with the boat. There was nothing they could do."

Cat nodded, and his eyes filled with tears.

"Your brother-in-law is here, staying in our bachelor officer quarters; I've sent for him. Do you think you can tell me about it now? I want to do everything I can, but I need the details." Adams produced a small tape recorder.

Cat got hold of himself and began at the beginning.

When Cat woke up again, Ben Nicholas, Katie's brother and Cat's business partner, was sitting next to the bed, his normally open, friendly face showing the shock. Before Cat could speak, Ben took his hand.

"You don't have to tell me about it," he said with some difficulty. "Lieutenant Adams played the tape recording for me. He was very impressed with how thorough you were."

"Thank you, Ben," Cat said. "How long have you been here?"

"I got in last night. They flew me in a Navy plane from Miami. They've made me comfortable. Never thought I'd get to Cuba."

"Me, either. Does Dell know?"

"The doctor says we can move you to Atlanta in a day or two. I've got an air ambulance standing by in Miami. They'll hop over here when we get the word."

"Have you told Dell?"

Ben shook his head. "I couldn't find him, Cat. There was an answering machine on his phone; I didn't want to tell him that way. I went around to his place, in that high rise; nobody answered the bell. Doorman said he hadn't seen him for a couple of days. Liz is calling him every hour. She wants you to stay with us until you're better. She'd been here herself, but her mother's in the hospital again. The P.R. guy at the office has been dealing with the press. Some wire-service reporter got onto it, from the Coast Guard, I guess, then a business reporter at *The New York Times* recognized your name, then the Atlanta papers went with it, and . . . well, all hell broke loose. There wasn't any way to avoid having the details made public. It was just too sensational a story — well-known businessman-inventor, all that."

Cat nodded. "Ben, it's my fault; I did it to Katie and Jinx."

"No, no, Cat, you mustn't think that. You didn't deliberately put them in danger; you couldn't have foreseen this."

"I took them into that place. Katie didn't want to go, I talked her into it, I pushed her."

"Listen to me, Cat," Ben said. "I know how much you loved Katie and Jinx. You just did what you thought was best, and it went wrong. It happens like that sometimes; you can't see something like that coming. It's nobody's fault but the people who did it. Katie would see it that way; Jinx, too. That's the way you've got to see it. You'll go nuts if you don't."

They both began crying. Cat got an arm around Ben, and they sat that way for a moment, sobbing. After they had composed themselves and Ben had gone, Cat knew he would not cry anymore. He couldn't allow himself that much self-pity again, not if he was to go on living.

His memory began to pluck at him, but he pushed it aside, blanked it out. He couldn't bear to see that scene on the yacht again. An image forced its way into his head, though, skirting his defenses. The handprint stood out, vivid and red. Then the anger began. And through the anger came a question: Why? Not just why him or why Katie and Jinx, but why at all? His best memory of the yacht after those people had left was that it was absolutely intact. All the expensive electronics were in place, the boat had no appearance of having been ransacked. They had many possessions on board that a thief would have wanted, but none of them had been taken. He had no enemies that he knew of, and anyway, this thing couldn't have been planned, because the decision to sail into Colombian waters had been made on the spur of the moment. Not until the dawn of that terrible day had he, himself, known that they would be sailing into Santa Marta.

To all appearances, these people had committed a wanton act of piracy and two murders — three, they thought — for no gain except a twenty-five-hundred-dollar Rolex wristwatch. It made no sense whatever, and that made Cat angrier still.

He knew that Katie and Jinx were lost beyond hope, that he could never have them back, but almost as much as he wanted the people who had killed them, he wanted to know why it had been done.

He began building toward a state of new resolve: He would spend every dime he had and the rest of his life, if necessary, to find out.

6

Cat climbed out of the pool behind his house and walked up and down on the flagstones for a moment, breathing deeply. This was so much easier than it had been in the beginning, he thought. He'd been as weak as a kitten when he had gotten out of the hospital. He'd started swimming laps to stretch his chest muscles, damaged by the shotgun blast, and he'd learned to enjoy the workouts, as much as he was capable of enjoying anything. It was better than sitting in a chair, staring straight ahead. He'd done enough of that.

He had lost thirty pounds in the hospital and nearly another twenty since. He weighed the same as he had the year he graduated from high school, and he felt in better shape, strong, tanned, and fit. He still surprised himself when he encountered a mirror — slim, clean-shaven, and close-cropped for the first time in years. He had gained the new fitness with swimming and with hitting tennis balls back at a machine. They were both suitably solitary activities. He had played tennis a couple of times at the club and discovered he didn't want the company; he preferred to sweat in solitude.

Someone called to him from the back of the house. Cat turned to see Wallace Henderson, a retired Atlanta police captain, now a highly regarded private investigator, approaching. With a feeling of dread, he shook the man's hand and offered him a chair at poolside while he got into a terry-cloth robe. He knew what was coming.

"It's come to this, Mr. Catledge," Henderson said. "My people and I have spent nearly three months and a considerable sum of your money running down every conceivable lead and theory of this case. We have telephoned or seen every dentist in San Diego and the surrounding Southern Californian communities and found two who have a son named Denny; one was a junior in high school and one was three years old. We have checked the crew lists for the last ten years on the yacht races this Denny says he sailed. Nothing there. We have liaised with the State Department and the Colombian police; the Colombians have distributed the artist's sketches based on your descriptions of the two men — you didn't get a good enough look at the woman for a description; they've circulated a description of your wristwatch and the engraving on the back. We've had the Colombian Navy and the U.S. Coast Guard on constant lookout for a sportfishing boat called *Santa Maria* — turns out that's a very common name for a boat in Latin American countries — and there's been no sign of such a boat. We've had a salvage company look at the possibility of raising your yacht and recovering the bodies, but she sank in more than a thousand fathoms of water and is unrecoverable.

"The fact is, sir, I don't think that I can, in good faith, take any more of your money. I was a police officer for twenty-five years, and I've been a private investigator for nearly ten, and I tell you, I have never dealt with a case with so little to go on and so many dead ends. Now, there's a chance that one or more of the queries we've made might produce some sort of answer sometime in the future — maybe they'll find the *Santa Maria,* for instance — but that is unpredictable and entirely out of our hands.

"I'm not going to tell you, Mr. Catledge, that you should forget that your wife and daughter were murdered and your yacht sunk; I'm not going to tell you that we'll never know why or that the people who did it will never be brought to justice. But I have to tell you that, right now, I don't know of a single other way to make that happen." The man shifted uncomfortably in his seat. "I just don't," he said with finality.

"Captain, we could send a couple of operatives down there," Cat said, trying to keep the desperation out of his voice.

Henderson shook his head. "No, sir — I mean, we could do that; I could, through some of my colleagues, probably find a couple of Latinos who could blend in down there, but the Colombian police — thanks to the pressure you brought on the State Department — did what I consider a first-class job of investigation in Santa Marta. You've read the translated reports; no outsider I could send in there could possibly do half as well. At least you've got the interest of the police down there. If they turn up something, we'll hear about it."

Cat heaved a sigh. "I suppose you're right," he said, wearily. "I've paid you for your skill and advice, and you've given me both, Captain Henderson, and I'm grateful to you." He stood. "I guess I'm just going to have to wait until something new turns up." He offered his hand. "Send me your bill for any work outstanding."

Henderson took his hand. "I want you to know, sir, that I consider this a personal defeat for me. But I've given it my best. I hope you'll call me if you hear anything new." The man left.

Cat got into the Porsche and drove. He was a fast driver and had the traffic tickets to prove it, but today he drove listlessly, carelessly. It had occurred to him more than once to take the car out somewhere and crash it into a tree or a bridge abutment and end the whole thing. All that had kept him going had been the hope of finding Denny and his cohorts, and now that seemed a remote possibility.

Ben and Liz had been wonderful, having him to dinner, inviting friends over, keeping him from becoming a recluse. There had even been a couple of attempts to fix him up with women, evenings that had fizzled. He simply had no interest in women, or, for that matter, anything else. Even the business, which had once given him so much satisfaction, had no further appeal for him. He had not spent more than a few hours at the office; the people there had tiptoed around him, and he hadn't felt in the least necessary. Ben had been getting feelers about a takeover by a larger company, and that was fine with Cat, not that he needed the money.

He suddenly felt ill and pulled the car over. He sat on the grass verge of the roadway, fighting nausea, trying to think of something else to do for Katie and Jinx, for some reason to go on living, and not having much luck. Suddenly, there was a loud roar overhead, and a shadow passed across the car. Cat looked up and discovered that he was parked at the end of a runway at Peachtree Dekalb Airport, a general aviation field on the outskirts of Atlanta. He watched the light airplane climb, turn, and start back toward the field.

Cat started the car and drove around to the main entrance of the airport. Passing through the gate, he immediately saw a sign reading "PDK Flight Academy." A few moments later he sat across a desk from a pleasant man who explained the flight-training program to him. Half an hour later he sat at the end of a runway in a Cessna 152 trainer and listened carefully to the fresh-faced young instructor seated next to him.

"Okay," the kid was saying, "full throttle, keep the airplane on the center line, watch your airspeed, and rotate at fifty knots."

Cat pushed in the throttle, and the little airplane started to roll. He steered with the rudder pedals, nervously watching the airspeed indicator. At fifty knots he pulled back on the yoke and the airplane leapt off the runway, leaving his stomach on the ground.

"Continue straight ahead and climb to three thousand feet," the instructor said. A few minutes later they were over Lake Lanier, forty miles to the north of the city, practicing turns. Flying was something he'd thought about off and on over the years, but he had never had the time. Now he had nothing but time. An hour later, Cat had been issued a flight manual and enrolled in the flying school.

That night he stayed up late reading the manual. The next day he took a two-hour lesson. The day after that, another. He began flying every day the weather was decent, studying the manual and workbook whenever he was grounded. He registered in a weekend seminar to accelerate his academic training and passed the FAA written examination the following day with a perfect score. He soloed ten days after beginning his training and began flying the airplane alone on practice sessions and on cross-country flights. His concentration was total. He read every flying magazine he could get his hands on, every book he could squeeze in. He clung to the training doggedly, obsessively. It filled his life, left no room to think about anything else, and that was what he wanted.

In the middle of his fourth week of training, his instructor met him at the airplane after a solo flight. "I've scheduled you for a check ride with an FAA examiner for your private pilot's license tomorrow morning at ten o'clock," the young man said. "I'll tell you, Mr. Catledge, you've set a record around here. I've never seen anybody work so hard and get so much packed into so short a time. I think you'll do just fine on your check ride." They spent an hour filling out forms and making sure Cat's logbook was up to date, then Cat went home, buoyed with the idea that tomorrow, after a flying test he was confident he could pass, he would be a licensed private pilot. He started thinking about training for an instrument rating.

Back at the house, he changed into a swimsuit and went out to the pool. He dived in and began swimming slow, steady laps, balancing his kicks on each side, measuring his strokes, working every muscle. He swam twenty laps, then heaved himself onto the side of the pool, sucking in deep breaths. There was water in his eyes, and it took him a moment to realize that somebody was standing at the opposite end of the pool, staring at him. The figure was tall and slim, rather like the man he had been seeing in the mirror lately.

"Hello, Dell," he said, finally, to his son.

The boy said nothing, just stood and stared blankly at him.

"You haven't been around," Cat said, trying to keep his voice neutral. "We've been trying to locate you. You've heard?"

Dell did not move any closer, but nodded. "I've been out of the country. I read about it in the papers when it happened."

"Why didn't you come home? There was a memorial service; a lot of people were there."

Dell seemed to think a moment before he replied. "I didn't come home because there was nothing I could do for Mother and Jinx, and because if I had come home, I might have killed you. You killed them, after all; that's how I see it."

Cat nodded. "For once, we agree on something."

"You accept responsibility then?" Dell asked, surprised.

"I do," Cat replied. "One of the things

about being an adult is, you have to accept responsibility for your actions. One of these days, maybe, you'll learn about that."

The boy's face contorted. "You bastard. I should kill you now."

"Maybe you should," Cat replied, evenly. "You might be doing me a favor, and it shouldn't bother you much. After all, in your business, people get killed every day."

"I simply supply a consumer need, just like you," Dell said.

"Sure, Dell, you go on telling yourself that. Never mind the human misery you and your kind cause. The money's all that matters."

"What about the misery you caused my mother and my sister?" he spat back.

"What about the misery *you* caused them?" Cat asked. "For two years your mother never went to sleep without fear of being wakened in the night by the police announcing your arrest or your murder. Your sister never mentioned your name outside the family, for fear of causing embarrassment to whoever might hear it. Your gifts to them were great — constant pain and suffering. The last night of their lives I sat at dinner and saw tears come to the eyes of both of them when your name was mentioned. To their credit, they both believed there might be something in you worth saving. I haven't shared their hope for a long time now."

"Well," Dell said, "you needn't devote any more of your time to thinking about me. You can think, instead, of how they would still be alive and well if you hadn't been so stupid."

"I'll do that," Cat said. "For as long as I live."

"I'm moving to Miami," Dell said. "You won't be hearing from me again. That's what I came here to tell you."

"Finally, some good news," Cat said, bitterly.

"Yeah, I'm moving on up," Dell replied. "I'm plugged in at the source now; no more low-level dealing — I'm in management. I'll bet I make more money this year than you do."

"No bets on that," Cat replied, trying hard to keep from running to the other end of the pool and beating his son to death. "Dealing in human misery has always paid well. All you have to do to win your bet is to live until the end of the year. From what I hear about your business, that won't be as easy as you think."

"We'll see," Dell spat at him, then turned and walked away toward the garden gate.

"We'll see," Cat echoed quietly to himself. He slipped into the pool again and began swimming long, slow strokes. Breathe deeply, he said to himself. Bleed the anger into the water. The boy was lost; forget about him.

It didn't work.

Cat spent the evening sitting, staring uncomprehendingly at the bedroom television set. The flight manual lay in his lap, open and unread. His flight test the next day, something that he had been eagerly anticipating, seemed remote and uninteresting. He went to bed at midnight, wide awake, longing for oblivion, but he remained conscious for a long time. Much later, when he had slipped into a light and troubled sleep, he suddenly jerked awake. Something had wakened him, but what? There had been no noise.

Almost immediately, the telephone rang. He must have anticipated it, he thought. He glanced at the bedside clock: just after 4 a.m. Who the hell? He felt an unexpected stab of panic. The phone rang again. Fully awake now, unreasoningly frightened, he picked up the instrument. "Hello," he said, rather unsteadily. He was greeted by a wave of static, coming, it seemed, from a great

69

distance. "Hello," he said again, this time more strongly.

Then, faintly but clearly, came a voice he would have recognized anywhere on earth, at any time of the day or night, awake or asleep, a voice he had given up hope of ever hearing again.

"Daddy?" the voice said.

Cat felt a great rush of adrenaline, a tightening of the chest and throat; he seemed unable to exhale.

Before he could speak, there was a turbulent scraping at the other end of the line, followed by a loud thud, then a distant, electronic chirp as the connection was broken.

He spoke repeatedly into the telephone, shouting, begging, until finally he was quieted by the persistent sound of a dial tone coming from the instrument.

He was left alone again, bereft, staring wide-eyed into the darkness.

7

"The senator is sorry he couldn't be here to see you, Mr. Catledge. He's chairing an intelligence committee hearing right now. I'm counsel to the committee, and I should be there myself, but the senator is very grateful for your past support, and he wanted to know what we could do for you."

They were in the small conference room adjacent to the office of Senator Benjamin Carr, Democrat, the senior senator from Georgia. Carr's chief administrative assistant sat across the table from Cat.

"I understand, of course," Cat said. "I've taken too much of his time already."

"Not at all," the man replied. "He's been very concerned about your situation." The younger man, fortyish, Cat thought, placed his elbows on the table, folded his fingers together, and rested his chin on them. "I've been doing all the liaising with the State Department, though, so it's just as well that you and I should talk. You've just come from Foggy Bottom, have you?"

Cat nodded. "I saw the head of the Colombian desk."

"Barker?"

"That's the one. He was very sympathetic."

"But . . . ?"

"But he says he's done all he can. The Colombian police are unwilling to open a new investigation on the basis of a single word spoken on the telephone from somebody who's been confirmed dead."

"I was afraid of that," the assistant replied. "After all, you saw her dead yourself, and the Coast Guard frogmen confirmed what you saw."

Cat shook his head. "What I saw was only for a fraction of a second, not long after I'd taken a shotgun blast in the chest. I wasn't a very reliable witness. I know I saw Katie; she was lying on her back on the port settee, but Jinx . . . the girl I thought was Jinx . . . was facedown on the saloon table, naked. I haven't seen Jinx naked since she was nine or ten, I guess, and as I said, I looked away immediately. Since we were the only three on the boat, I naturally assumed she was Jinx."

"Who was the girl you saw, then?"

"There was a girl on the boat with the Pirate, Denny's accomplice. Maybe she was somehow substituted for Jinx — I don't know, I know it doesn't make any sense. I only got a glimpse of her — I think she was probably older than Jinx and that she was Latin, but in the state I was in when I came to — well, it's the sort of mistake I could easily have made."

"I can understand that."

Cat leaned forward. "What I didn't make a mistake about was the voice on the telephone. It was Jinx. She said, 'Daddy.' It was almost the first word she ever said to me, and I've heard her say it all her life, at least until she started to grow up and decided to call me Cat. I'd know Jinx's voice anywhere, and I'd know it especially well saying that particular word. It *was* Jinx."

The assistant was staring down at his reflection in the table. "I believe you," he said finally. "What are your plans now? Are you going back down there?"

The mere thought of returning to Colombia filled Cat with panic. "I don't know," he replied. "Barker, at State, advised against it in the strongest terms. He says I'm not equipped to conduct my own investigation, and God knows that's true. He won't give me assistance of any kind if I do go. Says the department won't take any responsibility."

"So what are you going to do?" he asked, watching him closely.

Cat leaned back and sighed. "I'm going to go back down there," he said. "It's all that's left, and I could never live with myself if I didn't do everything I possibly could to find Jinx."

The man seemed to search Cat's face for doubt. "That's your final decision, then? You won't be dissuaded?"

"No. I'm going. I've got some money; maybe I'll go to the newspapers and offer a reward."

A twitch of alarm seemed to cross the assistant's face. He stood up. "Will you excuse me for a few minutes? Don't leave; I'll be right back." He left the room.

Cat walked to the window and looked out toward the Capitol dome. There really was nothing else left to do. He dreaded the thought, but he would have to go back to Colombia, to Santa Marta, and make a start. Somebody, somewhere in that country knew something. Maybe he could buy the information. The money was all he had left. They could have it all if they'd give Jinx back to him. He watched people enter and leave the Capitol, his mind growing numb with the fear of what was ahead of him.

Ten minutes passed. The assistant walked back into the room. "Sit down, will you?" he said.

Cat dragged himself back to the table.

The younger man placed his hands on the table in front of him and opened his fingers, as if to spread out some invisible map. "Let me be sure you understand this," he said. "Our conversation ended when I left the room a few minutes ago. I expressed my sympathies, said there was nothing further the senator could do, we shook hands, and you left."

Cat snapped back to the present, puzzled.

"This part of our conversation never happened," the assistant said, seriously, "and no one — not the senator, or anyone else — is ever to be told about it, do you understand me?"

"Yes," Cat said, his pulse accelerating. "Of course."

"You're staying at the Watergate?"

"Right, though I'd planned to check out before lunch and go back to Atlanta."

"Stay another night. Sometime tomorrow, probably in the afternoon, you'll get a phone call from someone who will introduce himself as Jim. Just Jim."

"Jim. Tomorrow afternoon."

"Maybe sooner. Don't leave your room until you hear from him. Don't expect too much, but he will probably have some advice for you. I can't promise you'll like the advice, but this is the only other thing I can think of to help you."

Cat stood up and offered his hand. "Thank you for believing me. Nobody else has."

The man took his hand. "Mr. Catledge, I only wish I could do more," he said.

Cat was asleep when the phone rang. He hadn't slept much the night before, and late in the afternoon he had dozed off in front of the TV. It took him two rings to orient himself. He glanced at the bedside clock as he picked up the phone. Just after six.

"Hello?"

"My name is Jim. I believe we have a mutual friend."

"Yes, we do."

"Come to 528 now."

"Where?"

"Room 528, here, in the hotel." The man hung up.

Cat threw some water on his face and slipped on a jacket. He rode the elevator down to the fifth floor, found the room, and knocked. The man who opened the door was in his late fifties, nearly completely gray-haired, and was dressed in a three-piece suit, button-down collar, and a paisley tie. He didn't look very fresh. He was wearing a day's growth of beard, his shirt collar had a sweat ring, and his hair was greasy. He beckoned Cat into the room and pointed at one of a pair of wing chairs.

"Take a pew," he said, walking to the other chair.

Cat sat down and glanced around the room. It didn't look occupied. "Thanks for seeing me," he said.

"Any friend of the senator's," the man said.

Cat relaxed a little. "Let me tell you about my problem," he said.

Jim held up a hand. "I'm acquainted with your problem," he said. "I read the newspapers. Just let me do the talking for a while."

Cat nodded.

Jim opened a briefcase, the smaller of two beside his chair, and took out a file folder. "Let's see," he said, flipping through pages. "Born Atlanta, Northside High, decent fullback — not good enough for college, though; Georgia Tech, Class of '53, missed Korea with a student deferment — smart move, let me tell you. Naval ROTC, took your commission in the Marines. Why?"

"I was young and stupid," Cat said, honestly.

Jim laughed. "Didn't you like it at Quantico?"

"Can't say that I did," Cat said.

"I was there a few years ahead of you," Jim said. "I guess I didn't like it much, either." He looked at the file again. "Still, you did okay. They had a nice word or two for you on your efficiency reports."

"I kept my mouth shut and did as I was told."

"That's not what it says here," Jim said, consulting the file. "Says here, 'Extensive use of personal initiative, tends to improvise.' That's Marine-ese for maverick, or sometimes just pain in the ass."

Cat shrugged. "Guess I wasn't cut out for the military."

"Is that why you turned down the Agency?" Jim asked. "You thought it would be too much like the military?"

"The Agency?"

"The Central Intelligence Agency. You've heard of that," Jim said dryly.

Cat's eyebrows went up. "Jesus, is that who that guy was? I thought he wanted me to reenlist! He kept going on about service to my country. I told him to get stuffed."

Jim laughed. "Recruiters in those days

were a little too subtle, I guess."

"Is that what you are? CIA?"

Jim ignored the question and returned to the file. "Let's see; out of Tech you worked for IBM, then Texas Instruments, then went off on your own with your financial whiz brother-in-law. Not cut out for the corporate life, either?"

"I guess you could say I made extensive use of personal initiative, tended to improvise. Big business didn't like it any better than the Marines did."

Jim nodded. "Then you got rich. Invented that printer, Ben took the company public. You paid all your debts, built a new house, built a boat. Net worth of a little over sixteen million, mostly in your remaining shares in the company, some real estate, money market, stocks. You've got a smart brother-in-law."

"You're pretty well informed," Cat said, squirming a little. "Do you know where my daughter is?"

Jim shook his head. "Sorry. You seem to think she's alive somewhere in Colombia, though."

"Yes."

"And you're determined to go down there and look for her."

"Yes."

"Colombia can be a very dangerous place," Jim said. "Is there anything I can say to talk you out of it?"

"Not unless you can tell me another way to get my daughter back."

Jim shook his head. "I'm afraid I can't," he said, "and if she were my daughter, I'd go after her, too." He rubbed his eyes with his knuckles. "Listen," he said, "why the hell not go down there? You're just as smart as the State Department guys and the Colombian police, who've done all the looking so far. Hell, smarter — you're rich! Your problem is, you're a little short of resources. But you can buy resources."

"Such as?"

"You're going to need some help down there, somebody who knows the territory. You don't speak any Spanish, do you?"

"No. None."

Jim opened the larger of his two cases and took out a hefty camera. He got up and removed a picture from the wall. "Stand over here," he said, taking off his necktie, "and put this on."

Cat did as he was told.

Jim continued talking while he snapped a picture, pulled a tab on the back of the camera, and glanced at his watch. "There's a guy who might be just the man, and

fortunately he's in Atlanta. He's an Australian, name of Bluey Holland; he's lived in
this country for a while — well, off and on,
anyway. He's spent a lot of time in Colombia, and he knows all the wrong people, if
you know what I mean."

"Do you think he might be free?" Cat
asked.

"Well, not exactly," Jim said. "He's in the
Atlanta Federal Penitentiary. But he's up
for parole soon. I can see that somebody
puts in a favorable word for him. You've
changed a lot since your last passport
picture was taken," he said, holding up a
sheet of four photographs of Cat.

"Well, apart from the beard and haircut,
I've lost about fifty pounds."

"That's good. Nobody's going to recognize you as the man who had his picture in
all the papers a while back."

"What's Bluey Holland in for?" Cat asked.

Jim returned to his chair, fished in the
large case, and came up with some sort of
small machine. "Old Bluey is a hotshot pilot
— Australian outback, bush flying in Alaska,
that sort of thing, and he's made not a few
runs between this country and various strips
in South America."

"I see," Cat said.

"This last time, though, Bluey got mixed

up with some Cubans on a deal — Jesus, nobody should get mixed up with Cubans these days — and they stuck him in Atlanta with them."

"Is this guy a hard criminal?"

"Well, let's just say that old Bluey has always taken a liberal view of U.S. Customs regulations. He doesn't hit people over the head and take their money, doesn't do contract killings. Bluey loves flying, preferably low and fast, and he prefers small, dark airports to big, brightly lit ones. He's a pretty capable sort of fellow, and as I've said, he knows the territory down there."

"How can I contact him?"

"I'll have him contact you when he's out. He won't know where the message came from. Tell him Carlos pointed you at him." Jim snipped the four photographs apart, took a small blue booklet from his case, and, using the machine in his lap, sealed a photograph into the booklet. "There's not a hell of a lot more I can do for you, except give you some thin cover."

"How do you mean, thin cover?" Cat asked.

Jim tossed him the booklet.

Cat opened it to find his photograph in the United States passport of one Robert John Ellis.

"You'll need this, too," Jim said, tossing something else.

Cat caught a well-worn wallet. Inside were half a dozen credit cards, a social security card, a Georgia driver's license, and other cards, much like the ones in Cat's pocket.

"Sign them and the passport."

Cat started signing.

"Ellis is a salesman with your company," Jim said. "Other than having a different name and address, he's a lot like you. His passport expires on the same date and it has the same stamps as yours, the same travel history. In fact, since you've lost so much weight and shaved the beard, his passport information is more like you than yours is."

"You really think I'll need all this?" Cat asked, a little nonplussed.

"I don't know, but if I were going where you are, I'd want some cover. The passport, the driver's license, and the credit cards are all real. You're on all the right computers as of today. If you go through Colombian or U.S. Immigration, the passport will hold up. If you charge dinner on the Ellis American Express Card, it will go on your company account. Oh, when you get back to Atlanta, have your company print some Ellis business cards, and tell your switchboard operator that if he gets any calls, to say he's in South America. You'd better brief your brother-in-law, too, but don't tell him about any of the ID materials, just that you might be travelling under the name of Ellis and to back you up."

"You've done all this since yesterday?" Cat asked, amazed. Now he knew why Jim was unshaven — he'd been up all night.

"All part of the service," Jim said. "Come over here to the window for a minute." He took some pieces of plastic from his pocket. "This is a Colombian entry stamp; you just pull off the plastic sheet, press it onto your passport on an empty page, then write in the date of your entry in ink. Be sure to use one on both your passports and on these." He went back to his briefcase and stapled photographs to two printed cards. "These are Colombian tourist visas for both your identities." He took two envelopes from the case. "This one is a passport for Bluey. He doesn't have one at the moment. Don't give it to him until you have to. He might use it to travel in another direction. Tell him he can keep it, just a little gift from Carlos." Jim held up the other envelope. "There are two passports here for Jinx, one in her own name, one in another; same photograph. If you find her, you'll want to leave in a hurry,

I expect."

"I'm a little overwhelmed by all this," Cat said.

"I wish I could do more," Jim replied. "I wish I could tell you how to find your daughter. But I think this stuff will improve your chances of getting in and out alive."

"I'm very grateful for your help, Jim," Cat said.

"Don't worry about it. Maybe one day you can do me a favor."

"Just ask. Anytime. Is there some place I can reach you when I get back? I'd like to let you know how it all works out."

"No." He started to pack up his equipment. "Give Bluey Holland a few days to spring himself, then he'll be in touch. Offer him fifty grand — ten now, and forty when you're back in the States. That ought to do it." Jim snapped a case shut. "You and I never met, of course."

"Right."

The two men shook hands. Cat opened the door.

"Listen, Catledge," Jim said with some feeling. "You're liable to be in some rough places. Watch your ass." He closed the door.

8

"Can I speak with Mr. Catledge, please?" The accent was broad and flat. He might have been calling from downtown Sydney.

"Speaking."

"This is Ronald Holland. I got a message to call you."

"Have you got cab fare?"

"Yes."

Cat gave him the address. "Tell the driver it's off West Paces Ferry Road, west of I-75."

"Right. About an hour, I guess."

Cat had somehow been expecting somebody on the scrawny, weasly side, but when he opened the front door he was confronted with a man of about six feet five, two hundred and fifty pounds. Cat, at six-three, didn't look up at all to that many people, but he looked up at this one. The face was round, open, cheerful; the sandy hair was receding. Cat put him at about forty-five. Bluey Holland held a small canvas suitcase in one hand.

"Holland," the man said.

"I'm Catledge; come on in."

Cat showed him ahead toward the study. On the way Holland got an eyeful of the large, handsomely furnished living room of the contemporary house. In the study, Cat offered a chair and sat down at his desk. Even though this man was his only hope at the moment, this was an employment interview, and Cat didn't want him to think he was going to automatically get the job.

"How do we know each other?" Holland asked.

"I understand you know your way around South America," Cat said, ignoring the question.

"Afraid not," Holland replied.

Cat felt a moment of panic. Had he got the wrong man?

"Just Colombia," Holland continued. "I know more about that place than the bloody Colombian Tourist Board."

"That'll do," Cat said, relieved. "How's your Spanish?"

"Useless in the libraries and classrooms of the world, crackerjack in Colombian bars and whorehouses," Holland said. "How'd you come by my name?"

"You available for a few weeks, maybe a

few months?"

Holland slapped his hands down on the arms of the leather chair. "Listen, mate, I've asked you twice how we come to be introduced, and you haven't answered me. I just did two years and seven months of a five-to-eight for doing business with people I didn't know, so I'll just push off . . ."

"A mutual acquaintance," Cat said. "Carlos."

Holland stopped talking, his mouth still open. "I know lots of blokes named Carlos," he said, warily.

Cat tried to keep his face still. He hadn't counted on this.

"Half the Latinos in the hemisphere —" Holland began.

"This Carlos isn't a Latino," Cat said quickly.

"The son of a bitch," Holland grinned. "I thought he was dead."

"Nope."

"Well, now I know how I got paroled first time at bat. You and Carlos work together, do you?"

"Just acquaintances," Cat said.

"Mr. Catledge," Holland said, relaxing into the chair, "my time is your time. What can I do for you?"

"How about a drink?" Cat asked, rising.

"I wouldn't spit up a scotch," Holland replied.

Cat picked up an old copy of *Time* magazine from his desk and dropped it in Holland's lap on the way out of the room. "Page sixty-one," he said. "That'll bring you up to date."

In the bar, Cat took his time about mixing their drinks. When he came back into the room, Holland was still reading. Cat handed him his drink and sat down on the sofa across from the man. Holland looked up, his face sad.

"I'm sorry," he said. "That was a bloody rotten deal."

"That's about the most complete account of the event the press published," Cat said, "but a lot has happened since then." He told the Australian in some detail of his efforts to find the pirates, then finally of the phone call from Jinx. "I'm going down there after her," he said. "I need help. Somebody who knows the territory; somebody to keep me out of trouble. Carlos says you're the man. Want to go with me?"

"Be delighted," Holland grinned.

"I'll pay you fifty thousand — ten up front and forty when we get back alive."

"That what Carlos told you to offer me?" Holland asked.

"Yep."

"Well, that seems fair, but how long are you reckoning on?"

"As long as it takes."

Holland made a sucking noise in his teeth. "That could be an awful long time," he said.

"I see your point," Cat agreed. "Tell you what; if it takes longer than a month, I'll pay you five thousand a week for as long as it takes."

"Done," Holland said. "Now what?"

"Let's go to Colombia."

"Now, let me get this straight," Holland said, holding up a hand. "You don't have any information you haven't told me about?"

"No. Now you know everything I know."

Holland rubbed his chin briskly. "Well, then, I guess we start at Santa Marta, then, since that's where this thing began, and since we haven't got a clue in the bloody world where else to start."

"Not a clue," Cat said. "I know it's a big country. Do you think we have any chance at all of finding her?"

Holland shrugged. "Listen, mate, Carlos thinks you've got a shot at finding her, or he wouldn't have put you in touch. If he thinks so, that's good enough for me. Sure, it's a big country, but when you're tracking down something as dirty as this, the geography shrinks. The people who do this sort of thing tend to congregate in certain parts of the country. We'll start in Santa Marta, because that's the beginning of the trail. I doubt if she's there, but somebody knows something. I know a couple of people there; we'll call on them. If I had to guess where she is, I'd say one of three places: The Guajira Peninsula, in the northeast; Cali, in the west; or in the Amazon country. If she's alive."

"She was alive a week ago," Cat said.

"That's your best hope," Holland replied. "If they didn't kill her when the boat went down, they want her for something."

Cat didn't want to think about why somebody might want Jinx. "Why those three places?" he asked.

"Because that's where the drugs get made, and sold, and smuggled."

"Why do you think this has something to do with drugs?"

"Because everything in Colombia — everything that's dirty, anyway — has something to do with drugs."

Cat had heard that before.

Holland reached down, unzipped his canvas bag, and removed a large magazine, printed on yellow newsprint, called

Tradeaplane. Cat had seen it around the flying school. "We're going to need an airplane," he said.

"What for?" Cat asked, surprised. "Don't the airlines fly to Colombia?"

"Oh, sure," Holland said, "but I don't have a passport; they took it away before my trial. And anyway, I expect my face would light up a few computers in both Colombian or U.S. Customs and Immigration. Then, once we're in the country, we have to be able to move around without the police paying too much attention to me. There's always police in airports."

"Then where would we land a light aircraft?"

Bluey grinned. "Well, there's airports and there's airports."

Cat remembered that he had a passport for Holland, but he remembered Jim's advice, too. "Okay, if you say so."

Holland waved a hand. "Your house, your car — you look as though you can afford a good airplane." He began flipping through *Tradeaplane.* "I reckon we'll need to spend somewhere between seventy and a hundred thousand bucks, depending on what's available locally. Of course if you want to go looking around the country, we could save some money."

"I'd rather save time. We'll get whatever you want."

Holland stood up. "I'll start looking today. You got a car I can borrow?"

Cat went to his desk and got some keys. "There's a Mercedes station wagon in the garage." He tossed Holland the keys.

Holland fingered his suit. "I'll need to pick up some gear as well."

Cat took a banded stack of bills from his desk drawer and tossed it to Holland. "There's your ten thousand," he said. "You've got yourself a job, Mr. Holland."

The Australian stuck out his hand. "Call me Bluey," he grinned.

Cat grinned back. "I'm Cat." He liked the man, but he still felt a little uncomfortable with him, knowing what he did about his past. Now he was giving him ten thousand dollars and Katie's Mercedes. What the hell, he thought, he could never do this on his own. He needed Bluey Holland, and he would just have to trust him.

That night Cat lay in bed and stared at the ceiling. He closed his eyes and conjured up Jinx's face, but it was not the face he had most recently seen. It was younger — twelve or thirteen. He could not quite form her image at a later age in his mind. He wondered if, eventually, he would not be able to remember her at all.

"I'm coming, kid," he said aloud into the darkness. "I'm coming to get you."

9

"Cat? Bluey. I think I've found our airplane."

"Great, Bluey. What's it going to run me?"

"The neighborhood of seventy-five grand — that's purchase price — we're going to need an annual inspection for five hundred to a grand, a loran navigator, and a fuel-flow meter — call that another six grand. Plus, we've got some fuel modifications to do south of here; say, a total of ninety grand all found."

"Okay, that sounds good. Can I have a look at her?"

"Sure, I'd want you to. I'm out at — what's this bloody field called?"

"Peachtree Dekalb?"

"That's the one. The airplane's sitting out in front of the tower. She's red and white; her tail number is 1 2 3 Tango."

Cat laughed. "I like her already. I'll be there in half an hour."

At the airport, Cat parked near the tower and started looking for a light twin-engine airplane with the right tail number, but to no avail. Then Bluey came out of a hangar and pointed. Cat's eyes came to rest on a single-engine Cessna, and he came to an abrupt halt. "Jesus, Bluey, you want to fly us over a thousand miles of open ocean in a *single?* That thing's not much bigger than the little trainer I've been learning in."

"Listen, sport," Bluey said indulgently, "let me give you a fact or two about airplanes. First of all, the fatality rate for singles and twins is identical. Second of all, if you have an engine failure in a twin, you have a very difficult airplane on your hands. It takes a lot of practice to fly a twin on one engine, and where I've been, they didn't offer that sort of leisure-time activity. And there are certain advantages in fuel efficiency with a single. Flying over water, I'll take a well-maintained single any day."

"Well . . ."

"This is a Cessna 182 RG, RG for retractable gear. It's one hell of a lot more airplane than the 152 you've been training in. She does a hundred and fifty-six knots — that's a hundred and eighty miles an hour — on about thirteen gallons of fuel an hour, and I can land her or take off in seven hundred and fifty feet of runway. She'll lift anything we can put in her with full fuel aboard, and not many airplanes will do that. She's only got four hundred hours on an engine that's designed to fly two thousand between overhauls, she's loaded with good equipment, and she's got long-range tanks. We're paying about five thousand over market value, but we're in a hurry, and airplanes this good aren't easy to come by. Now, if you want to hang around here for two or three more weeks while I find a decent twin and practice flying it on one engine, that's okay by me, but this is a damned good airplane. What do you want to do?"

Cat threw up his hands in surrender. "Sold."

"Good. How quick can you get back here with a cashier's check for seventy-five thousand dollars, made out to Epps Air Service?"

Cat glanced at his watch. "It'll have to be tomorrow morning."

"That's good. I'll get them started on the annual inspection. If the mechanic doesn't run into any unusual problems, we should be able to leave in about three days."

"As long as that?"

"Yep, that's good time for an annual and installation of the extra gear. We'll be stopping in Florida for a life raft and another modification or two on our way. I'll have you in Colombia in under a week's time, if there's not a hurricane in our way."

"Okay, you'll have your money first thing in the morning."

"Cat, you're going to need to take a lot of cash along."

"How much?"

"Well, the Florida modifications will come to a few grand, we're going to have to grease a lot of palms south of the border, and they don't take American Express in the Guajira or the Amazon. We're going to be buying goods and services from people who are used to dealing with customers who pay for things with fistfuls of hundred-dollar bills. You don't want to get caught short down there."

"I can probably arrange for my bank to wire me whatever I need down there."

Bluey shook his head. "We're liable to be in places where that won't be convenient, or even possible."

"Well, how much then?"

Bluey shrugged. "Well, I think you probably ought to have a hundred grand in walking-around money, just so people will take you seriously. Apart from that, well, we're talking about the possibility of ransom, aren't we? If we find your daughter alive, you may have to buy her from whoever has her."

"I see," Cat said, because he couldn't think of anything else to say.

Cat had a busy three days ahead of him. He paid for the airplane, then he saw his brother-in-law.

Ben listened quietly to what Cat had to say. "Cat, this is a crazy thing to do, but in your shoes, I guess I'd do the same thing. You really don't have another alternative, do you?"

"Thanks, Ben," Cat replied. "You've still got my power of attorney. Do whatever you think is best with the business."

"We've had a couple of feelers for a takeover. It would mean one hell of a lot of money for our remaining stock."

"Whatever you think is best, just don't commit me to an employment contract. I'm not sure I'll ever be able to concentrate on business again."

"I understand," Ben replied.

"I'll call you from down there whenever I get a chance."

"Good. I'll let you know whether there's anything important in the mail."

Cat saw his lawyer and made a new will,

leaving everything to Jinx, if she was still alive, a large bequest to his alma mater, and the rest to Ben, if Jinx was found dead. He specifically excluded his son from any inheritance.

On his way home from his lawyer's office he stopped at a camera store and bought a solidly built aluminum camera case, with combination locks, the size and shape of a large briefcase. At home, he cut a newspaper into a hundred small pieces, measured them, and made some calculations. He was surprised at the result. He called his stockbroker and gave him a sell order and some brief, firm instructions, then called the head office of his bank and asked to speak to the president.

"Mr. Avery's office," a secretary said.

"My name is Wendell Catledge. I'd like to speak with Mr. Avery," Cat said.

"What is this about, sir? Does Mr. Avery know you?"

"I'll discuss that with Mr. Avery. We've never met."

The secretary became officious. "I'm afraid Mr. Avery is in a meeting. If you'll leave your number . . ."

"I have a business account with the bank. The company name is Printtech. Please go and tell Mr. Avery that Wendell Catledge wishes to speak with him at once."

"I'm very sorry, but . . ."

"Please don't make it necessary for me to come to his office."

There was a short silence. "Please hold," she said, exasperated.

There was a longer silence, then a man's voice. "Mr. Catledge? Cat Catledge?" The man had been reading his *Fortune* and *Forbes.* "I'm sorry you were kept waiting. How can I be of service?"

Cat identified himself with the Printtech account number and his personal account number. He told the banker how he could be of service, explaining that the man could verify his instructions by calling him at the home number listed on his account records.

The man was uncomfortable. "May I ask . . . you understand, Mr. Catledge, that by law this sort of transaction has to be reported to the federal government."

"I quite understand. I'll be at your office at eleven tomorrow."

The banker was still balking. "This sort of thing takes time, you know."

"Mr. Avery," Cat said, becoming exasperated himself, "you have nearly twenty-four hours. All I really want to do is cash a check. I'll be at your office at eleven tomorrow morning."

"Yes, sir," the banker said.

Promptly at eleven the following morning, Cat presented himself at the bank. Avery took him into his office, then into an adjoining conference room. Another bank officer and a uniformed security guard were standing at the end of the table.

In the middle of the table was a stack of money.

"Twenty thousand hundred-dollar bills," Avery said, still sounding doubtful, "banded into bundles of five hundred, as you requested. Do you wish to count it?"

"No," Cat replied.

"There are some papers to sign."

Cat placed his aluminum briefcase on the table and opened it. "Please put the money into this case while I sign the papers," he said to the guard. Avery nodded and the guard began to pack the money.

Avery shoved some papers toward him. "First, please sign a check for two million dollars," he said.

Cat signed the check.

"Then, I have prepared a release of all liability on the part of the bank. We don't usually transact business this way, as you can understand."

Cat signed the release. He noticed that

the money fit nicely into the case, with a little room to spare. He had calculated correctly.

"That's all in order, then," Avery said. "I'd like our guard to walk you to your car. This is not the safest of neighborhoods, you know."

"Thank you," Cat said. "And thank you for doing this so quickly."

Avery walked him to the door. "Mr. Catledge, if you're in some sort of difficulty, I'll do anything I can to help," he said earnestly.

"Thank you, Mr. Avery," Cat smiled, "but it's nothing like that. I just have to do some business in a place where ordinary banking facilities aren't available. Please don't concern yourself further."

The guard walked him to his car, looking nervously about them. Cat thought he might have been less conspicuous alone. When he walked into the house the phone was ringing.

"Hello?"

"It's Bluey. We're on for tomorrow morning. You all squared away?"

"I think so. I've just got to pack. What will I need?"

"Summer clothes for everywhere except Bogotá, if we end up there. Bogotá is at better than eight thousand feet of elevation, cool and rainy. A raincoat will be heavy enough. Bring a business suit, in case we have to impress somebody."

"Okay. Anything else?"

"You own a gun?"

"No."

"Buy one. Buy one for me, too, come to think of it. Get me a .357 magnum with about a four-inch barrel and a shoulder holster. Get yourself whatever suits you."

Cat felt a little queasy at the thought of firearms. He had been shot with the last weapon he had owned. "You really think I ought to be armed?" he asked.

"Too bloody right. I'd take a bazooka if I could get it in a shoulder holster."

Cat went to the gun shop where he had bought the little shotgun for the yacht. The place was a wonderland of death, with every conceivable sort of weapon. He picked out a magnum for Bluey, but balked when choosing something for himself. The only handgun he had ever fired was the .45 automatic the Marines had given him, although he had fired Expert with the pistol and a carbine. He didn't want anything as big as Bluey's magnum, and finally he accepted the salesman's recommendation of a very expensive Hechler & Koch 9-millimeter automatic pistol, because it was light and held a fifteen-round magazine. He bought the appropriate shoulder holsters and a box each of ammunition and left the shop with everything in a brown shopping bag, feeling foolish.

By seven in the morning they had the airplane loaded, and Cat followed Bluey around the aircraft, learning the preflight inspection.

"You been taking lessons, huh?" Bluey asked. "How many hours you got?"

"About sixty. I was supposed to take my check ride for my private license a couple of weeks ago, but all this got in the way."

Bluey nodded. "Okay, you fly her. Let's see how good you are."

"What?"

Bluey shoved him into the left seat and climbed in beside him. "It's not all that different from the trainer you learned in. You've got a couple extra knobs, that's all, for the landing gear and the constant-speed propeller. Anyway, I'm the hottest instructor who ever came down the pike."

Cat shrugged. "Well, I guess my student license is good." He buckled in and, with Bluey reading the checklist and pointing at things, got the engine started. The tower wasn't open yet, so they checked the wind sock and taxied to the runway. Bluey announced their departure on the Common Traffic Advisory Frequency and nodded. "We're off. Full throttle."

Cat shoved the throttle all the way in and marveled at how the airplane accelerated, compared to the less powerful one he had been flying. As instructed, at sixty knots of airspeed he pulled back on the yoke and the craft rose into the air.

"Retract the gear," Bluey ordered. "Flaps up. At five hundred feet reduce throttle to twenty-three inches of manifold pressure — there's the meter, there — and trim the propeller back to twenty-four hundred rpm." He glanced at a chart. "Now start a turn to the left and aim for Stone Mountain. Climb to three thousand feet."

Cat did as he was told and picked out the giant granite lump that was Stone Mountain, rising through a patch of early morning mist.

Bluey got on the radio and called Atlanta Flight Services and opened the flight plan. "I filed for Everglades City," he said, winking, "but we're not landing there."

"Where are we landing?" Cat asked, while trying to concentrate on leveling out at three thousand feet.

"A little place near there. A friend of mine

runs it," Bluey said mysteriously. "You'll see when we get there. When you get to Stone Mountain, turn right to one eight zero degrees and hold your altitude. We've got to get past the Atlanta Terminal Control Area before we can climb to cruising altitude."

Twenty minutes later, Cat climbed to nine thousand feet and leaned out the engine. Bluey switched on the loran navigator and punched in the three-letter code, X01, for Everglades City. He pressed two buttons on the autopilot and sat back.

"Okay, let go the controls," Bluey said.

Cat let go and the airplane flew itself.

"Great thing, loran," Bluey grinned. "Now it will fly us straight to our destination at nine thousand feet, giving us ground speed and distance remaining. I'm going to grab a nap. Wake me when we're fifty miles out of Everglades City." He cranked the seat back, pulled the brim of his hat down over his eyes, and seemed to be instantly asleep.

Cat sat and stared at the instrument panel of the self-operating airplane. This was the biggest aircraft he had flown, and he was very pleased with himself. A decent takeoff, a good climb — his instructor would be proud of him. He sat back and gazed out over the clear, Georgia morning, at the green, lake-dotted earth below him. The loran clicked out the distance remaining and their ground speed, a hundred and sixty-seven knots. They must have a tail wind, he thought. It seemed a good omen.

When they were over South Georgia and the Okefenokee Swamp, Bluey opened an eye, glanced at the instrument gauges, then went back to sleep. The Gulf Coast of Florida appeared on their right, then the Tampa/St. Petersburg area. After three hours of flying, Cat woke Bluey.

"We're fifty miles out of Everglades City," he said to the Australian.

"Right," Bluey said, yawning. He scanned the instruments again, then pulled out a sectional chart of Florida and pointed to an area west of Everglades City. "Spike's place is about here," he said.

Cat looked at the chart. "That's the Everglades swamp," he said. "How the hell are we going to land there?"

Bluey grinned. "Oh, we'll put her down on a crocodile, if we have to," he said. A few minutes later he turned to Cat. "Reduce power for a five-hundred-foot-a-minute descent," he said. "The loran and the auto-pilot are still aiming us at the airport."

Cat eased back on the throttle, and the nose of the aircraft dropped. "I see an airport dead ahead," he said after a few minutes.

"That's our supposed destination," Bluey said. He waited another five minutes, then called Flight Services. "This is One Two Three Tango; I have the field in sight; please cancel my flight plan." He changed frequencies and announced, "Everglades traffic, One Two Three Tango, on a five-mile final for Runway One Five." He turned to Cat. "Switch off the autopilot and line up with one five. Make a normal, straight-in approach." Two miles out, he said, "Drop the gear and put in ten degrees of flaps. Let your airspeed drop to one hundred." One mile out, Bluey said, "Twenty degrees of flaps, eighty knots. Keep her at that speed and aim for the end of the runway."

Near the end of the runway, Cat started to flare for a landing, but Bluey took hold of the control column.

"Give me the airplane," he said. He punched the transmit button. "Everglades traffic, One Two Three Tango going around." He pushed in full power, flipped up the flaps a notch, and retracted the landing gear. He climbed to a hundred feet and made a sharp left turn. "Take the airplane," he said to Cat. "Maintain one hundred feet."

"One hundred feet?" Cat took the controls as Bluey began to tap a new longitude and

latitude into the loran.

"There we go," he said, flipping on the autopilot and pressing the altitude hold button. "Let the autopilot take it and keep a sharp lookout for radio towers."

Cat stared wide-eyed at the low swampland rushing past the airplane. "Jesus, Bluey," he said, "we're supposed to maintain five hundred feet above the nearest obstacle. Do you want to lose your license?"

"Are you kidding?" Bluey snorted. "What license?"

Cat tried to stop thinking about Federal Air Regulations and look for obstacles in their path. The distance to destination read twenty-seven miles on the loran.

A few minutes later, when the distance was down to three miles, Bluey said, "I've got the airplane." He switched off the autopilot, dropped the gear, and put in ten degrees of flaps. "Watch for traffic," he said, "although I don't think there'll be any."

Cat looked around them. It all looked like swamp to him. Where the hell was Bluey planning to land? His answer was a sixty-degree bank to the left and a loss of altitude. Then, as the wings came level again, he saw what seemed like an extremely short expanse of treeless ground, a small clearing, really, dead ahead of them.

"Full flaps, airspeed sixty-five knots, cut throttle," Bluey recited aloud to himself. The airplane skimmed some treetops, then dropped into the clearing. The landing gear touched the ground, and the moment the nose wheel touched, Bluey dumped the flaps and shouted to himself, "Brake hard!"

Cat held his breath as the trees on the other side of the clearing rushed toward them. The airplane seemed to float for a moment, then Cat felt his safety belt press into his chest as the brakes quickly brought their speed down. He took a deep breath and exhaled slowly. It had been a textbook short-field landing. He began to feel some confidence in Bluey Holland.

Bluey turned left and pointed at some more trees. A man waved from their shelter.

"There's old Spike," Bluey chortled. The man was waving them toward him. Finally, he held up crossed arms. Bluey spun the airplane a hundred and eighty degrees and killed the engine.

Cat climbed down from the airplane. Bluey waved him over to where Spike was standing.

"Spike, meet me mate —"

"Bob," Cat said quickly, sticking out his hand. He had already decided to use the Robert Ellis cover in Colombia. He might as well start now. From the looks of this place, the cops could arrive at any moment.

Spike was small and scrawny, but his hand was surprisingly big. "Howyadoin'?" he asked, as if he didn't really care. "Let's get this bird into the trees."

The three men pushed the airplane backward under a camouflage net.

"Welcome back to the world, Bluey," Spike said when they had finished. "What can I do you for?"

"Oh, let's see: a fifty-gallon auxiliary tank, a raft, a couple jackets, and some new paperwork and numbers ought to do it. Fuel, too. What'll that run me, and when can I get out of here?"

"Two grand for the tank, three for the raft and jackets, five for the paperwork and numbers, and ten bucks a gallon for the fuel. I got to bus it in here on an airboat. I'll throw in a bed and a steak."

"How quick?"

"I'm not too busy. You can take off tomorrow night."

"Do it, sport!" Bluey bellowed. "Now, point us at the beer. I want to get outside a pint or two in a hurry."

A few minutes later they were settled into a small, comfortable cabin with a supply of Swann's Lager, an Australian beer. "Spike was down under a few years back," Bluey chortled, "and now he won't drink anything else. Christ knows where he gets it."

Shortly, Spike joined them. "Where you bound for, Bluey?"

"I need a window at Idlewild the day after tomorrow."

"I'll make the call after dark," Spike said, sucking on a beer. "Jesus, Bluey, I thought you got hard time for that last one. What you doing running around loose?"

"Parole, mate. Model prisoner, and all that," Bluey laughed.

Spike turned to Cat. "Hell, Bob," he said, "this crazy old digger put down a DC-3 in a farmer's field up at Valdosta, Georgia, a couple years back. No engines! At night!"

"Didn't put a scratch on her, either," Bluey added, graciously accepting the praise.

"Shit, they should of give him a medal!" Spike crowed.

Cat looked at Bluey. "A DC-3? You mean a C-47? With no engines?"

Bluey nodded. "Worst piece of luck I ever had," he said. "Little miscalculation on the fuel."

Cat winced at the idea of putting the big twin-engine airplane down dead-stick in a field at night. He hoped Bluey would do a better job of calculating fuel the following night.

Spike left the cabin, and Cat turned to Bluey. "What's this about a 'window at Idlewild'? You talking about Kennedy Airport in New York?"

Bluey shook his head. "Nah. Now Idlewild is an airfield in the Guajira Peninsula of Colombia, a sort of aeronautical Grand Central Station for blokes in the business." He took a long swig of the Swann's. "Spike'll call down there tonight on his handy little high-frequency radio and get us a window, half an hour or so when we can land. It's the sort of place where it's best to be expected."

Cat nodded. "I think I'll take a little run around the clearing out there. That okay?"

Bluey nodded. "Stay near the trees, though. If you hear an aircraft, get yourself under some cover. Spike would like for folks to continue to think of this place as a deserted chunk of the Everglades."

Cat changed into some shorts and running shoes and left the cabin. He walked past an open-sided hangar where a twin Piper was being worked on by a man. There were already two men working on 1 2 3 Tango. He reached the clearing and started to jog. It was high noon, hot and sticky, but

Cat wanted the exercise. He didn't like running — he had done too much of it in the Marines — but there was no pool here, and the nearest water had unfriendly creatures in it.

He wanted to run, too, because he felt the paralysis of fear sneaking up on him, and it was best to move around when that happened. He tried to think of the last time he had felt that feeling coming over him and realized it must have been at boot camp, a long time ago. For Cat, exercise had always been an antidote for fear, and fortunately, as a shavetail ROTC lieutenant, there had been plenty of exercise available, because there had been plenty of fear to go around, too: fear of the drill instructors; fear of not being able to do what they wanted him to do; fear of humiliation before the rest of his company; fear of dying of what they had done to him — done to everybody — at Quantico.

Now he felt the fear he had associated with Colombia since the yacht had been sunk. He didn't want to go back there, and he especially didn't want to go back there in a single-engine airplane with a convicted drug smuggler. He had to go, he knew that, but now he was thinking of getting himself to Miami and taking Eastern

Airlines to Bogotá. He could meet Bluey later. But what would Bluey do if he was left here with ten thousand dollars and an airplane with new numbers and papers? Jim had told him not to give the man a passport until necessary. Wasn't money and an airplane even more tempting than a passport?

After two laps around the clearing in the heat and humidity, Cat was dragging. He went back to the cabin, took a cold shower, and lay down on his bunk for a few minutes, wrestling with this one, last decision. Bluey sipped a Swann's and read a paperback spy novel.

Finally, Cat got up, went to his luggage, and got the brown paper bag. "Here," he said, tossing the .357 magnum to Bluey.

Bluey caught it and nodded with approval.

Cat tossed him the shoulder holster and ammunition, then sat down at the table in the middle of the room with the 9-millimeter automatic. He took a deep breath, opened the manual, and started to fieldstrip the weapon.

Bluey watched him appraisingly from across the room. "You've done that before, have you, mate?"

Cat nodded. "A long time ago, in a galaxy far away."

He hadn't thought he would ever have to do it again.

10

It was just after eleven, and with no moon the darkness weighed heavily upon them. Cat looked nervously about him as Bluey, strapped into the left seat for the first time, did his run-up of the airplane. In the dim light from the instrument panel, Cat could see the bulky, fifty-gallon fuel tank in the rear compartment, where the luggage usually went, and the luggage piled into the back seat. On top of the luggage was the life raft, surprisingly compact, but heavy. Cat reckoned they were at least ten percent over the rated maximum gross weight for the airplane.

Both men wore deflated yellow life jackets and shoulder holsters with their respective weapons. ("Don't wear that thing under your jacket," Bluey had said. "Where we're going, you want everybody to know you're carrying.") Under his right arm Cat wore another kind of shoulder holster, a large, soft, leather wallet containing a hundred thousand dollars in hundred-dollar bills, this in addition to the two million dollars in the aluminum case lying next to the life raft, at the top of the pile of luggage. If they had to ditch this airplane, Cat intended to be sure that case went into the life raft with them. On the floor between the seats lay an Ithaca riot gun — a short, 12-gauge shotgun holding eight double-aught buckshot shells — that Bluey had bought from Spike. ("Scarier than a machine gun," Bluey had declared.)

In the shoulder holster with the money was Cat's Robert Ellis passport; the matching wallet was in his hip pocket. His own passport and wallet were in the aluminum case with the money. Cat now possessed a forged FAA Temporary Airman's Certificate, in each of his two names, declaring him to have recently passed his instrument rating. That was a joke, Cat thought, since he hadn't even earned his private pilot's license. (Spike had explained that the certificate was what a newly qualified airman was issued on completion of his examination. It was good for six months, and a hell of a lot easier to forge than a permanent certificate.)

They were loaded for bear, Cat thought,

and that gave him some reassurance, but the airplane was loaded, too, and that was making him very nervous. He watched as Bluey switched on the taxi and landing lights, flipped in twenty degrees of flaps, trimmed for takeoff, and shoved the throttle in. They sat with the brakes on, vibrating, until the engine reached full power, then Bluey released the brakes.

Cat was appalled at how slowly the airplane seemed to be gathering speed. The clearing couldn't be much more than a thousand feet long, and they were using up ground fast. Ahead, in the beams of the airplane's lights, the trees were growing alarmingly close. Then, at fifty-five knots, Bluey hauled back on the yoke, and the airplane staggered into the air at what seemed to Cat an impossible angle of ascent. Surely the aircraft would stall. Bluey brought the landing gear up and the angle increased even farther, and suddenly they were over the trees, and the Australian was pushing the yoke forward, letting the airplane gather speed.

Bluey grinned at him. "That's your actual short-field-takeoff-over-an-obstacle," he said, pleased with himself. "You want to remember how that felt, the angle and all. Might come in handy one of these days."

"Thanks for the demonstration," Cat replied, mopping his brow with his sleeve. The real thing had been quite different from practicing on a nice, long runway.

Bluey turned sharply toward Everglades City and kept the airplane flying low. A few minutes later, with the airport in sight, he began an ascent, simultaneously calling Flight Services on the radio. They had just departed Everglades City, he explained, and would like to file for Marathon, in the Florida Keys. The flight plan filed, Bluey relaxed.

"I told you it would lift anything you could put in it," he grinned at Cat.

"I believe you," Cat replied. "Why are we landing at Marathon?"

"We're not," Bluey said.

Silly question, Cat thought. He should be getting used to this by now. Bluey had pretended to take off from Everglades City, and now he would pretend to land at Marathon. His flight plan was on record. Their next stop would be the Guajira Peninsula of Colombia.

An hour later Bluey set up a landing at Marathon, called Flight Services and canceled his flight plan, then roared down the runway, ten feet above the ground. He switched off the rotating beacon, the navigation lights, the landing light, and the wingtip strobes, climbed to two hundred feet, and turned steeply to the southeast, flashing over the narrow island. Immediately, clear of the land, he pushed the yoke forward and dived at the water, causing Cat to close his eyes and grit his teeth in anticipation of the impact.

When nothing happened, he opened his eyes. "What's our altitude?" he asked shakily.

"About fifteen feet, I reckon," Bluey drawled.

Suddenly they blew past a sailing yacht, no more than a hundred feet from the wingtip on Cat's side.

"Watch out for boats," Bluey said, tardily.

"Sure thing," Cat said. "How long are we going to maintain this altitude?"

"All the way past Cuba to Hispaniola," Bluey said. "Take the airplane."

Cat lunged for the yoke as Bluey turned his attention to the loran, punching in another set of coordinates.

"Don't let her climb!" Bluey commanded.

Cat realized he had been unconsciously pulling the yoke back. He tried to settle down.

"Watch the water, not the altimeter," Bluey said. A moment later he took the controls back from a relieved Cat.

Bluey had told Cat they would be flying around Cuba, down the Windward Passage between that island and Haiti, but he had not told him they would be doing it at fifteen feet. Cat found it impossible to relax.

"There's a balloon back in the Keys on a fourteen-thousand-foot cable," Bluey said. "They run it up and use it to look down with radar. It's not up tonight, but we've got to stay under both the American and Cuban radar until we're in the clear. I don't want a couple of Fidel's MIGs using us for target practice."

For nearly two hours the airplane skimmed the sea, while Cat's eyes roamed the dim horizon looking for ships and small craft. At one point he saw some lights off to the right. He assumed they were Cuba, but he didn't want to distract Bluey by asking. Later, lights appeared dead ahead.

"There's Haiti," Bluey said. "We'll be climbing shortly."

The lights drew closer, and Bluey climbed a couple of hundred feet. Then a beach flashed beneath them, and the airplane began to climb in earnest.

"There's a nine-thousand-foot mountain out there," Bluey explained.

"Is nobody going to notice a strange

airplane over Haiti?" Cat asked.

"Oh, sure," Bluey said. "We're on American defense radar now. They'll think we're a Haitian airplane taking off. We're on Haitian radar, too, if they're awake, which I doubt, but Haiti doesn't have an air force, so what the hell?"

Clear of the island, Bluey set the autopilot's altitude hold at nine thousand feet, leaned out the engine, and tapped in a new longitude and latitude. "That's Idlewild," he said. "We'll be there in about six hours. Our window is between seven-thirty and eight o'clock. I built us an extra half hour into the flight plan for safety."

"Safety?"

"If you arrive early or late at Idlewild, they shoot you down when you try to land," Bluey explained cheerfully. "Touchy lot."

"I see," Cat said. "Have you flown in there often?"

"I guess I've made a couple dozen round trips."

"How will they know who we are?"

"We've got a code. Idlewild is Bravo One, we're Bravo Two. How'd you meet Carlos, Cat?"

"We had a mutual friend. How'd you meet him, Bluey?"

Bluey laughed. "I was dusting crops in

Cuba in '59. Batista was still in power, but Fidel and his merry band of men were pressing hard. A lot of foreigners — a lot of Cubans too — were leaving the country, but I stuck around. There was money to be made, and I was young and foolish. One day, I was gassing up the airplane, and this Cuban peasant sidles over to me and asks me if I want to make some extra money. Asks me in an American accent. I do a double take, then I say, sure, I'd like to make some extra money. He gives me a camera and says he wants some pictures of a beach near the cane field I was spraying, wants 'em from less than a hundred feet, a couple hundred yards offshore. I made two or three passes, got the pictures, got paid. We had a few beers, got along. The beach was at a place called Bahia de Cochinos. Bay of Pigs."

Bluey poured himself some soup from a thermos Spike had given them, then continued. "When Castro broke out, I flew the crop duster to Key West — liberated it, you might say — and started a little business in Florida. Couple years later, when I'm pretty sick of crop dusting, I get a call from Carlos. God knows how he found me. Next thing I know, I'm in Guatemala, where they're training Cubans for the party at the

125

Bay of Pigs. During the invasion I dropped supplies onto the beach from a DC-3, not the most fun I ever had, and I took a little shrapnel in the ass doing it. I ditched in the ocean and got picked up by a landing craft. Carlos was waiting for me when they took me aboard ship. Over the years since, he's popped up now and then with a job, always for good money."

"He's CIA, then?" Cat asked.

"If you say so," Bluey chortled. "He never once showed me his credentials, just his money. That was always genuine, so I never asked questions. He's a good bloke, though."

"I guess he is, at that," Cat said. "He's all right with me, anyway."

"You sleepy?" Bluey asked.

"Are you kidding? My adrenaline is still pumping from your low flying."

"You take the airplane for a while, then. I'll grab a nap. Just keep scanning the oil pressure, cylinder-head temperature, and oil temperature." He pointed out the gauges. "If anything gets out of the green, or if you're worried about something, wake me up." He wound his seat back and tipped his hat over his eyes.

Cat glanced around the instrument panel. With the loran navigating and the autopilot flying, there wasn't much to do. He ate a sandwich and drank some coffee. The engine droned reassuringly on, and the gauges held rock steady. The moon came up and reflected on the sea below, silver on blue. The stars wheeled above in a cloudless sky. Cat felt a kind of contentment from knowing that he was doing all he could do — at least as close to contentment as he had come since the yacht went down, and he savored the moment as best he could with Jinx still in the front of his mind. Once in a while he still got an involuntary flash of the bloody palmprint, even though he now knew that the body had not been Jinx's. He wondered who the poor girl had been and why she had been murdered with Katie. It made no sense at all, and that bothered him. Had he imagined the voice on the phone was Jinx? Had she really gone down with Katie and *Catbird*? Was he risking his life and his liquid wealth on a fool's errand to find a girl who couldn't be found because she was at the bottom of the sea?

A couple of hours out of Haiti, Cat stirred himself from his reverie to check the instrument panel, as he had every few minutes since Bluey had gone to sleep. The gauges still held steady, and their true airspeed was right at a hundred and fifty-six knots, just where it should be. Fuel flow was twelve and a half gallons an hour, and there were something over five hundred miles remaining to Idlewild. The ground speed, though, was displayed on the loran as a hundred and twenty-eight knots. Startled, he quickly checked the other instruments again. Everything was normal. He gave Bluey a shake.

"What?"

"The loran is showing a lower ground speed than our true airspeed. Have we got a head wind?"

Bluey glanced at the instruments. "Too bloody right, we've got a head wind. Damn near thirty knots of it." He checked their time to destination on the loran against their remaining flying time on the fuel-flow meter. "Shit," he said. "If we go higher, we might get even more head wind; if we go lower, the head wind might decrease, but we'd be burning a lot more fuel at a lower altitude. We're best off where we are, but that ain't so hot. Our reserve is going to get eaten up. I calculate that if the wind holds where it is and we cut, we'll make the coast with six minutes of fuel remaining."

"Is that enough to make Idlewild?" Cat asked, alarmed.

"Maybe," Bluey replied, looking dour. "We're past the point of no return; we've

128

got to go on and hope for the best." He reduced power slightly. "We'll cut power to fifty-eight percent. That's our most efficient setting, but it's cutting another four knots off our airspeed, and that's cutting into our time reserve for our window at Idlewild. We sure as hell don't want to be late there. Maybe the wind will drop. Maybe the fuel-flow meter is inaccurate in our favor."

Or, Cat thought, maybe the wind won't drop and maybe the meter is inaccurate and not in our favor. Maybe we'll have to ditch, or maybe we'll be late at Idlewild and get machine-gunned for our trouble.

"Let's start pumping our auxiliary fuel into the wing tanks," Bluey said, fiddling with the fuel pump.

They flew on in silence for another hour, and their ground speed dropped another three knots. Their head wind was rising.

Bluey shoved the throttle in again. "We've got to go back to full power," he said. "We're at the outer limits of our time reserve now."

The airplane flew on toward South America, and soon pink began to show in the eastern sky. Bluey did some more work with the loran. "Now it looks like four minutes of fuel when we cross the coast," he said.

Cat said nothing. He was willing the airplane to fly faster, the wind to drop, the engine to use less fuel.

With eighteen minutes of fuel showing on the meter, Bluey let out a shout. "The coast! The bloody coast! We're not going to have to swim ashore, anyway."

Cat looked up to see a brown line of land ahead, lit by a rising sun.

Both men's eyes alternated between the fuel-flow meter and the Colombian coastline, which seemed to be nearing at all too slow a rate.

"Bravo One, this is Bravo Two," Bluey said to the radio. He was greeted by nothing but static. "We're still too far out," he said. Then his face fell, and he pointed at the loran. A red light had come on. "That means the signal is unreliable." The red light went off. So did the loran display. "We're at the outer limits of the loran chain." The display came back on, then went off again. "Bravo One, this is Bravo Two. Do you read?" Static.

They crossed the coastline, and Cat looked at the fuel-flow meter. Two and a half minutes' fuel remaining.

"I'm going to hold this course for another five minutes, then start a descent," Bluey said, grim-faced. He switched on another navigation radio. "Maybe I can get a radial and a distance from the Barranquilla VOR." He fiddled with the radio. "Dammit, we're getting the VOR signal, but not the distance-measuring equipment. Out of range. Maybe . . ." As he spoke a red flag appeared on the instrument. "Correction," he said, "we're not getting the VOR, either. What else can go wrong?"

As if in answer to his question, the engine sputtered, then caught again. The fuel-flow meter was showing a minute and fifteen seconds. The engine sputtered again, and the meter read zero. The engine ran for another half a minute, then gave a final sputter and died. The nose of the airplane dropped.

"We're landing this airplane," Bluey said, somewhat unnecessarily, Cat thought. "Check your side for a place to put her down. Bravo One, this is Bravo Two. Cat, you make the radio call. I've got to turn this crate into a glider."

Cat began speaking the code words into the radio while looking desperately out the window for someplace to land. "It looks pretty flat down there," he said to Bluey. There was brown, dry-looking land, dotted with scrub brush, all around them.

"It is flat," Bluey came back. "The Gua-jira Peninsula is shaped like Florida and looks like Arizona. It's a desert down there, and I can put us down in one piece, more or less, but I don't want to land in the middle of nowhere with no transportation, no refueling, and at the mercy of any bastard who's inclined to shoot us for our shoes." He had the airspeed down to eighty knots now, the airplane's best glide speed. The altimeter was showing a steady decline, and the earth was getting closer.

"Bravo One, this is Bravo Two," Cat repeated. "Bravo . . . Jesus, Bluey, what's that?" He was pointing just ahead of the right wing, a couple of miles ahead in the bright morning sunshine.

Bluey rolled the airplane to the right slightly and looked where Cat was pointing. "I'll tell you what that is," he crowed, "it's a goddamned dirt strip! Looks like an old crop duster's field!" He pointed the airplane at the gash of earth. "We've got enough altitude, too. We're going to make it! Oh, Jesus, I hope they've got fuel!"

"Bravo One, this is Bravo Two," Cat said, mechanically, keeping his eyes glued to the strip. They passed over it at a couple of thousand feet.

"Is that some sort of tank down there?" Bluey asked, pointing.

Cat looked and saw what looked like a

large metal cylinder lying on its side. "I hope it's not a water tank," he said.

Bluey made a three-hundred-and-sixty-degree turn to lose some altitude, then lined up with the dirt runway and let the airplane glide toward it. When he was sure they had it made, he lowered the gear and some flaps, and the airspeed came down to seventy knots. "Picture-book approach!" he chortled. They landed smoothly enough, and Cat marveled at how quiet it was with no engine. The runway was rough, but passable. Bluey let the airplane roll until it came to a stop on its own. Ahead of them about fifty feet, just off the strip, was what looked like about a five-hundred-gallon tank set on a wooden cradle about ten feet off the ground. "That's fuel," Bluey said, pointing. "Look, there's a hose. Quick, let's get the airplane over there."

They scrambled out of the airplane and began pushing on the wing struts. The aircraft moved slowly across the pebble-strewn dirt strip. Cat looked around but saw only a shack with a tin roof about fifty yards on the other side of the tank. Was it really a fuel tank? Was there anything in it?

Finally, they were within reach of the hose. As Bluey ran for it Cat saw some letters roughly painted on the side of the tank:

100LL. It was aviation fuel.

"Quick!" Bluey whispered, glancing at the shed. "There's a collapsible stepladder in the luggage compartment with the auxiliary fuel tank. Get it, and be quiet about it! If there's anybody sleeping in that shed, I don't want to wake them."

Cat ran around the airplane, opened the compartment, and found the little stepladder. He ran back to the right wing, set up the ladder and stood on it, taking the fuel hose from Bluey. He got the tank open and the nozzle inside.

"It's not even locked," Bluey said in a loud whisper.

Cat squeezed the handle and fuel began to flow. The tank was about half full when Bluey tugged at his trouser leg.

"Get down from there; get the shotgun and cover me."

Cat looked over his shoulder and saw four sleepy-looking Indians approaching them from the direction of the shack. Three of them had pistols. The fourth was wielding a light submachine gun. Quickly, he got the cap back on the fuel tank and jumped down.

"Give me some money," Bluey said hoarsely.

Cat dug into his shoulder holster and snatched out a bunch of fresh, new hundred-dollar bills. He gave them to Bluey, tossed the collapsible stepladder into the airplane, and grabbed the shotgun. He stood under the wing, his feet apart, with the weapon held at a stiff port arms, and tried to look calm.

"Amigos," Bluey cried out, waving to the men. They stopped, and one of them began to talk rapidly. He stopped.

"What's he saying?" Cat asked out of a corner of his mouth.

"I don't know," Bluey said, "but he's pretty mad."

"What do you mean, you don't know? You said you speak Spanish!"

Bluey shook his head. "Yeah, but this is some kind of dialect."

The Indian started talking again, and the man with the submachine gun cocked it ominously. Cat, somewhat to his surprise, worked the pump of the shotgun noisily. The four men all stepped back, staring at it. Bluey had said it was scary.

Bluey stepped forward and held up a hundred-dollar bill. The Indian stopped talking, then waved him forward. Bluey began to speak in Spanish, smiling, waving the money. Cat heard the word "amigos" used several times. The Indians were glancing at each other.

Bluey called over his shoulder without taking his eyes from the men, "How much fuel did you get into the tank?"

"Maybe half full," Cat called back.

Bluey continued to talk. Now he was peeling off hundreds, counting loudly in Spanish. One of the Indians stepped forward, nodding, and took the money. The man with the submachine gun still looked threatening.

Bluey turned and began to walk toward the airplane. "Just keep standing there with the shotgun," he called to Cat. "I'm going to turn the airplane around, then we'll get the hell out of here." He walked to the rear of the plane, pushed down on the horizontal stabilizer, lifting the nose-wheel off the ground, and spun the airplane on its axis. When it was pointing down the runway again, he began to climb inside. "When the engine starts, get your ass in here," he called to Cat.

"Right," Cat replied. A moment later the engine cranked, then fired. Cat, half backing, made his way around the airplane, waving and smiling at the four Indians. They remained impassive and suspicious. Cat leapt into the airplane, and it started to move.

"No time for a run-up," Bluey said, shoving the throttle to the firewall. "Here we go. I hope those bastards don't start shooting."

The airplane rolled down the short strip, picked up speed, and lifted easily into the air, lightened by its lessened fuel. Cat let out a long sigh.

"Okay," Bluey said, "we've got a little more than an hour of fuel. Let's find Idlewild. Bravo One, this is Bravo Two."

To Cat's astonishment, a voice immediately said, "Bravo Two, this is Bravo One. How far out are you?"

Bluey let out a whoop. "Stand by," he said into the radio.

He pushed a button on the loran, and it came to life. "Bearing one three five degrees, distance twenty-two miles," he said into the radio. "Sorry we're late."

"Exactly how late are you?" the voice asked, suspiciously.

Bluey glanced at his watch. "Thirty-one minutes," he replied.

There was a pause, then: "Right, you're cleared to land, Bravo Two," the voice said.

Bluey and Cat looked at each other.

"Does that mean we won't get shot at?" Cat asked.

"Looks that way," Bluey grinned.

Five minutes later, Bluey pointed dead ahead. "Field in sight!" he shouted.

Cat looked at the long strip of dirt ahead of them and smiled weakly. "How much was the fuel?" he asked.

"A thousand bucks," Bluey said, dropping the landing gear and lowering the flaps. "Do you mind?"

"A bargain," Cat said, and meant it.

11

A man waved them to a parking place alongside half a dozen other aircraft — a DC-3 and some light twins. They turned the airplane and pushed it backward under a camouflage net. Cat was surprised to find himself on pavement. The airstrip was evidently covered by a thin layer of dirt, and not by nature's design. As Cat watched, a small house on a trailer was hauled into the middle of the runway, and brush was placed in other strategic places.

"Makes it hard to spot from the air," Bluey said. "They don't uncover unless they're expecting you, and anybody else who tried to land would have to run right through the house." He led the way to a low building under more camouflage netting. Inside, a man at a desk looked up. He was at least seventy, skinny with a thin, white beard.

"Bluey," he said. He looked as if nothing

could surprise him. "What do you need?"

"Hi, Mac." Bluey flopped down in a rickety chair and gazed at the ceiling fan whirling above him. "Fuel, a car for a couple days, some stamps on my papers."

"How much fuel?"

"Just the wing tanks. About eighty gallons, I guess."

"A grand in advance, and five grand deposit on the car. You can make your own deal on the stamps." He picked up a microphone and said something in Spanish. His voice boomed across the strip over loudspeakers. "There's a *capitán* around somewhere."

Bluey peeled off most of the rest of the money Cat had given him. "Right. What kind of car?"

Mac tossed him some keys. "There's a newish Bronco outside. You bend it, you buy it, and it's expensive."

"Right."

The door opened and a uniformed Colombian police officer came in. Cat tensed, but Bluey stood up, shook his hand, and held a brief conversation in Spanish. There was some bargaining, and Bluey turned to Cat. "Give me a couple thousand."

Cat handed him another wad of bills. Bluey produced the airplane's papers. The policeman opened a briefcase, stamped the documents in several places, then made out a lengthy form, occasionally asking Bluey questions. Cat thought he heard a reference to passports, and Bluey shook his head. Cat produced his Ellis passport and Bluey's, and the man blithely stamped them, hardly looking at them before returning them to Cat. He had been paid, and he couldn't care less whose passports they were. Bluey looked puzzled but paid the man without comment.

"Come on," Bluey said when the policeman had gone, "let's get our gear into the car and get out of here."

Cat handed Bluey his passport. "A little present from Carlos."

Bluey looked at it and laughed. "Oh, he's wonderful, he is. I've been travelling in Europe these past couple of years, according this. I'll bet he told you not to give it to me until you had to."

"He did."

"Ever cautious, Carlos." He looked at Cat quizzically. "Why now, then?"

Cat returned his gaze. "Because I think I can trust you."

"Thanks, mate," Bluey said. "Feels nice to be legal again. Now both our passports and the airplane have been cleared through

Cartagena, all perfectly legal, thanks to that bloody bent copper back there. We can go anywhere in Colombia, and no sweat." They walked back into the little office.

"How long you tying down, Bluey?" Mac asked.

"Just a couple days."

"It's a hundred a day. You can pay when you leave. You need any work done on the bird?"

"Nah, she's fine. I'd like it if she was in one piece when I get back. Tell me, Mac, is Florio still working out of the Excelsior in Riohacha?"

Now Mac had found something to look surprised about. "You changing your habits, Bluey?"

"I wouldn't be down here in a light single."

"Yeah, he's still there. Don't show him any money, though, not until he's showed you something."

"Too right. Thanks."

In the car, Bluey produced a road map. "We're here, near the thumb of this mitten-shaped peninsula, about thirty miles inland. We'll drive down to Riohacha, on the coast, and nose around a bit."

"Why not just go on to Santa Marta?" Cat asked. "It's early and it doesn't seem all that far." He pointed to the town and measured the distance against the scale. "About two hundred and fifty miles."

"Before we start doing detective work down there, I want to feel around out here in the Guajira a bit, see what we can turn up," Bluey answered. "I've been away a while, you know, and I want to get my feet on the ground again and see what's happening before we charge into Santa Marta and start asking questions. Okay?"

Cat nodded. "Whatever you think best. What was that business between you and Mac, about you changing your habits?"

"Florio is a coke dealer. I'm known down here as a grass man. I've never run anything else. Shitty stuff, cocaine, screws people up. I've never wanted any part of that."

"What do we want with a cocaine dealer?"

"Well, there ain't any tourists in the Guajira," Bluey said. "Out here, people make a pair of gringos as either buyers or narcs. People they think are narcs don't live long, so we want to establish ourselves as buyers right off."

"I see." The idea of being thought of as a drug buyer didn't rest easily with Cat, but the idea of being dead was worse.

They climbed into what seemed a brand-new Ford Bronco, a four-wheel-drive vehicle with a leather interior and air-conditioning, and were let out a gate in a chain-link fence. Shortly, they came to a ramshackle settlement, and Bluey stopped in the only street in front of a mud building.

"I just want to pop into the cantina here and pick up a cold beer. You want anything?"

Cat shook his head. "It's early for me, but I'm going to be hungry pretty soon."

"I'll get some food, too. You stay with the car, okay?" He got out and went inside.

Cat looked around him. The settlement was nothing more than two rows of mud houses with tin roofs and shanties, made of almost anything, on either side of a dusty, rutted road. A pig was rooting in the road a few yards away, and a couple of dogs lay sleeping in the morning sun. A few minutes passed, and Cat saw a truck appear a hundred yards down the road, in a dusty haze of rising heat, driving slowly toward him. There were half a dozen men standing in the back, and they appeared to be armed. The truck came slowly on, weaving a bit, as if the driver was drunk. Suddenly, there was a popping noise, and the ground around the pig erupted. The animal screamed and went down. He struggled to his feet again and ran off the road, dragging a useless leg.

Cat could see two bullet holes in his rump, pouring blood. There was more noise and mud flew from some buildings across the road.

Bluey came to the door of the cantina. "Get in here, quick!" he shouted.

Cat jumped out of the car and ran inside. He joined Bluey, pressed flat against the wall facing the street. "What the hell is going on?" he whispered to Bluey.

"Some of the locals had a little too much up the nose, I expect," Bluey replied. There was another burst of automatic gunfire, and a large picture on the back wall of the cantina exploded, then fell from the wall. "They get paid what for them is fabulous amounts of money, then they snort up everything they can get their hands on. It's a bit like the Old West out here."

Cat heard the truck move on and more gunfire. After another minute, Bluey stuck his head out the door.

"All clear; let's go." They got into the car and drove on. Miraculously, it was unscathed. "What you've got to understand," Bluey explained, "is that out here there's too much money and cocaine, and no law at all. Even the army doesn't poke into the Guajira very often."

"Christ, is the whole country like this?"

"Oh no, no. It's a lovely country, most of it; lovely people. It's just the Guajira that's wild. Mind you, you can get your pocket picked or your throat cut just about anywhere. You just have to exercise the same caution you would in, say, New York City."

This, Cat thought, was the country to which he had brought two million dollars in a briefcase. And, he reflected, where somebody had taken his daughter from him for God knew what reasons.

They bounced along a dirt track, through scrub brush and cactus for some time, then broke onto the coast road at a place Bluey identified as Carrizal. The track became a road here, but not much of one. Bluey made the best time he could, and Cat gazed out drowsily at the blue Caribbean on his right. The sun was well up now, and the heat was bearing down. Cat rolled up his window and switched on the air-conditioning. They passed through a collection of ramshackle buildings known as Auyame, then came to a place called Manaure. Cat was contemplating the sameness of these places, when suddenly he jerked upright in his seat, pointing.

"Out there, Bluey, anchored just beyond the trawler."

"The white one?"

"Right. The sportsfisherman." Cat's heart

146

was pounding. "Jesus, I think that's it."

"What?"

"The *Santa Maria,* the boat the Pirate was on."

Some buildings blocked their view for a moment, then Bluey turned down a side street toward the sea. After a moment, the water appeared again. They were facing a harbor, open to the east, but bound by a long point of land to the north. An assortment of boats rode at anchor, some of them looking very fast indeed.

"A lot of these are runners," Bluey said, maneuvering the car to the side of the road and stopping. "They take bales of grass out to ships waiting offshore." He pulled a new pair of binoculars from his luggage. "Have a look through these."

Cat, trembling, put the binoculars to his eyes and focused. Could they have gotten lucky this fast? The boat came into sharp focus, and immediately, Cat saw a man sitting in the fisherman's chair, aft, smoking a cigar. The man seemed Anglo, gray hair, in his fifties. Not familiar. He panned slowly the length of the boat. Something was wrong, he wasn't sure what. He closed his eyes and ran the scene again in his head. The boat was approaching *Catbird* off her starboard quarter; the name, *Santa Maria,* was clearly visible on her bows. He opened his eyes again. There was no name on the bows of this boat, but that could have been changed. There was something else, though. The davits, aluminum arms for bringing a dinghy aboard. The *Santa Maria* had had no davits on her stern. They could have been added, though. Cat watched as the wind shifted, and the boat began to swing her stern toward them. As she came around, a name appeared on her stern, *Mako,* out of Guadeloupe. A stab of disappointment hit Cat, but it wasn't the name that did it. He could see into the wheelhouse. The boat's wheel was on the port side, and he had a clear memory of the Pirate steering the *Santa Maria* from the starboard side. As she had approached *Catbird* the man had stuck his head out over the gunwales while turning the wheel and throttling back.

"I'm wrong," Cat said. "This boat's newer, too. The *Santa Maria* was seedier."

"You're sure?" Bluey asked.

"I'm sure. Sorry for the false alarm."

"That's okay. Shows you're on your toes. You were half asleep when that boat hove into view."

Cat lay his head back as Bluey drove away. He was tired from being up all night on the airplane, and now the adrenaline charge from seeing the boat was draining away, leaving him feeling washed out. He dozed.

Bluey woke him on the outskirts of Riohacha; he pulled over and shrugged out of his shoulder holster. "Time to put these under the jacket," he said.

Cat sleepily followed his instructions, pulling a light bush jacket on, covering the pistol. He looked around him. The shacks on the outskirts of town gave way to real buildings of stucco with tile roofs. The shops were opening, and traffic, what passed for rush hour in Riohacha, was on the move.

Bluey drove into the center of town, which somehow combined being sleepy with being busy, and pulled up in front of the Excelsior Hotel, which did not live up to its name.

Cat was annoyed to see Bluey slip a hundred-dollar bill to the boy who took the car away, and another to the boy who brought in the bags.

"You're going to have to trust me on this, sport," Bluey said, noting his expression. "These people are not going to render a hell of a lot of service for the money, but unless we're generous, we'll come back and find the car stripped and the bellhop looking the other way."

Shortly, they were ensconced in a large room at a corner of the hotel overlooking the sea. The place had a certain seedy elegance about it, and Cat did not doubt that it had once been grander. At least the hot water worked, and a soak in the tub cleansed away the Guajira dust and soothed his cramped muscles. They had been in the airplane and car for more than twelve hours. Totally drained, Cat made it to the bed before losing consciousness.

It was dark when Bluey shook him. "Come on, mate, it's dinnertime."

Cat got his feet onto the floor, but his head felt better in his hands. "What time is it?"

"Going on nine. Our table's in five minutes."

Cat struggled into some clothes. "Listen, I could have slept straight through until morning. I think I'll pass on dinner."

Bluey shook his head. "Dinner's important. We'll get our first look at Florio."

Cat followed Bluey downstairs to the Excelsior dining room, which also carried hints of former glory. The headwaiter's dinner jacket was a little small, but he was not short on dignity. Bluey ordered roast meats and a bottle of Chilean wine. The food was better than Cat had expected, and he ate hungrily.

In the middle of their dinner, Bluey

nudged him under the table. Cat looked up to see a party of eight entering the dining room. At the obvious center of the group was a carefully barbered Latino in a cream-colored suit, wearing a great deal of gold jewelry.

"Florio," Bluey said under his breath.

The party settled at a large table in the corner of the dining room and began looking at menus. Florio's three male companions were lesser versions of him, and the women were dark and flashily dressed.

Cat tried not to stare, but he had never seen a big-time drug dealer before, if he didn't count his son. The man was the center of attention and enjoying it, the headwaiter and his staff fawning over him.

"You finished?" Bluey asked.

Cat nodded. "I don't think I could handle dessert."

Bluey waved the headwaiter over. "You got some Dom Pérignon?"

"Of course, señor. Always."

"Send two bottles over to Florio's table with my compliments."

The man scurried away.

"That'll be our calling card," Bluey said to Cat. "Now, let's turn in."

They were having breakfast in their room

the next morning when there was a knock on the door. Bluey answered it, and there was a brief conversation in Spanish. He returned to the table. "We have an appointment with Florio in half an hour," he said, buttering some toast. "Don't wear a gun, and let me do the talking."

They presented themselves at Florio's suite at the appointed time and were thoroughly searched by a stone-faced man who had been at the table the evening before. When he was sure they were wearing no weapons, he ushered them into a sitting room and waved them to a chair. It was obvious that Florio had furnished the place himself. The furniture was heavy, overstuffed, and covered in various bright shades of synthetic velvet. One wall was dominated by a large and awful painting of a bullfighter, done in iridescent acrylics. Shortly, Florio entered the room, wearing a red silk dressing gown. He arranged himself on a sofa before them and stroked his thin Pancho Villa moustache. His face was puffy and paler than it had seemed the night before, and Cat wondered if he had been wearing makeup.

"Ah, Mr. Holland," Florio said, smoothing the gown and not looking directly at them, "I had understood we were not in quite the same business." His English was heavily accented but quite good.

"I've recently changed businesses," Bluey replied.

"Oh?" Florio said, lifting his eyes to gaze languidly at the Australian. "How can I be of assistance?"

"I'm not at all sure that you can," Bluey replied. "I'm in the market for two hundred kilos of the purest."

All expression left Florio's face, and Cat could not tell if he was stunned or if his mind were racing.

"The market price is twenty-one thousand a kilo these days," Florio said finally.

Bluey shook his head. "I don't expect to pay that for quantity," he said. "I might go to thirteen thousand."

Cat was calculating rapidly in his head. Two hundred kilos at thirteen thousand dollars a kilo was two million, six hundred thousand dollars, which they didn't have. Was Bluey trying to get them killed?

Florio was silent for another long moment. "One assumes you have the money readily available."

"Of course not," Bluey said. "I can arrange it on forty-eight hours' notice, though, to be exchanged for the merchandise in an agreed fashion."

Florio was quiet again. A slight expression of distress crossed his face, and finally he shrugged. "Señor, I am afraid that I cannot be of assistance to you. The market is, well, difficult at the moment. I could manage only a small part of what you wish."

Bluey nodded. "Thank you for being frank with me."

"Is there any other way in which I might assist you?"

Bluey was about to rise, but stopped. "Perhaps," he said, pausing on the edge of his seat. "I understand there are people from whom a beautiful young woman might be purchased."

Cat resisted the impulse to lean forward. Instead, he watched Florio's face carefully.

Florio laughed aloud. "But of course, señor, such people are on every street corner in Riohacha, or the bellman could assist you. But why do you ask this of *me?*"

Bluey shook his head. "I beg your pardon, I have not made myself clear. I am not interested in a local prostitute, but in a more permanent purchase. An Anglo, perhaps."

Again, Cat watched the man's face closely.

Florio looked at them blankly. "I am most sorry," he shrugged, "but you ask me something of which I have no knowledge. I deal in quite a different commodity."

"Of course," Bluey said, rising, "I wished merely to ask your advice."

Florio rose with him. "I am flattered that you would ask me, and I am sorry that I cannot help. I hope we might at some future date do business, when the market is better, but at the moment I am afraid you are talking about Anaconda Pure, something that does not come my way."

Bluey had turned toward the door, but now he stopped. "Anaconda Pure?" he asked. "I am not familiar with that."

"Ah, well, this is rumor," Florio said. "One hears of large amounts of the finest merchandise being moved, but perhaps it is only rumor. Still, the last couple of years, one hears the name often. If the rumors are true, then surely the merchandise is shipped through Guajira, but none of it stops here."

"Where does it originate?" Bluey asked.

Florio spread his hands. "There are not even rumors about that," he said.

They all shook hands, and the stone-faced bodyguard let them out of the suite.

"A very courtly fellow," Cat said as they walked back to their own room.

"If he had thought we had that much money on us, he would have had our throats cut on the spot," Bluey replied.

Cat gulped. "You gave me a start, there,

when you were talking about two hundred kilos at thirteen thousand a kilo. I didn't bring that much money."

"Ah, that was all bluff," Bluey said. "Florio never dealt more than ten kilos in his life. I blew him right out of his socks with talk of two hundred. I knew he wouldn't even pretend to have access to that much; he's strictly a small-timer. I just wanted to ask him about girls."

"I was glad you told him we'd need forty-eight hours to get money, too," Cat said.

"Well, you want to distance yourself from that much money, otherwise you might meet one of Florio's blokes in a dark alley. Say, how much did you bring with you, anyway?"

"Two million dollars," Cat said.

Bluey stopped and stared at him. *"What?"*

"Plus the hundred thousand pocket money you suggested," Cat said.

"Jesus H. Christ!" Bluey whispered hoarsely. *"Where is it?"*

"In the room," Cat said, surprised at his reaction, "in that aluminum case of mine. You did say to bring a lot of money, Bluey."

"I meant two or three hundred thousand," Bluey said, walking faster. "Jesus, now I'm not going to be able to relax for a minute."

He opened the door to their room. "Good

God, it's just sitting there!" he said, pointing at the case.

"Well, it has a combination lock," Cat said. "I thought it would probably be safer just sitting out than if I hid it under the mattress."

Bluey sat down on the bed and mopped his brow. He jumped at a soft knock on the door.

Cat, who was nearer the door, opened it. The bodyguard from Florio's suite stepped in and walked over to Bluey.

"Señor, you are interested in a girl?" he asked. "I hear you say this, yes?"

"Not a whore," Bluey replied.

The man's eyes narrowed slightly. "I think you are looking for a girl . . . particular," he said.

"Oh?" Bluey said, feigning indifference. "How do you mean?"

"I think you look for a girl you know. Just this one girl."

Bluey said nothing.

"I know a man who has such a girl," the man said.

Cat's heart leapt.

"What girl?" Bluey asked, shooting Cat a cautionary glance.

"An Anglo girl. A beautiful one. I see her, myself."

"Where is she?"

"Here, perhaps three kilometers from the town. In a very rich house."

"What is this girl's name?" Cat asked, taking care to keep his voice steady.

"Her name is Kathy, señor. This is Anglo, no?"

"Perhaps. What does she look like?"

"She is very beautiful, señor. Tall, like this." He held a hand to his eyebrows. "Her hair is gold, but not at the bottom." He placed a finger at the part in his own hair. "Here it is darker."

"How old is she?"

The man shrugged. "She is young. Her skin is very smooth."

Ignoring Bluey's wary expression, Cat removed a photograph from his wallet, a year-old picture of Jinx in tennis clothes. It was the most recent one he had. "Is this the girl?" he asked, handing the snapshot to the man.

He regarded it for a moment, then nodded. "I think this is so," he said. "The hair is gold, but I think it is this girl."

Bluey stood up. "Will you take us there? There's money in it for you."

The man held up a hand. "Not now," he said. "Too early. But there is party tonight. I can get you invitation. For one thousand dollars American?"

"I'll give you five hundred when we get inside the party," Bluey said, "and five hundred if the girl is what I want."

The man nodded. "I come for you eleven o'clock tonight. You must wear suit, tie."

Bluey nodded his agreement, and the man left. Bluey turned to Cat. "You're rushing this," he said. "I don't like it. It's too good to be true."

"No, it's not," Cat replied.

"What do you mean?"

"There's something I haven't told you," Cat said. "Jinx is a nickname. When she was small she was always breaking things. Her name is Katharine, after her mother."

12

Stoneface, as Cat had come to think of him, arrived on time, at eleven that evening. In front of the hotel, the man called for his car. "You drive your car," he said. "When you are in the house, you give me five hundred, okay?"

Bluey nodded. "Okay."

"When you see girl, you give me five hundred more."

"If I want the girl," Bluey said. "If it is the girl in the picture."

The man nodded and held up a finger. "I leave when you see this girl," he said. "I don't help you take this girl."

Bluey agreed.

"These *hombres*, they are quick," he said, making trigger motions with his index finger. "It is dangerous, *comprende?*"

"*Comprende*," Bluey said. The cars arrived.

They drove east for ten minutes or so. Neither Cat nor Bluey said anything. The houses thinned out, and they came to a large iron gate. A policeman stood guard. Stoneface stopped, exchanged words with the policeman, gestured at the car behind him, and both cars were waved through. The house was a couple of hundred yards from the street, behind an unruly growth of stunted trees. A wide area in front was filled with a jumble of vehicles, including a number of Cadillacs and Mercedeses. Bluey turned the Bronco around and parked it facing the gate, a little away from the rest of the cars. The house was a large, apparently old, stucco structure, in good repair. Lights flashed from the windows, and music with a heavy beat could be heard from inside. They met Stoneface at the steps.

"Now," he said, rubbing his fingers together.

Bluey gave him five hundred dollars, and they walked into the house together.

A wall of noise and heat met them. There was music of more than one kind being played, and Cat was temporarily blinded by flashing strobe lights. He held up a hand to protect his eyes and tried to become accustomed to the light and sound. A large room ahead of them was filled with people dancing with abandon to rock music. Another room to their left had a live band playing something South American just as noisily. Bluey grabbed a couple of glasses of champagne from a passing waiter and gave one to Cat. "Take it," he said. "We'll look odd without a drink." He turned to Stoneface. "Where's the girl?" he shouted over the din.

Stoneface made a circular motion with his hand. "We must look," he shouted back. He led the way into the room before them, skirting the dancers. Another waiter approached, this time with a tray bearing a crystal bowl containing a white powder. Stoneface took a tiny spoon from the tray, dipped it into the powder, and sucked it into his nose. He grinned widely at Bluey and Cat, exposing a set of badly stained teeth. He held up a thumb and motioned for them to help themselves.

Bluey and Cat shook their heads. Stoneface shrugged and moved on into the room, searching faces. He was beginning to move in time with the music. Cat and Bluey followed, bombarded by the volume. They circled the room twice, then moved into the room with the live band. The volume was more tolerable there, and the dancing slightly more restrained. They moved slowly through the crowd, Stoneface occasionally stopping to have a word with someone.

Then, moving his head to the music, he led them into another large room beyond.

It was nearly unlit, and the music was different — still South American, but slower, though just as loud. Most of the light in the room came from a large projection TV at the far end, on which a pornographic movie was playing. There were a few tables, but more cushions and mattresses on which couples and groups were arrayed, most of them naked. Stoneface motioned them to a table.

Cat sat stiffly, watching the action around him, made nervous by what he saw. He was not a very good voyeur, he discovered. As his eyes became accustomed to the gloom, he found the activity more embarrassing than erotic. Why did they have to sit through this? He leaned forward to speak to Stoneface, but Stoneface was already speaking.

"Close to the video," he was saying. "That side." He nodded toward a corner. "Here is Kathy."

Cat and Bluey followed his gaze to a girl who seemed to be kneeling, some fifteen feet away. There was a large thump inside Cat's chest as he recognized the familiar profile. His pulse quickened, then he flinched as he realized she was not kneeling but astride a man, moving rhythmically back

163

and forth. Cat started to rise, but he felt Bluey's restraining hand.

"First, let's be sure," he was saying. "Is it her?"

Cat stared at the girl. She turned her head, and she was illuminated sporadically by the light from the video screen. Her hair was blond and fairly short, but that could have been dyed and cut. Her figure startled Cat, though. Her shoulders and breasts were so familiar. Maddeningly, though, she was wearing a gash of thick red lipstick and very heavy eye makeup. It might as well have been a mask. "I can't tell from here," Cat said. "We've got to get closer."

Stoneface shook his head. "No, not here. We wait."

They sat at the table for some minutes longer while the sex act ground on. Bluey feigned interest elsewhere in the room, and Stoneface's interest was not feigned, but Cat's eyes remained riveted to the girl, willing her to see him, to show some sign of recognition. As if in answer, she turned her head and seemed to stare directly back at him. Suddenly, she smiled, and Bluey had to restrain Cat again.

It was Jinx. He knew it, and it was killing him, seeing her here in this place, this way. Her smile remained fixed as she looked away from Cat and down at her lover, whose motion seemed to be quickening. She was on some drug, she had to be. Then the man sat up and rested on his hands. He said a few words to her, and the smile faded. They got up and he began to lead her toward a door at the other end of the room. She looked back toward Cat again, smiling, and then they were gone.

Cat rose to follow, but Stoneface herded them back the way they had come. "This way," he kept saying. He guided them back into the rock-music room, through another room where food was stacked on a long table, and out another door.

They found themselves in a garden, following Stoneface toward a hedge. Even though it was a hot evening, the air outside was cooler than that in the house. There was a glow of light through the thick growth, and Cat heard a splash. They reached the end of the hedge and came around it facing a large swimming pool, lighted underwater. She was standing on the edge of the pool, tall, slim, and naked, looking toward the man in the water, who was beckoning her to follow him in. She dived into the water and surfaced, scrubbing her face with her hands, rubbing the makeup away. She ducked under to sweep her hair back and, eluding her companion, made for the side of the pool and pulled herself out in one smooth, clean motion. Cat stepped into the open; she saw him and smiled. They were farther apart than when they had been inside, but the makeup was mostly gone, and the glow from the pool lit her face from below.

"It's Jinx," Cat said, with finality.

Bluey stopped him from moving toward her. "Not yet," he said.

"My money, señor," Stoneface whispered.

Bluey gave him the money, and Stoneface walked quickly away.

Bluey pulled Cat back behind the hedge. "We've got to do this clean," he said. "We're the strangers here; this guy is a guest, maybe even the host. I don't think he's armed, though," he chuckled.

As Bluey spoke the naked man pulled himself up the ladder to poolside, grabbed her by the wrist, and pulled her toward a reclining chair. She came reluctantly along, looking over her shoulder toward where Cat had been standing. The man pushed her roughly onto the chair and began to climb on top of her. She watched, wide-eyed, as Bluey emerged from behind the hedge, followed by Cat, and began to walk quickly, softly toward them.

Cat saw Bluey reach inside his coat as they approached the recliner.

She looked at Cat and smiled. "Well, hi there," she said, sounding a little drunk, "what took you so long?"

Something is wrong, Cat thought. The man turned to see who she was speaking to.

"Evening," Bluey said as he swung the heavy pistol. The barrel caught the man behind the ear, and he rolled sideways off the lounge.

Cat's eyes went back to her as her expression began to change. The accent. Something had been odd about the accent.

"You bastard," she said. Then she opened her mouth and screamed.

Bluey hit her with his open hand, rolling her off the lounge on top of her lover. He grabbed her wrist and snatched her to her feet, and she began screaming again.

Cat went to her and took her face in his hands. The remnants of the heavy makeup streaked her face. "Jinx," he said, "be quiet, listen to me."

Her mouth drew back into another scream, revealing a row of small yellow teeth. In the instant before the scream came, Cat was jerked back to reality. Her accent had been hard, Midwestern. Jinx's was Southern. Jinx had large, very white teeth, not these teeth. Cat dropped his hands and stepped back from her in horror, blaming her for not being Jinx.

Bluey jerked Cat around to face him. "Isn't it her? Isn't it Jinx?"

Cat shook his head. She screamed again.

Bluey hit her, hard, with his fist. She stopped screaming. "Come on," he said to Cat, "we're getting out of here." He ran back toward the hedge, back the way they had come.

Cat looked up to see people staring at them from the door to the orgy room. They began spilling out toward the pool. Someone was shouting in Spanish.

Instead of going back into the house, Bluey led the way around it. It was bigger than it had seemed. They pushed their way blindly through shrubbery, Bluey cursing all the way. Finally, they came to a corner of the house and Bluey stopped and peered toward the front door. All seemed quiet there. "Come on," he said, and began to walk briskly across the graveled parking lot.

Cat followed, catching up and walking beside him.

"Not too fast," Bluey said, holding out a restraining hand. They picked their way through the cars and made for the Bronco. Behind them there was a hubbub at the front door of the house.

"Don't look back," Bluey said, "just keep walking."

They made the Bronco as the sound of running feet struck the gravel forty yards behind them. Bluey got the car started and into gear. He drove rapidly, but not wildly, down the drive, slowing as they approached the policeman at the gate. He smiled and waved to the man, who saluted. "Thank Christ they don't have walkie-talkies," Bluey said as he turned toward Riohacha and floored the accelerator.

Cat was limp beside him, reliving the moment when he knew the girl was not Jinx. She had not even looked that much like her. He had wanted too badly for her to be Jinx.

At the hotel, Bluey told the boy to keep the car ready. "Come on," he said to Cat, "let's get our gear together and get out of here." Fifteen minutes later, they had paid their bill, thrown their hastily packed belongings into the back of the car, and were driving away.

"Where are we going?" Cat asked.

"Back to the airplane," Bluey replied. "We were seen back there, and we don't even know who that guy was, how much trouble we're in, or how hard he'll look for us. But they saw us and the car, and we're getting out of the Guajira."

Cat rested his head on the seat back. He didn't much care what they did next. He'd been so sure, had had his hopes so high, and now he was weak with disappointment.

"Okay, so we blew it," Bluey said, consolingly. "Hell, that's okay, we might blow it again, even. But we'll keep on looking. Santa Marta's next. That's where this whole thing started, anyway. We only came to Riohacha because it was on the way. Now we'll go on, and we'll find something in Santa Marta."

13

They slept at Idlewild, in a small bunkhouse attached to the office. An Indian woman made them some breakfast, then Bluey asked Cat for more money. "We've got to get a flight plan filed for us at Cartagena for Santa Marta. Our papers are okay, but you have to file in this country, and we can't arrive at Santa Marta from out of nowhere. It's going to take a thousand to get it done. We've got to pay for fuel and tie-down, too."

Cat gave him five thousand dollars. "You're going to need something for tips," he said, dryly.

Bluey winked at him and went to make the arrangements.

Before takeoff, Bluey piled their luggage on top of the now-empty plastic ferry tank. "A spare tank sets off alarms with the cops or the army," he said. "We don't want to have to bribe somebody unnecessarily."

Cat was grateful Bluey was being concerned about money. They had already put a sizable dent in his hundred thousand dollars.

They took off at midmorning and headed out to sea.

"We'll circle around and approach Santa Marta from the west, just to look good," Bluey explained. "It's less than a hundred miles as the crow flies, and we'll add another fifty to the trip."

They had a brief glimpse of the nineteen-thousand-foot Sierra Nevada de Santa Marta before the building clouds obscured them. Cat remembered an earlier glimpse of the mountains from offshore, the day he had first sailed *Catbird* into Colombian waters. He tried not to think about what life would be like now if he had sailed on to Panama.

Santa Marta airport was a single, long, asphalt strip, and Cat, who was flying left seat at Bluey's insistence, listened as the Australian read him the checklist for landing. It was the first time Cat had landed the airplane. As soon as their wheels touched the runway, Bluey shoved the throttle in and reduced the flaps.

"Go around," he grinned. "Let's get you some touch-and-go's."

There was a strong crosswind blowing,

and Cat sweated out that and the unaccustomed controls and final checks through a dozen practice landings, including a couple of short field takeoffs and landings. Gradually, he became accustomed to the airplane, heavier, faster, and more complex than the trainers he had been flying. "I reckon you're checked out in this airplane," Bluey said when he had finally allowed Cat to taxi to the apron. "I'd sign your logbook if I was still certified."

A policeman gave their papers a perfunctory glance and waved them through the barrier into the small terminal. In the taxi Bluey said, "I reckon we'll stay out at El Rodadero, the beach area. There's nothing all that great in the town." He had a brief conversation in Spanish with the driver. Shortly they pulled into the drive of what seemed a modern hostelry, a cluster of low buildings hugging the beach. Cat was glad for the change. He had begun to think that Colombia was filled with nothing but seedy Excelsiors and drug runners' bunkhouses. At the front desk he registered as Ellis and shortly they were in a comfortable two-bedroom suite. Cat drank in the air-conditioning.

"I'd like to get some sleep before we go into town," Bluey said, yawning.

Cat glanced out the window at the blue Caribbean. "I think I'll see if they have a swimsuit in the shop downstairs." He hadn't showered that morning, and he was feeling hot and grimy. When he had changed, he walked downstairs, through the lobby and a courtyard containing a large pool and a thatched bar. It all seemed oddly normal after the past few days. He walked on to the beach, dropped his towel, and ran for the water. It was perfect. He swam out a hundred yards, then did slow laps up and down the beach for half an hour, working out the kinks, happy for some exercise.

Back on the beach, he flopped down onto the sand and ordered a piña colada. He drank the icy, sweet rum drink in record time and stretched out on the towel. It seemed nearly like a vacation. Down the beach a group of children were building a sand castle while their mothers chattered under a large thatched umbrella. An attractive woman with short dark hair waded out of the sea and walked to within a dozen yards of where he sat. She was in her early thirties, he reckoned, lithe and athletic-looking. She dried herself, then sat down and began to apply tanning lotion to her shoulders. He had a sudden urge to speak to her, but balked. Would she speak English?

And anyway, how long had it been since he had approached a woman? He and Katie had been married right out of college, and he had never needed anybody else. The thought of approaching her made him suddenly anxious, but he was surprised that he wanted to at all. Was this some sign of healing? He dismissed the thought. Nothing could ever heal until he found Jinx, he was sure of that.

He dozed, and when he woke she was gone. He felt relieved. He got up, dusted himself off, and walked back to the pool bar. The dark-haired woman was sitting at a table nearby. He ordered a sandwich and a beer and tried not to think about her.

Bluey turned up, looking refreshed, and ordered a sandwich, too. "Fairly nifty Sheila," he said, nodding at the woman.

Cat laughed. "Is that your down-under way of expressing approval?"

"Too right, mate. I have always found Latin women fairly nifty, and you're forgetting where I've been the last couple of years."

"I am at that," Cat replied. "Go ahead, if you're in the mood."

Bluey shook his head. "I'm not her type," he said ruefully. "After a lifetime, I know the sort I turn on, and she's not it. I'm not so sure she's my sort, either. A little too classy."

"If you say so, Bluey."

They finished their sandwiches.

"How about we bomb into Santa Marta and take a look around?" Bluey said.

Cat gave the woman a last glance. "Okay, let's do it." When he had found Jinx, then he could think about women.

They got a rent-a-car at the desk and drove the few miles to the town. It was busier than Cat remembered. He had gone no farther than the waterfront on his first visit, and now they were entering the town from the land, making it seem quite different. They passed the cathedral, then a colorfully painted old locomotive preserved as an exhibit near the railway station. Cat didn't feel like a tourist. His anxiety level was rising. He was back where it had all begun.

Bluey parked the car near the cathedral. "Let's nose around, see if we see anybody we know."

They walked slowly through the town for an hour, looking into cantinas, both men searching faces. Cat half expected to turn a corner and see Denny or the Pirate sitting at a sidewalk table sipping a *cervesa*. It didn't happen. They got back into the car, drove to the waterfront, and parked again.

"Show me where you met Denny," Bluey said.

They walked unmolested past a young policeman at a gate in a chain-link fence separating the docks from a large square. Keeping to the water, Cat finally brought them to the spot where they had tied up. He stared at the rusty ladder he had climbed on his last visit. A fishing boat was tied to it. Cat tried to swallow the lump in his throat.

"Let's ask around," Bluey said, buttonholing a man who was busy applying a fresh coat of yellow paint to a rusty boat engine. The man nodded. "He knows Denny," Bluey translated. The man shook his head. "Hasn't seen him for a long time — several months." Bluey asked another question and got a negative reply. "He doesn't know the guy you call the Pirate or a sportsfisherman called the *Santa Maria*."

They continued to stroll along the concrete wharf. There were a handful of foreign yachts tied up, and Cat resisted an urge to find the skipper of each one and tell him to get the hell out of Santa Marta. Bluey approached a dozen people and, finally, got what seemed to Cat a positive response from a young fisherman when the name *Santa Maria* was mentioned.

Bluey thanked the man and rejoined Cat. "He says he saw such a boat less than a month ago anchored at Guairaca, a fishing village seven or eight kilometers east of here. He's sure of it. Let's go."

They began driving, and Cat tried to keep his hopes down. Everything so far had been a red herring. They climbed into the hills east of Santa Marta, passing a large shanty town on the edge of the city. Houses had been thrown together from all sorts of materials — packing crates, sheets of tin, cardboard. They were little better than tents. "Jesus, what a way to live," Cat said.

"Barrio," Bluey replied. "A lot of people in this country live like that. Look." He nodded at a roadside sign. "Some politician has put his name on this one. Probably got them a water tap or something."

Soon they crested a hill and found a beautiful bay below them with a village nestled at its shore. Cat thought that any American real estate developer would love to get his hands on the site, it was so beautiful. The road fell rapidly away toward the village, and shortly they had drawn up to the beach.

"Look," Bluey said, pointing. "There's the *Santa Maria.*"

Cat followed his finger to the spot. Half

numb, half frightened, he got out of the car and walked quickly down the beach, forty yards, to the boat. The name was clearly visible on her bows.

"That's the boat," Cat said as Bluey fell in beside him. "No mistake, this time."

The two men stopped and stared together. The *Santa Maria* lay beached, a weedy mooring line still running, quite unnecessarily, from her bows to a large rock at the top of the beach. She was heeled sharply to port, and as they moved, her starboard side came into view, the hull charred and burned away, her interior exposed. She had been stripped of anything of possible value. Not so much as a cushion was left. Bluey walked over to a group of half a dozen men who sat on the sand mending nets.

Bluey translated as they spoke. "The skipper was a man named Pedro. Rough-looking fellow. That's your Pirate. No one has seen him for months. He left the boat here and didn't come back. Finally some robbers stripped her gear and set her afire. The men from the village tried to save her, beached her, but she ended up as we see her. No one knows where Pedro went. No one knows his last name." He continued to talk with them a moment more. "He didn't seem much interested in sportfishing. Nobody comes here looking for sportfishing, anyway. They naturally assumed he was running drugs. Nobody worries much about that around here, there's so much of it." They conversed for another few minutes, then Bluey waved Cat away, and they walked back to the car. An old woman carrying a large fish fell in step with them, talking rapidly, obviously trying to sell them the fish, grinning, revealing a toothless mouth. Bluey gave her some money, not even slowing down.

"He was always alone, they said. Nobody ever saw him with a girl or anybody else. I think that's the whole story. In a village this size, everybody knows everything, and if there was anything more to it, these blokes would know it. They wouldn't miss a thing around here, especially anything to do with a boat."

Cat stood, watching a group of small boys play an impromptu soccer match in the street along the beach. "So we're back to square one again?"

"Not quite. At least we've got a name we can put to the face around Santa Marta. We might turn up something in the cantinas."

"Come on, Bluey, half the male population of South America must be named Pedro, and anyway, it's probably not his real name, not if he was running drugs."

"Doesn't matter. If he called himself Pedro here, he used it somewhere else."

The two men trudged back to the car and started for Santa Marta. They were quiet for a while.

"How long since you were in Australia, Bluey?" Cat asked. He didn't want to think about Pedro any more today.

"Strooth," Bluey chuckled. "Mid-fifties, I guess. I think of myself as American these days. Got my citizenship in '64."

"You got any people back there?"

"Tell you the truth, I don't even know. My folks are dead. I had a brother and a sister, both older. I hadn't seen them for a couple of years when I came to the States. I got an ex-wife and a little girl in Miami, but I haven't seen them in a while, either. The lady's name is Imelda; she's Cuban."

"I thought you said you'd always been a bachelor."

Bluey grinned. "Well, for all practical purposes. I wasn't very good at being married, I guess."

"How old is the little girl?"

"Marisa is eight now. I send her Christmas and birthday presents; that's about it. Imelda remarried about three years ago. Seems happy and settled. She wanted a slightly more stable citizen than me, I reckon. Still, it's good for the kid. I have this fantasy that when she's eighteen, I'll pop up and send her to college, if I ever get a few bucks ahead."

"What will you do with the money you're making on this trip?"

Bluey smiled. "That's all spent, in my head, anyway. I got an old mate over in Alabama has a little airplane refurbishing business, paint and interiors. I've got a few ideas for some modifications to Cessnas and Pipers. I'd like to move into his shop and work on those, maybe teach a little flying, if I can get my ticket back. I've always liked showing other people how to do it. Don't know why."

"All finished with the grass business, then?"

Bluey snorted. "You betcha. This is my last trip south. I want to have someplace to go home to at night, you know?"

Cat knew. He wasn't sure he had that, himself, anymore.

They drove back into Santa Marta. Bluey suggested they take up the chase tomorrow, and Cat agreed. He was tired and wanted some dinner and a good night's sleep.

They stopped at a traffic light. It was rush hour in Santa Marta, and the streets were teeming with an assortment of cars, motor-bikes, and the garishly painted American school buses that passed for public transport in Colombia. Cat glanced to his right at a kid on a motor scooter who had pulled up next to them. The boy couldn't be more than twelve, Cat thought; his feet barely reached the pedals, and he had to lean way forward to manage the handlebars. Cat wondered where a kid that age got a motor scooter. Not only that, he thought, looking at the boy's arm, but an expensive wrist-watch, too.

"Jesus Christ!" he shouted, throwing open the door and leaping out. The light changed and the boy on the scooter accelerated and turned right. Cat sprinted after him shout-ing, "Hey, stop! I want to talk to you! Hold it!" He could hear Bluey shouting behind him, and the chorus of horns that said he was blocking an intersection.

The boy looked back and saw Cat gaining on him. He revved the engine, and sprayed sand and gravel in Cat's face.

"Hold it! I just want to talk!" But the scooter was half a block ahead of him and gaining.

Bluey pulled up in the Bronco. "What the hell are you doing, Cat?"

"Catch that kid on the scooter up there,"

Cat shouted at him. He looked down the block, but the scooter was gone. The boy must have turned into a side street. "Come on, Bluey, move it! That boy was wearing my Rolex wristwatch, we've got to find him!"

Bluey got the car in gear, and they began methodically cruising every side street, passing a strange mixture of hovels and mansions.

"Listen, Cat," Bluey said, shifting gears, "you're getting too excited about this. So the kid had a Rolex. He stole it, and he stole the scooter, too, probably, but half the drug runners in Colombia have Rolexes; they're a big fad down here."

Cat knew what Bluey was thinking. First he had seen the wrong boat, then the wrong girl, now the wrong watch. "You don't understand, Bluey," he said, swiveling his neck to peer down an alley. "Most of the Rolexes you see are the old self-winding, mechanical models. Mine is a newer type, a quartz movement. They look different, and there aren't that many of them around. I'll bet that's the only one in Colombia. All I want to do is look at it. There's some engraving on the back of mine."

Bluey sighed and kept on driving. They turned another corner, and a block ahead of them they saw a small crowd of kids on a corner. A woman with some sort of movie camera was taking their picture. Bluey slowed so they could check out the group, but the boy on the scooter was not there.

Cat suddenly realized that the woman with the camera was the one he had seen on the beach that morning. "Stop the car," Cat said. He rolled down the window. "Excuse me, señorita, do you speak English?"

"Well, yeah, a little," she said.

Cat winced. The woman was American.

"We're looking for a boy of eleven or twelve on a motor scooter. Could you ask these kids if they've seen him?"

The woman looked amused. She turned to the children and spoke to them in excellent Spanish. Their faces went blank, and they shook their heads gravely in unison. "Sorry," she said to Cat. "Nobody's seen him."

Cat looked at her closely. He felt there was some sort of conspiracy between the woman and these children, some silent secret. He thanked her, and they drove on, searching vainly for a boy, a motor scooter, and a Rolex wristwatch.

After an hour of this, when it was getting dark, Cat turned to Bluey. "Listen," he said,

"I've had enough of this for one day. Why don't we start again tomorrow? The boy will still be around."

"Yeah, I know you must be bushed, Cat. Listen, I had a nap this afternoon when you were swimming, so I'm okay. Why don't you take a cab back to El Rodadero and have a drink? I'll keep at it for a bit, ask some questions around the cantinas. Maybe somebody knows the kid."

Cat nodded. "Okay, if you're game."

Bluey drove him to a taxi stand and left him. Cat got into a cab and gave the driver the name of the hotel. Suddenly he had the odd feeling that he would not see Bluey again. He looked over his shoulder in time to see the Bronco turn a corner and disappear. It was the first time they had been separated since they had arrived in Colombia. Cat had come to trust the Australian, but some tiny corner of his mind still seemed to fear abandonment. Cat chased the thought from his head.

14

Back at the beach, Cat showered and changed into cool cotton clothes. The evening was warm, and he didn't bother with a jacket. He strolled down to the pool bar and ordered a piña colada. He loved the drink, and he made a point of never ordering it unless he was in some tropical place. He had taken only a sip when someone sat down on the adjacent barstool.

"Pardon me," she said.

He turned and looked at her. She had changed into a strapless flowered cotton sheath, and instead of speaking, he simply enjoyed looking at her for a moment.

"Why did you want the boy?" she asked.

"I had the feeling this afternoon that you knew him," Cat replied.

"I know a lot of the *gamines*," she said.

"The who?"

"Street children. Most of them have no family. They live any way they can. I'm doing a film about them. Why did you want the boy?"

Cat looked closely at the woman. Her dark hair was still wet from the shower, and her tan glowed against the bright yellow of the dress. There didn't seem any reason not to tell her. Maybe she would know something. "I had a wristwatch stolen some time back. The boy was wearing a watch this afternoon that looked like mine."

"So you wanted to catch him and take it back?"

"If it was mine, I was willing —"

"Señor," the bartender interrupted. "You are Señor Ellis?"

"Yes."

The bartender set a telephone on the bar.

Cat picked it up. "Hello?"

"It's Bluey. I'm at a bar on the beach just off the square called Rosita's. The boy comes here every evening selling stolen goods, keeps a pretty regular schedule, the bartender says. He's due here any minute."

"I'm leaving right now," Cat said and hung up. He turned to the woman. "Please excuse me. I have to leave."

She caught his arm. "Is this about the boy?"

He was about to tell her it was none of her business, but she anticipated him.

"I know him," she said. "His name is Rodrigo. I may be able to help."

"Come with me then."

They got a taxi at the front of the hotel. Cat's mind was racing. Finally, a link to Denny and Pedro, something concrete.

"My name is Meg Garcia," the woman said.

"Bob Ellis," Cat replied. "Tell me about this kid."

She shrugged. "He's one of the bunch I've been filming. They're lost, these children. They've no families, no schooling. They hardly know the name of the country they live in. They're like a pack of little animals, except that they take care of their own. It's quite touching, really. But, like animals, they can be very mean in packs or when cornered. Has your friend found Rodrigo?"

"He's at a bar called Rosita's. Apparently, the boy comes there regularly selling stuff."

"I know the place. Look, if we see the boy, let me talk to him. It's important that you don't try to take the watch from him. He won't let you have it without a fight. He's very proud of it."

"Do you think he might sell it?"

"Maybe. I'll talk to him about it. How will you know if it's yours?"

"There's engraving on the back. I have to

189

know exactly how he got it. I'm looking for the people who stole it from me."

The cab pulled up in front of Rosita's, and they got out. It seemed an ordinary enough place. There were some sparsely populated tables along the sidewalk, and inside, more tables and a bar. Bluey was nowhere to be seen.

Cat turned to the woman. "Will you ask the bartender where my friend is? He's a big, heavy fellow, an Anglo."

She spoke briefly to the bartender, then turned and ran from the place. She stopped and whipped off her high heels as Cat caught up with her. "He chased Rodrigo this way." She started running down the street.

Cat was unprepared for how quickly she could run in the tight dress, but he managed to stay close behind her. Ahead half a block, across the street, he could see a small crowd of people gathered, looking into an alley. Suddenly they were moving back, away from the alley, and there was a woman's scream. As Cat and Meg Garcia reached the spot, Bluey staggered out of the alley into the street, holding both hands against his chest.

Horrified, Cat watched as, with a great effort, Bluey pulled his hands away. In his right hand was a knife, and the front of his shirt was red and shiny. As Cat reached him the Australian sank into a sitting position, one leg collapsed under him. Cat grabbed his shoulder and took Bluey's weight against him. With his other hand he ripped open the sodden shirt to find a spurting wound.

"Quick," he said to the Garcia woman, "get an ambulance." At that moment, a police car pulled up, and she began talking rapidly to the policeman, who said something into a radio. Cat got a handkerchief from his pocket and pressed it against the wound, trying to stop the bleeding.

Bluey wore a look of astonishment. "Cat," he managed to say, "I wasn't expecting . . ."

"Shhh, Bluey, it's going to be all right. An ambulance is on the way. We'll get you patched up in a hurry." Cat knew it was a lie, even as he said it. The wound was near the center of the chest and was spurting. It had to be the aorta.

"Cat," Bluey was saying, but more weakly, "Cat, Marisa — it goes to Marisa, she's the only . . ." He stopped in mid-sentence, coughed up some blood, and stopped. There was a streetlamp above them, and as Cat looked into Bluey's eyes, he clearly saw the pupils dilate. He removed the handkerchief from the wound; it had stopped spurting. He felt at the neck for a pulse; there was none. Cat closed Bluey's eyes and stayed there, holding him until the ambulance came.

Cat was at the police station until midnight, numbly answering questions translated by Meg Garcia. Bluey's body was placed on a bench in a back room until an undertaker came and took it away.

"I must send the passport with a report to the American Consul in Barranquilla," the policeman was saying. "Is there a next of kin?"

Cat nodded. "He has a daughter in Miami, Florida."

"Will you act for her?"

"Yes, I'll see that she receives his personal effects."

The policeman handed him a brown paper bag. "Do you have the address?" he asked.

"No," Cat replied.

"Do you think it might be with his effects?" Meg Garcia asked.

Cat emptied the bag onto the desk. There were a fat wallet, the keys to the car and the airplane, some coins, and a small notebook. Cat leafed through the notebook. He wanted to leave this place.

"Here it is," he said. "Marisa Holland, in

care of Mrs. Imelda Thomas." He read out the address in Miami.

The policeman duly noted it in his report. He handed Cat a sheet of paper. "Here is the name of the undertaker, and the telephone number of the American Consul. You must make arrangements tomorrow."

Cat nodded. "Yes, of course. May we go now?"

"There is nothing more to do."

"Will you catch the boy who did this?"

The policeman shrugged. "No one actually saw the stabbing occur, no one who will say so, anyway. It will be very difficult."

They didn't talk much on the way back to the hotel. When they parted she said, "You look exhausted. Try and get some sleep and I'll meet you here tomorrow morning and help you make the arrangements," she said.

"Thank you, I appreciate that," he replied. "Do you think you might still be able to get the watch?" It was his last shred of hope. He had to have it.

"I'll try. It may not be possible now. We'll talk about it tomorrow."

Cat's body and mind cried out for rest. He managed to get to sleep without thinking.

15

Cat moved, trance-like, through the horrors of dealing with the undertaker and the American Consul. The undertaker was professionally sorrowful, the Consul, on the telephone, was brisk. It was not the first American corpse he had dealt with.

"Do you have any reason to suppose there is anyone in the United States who would want Mr. Holland's body returned there?" he asked.

"No, I don't believe I do."

"Well, then, my advice is to have the undertaker bury him in Santa Marta. This is a hot climate, and even with embalming, well . . ."

"I see your point. I'll make the arrangements."

"Was there anything of value among his effects?"

"There was some money."

"Do you want me to send it to the daughter, or will you?"

"I'll take care of that."

"Good." The man sounded relieved.

The undertaker found a priest, and there was a brief, graveside service attended by Cat, Meg Garcia, the undertaker, and two gravediggers. When it was over she said, "That's it, there's nothing more to do."

"There's the watch," Cat said. "Will you try?"

"Do you have a thousand dollars?"

"Yes."

"Give it to me. I'll try to find him. Wait for me at the hotel."

Lying on his bed with the air-conditioning turned up high, Cat tried to think. Everything depended on the wristwatch; he couldn't leave Santa Marta without knowing about that. If the Garcia woman could find out where the boy had gotten it, there might be a thread to follow, although he was ill-equipped to follow it.

He kept expecting to hear Bluey's voice from the next room — gruff, cheerful, practical, knowledgeable — always with an idea of what to do next. Cat didn't know what to do next. He got up and went into Bluey's room. The clothes he had bought in Atlanta were neatly hung in the closet and tucked into drawers. He collected them and packed them into the single canvas bag Bluey had brought with him. There was about seven thousand dollars in the jacket, the remainder of the ten thousand Cat had paid Bluey in Atlanta.

In Bluey's wallet he found a school photograph of a small, dark little girl, very pretty. Except for a few hundred dollars, the new wallet was strangely empty — no credit cards, no driver's license, just a few scraps of paper with unfamiliar phone numbers and incomprehensible jottings. He tossed all of it, except the photograph, the money, and Bluey's .357 magnum, into the bag and zipped it shut. There was nothing worth sending back to the States; he'd give it all to the porter. He staggered back to his bed and slept.

There was a soft knock on the door. Cat struggled up, glancing at his bedside clock. Early evening. He had slept the whole afternoon away. He went to the door.

"May I come in?" the Garcia woman asked.

"Sure, have a seat. Did you have any luck?"

She sat down on the living-room sofa, opened her handbag, and handed him a

Rolex wristwatch. "He took your thousand dollars," she said.

Cat turned over the watch, holding his breath, and read the inscription on the back. "For Cat and *Catbird,* with love, Katie & Jinx." He swallowed hard. "Did you find out where he got it?"

"Yes. He stole it from a man, a man with an eye patch. Does that mean anything to you?"

"Yes, yes, it does," Cat said, growing excited. "Does he have any idea where the man is now?"

"He's dead. The *gamines* killed him for the watch. A dozen of them trapped him in an alley, and . . . well, he wasn't the first, and your friend, Holland, won't be the last."

"Did the boy know anything about the man? Anything at all?"

She shook her head. "Nothing at all. He was drinking at one of the cantinas, sitting near the sidewalk. They saw the wristwatch. When he left, drunk, they followed him. That was it."

Cat sank into a chair. This was the end of it all. If Pedro the Pirate was dead, he had nowhere else to go in this thing, not without Bluey Holland. He felt stripped of his power to do anything about anything. In his mind, he listened once again to the voice on the

197

telephone and the one word it spoke, and he was no longer sure. He had mounted this expedition on a wisp of a hope that his mind had conjured up, just as it had conjured up Jinx's face on the girl in Riohacha. He had gotten a good man killed for a mindless compulsion and a wristwatch. He tried not to weep.

"What will you do now?" she asked.

"I'm going home," he said wearily. "I've got all there is to get, I'm afraid." He looked up at her. "You've been very kind to me. Is there anything I can do for you?"

"Yes, you can buy me dinner tonight and tell me the whole story." She paused. "I know who you are, Mr. Catledge. The inscription on the watch told me. I read all about it at the time. You've changed a lot from the pictures I saw."

Cat nodded. "Of course I'll buy you dinner. I owe you a great deal more than that."

"An hour then? At the pool bar?"

"Yes, fine. I could use a shower, and I want to make some travel arrangements and call home."

She left, and Cat called the front desk and asked about flights to Miami.

"There is a flight from Cartagena the day after tomorrow, señor, or there is the daily Eastern flight from Bogotá. There is a connecting flight from Santa Marta tomorrow morning at ten o'clock."

"Will you try and get me on the flight from Santa Marta, please? And will you ask Eastern to get me on a connecting flight from Miami to Atlanta, Georgia?" He'd leave the Cessna; maybe there would be some way to get it back later.

"Of course, señor."

"And I'd like to make a call to Atlanta." He gave her Ben's number.

"I will have to place the call with the international operator, and that will probably take at least an hour," she said.

"Fine, I'll either be at the pool bar or in the dining room." He hung up and got into a shower.

She was wearing a white silk sheath this time, and she looked even better, the whites of her eyes startling against her tanned skin. "Let's go straight to the dining room, shall we?" he said, taking her arm. "It suddenly occurs to me that I haven't eaten since lunch yesterday, with all that's happened." He took her arm and guided her to a table, noticing how pleasant her cool skin felt to his touch.

When they had ordered drinks and dinner, she took a sip of her martini and put it down. "Before you tell me what's happened, there's something I must tell you," she said.

"I'm all ears."

"I'm a television journalist — free-lance. I sell my stuff to the American networks. My proper name is Maria Eugenia Garcia-Greville, but I use Meg Greville for my work."

A light went on in Cat's head. "Of course, I've seen some of your stuff — on the *Today* show, wasn't it? Something about Central American guerrillas?"

"That's me."

"But you never appear on camera, do you?"

"No. I was working at a local television station in Los Angeles during the early seventies, and I talked them into sending me to Vietnam with a cameraman and sound man — not for war reporting, but for human-interest stuff — talking to kids from L.A. in hospitals — 'Hi, Mom' — that sort of thing. We had hardly arrived when there was an attack on Saigon. My cameraman and sound man and I took a mortar shell behind a wall where we were hiding. Both my crew were killed, but I wasn't badly hurt. I salvaged some of the gear and did my own shooting, narrating it as I went. I kept it up through the whole attack, and when I got back to L.A. it ran — first on the local station, then on the network. I got a Peabody for it.

"After that, I never worked any other way. The subjective camera, voice-over, turned into a personal trademark for me, and over the years the equipment has shrunk and gotten a lot lighter, so it's easier than it used to be."

"You're free-lance, you say? You don't work for a network?"

"Nope, I like my independence. It pays well, and I can pursue whatever interests me. Mostly I've reported from South and Central America and from the Philippines. I came down here the first time to do a story about an Indian family in the Amazon who run their own little cocaine factory — just a man, his wife, and two sons. I met some people, established some sources, fell in love with the country. I bought a little piece of property near Cartagena and built a beach house. I keep an apartment in New York, but the house is where I come when I'm tired. I heard about the *gamines* in Santa Marta, and I've been up here for a little over a week, shooting stuff on them. It'll make a good piece for the *Today* show, I think. I'm all wrapped up now; I was shooting my last footage when I ran into you yesterday on the street."

"Sounds like an interesting life."

She nodded. "It is." She paused. "I like to be up front on a story. I wanted you to know, going in, that I'm a reporter."

"You want to do a story on what I'm doing here?"

She shook her head. "No, I wasn't around to shoot any tape, so for me there's no story. You're going home, anyway, you said. No, I'm just curious, having landed in the middle of all this. But I am a reporter, and I want you to know that if you tell me something, it might end up in a story sometime."

"Fair enough. I'll skip the part about losing the yacht, since you've read the reports on that, anyway."

"What I read was the *Time* story. I was in Honduras at the time."

"That was accurate reporting, so I'll start a few months after that, in fact, less than a month ago." Cat took her from the phone call to the present, giving her as much detail as he could, remaining vague about his contact with Jim. He found that telling her the story was helping to put the whole thing into perspective. If he had had any doubts that he was at the end of his rope, they dissolved as he recounted the details.

"And exactly how did you meet Bluey Holland?"

"Friend of a friend. I'm afraid I can't tell you any more than that."

"And now you feel that your daughter is really dead?"

Cat sighed. "I'm not sure about the voice on the phone anymore," he said, "and apart from that, I don't have the slightest shred of evidence that she might be alive. I do know, thanks to you, that one of her murderers is dead, though, and that's half the job done."

"Would you finish the job if you could find Denny?"

A little flash of anger went through him as he thought about Denny. "If he were sitting here right now, I don't think I could answer for myself. But I wouldn't know where to start looking for him. Would you, in the circumstances?"

She shook her head. "It's a big country, and he might not even be in it. I wish I could suggest something."

Dinner came, and they ate slowly, making small talk about Central America and Colombia. As the busboy took away the plates, a waiter appeared.

"A telephone call, Señor Ellis," he said.

Cat rose. "Excuse me, I placed a call to my brother-in-law earlier. I'll be right back."

He followed the waiter to a phone. The connection was excellent.

"Jesus, I'm glad you're alive," Ben said. "We've been worried sick."

"I'm just fine, Ben, and I'm coming home tomorrow. Everything here has come to a dead end."

There was a short silence, then Ben said, "Listen, a guy in Senator Carr's office called here a couple of days after you left."

"Yeah? What did he say?"

"He said he had a message from Jim. Do you know a Jim?"

"Yes. What was the message?"

"There were two pieces of information he wanted passed on to you when we heard from you. First, he said that a guy you were in the Marines with, named Barry Hedger, is working in the American Embassy in Bogotá. He thought that might be a good contact for you if you had problems."

Cat remembered Barry Hedger well. He had been a fellow platoon leader in the company, a gung-ho, straight-arrow Naval Academy man who none of the ROTC officers had liked very much. "Well, I guess that information won't be of much use now," he said. "What was the other thing?"

"The other thing," Ben said, "was the phone call you thought you got from Jinx."

"What about it?" Cat asked.

"This guy, Jim, says it was traced to a hotel room in Cartagena —"

"What?"

"He was very emphatic about it, said it was confirmed that the phone call came from" — a paper rustled — "from the Caribé Hotel in Cartagena."

Cat grabbed a nearby chair and sank into it, his knees weak.

Ben was still talking. "I don't know how the hell a thing like that could be confirmed," he said, "but the senator's aide said you could take it as gospel. Listen, Cat, I owe you an apology. I thought you were hallucinating or dreaming or something."

Cat's heart was pounding, his mind racing. He thought for a moment he might faint.

"Cat? Are you there?"

Cat got hold of himself. "Yes, Ben, I'm sorry, I was just having a little trouble absorbing that information." He dug into his coat pocket for Bluey's notebook. "Listen, Ben, I want you to do something for me, something important, okay?"

"Sure, anything."

He gave Ben the address of Bluey's daughter and ex-wife. "I want you to confirm that Marisa Holland is the daughter of one

Ronald Holland, and I want you to tell her mother that Holland was killed in a mugging in Colombia, all right?"

"Sure, all right. You didn't get mugged, did you, Cat?"

"No, just Holland. He was helping me out down here. Something else: I want you to send her ten thousand dollars immediately, then I want you to set up something for the child's future; get hold of my lawyer, and put a hundred thousand dollars into a trust. Make her mother and me the trustees; I want to keep in touch with the child. You've got my power of attorney; can you get all this done right away? I won't be coming home just yet, not after the news you've given me."

"Sure, Cat, I'll get on it tomorrow. Anything else?"

"That's it for now. I'll call you when I've had a chance to check out the Caribé Hotel. And, Ben, thanks so much for this news."

He hung up and returned to the table. "I'm not leaving tomorrow," he told Meg. He explained what he had just been told.

Meg leaned forward and rested her elbows on the table. "Do you know anybody in any of the American intelligence services?" she asked.

"Sort of. Why?"

"Well, that phone call is the sort of thing that only the National Security Agency could track down. They're constantly recording all sorts of international telephone calls."

Cat nodded. "Maybe that's how it was done. You say you're finished in Santa Marta?"

"Yes, all I've got to do is edit my videotape when I get back, then lay a voice track over it. No rush about that, though. I haven't sold the piece yet."

"Will you come to Cartagena with me tomorrow, then? I could really use the help of somebody who knows the territory."

"Can I come as a reporter? Can I shoot if I want to?"

"All right."

She offered him a firm handshake. "You've got a deal. If I can help you find her, I will. I just want it all on tape."

It seemed a small price for her help, Cat thought. And quite apart from that, he was glad she would be around for a while longer.

16

With Meg Greville's help, Cat managed to file a flight plan for Cartagena and get a weather forecast. He was relieved to have good flying weather, since, in spite of the instrument rating on his forged license, he didn't want to have to make an instrument approach.

On the taxiway, he went slowly and carefully through the checklist, doing the procedure as Bluey had taught him. "Listen," he said to Meg, "the international language of air traffic control is supposed to be English, but if I get into trouble, jump in and save me, okay?"

"Sure. I don't fly, myself, but I've got a lot of hours as a passenger in light planes in Latin America. I know the drill pretty well."

Cat called the tower and reported ready for takeoff. He was relieved to get permission in clear English. He taxied onto the runway, noting the time, glad to have the

Rolex back on his wrist where it belonged, and shoved the throttle forward, watching the airspeed indicator carefully. At sixty knots, he pulled back on the yoke and the airplane rose into the air. He climbed to his filed altitude of four thousand, five hundred feet and turned southwest, working through his checklist. He leaned out the engine, set a course, and switched on the autopilot and altitude hold. He relaxed a little, feeling as if Bluey were still seated beside him, issuing instructions.

Cat chose to fly over the sea, a mile or so offshore, to get a better view of the coast. In an emergency, he could always set down on the beach. The coastline looked ordinary enough. There was an occasional tiny village, hard against the beach, and the large city of Barranquilla with its VOR beacon. He hardly needed radio navigation, though. It was simply a matter of hugging the shore until Cartagena hove into view.

Just before Barranquilla, Meg pointed ahead and down. "Can you make out a twin-engine airplane just inshore of the beach?"

Cat looked for a moment and found it. The aircraft was sitting only a few yards from a house.

"Drug runner inbound from the States,"

she said. "Probably aiming for the Guajira, got lost, and ran out of fuel. He put it down on the water, skipped a couple of times, plowed across the beach, and came to rest in somebody's front yard."

Cat was thankful he'd been with somebody as capable as Bluey on his inbound trip.

An hour or so after leaving Santa Marta, Meg pointed again. "There's Cartagena Airport."

They were five miles out, and the single long strip was easily visible. Cat started a descent and called the tower. Shortly, he was on final approach, running through the last of his checklist. He bounced once, then settled the airplane down. Soon he wished he'd aimed for the middle of the ten-thousand-foot runway. It was a long taxi to the terminal. A lineman guided him to a parking spot, and Meg ordered fuel. A policeman appeared, but the forged papers and a smile from Meg got them cleared quickly. A teenage boy turned up with a cart to carry their luggage.

"Where do we get a cab?" Cat asked Meg.

"My car's in the parking lot," she said.

The car was a dusty, elderly Mercedes sedan, from which the radio had apparently been stolen. Soon they were entering the city, driving along a high, stuccoed wall.

"What's behind the wall?" Cat asked.

"The Old City. I'll show you later."

They came to a stretch of beach rimmed by a string of high-rise hotels disappearing into the distance. Modern Cartagena, at least the beach portion of it, looked very like a Florida resort city. The Caribé stood out among the modern hotels, an older, lower building of pink stucco. Meg pulled into the driveway and under a portico. A doorman took the car, and they entered the cool lobby of the Spanish-style building and approached the front desk.

"May I speak with the manager, please?" Cat asked a woman at the front desk.

"He is occupied, señor," she replied. "Will you wait a few minutes?"

"We'll be at the pool restaurant," Meg said quickly. "Mr. Ellis is the name." She turned to Cat. "I'm hungry. Let's get a sandwich while we're waiting."

They walked out of the lobby, through a densely gardened area, and up some stairs to the pool.

Cat was impressed. "I wasn't expecting anything quite like this in Colombia," he said, gazing at the large, handsome pool and the beautiful bodies surrounding it. "This reminds me of the pool at the Beverly Hills Hotel."

"Oh, this can be a very pleasant country," Meg said, sitting down at a poolside table. "This hotel is my favorite in Cartagena. It was designed by a Cuban just after World War II, and I think it must be a bit like Havana before Castro."

As they were finishing their lunch, a young man in a suit approached them. "Excuse me, Mr. Ellis? The manager will be occupied for some time. My name is Rodriguez, may I be of assistance?"

Cat offered the man a chair. He had his story ready. "Earlier this month, I believe my niece may have been staying here. I had a brief telephone call from her — a very bad connection — and then we were cut off. I was unable to get through that day, and when I finally did I was told that she was not registered. I'd like to locate her; her mother is worried about her."

"What was your niece's name, señor? I will check my records."

"Her name is Katharine Ellis, but I think she was travelling with friends, so she may not have been registered. I think if I could learn who she was travelling with, I might be able to contact her through her friends."

Rodriguez looked puzzled.

"What I wonder if you could help me with

is, would it be possible to check your telephone records for the date and learn from which room the call was made? Then we would know to whom the room was registered. The call was made on the second of this month."

Rodriguez now looked doubtful, and not a little suspicious.

"I am afraid this is irregular, señor. We do not divulge the names of our guests to informal inquiries. In any case, the hotel was filled to capacity on that date, and that would mean searching the records of more than two hundred rooms."

Cat jotted a number in his notebook, ripped it out, and pushed it across the table, covering two one-hundred-dollar bills. "Here is the number she telephoned. It is in Atlanta, Georgia, in the United States. I know this is a great imposition, but I wonder if you might take the time to have a look through your records?"

Rodriguez glanced quickly about him, then pocketed the number and the bills. "Well, perhaps I could take a look through the telephone records this evening, when I am off duty."

"Thank you so much," Cat said.

"Where may I reach you, Señor Ellis? This may take a few days, unless I am lucky."

Meg cut in and gave the man a phone number.

Rodriguez stood and bowed. "I shall be in touch as soon as possible, Señor Ellis," he said.

"Thank you," Cat replied. "I will be equally grateful when you have found the information."

The young man smiled and left.

"What was that number you gave him?" Cat asked.

"My place. You may as well stay out there. There's a lot of room."

"You're sure I'm not putting you out? I could get a room here."

"Not at all," she said.

They finished lunch and left the hotel, driving along the beach.

"We'll take a turn through the Old City," she said, maneuvering through cars, brightly painted schoolbuses, and horse-drawn carriages. She drove through a gate in the fifty-foot-thick walls, and the character of Cartagena changed dramatically. Suddenly, they were in an earlier century. They wandered through narrow streets and elegant squares. The buildings were beautifully restored and maintained, made of the same masonry and stucco, with the same tile roofs. There was a harmony of design that grew from centuries of tradition and slow change.

"This is one of the most beautiful places I've ever seen," Cat said. "I expected this whole country to be one great big hovel, but I was wrong."

"This part of the city goes back to the early sixteenth century. This was the strongest fortress in South America, the port from which most of South America's treasure was hauled away by the Spanish."

They left the walled city and drove northeast along the coast on a two-lane tarmac road. A few miles out of Cartagena, Meg turned left onto a rough dirt track and slowed enough to manage the potholes.

Cat had been impressed with the Caribé Hotel and looked forward to comfortable arrangements for the night. Now, as the Mercedes banged along the track through the cactus, he saw that hope vanishing. He began to think in terms of hammocks slung under thatch. His hopes were not improved when Meg got out to open the padlock on a battered steel gate. After that, though, the road smoothed out and showed signs of having been graveled. Shortly a large tree appeared before them, and as Meg swung the car around it, the house came into view.

It was no more than a few years old, of the traditional white stucco and red roof tiles. Meg used several keys on a sturdy oak door, then they were inside a large, sunlit space, stiflingly hot.

"Jesus, let's get some air in here," she said, and began unlocking large sliding glass doors opening onto a wide veranda. The sea breeze swept into the house, quickly cooling the interior. The living-room furniture was a mixture of Bauhaus leather and steel and soft pieces upholstered in pale Haitian cotton. "You're this way," she said, waving him into a large, sunny bedroom with a large bed and wicker furniture. "Say, do you play tennis?"

"Sure," he said, dropping his bags on the bed. "I don't have any gear, though. Tennis wasn't what I had been expecting from Colombia."

She laughed. "In Colombia, expect the unexpected. Look in the second closet, there. I think you'll find what you need."

Cat opened the closet and found tennis clothes and bathing suits in a variety of sizes, men's and women's. He found some shoes and changed. He could hear her in the kitchen as he came out of the bedroom.

"Just thawing some steaks for dinner," she called out.

He had another look around the living room. He hadn't noticed the pictures before. They were very South American-looking, mostly primitives. He liked them. The effect of the whole place was pleasing, much like its owner.

A moment later she joined him and led the way out the front door and along a path to a nicely built hard court. "This is my pride and joy," she said. "I never have guests who don't play tennis." She blew the surface clean with an electric blower, and they began to hit balls.

She played more like a man than a woman, he thought, feeling it in his wrist as he returned one of her forehands. She won the serve and aced him twice before he even got a racket on a ball.

"Sorry about that," she called out. "I get worse as it goes on."

She wasn't sorry about it, and she didn't get worse. Cat thought if he had not been working out so much the last few months, she'd have run him off his feet. She took the first set six-one, and he stopped feeling guilty about wanting to beat a woman. Playing as hard as he could, he squeaked through the next set, winning it seven-five. At four-four in the third set, she broke his serve, and he reached down inside himself for something more. He had a brief flash of memory, of Quantico and a ten-mile run, surely the last time he had had to try this hard at anything. He broke her serve, then lost his again, then took hers again. His concentration was total now; he might have been playing at Wimbledon. He aced her to get to seven-six, then hit four of the hardest returns of service he had ever hit to beat her, eight-six.

They flopped onto a bench at courtside, both pouring with sweat and breathing hard.

"You sonofabitch," she said conversationally. "Do you always play so hard against girls?"

"Girl? You're the goddamned Bionic Woman. Don't you have any pity?"

"You're the first man to beat me in a long time."

"The first *man?* What women have you been playing — Navratilova?"

"How old are you?" she asked.

"I'm . . ." He stopped, tried to unscramble his brain, finally looked at his watch. The twenty-ninth. "Good God, I'd forgotten."

"Forgotten what?"

"I'll be fifty tomorrow."

"Fifty?"

"I may be the boy in this match, but you've got what, twelve years on me?"

"I've got *fifteen* years on you, buster."

"Oops, sorry."

"Race you to the beach," she said, and sprinted off.

He staggered after her down a narrow path to the sea, and as he came around a large boulder, he saw a trail of tennis clothes stretching across the sand and, hitting the water, a lithe, naked form. He hopped along on one foot, struggling with a shoe, then another, then his shorts and shirt. He hit the surf sprinting, loped a few steps through the water, then dived flat and started swimming. She had fifty yards on him but was moving more slowly than he. He caught her a hundred yards out.

"As a swimmer, you're a great tennis player," he said, overtaking her at last.

She shoved water in his face and began swimming slowly back toward the beach. He followed a few strokes behind. She found the bottom, waded from the water, and flopped on her back on the wet sand. He fell down beside her. They were both breathing hard from the tennis and the swimming, and he was very conscious of her nakedness, particularly her full, tanned breasts as they heaved with her breathing. There were no untanned strips anywhere. He suddenly found it necessary to roll onto his stomach to conceal his growing concern with her body.

"God, I haven't had such a workout in ages," she said, still breathing hard.

"Neither have I," he said, breathing, if anything, even harder. He knew he was staring, but he could not help himself.

She seemed unconcerned with her nakedness or his. "It'll be dark soon," she said, shivering a little. "I'd better go start dinner."

"I'll stay here for a minute and recover my health," he said, embarrassed to move.

She got to her feet and jogged toward the house, collecting their clothing as she went. He watched as she paused to rinse herself under an outdoor shower. The setting sun turned her body a hot shade of coppery gold. Then she was gone.

It took a couple of minutes of thinking about something else before he felt it was safe to stand. He trotted to the shower, grabbed a towel on the veranda, and let himself into his room through the sliding doors. He shaved, took a hot shower, and stretched out on the bed, just for a moment.

She placed the cool back of a hand on his face to waken him. It was dark in the room. He lay on his back, the towel covering his crotch. "How about a drink?" she suggested. "Dinner's in half an hour."

He looked at his watch. He had been asleep for an hour and a half. "Sure. Make me something local."

He unpacked his clothes and dressed in light cotton clothes and deck shoes. She had a rum punch waiting for him in the kitchen while she grilled some steaks and worked on dinner.

"I'm afraid it's frozen vegetables," she said. "There's nothing fresh in the house but potatoes, which are baking even as we speak." She was wearing a loose-flowing caftan of a soft beige material that occasionally revealed the outline of her body as she moved about the kitchen.

"I thought you might be ready for an American meal," she said.

"Sounds good. The house is wonderful."

"It's the only thing I own, except for the Mercedes," she said. "I've been putting it together for four years. It's just about where I want it now."

"I should have guessed. It's like you. Why did you bring me here? You don't know me."

"Yes, I do — better than I did yesterday, anyway. Want an instant character analysis?"

"Why not?"

"Well, of course, I know the general stuff about you, the business you built, and all that."

"I'll tell you a secret. My brother-in-law built the business. I just worked on the technical stuff."

"When I met you, you were wound pretty tight. I thought you might break when your friend was killed."

"I did break," he said. "I was in a state of complete despair, didn't know what to do next. I was about to pack it in and go home."

"But you didn't. When you got that phone call, you came back fast. That told me a lot — that, and the way you played tennis this afternoon. I beat you pretty easy the first set; then you decided you wanted to win. I was very impressed the way you played the last couple of games of the last set."

"Don't expect that sort of performance again. I don't think I've ever played that well."

"I don't mean how well you played; I mean how *hard* you played."

"Well," he chuckled, "I couldn't let myself be beaten by a mere slip of a girl."

"A mere slip of a girl who had a year on the pro tour. I was never ranked very high; I overtrained for too long, and my knees went on me."

"It doesn't surprise me to hear that. You strike me as somebody who goes after things pretty hard."

"That's something you and I share," she said.

He shook his head. "I don't think I've ever had to go after things hard. I had it pretty easy, except in the Marines, and nobody had it easy there."

"I learned something else about you during that tennis match, something you probably don't know yourself. Not yet, anyway."

"What's that?"

"You have it in you to be completely ruthless. It didn't take you long to put aside the fact that I was a woman, and that it might not be very graceful to play your best game."

He laughed at that. "You're right, you know; I am capable of ruthlessness, but apart from this afternoon, I can only remember once when I let it get the best of me."

"Dinner is served," she said, "but keep talking." She got the steaks, vegetables, and potatoes on the table and handed him a bottle of red wine to open. "Come on, when were you ruthless?"

"It was in the Marines. I had a Naval ROTC commission from college, and I was one of four platoon leaders in my company — two other ROTC guys and one Academy man, a guy named Hedger. Hedger looked down on us ordinary college boys, thought

223

of himself as infinitely superior. Our commanding officer, a major and an Academy man himself, shared Hedger's view.

"Now you have to understand, you have to be a little crazy to survive in the Marine Corps, and if you're not, you have to find a way to get a little crazy. Barry Hedger was my way. I lived to beat him, beat him at any and everything. I worked my ass off, day and night, to beat him at tactics, small-weapons training, personal combat — I even beat him in report writing, something an Academy man really does well. My platoon beat his platoon on the obstacle course, on the rifle range — even in keeping their barracks clean. My platoon sergeant knew what was going on between Hedger and me, and he used it to fire up the men. Christ, they reveled in it! The C.O. was on Hedger's back constantly to beat me in something. How could an Academy man — one of the top ten in his class, yet — allow himself and his platoon to be bested by a Rotsie officer and his platoon?

"Finally, Hedger snapped, invited me outside one night at the officers' club, promised to clean my clock. Everybody poured out of the bar, we stripped our blouses, and got down to it. Hedger came at me sort of karate style, half squatting, waving his hands around, making little noises. It's funny, I hadn't had a fistfight since grammar school — haven't had one since, but I kicked him in the knee and hit him once — broke his nose. Oh, Jesus, there was a lot of blood and all, and then some colonel came and broke it up, chewed us both out good, made us shake hands. Didn't report us to our C.O.

"On Review Day my platoon won all the silver, and Hedger marched with a limp and a taped nose. And then I realized what I'd done. I — an unmotivated, short-time officer, who couldn't wait to get out of the Corps — had ruthlessly, *gleefully,* pursued a good officer — not a very nice guy, but a good officer — pounded him into the ground, inch by inch — for the sheer hell of it. Oh, I didn't ruin his career, I guess — his platoon finished ahead of the other two and close behind mine — but the commendation that went in my record would have meant a hell of a lot more to him than it did to me. After I thought about it, I was ashamed of what I'd done.

"We got different assignments after that, and I never saw him again. And you know what? Part of the news in that phone call from my brother-in-law last night was that Barry Hedger is working in the Bogotá embassy. He's my contact if I need help!"

Meg laughed. "I sure as hell hope you don't need it!" She began clearing dishes away. "Here, take the brandy into the living room."

He poured two glasses and sank into the large sofa. As he did the lights went off.

"Oh, damn," she said, settling into the sofa beside him, her feet tucked under her, "the power's always going out. It'll probably be out all night."

"Never mind," he said, pointing outside, "we've got another source of light." A large moon had risen from the sea, illuminating the room in a patchwork of astonishingly white light.

She rose to her knees, reached down, took his face in her hands, and kissed him. "I didn't think you'd do this first," she said.

"I wish I had had the guts," he replied, kissing her back. He reached for her, and his hand fell squarely on a breast. She made a small noise, and he left it there.

Then, in one smooth motion, she hoisted the caftan over her head and let it drop to the floor. The moonlight made her naked body glow like marble as she helped him with his clothes. They stretched out together on the wide sofa, and in a moment were locked hungrily together.

When they had finished and were lying, spent, Cat felt as if he had taken a great leap across a wide chasm and safely made the other side. He tried to think more about it, but sleep overwhelmed him.

Much later, he woke. The moon was high over the house now, and the room was dark; the veranda and the beach were nearly as bright as day. He thought about himself, thought about the way he had been in the months since Katie had died. With his right hand he felt his wedding ring; he had never taken it off since the day he had been married.

He gently extricated himself from the sleeping Meg and walked out onto the terrace. He continued down to the beach, a warm breeze playing about his naked body. At the water's edge, tears streaming down his face, he dipped his hand into the water, for lubrication, then, with difficulty, worked the gold band over his knuckle. He stood still for a moment, then drew back and threw the ring as far out into the sea as he could, out to where Katie slept in *Catbird.* For weeks he had not been able to recall her face clearly, but now he could, this last time. Finally, he could let her go.

"Goodbye, Katie," he said aloud to her. "Peace."

He turned and walked back toward the house.

17

When he woke the following morning, the house was empty. He went down to the beach for a swim, and when he came back the smell of bacon greeted him.

"Morning," she called out. "I had to pick up some groceries. I didn't want to wake you. Breakfast in ten minutes."

He showered and got into some shorts. When he came out breakfast was on the table.

"Happy birthday! You were really sleeping this morning," she laughed.

"Can you blame me?" he asked. "The tennis alone was enough to render me unconscious."

She looked up from her breakfast. "Am I the first woman you've been with since your wife died?"

"Yes."

She turned back to her food. "Good."

"That was some birthday present," he

said, and he meant it.

After breakfast he asked about a phone. "I want to see how Rodriguez is doing with the telephone records."

"In my study, through there."

The study was also an editing room. A number of videotape machines occupied one end of the space, and everything was pin-neat, very professional. He called the Caribé and asked for Rodriguez.

"Who is calling, please?"

"Mr. Ellis."

"One moment." The operator was gone for a few seconds, then came back. "Mr. Rodriguez is not available."

"Ask him to call me, please." He gave her the number.

He lay around the house, read for a while, went for a run along the beach while Meg edited her Santa Marta tape on the *gamines*. When, at five o'clock, Rodriguez had not called back, he rang again and was told the man was still not available.

That night they drove into Cartagena and had dinner at a lovely place in the old city, a restaurant in an open courtyard. The heat and humidity were high, even in the evening, but the food and wine were excellent. Cat found himself relaxing into the relationship with Meg. She was now more than just a lover, she was a friend. Back at home, they made love again, and Cat found it even better than the first time. They were getting to know each other. The following morning he telephoned Rodriguez again and got the same answer from the operator.

"I feel as though I'm getting the runaround," he told Meg.

"Let me try," she said. She called the hotel and asked for Rodriguez in Spanish. He came onto the line almost immediately. She handed the phone to Cat.

"Hello, Mr. Rodriguez," he said. "This is Mr. Ellis. I've had difficulty reaching you."

Surprised, Rodriguez waffled for a moment, then said, "I am very sorry, señor, but a search of our records shows no such telephone call. I will be unable to assist you further." He hung up.

Cat told Meg what the man had said. "I don't buy it, do you?"

"Let's go look him up," she said.

Cat went to change. As he was leaving the room, he hesitated, then slipped into the shoulder holster and put on a bush jacket. At the hotel, he didn't ask for Rodriguez but walked around looking for him. Presently they saw the young man talking to a table of guests at poolside. When he turned to walk toward the main building, Cat stepped behind a large palm and waited.

"What are we doing?" Meg asked, getting behind him.

"I don't want him to see us until it's too late." Cat saw the man approaching and stepped out to meet him.

Rodriguez seemed very unhappy to see him. "What is it you want, señor? I must go to a meeting now."

"Tell me about the telephone call," Cat said, pleasantly.

"I told you, señor, we have no record of such a call."

Something snapped in Cat. This man knew something about Jinx, and he wanted to know it. Down a few feet of path from where they stood was a maintenance closet, its door open. A mop and pail were visible inside. Cat grabbed the smaller man by the necktie and hauled him into the closet. Meg was close behind, shutting the door.

"Tell me," Cat said, trying not to clench his teeth.

"There was no phone call!" the man said. Sweat was pouring down his face.

Cat pulled out the pistol and shoved it hard up under the man's jaw. "Tell me," he said.

"I could be killed for talking to you again," Rodriguez stammered. "Please, you must

232

go away."

"You are about to be killed for *not* talking to me," Cat said, cocking the pistol.

The man's eyes bulged. "Suite 800," he said quickly.

"And who was occupying Suite 800?" Cat asked.

"Please, señor, I can —"

Cat pushed the pistol harder against the man's neck. "Tell me all of it right now," he said. "I'm not going to ask you again."

"Suite 800 is permanently rented," Rodriguez managed to say. "Please, señor, you are hurting me."

Cat lowered the man from his tiptoes, held him against the wall with one hand, and put the pistol to his forehead. "Go on."

"A business rents the suite. I don't know any names."

"What business?"

"The Anaconda Company."

"And what business are they in?"

"I don't know, señor, nobody knows for sure."

"But you have an idea."

"I think, perhaps, an illegal business."

"Drugs?"

"I think, perhaps."

"Where is the company located?"

"I don't know."

"Where are the bills sent? You must know that."

"The bills are paid in cash. They come, they go in a jet airplane. They always have much cash."

"Who is the head of the company?"

"I swear to you, señor, I don't know any names. I don't deal directly with these people. Not even the manager does. They come, they sit around the pool, they order room service, they pay cash, they go away in their jet."

Cat produced the photograph of Jinx. "Did you see this girl?"

Rodriguez looked fearfully at the photograph.

"Don't lie to me, Rodriguez."

"Yes, once, when they arrived. She was taken immediately upstairs to the suite. She never came down again. I didn't see them leave. I think she . . ." He paused.

"Tell me."

"I think she was drugged. She looked . . . sleepy. They took her upstairs very quickly. When they left it was at night. I wasn't on duty."

"How long were they here?"

"They left on the third of the month. The day after the telephone call."

"Who is in the suite now?"

"No one. No one has been here since the third."

"All right, now listen to me carefully, Mr. Rodriguez. You and I and this lady are going up to the eighth floor and have a look around this suite. We'll use your passkey."

"*Dios,*" the man said, quaking, "I cannot do this. I will be seen. I will lose my job, my life even. You do not know these people, señor."

"Give me your passkey," Cat commanded.

Rodriguez fumbled in a pocket and produced a key.

Cat handed Meg the pistol. "Keep him here. I'll be as quick as I can. If he gives you a problem, kill him." He winked.

Meg took the pistol. "Sit down on the floor," she said to the man, holding the pistol to his temple.

"Which way?" he asked Rodriguez.

"In the old part of the hotel," the man replied, breathing hard. "Into the lobby and turn right to the elevators, the one at the far end. For God's sake, señor, don't let anyone see you. It is my life."

Cat left the maintenance closet and closed the door behind him. He walked back into the hotel lobby, went to the right-hand elevator, and looked around him. Only one woman was at the desk, and she was dealing with a guest. He pressed the button, and the doors opened immediately. He got in and reached for the button for the eighth floor. There was no button, just a keyhole. "Shit," he said aloud to himself. He tried the passkey; to his relief, it worked. The elevator rose. The doors opened into a vestibule. Cat strode to the door of the suite and inserted the key. It opened easily. Instinctively, he reached for the pistol, then remembered he had given it to Meg. He entered a large sitting room, decorated, he imagined, to the owner's taste. It certainly was not standard hotel decor in the tropics. The furniture was well chosen, with some antique pieces, and there were good pictures on the walls. It had the look of the home of an old-line investment banker, he thought.

Hallways led, left and right, off the room. Cat turned right. He came into a comfortable, panelled library, filled with books, many of them leather-bound. There seemed to be nothing in the room of a personal nature.

He went back to the living room and tried the other hallway. It turned and ran along the rear side of the hotel. Opening doors as he went, he found four large bedrooms, all elegantly decorated, but devoid of anything of interest. At the end of the hall he came to a large door, which was locked. He tried the passkey. It worked. The bedroom inside was as large as the living room and decorated even more richly. There was a large television set, a bar, a couple of sofas, a fireplace, and a huge bed with a canopy. There were closets on either side of the bed. The first held a wardrobe of negligees and expensive dresses. There seemed to be at least three different sizes, and there were labels from Bergdorf Goodman and Bonwit Teller. Shoe racks held at least a couple of dozen pairs of shoes with Charles Jourdan and Ferragamo labels, again in several sizes. A bank of drawers held lacy underwear.

The closet on the other side of the bed held a dozen men's suits in tropical fabrics. There were no store labels, so Cat looked for a tailor's label inside a pocket. They were all from Huntsman, in London, and had been made in the last year, but there was no customer's name in the usual place on the label. There was a stock of shirts and shoes from London makers as well, and a rack of neckties. In the drawers there were underwear and beach clothes, all custom-made. There was nothing in the closet to reveal the identity of the owner, but on all the shirts, there was a monogram, an A.

Cat went methodically through the room,

looking for anything else with a name, but found nothing. There was a telephone on a desk, with a card describing in English and Spanish how to make an international call. Cat felt he was where Jinx had been. Next to the phone was a large crystal ashtray and two books of matches. One was the hotel's, the other, different. It was a large matchbook, made of heavy, enameled black paper. Stamped in gold on the front was a rather good drawing, Cat thought, of a large snake dangling from a tree. On the back was a monogram, an A. He slipped the matches into his pocket.

What else could be in the suite? A kitchen, perhaps. He retraced his steps, and as he entered the sitting room he heard a key scrape in the lock of the front door. Not breaking his stride, he continued straight across the room, down the hall, and into the study. As he ducked into the room, he heard the voices of a man and woman, speaking quietly in Spanish. As far as he knew, there was not another entrance to the suite, but he thought there must be a fire escape. He was about to look for it when a loud noise interrupted the thought. A vacuum cleaner.

Placing the noise in the living room, he walked in that direction and peeped into the room. A woman was pushing the machine a few feet from him, and a man was dusting furniture. Both had their backs to him. He made quickly for the front door. Then the vacuum cleaner stopped.

"Buenos días, señor," a man's voice said.

Cat stopped and turned. The man and woman were staring at him. The man spoke again, asking a question in Spanish. Cat had no idea what he was saying.

"It's okay," he said, waving a hand at the room. "Go right ahead. I'm just going out for a while."

"Si, señor," the man said, smiling. *"Gracias."*

"De nada," Cat said, smiling back at him. He closed the door behind him. The elevator was waiting, its doors open. He inserted the key, turned it, and the elevator started down. Cat took a deep breath and released it. Sweat stood out on his forehead, and his knees felt weak.

In the lobby, he made briskly for the rear door. No one seemed to notice him. He walked quickly along the rear of the building to the maintenance closet, looked around, then opened the door. Rodriguez and Meg were gone.

He swore to himself. If the hotel security people had Meg, the police were already on the way. He left the closet and closed the door behind him, looking desperately about. He hadn't seen them in the lobby, so he started for the pool. As he came out of the garden, he spotted Rodriguez and Meg across the pool, sitting at a table. Meg had a tall drink, and they were chatting amiably, even smiling. He got there as quickly as he could without running.

"Oh, there you are," Meg said gaily, then under her breath, "What the fuck took you so long?"

"Sorry, it couldn't have been done any faster."

"Mr. Rodriguez and I have just been having a chat," she said.

He noticed that her hand was in her pocketbook. "Fine," he said. "Let's get out of here." He turned to Rodriguez and shook his hand, pressing five hundred dollars into it.

"Now listen," he said, smiling, "we're going to leave quietly, and I don't want any fuss from you. If we have any problems about this, I'll simply tell them I bribed you for your passkey, understand?"

Rodriguez smiled weakly and nodded. "Of course, señor, I do not wish to make problems for you. Please, please do not let anyone know how you got this information."

"I have no intention of telling anyone," Cat said, handing the grateful man his passkey. "Let's go," he said to Meg.

They walked quickly from the pool, through the hotel lobby, and asked for their car, waiting nervously for it to arrive. He had visions of security guards pouring out of the hotel, with Rodriguez screaming and pointing. The car came, and they drove away.

"I believe this is yours," Meg said, handing him the pistol. It was still cocked. "If I had any doubts about how serious you were, I don't anymore."

Cat eased the hammer down and engaged the safety. "I wasn't going to shoot the guy, but I didn't want him to know it. Why did you leave the closet?"

"A maintenance man came back for his mop. I just barely managed to get the gun into my handbag. Rodriguez talked us out of there. I thought we were better off in the open. What did you find out?"

"Not a hell of a lot. The place looks like William F. Buckley, Jr. lives there, except for the master bedroom, which looks like Hugh Hefner lives there. There were a man's suits — on the small side — and clothes for several women. Looks like an assortment to handle whoever's in residence.

The man's stuff had a monogram, A. And there was this." He handed her the matchbook.

"A for Anaconda," she said.

"Right. When we were in Riohacha, Bluey and I had a meeting with a local drug dealer. We were pretending to be buyers. He mentioned something called Anaconda Pure, a sort of brand-name cocaine, I guess. He spoke of it almost reverently. Where are we going?" She had turned along the sea, past the old city.

"To the airport. We know the jet left on the third of the month. Let's see if we can find out where it went. There isn't all that much traffic out of there. Somebody might remember it."

"You have to file a flight plan in this country," Cat said. "I wonder how long they keep them on file."

At the airport, it took Meg fifteen minutes and a hundred-dollar bill to get copies of flight plans of the only two jets that had left Cartagena on the third of the month. "There was a Lear for Bogotá and a Gulfstream for Cali," she said, translating the papers. "There's no information about who owns the planes, just the pilot's name and a phone number."

242

They drove back to Meg's house.

"Okay," she said, sitting down at the phone. "Which one is it going to be?"

"Well, from the looks of the hotel suite, they like the best of everything. A Lear is a comparatively cheap jet. A Gulfstream costs twelve or fifteen million dollars. Let's try Cali first."

"Sounds good," she said, dialling. "Cali has a reputation as a center for the drug trade, too." The number answered, and she spoke in rapid Spanish for a couple of minutes, then hung up. "Bingo, maybe," she said. "The number is the service company that hangars and maintains the jet. I pretended to be a girlfriend of the pilot, and I think they bought that. When I asked them for the name of the company that owns the plane so I could call him, they got cagey, said I could leave my number. Let's try Bogotá."

She went through the same routine with the Bogotá number, then hung up. "The airplane is owned by a construction company that does a lot of government work — roads, bridges, that sort of thing. Doesn't sound nearly as likely. Looks like we're off to Cali."

"I'm glad you said 'we.' "

"You're not going anywhere without me

and my camera," she said, kissing him. "I got the whole scene in the maintenance closet."

"What?"

She reached into her handbag and pulled out something the size of a large paperback book. "The latest in Japanese technology," she said. "I try new stuff out for them occasionally." She led him to the tape machines, popped out a tiny cassette, and shoved it into a machine. A moment later, Cat watched himself, from a low angle, terrify Rodriguez. The sound was hollow, but every word came through.

"Gosh," he said, "I never knew I did such a good George Raft."

18

Cat spent considerable time on his flight planning that evening. The longest nonstop flight he had ever made as pilot-in-command had been a little over a hundred miles, a solo cross-country during his flight training. Cali was south, in the western part of the country, some five hundred nautical miles from Cartagena.

He checked the range of the aircraft in the owner's manual and satisfied himself that the wing tanks held more than sufficient fuel for the trip. Using Bluey's charts and books, he determined that Cali was in the mountains, and all he knew about mountain flying was what he had read during his training. He satisfied himself that he could find the city, in decent weather, simply by following the Rio Cauca upstream from where it branched off the Rio Magdalena all the way to Cali, should his radio navigation equipment fail.

He calmed his nervousness about the flight with attention to detail. He had been taught all the essentials of flight planning; all he had to do was to remember it and do it right. And he was not about to fly commercial. The airlines had metal detectors, and he wanted the weapons with him more than ever.

Meg called the airport for a weather forecast. "Good," she said. "Only scattered high clouds at twenty thousand feet en route. Cali ceiling should be unlimited. We'll have a ten-knot tail wind. Could hardly be better." Looking over his shoulder, she pointed to the airport guide, open to Cali. "Here, this is the company I called to find out about the Gulfstream jet. Aeroservice. It says they have fuel, engine, and airframe repairs for Piper and Cessna aircraft and Lycoming, and Continental engines. It seems to be the only service for private aircraft on the field."

"Well, at least we have someplace to start, and a legitimate reason for being there," he said.

They took off at nine the following morning, into sunny skies and unlimited visibility. Minutes after departing Cartagena, they picked up the Rio Magdalena, Colombia's principal river, which divides a wide, green plain that is swampy in many places. Cat was beginning to feel quite confident as pilot-in-command. He thought Bluey would be proud of him. In less than an hour they had found where the Cauca branched off. Cat climbed to ten thousand five hundred feet in order to have plenty of altitude when the mountains presented themselves. The land rose to meet them as they approached and passed Medellín, Colombia's second largest city, and after Medellín, a railway ran alongside the Cauca and further confirmed their position. Piece of cake.

Cat had calculated a time en route of just less than four hours. They were less than an hour out of Cali when the first clouds appeared. They were in and out of them, which, technically, was illegal when flying under visual flight rules, or VFR, but Cat pressed on. He had no intention of landing at some other airport, not when Jinx might be waiting in Cali.

When they were handed off from the Center radio operator to Cali Approach, the operator said, "Call is three hundred overcast, wind two six zero at six. Expect the ILS for two seven zero."

Cat froze. ILS was an instrument approach. He had never flown an instrument approach and knew little about how to do it. He racked his brain for what his instructor might have told him.

"Turn right to zero nine zero," the controller said suddenly. "Vectors for the ILS."

Cat acknowledged the transmission. The controller was going to put him onto the approach. Now he remembered. The ILS was the instrument landing system, the one where you used two needles, one vertical and one horizontal, to stay on the approach. He tried to be calm. The autopilot was keeping the airplane straight and level in the cloud. He was all right for the moment, but he needed a radio frequency. He turned to Meg, trying to stay as calm as possible. "Say, look in that airport directory, will you, and give me the frequency for the ILS."

Meg consulted the book. "It's one, one, zero, point one."

"Descend to seven thousand feet," the controller said.

Cat started a descent with the autopilot, fighting panic. He dialed in the frequency for the ILS. As he did so he watched the instrument before him. The vertical needle swung sharply to the right, and the horizontal needle rose to the top of the dial.

"Turn right to two four zero degrees and intercept the ILS," the controller said.

Cat quickly turned the autopilot control to the correct heading and watched as the airplane turned itself and the vertical needle, which represented the centerline of the runway, moved closer and closer to the center of the dial. He had to do something, abort this approach, land somewhere else. He wasn't qualified to fly this airplane down to three hundred feet in cloud. He would kill them both. He was about to call the tower and abort when he noticed a button on the autopilot that read "APPR." It was worth a try. He pushed the button. Immediately, the airplane turned left and the vertical needle centered. They were on the runway centerline, and the autopilot was still flying the airplane.

"Outer marker in two miles," the controller said.

What the hell was the outer marker? Cat, frozen, watched the horizontal needle, the glide slope, move down toward the center of the needle. Suddenly an alarm went off, and a light flashed on the instrument panel. The airplane started to descend again, and both needles were centered. The outer marker must have been where the glide slope began.

Cat had just breathed a sigh of relief when he noticed that something was wrong. The airspeed had crept into the yellow arc on the dial and was headed for the red. Quickly, he eased the throttle back, and the airspeed returned to the green arc. He put in ten degrees of flaps, and the airplane slowed further. The needles were still centered. The autopilot would fly the approach, but it couldn't control the throttle.

Suddenly, they were out of the cloud, and the runway centerline was a mile dead ahead of them. Gratefully, shakily, Cat reduced speed further and came to twenty degrees of flaps. He switched off the autopilot and began flying the airplane himself. A moment later, they were on the ground.

"Hey, that was a pretty slick approach," Meg said.

"Thanks," Cat managed to reply, between deep breaths. His shirt was wet under the bush jacket. He had just done something very stupid; he had, with no experience at all, risked their lives on a complex procedure. He vowed he would never do anything in an airplane again until he had been thoroughly trained to do it.

As the airplane rolled down the runway, he saw a hangar with the name "Aeroservice" painted on it. He turned off the runway at the next taxiway and headed toward it. As he approached the hangar, a lineman ran out and directed him to a parking spot. Cat cut the engine and looked up. Ahead of them and to their right, he could see inside the hangar. He tensed.

"Look," he said, nodding at the airplane parked inside.

"Is it a Gulfstream?" Meg asked.

"Yes. I've seen a couple of them at the airport I fly out of in Atlanta. It's the biggest private jet available."

They climbed down from the airplane and unloaded their luggage. Cat asked the lineman for the office, and the man pointed to a glassed-in room inside the hangar. They walked slowly past the big jet, and Cat noted the tail number. It began with an N; that meant it was American registered. On the tail was a much larger version of the drawing of the snake in the tree on the matchbook in his pocket.

He made arrangements for tie-down and fuel with the young man at the desk, who seemed very friendly. "Say," he said to the man, "isn't that a Gulfstream out there?"

"Yes, señor. It is beautiful, no?"

"Yes indeed. I've never seen one up close. Who owns it?"

"A local business here in Cali."

"But it has an American registration number."

"Ah, yes. The company headquarters is in the States, you see."

"I wonder if we could have a look inside her? I've never been aboard one before."

The young man was shaking his head, but he stopped when he saw the hundred-dollar bill Cat was pushing toward him on the desk. "Just a moment, señor." He left the office and had a careful look outside the hangar, then returned. "You may go aboard her for just a moment, señor," he said. He led the way out of the office and toward the airplane. The door, incorporating a boarding ladder, was open.

Showing Meg ahead of him, Cat climbed aboard the jet, followed by the young man. They found themselves in a large cabin decorated in black leather and rosewood. The carpet was thick under their feet.

"See if you can occupy this guy back here for a moment," he whispered to Meg.

She nodded. "Is this the bar?" she asked, pointing to some cupboards.

"Yes, señora." The young man opened the doors to display a collection of liquor bottles.

"And where is the galley?" she asked.

"Back here, señora," he said, leading the way.

Cat walked quickly through the airplane

to the cockpit, which was a maze of dials and instruments. Breathing hard, he searched for something he knew must be there. A.R.R.O.W., he told himself. Airworthiness certificate, radio license, registration, Operator's handbook, and weight and balance restrictions — the documents that had to be aboard every aircraft.

He found them in a plastic envelope fixed to a bulkhead and quickly went through them.

"Señor!" The voice was sharp behind him.

He slipped the documents back into their envelope and turned around.

The young man was irate. "You must not tamper with the cockpit!"

"I just wanted to see what it was like up front," Cat smiled. "Gosh, there sure is a lot of equipment, isn't there?"

The young man relaxed a bit. "Yes, I suppose so. We must leave the airplane now. Someone might come, and I would get into trouble." He led them back down the boarding ladder.

"I've seen this symbol before," Cat said, pointing to the tail.

"Yes, señor, the Anaconda Company. It is very big in Cali."

"What business is it in?"

The young man shrugged. "Who knows?

253

Whatever it wants to be in, I think. They own Aeroservice; they own me, you could say. Would you like a taxi?"

"Yes, thank you. What's a good hotel?"

"The Inter-Continental is good. Shall I ring for you?"

"Yes, please, a suite, if they have it. The name is Ellis."

He went to telephone.

"The airplane is registered to an outfit in Los Angeles, Empire Holdings," he said to Meg. "Did you see anything else in the airplane that might be helpful?"

"Nope. Whoever owns it likes the best of everything, though. Do you want to show this guy the picture of Jinx?"

Cat shook his head. "I think we're a little too close to the center of things here to start flashing a photograph around. If he has seen her, he might mention us to someone, and we don't want to attract that sort of attention. Anyway, it seems pretty certain that she came to Cali on this airplane, from what Rodriguez and the flight plan told us. Maybe she's still here."

The young man returned. "Your suite is booked, and your taxi will be here shortly."

Cali seemed a large and prosperous city, and the Inter-Continental was large, modern, and comfortable. The suite had a terrace overlooking a large swimming pool, and Cat began to itch for some laps.

"Listen," Meg said, reading him easily, "I want to go to the local newspaper's office and see what I can find out about the Anaconda Company. If they're as big as they seem to be, there'll be something in the business pages about them. Why don't you go for a swim?"

"Okay, how long will you be?"

"A couple of hours, maybe."

She left, and Cat started to undress, then changed his mind. He felt restless, being in the city where Jinx might be; it didn't seem the right time for a swim. He called the concierge. "Can you find me a taxi driver who speaks English? I'd like to take a tour of the city."

"Of course, señor. You may leave whenever you wish. The doorman will find you the right man."

When Cat came downstairs, a man approached him. "You Mr. Ellis, who wanted an English-speaking driver?" He didn't sound Colombian; he sounded like a New Yorker.

"That's right."

"My name's Bill. I'm your man."

They got into the cab and drove away from the hotel.

"Anything in particular you want to see?" Bill asked.

"Nope. This is my first time here. Whatever you want to show me. Are you Colombian?"

"Yeah, I was born here, but I lived in New York for a long time. Pushed a hack there."

"What brought you back?"

"Well, I saved some money, and it goes a lot farther here than it did in New York. Now I own my own cab, and I live pretty good. Say, why don't we start at the top of the city and work down, okay?"

"Okay, whatever you like."

Bill pushed the taxicab higher and higher into the hills until he came to a large statue of a man looking out over the city. Both men got out of the car.

"This is the statue of Belalcázar, the guy who founded the city," Bill explained. "He was a Spanish grandee."

Cat took in the panorama, then his eye came to rest on a modern office tower. At the top was the Anaconda symbol. "Bill, what's that building? Something to do with the Anaconda Company?"

"Yeah, that's their headquarters."

"What business is the company in?"

"Agriculture I think. I don't know much about it, really. Tell you what, though, there's a good restaurant at the top of the building. Terrific view of the city at night."

"Are there a lot of drugs in Cali, Bill?"

"There's a lot of drugs everywhere in Colombia. Listen, if that's what you're interested in, you've got the wrong guy. I'll get you another driver if you want."

"No, I'm not interested in buying drugs. Just in what goes on in Cali. I'd heard drugs were big here."

"Come on," Bill said, "I'll show you something."

He drove the cab a few blocks from the statue, but not much downhill, then stopped. "The rumor is, the biggest drug dealer in Colombia lives right there," he said, pointing.

Cat looked down onto the house, a hundred and fifty yards below them. He couldn't see much except a lot of roof and trees and the corner of a tennis court. The place seemed to be contained in a walled compound that covered two or three acres. As he watched, a woman with a ponytail in tennis whites chased a ball to the edge of the court, then ran back to the part blocked by the trees. Just for a moment, Cat hoped, but the woman was shorter and stockier than Jinx. Quite masculine in the way she ran. He watched for a couple of minutes,

257

but he could see no other human being. A street seemed to run completely around the house. It sat on a sort of island in a neighborhood of other large houses.

"Bill, drive me around the house, slowly, will you?"

"Sure thing," Bill said, and put the car in gear.

As the taxi slowly circled the house, Cat rolled down the window and got a good look. It was built considerably above street level, a wall rising up from the streets to be topped by wrought-iron fencing all the way round. There were two gates, and large men in dark suits manned each of them. At one point a large Alsatian dog came to the fence near a gate and snarled loudly at the cab. The houses surrounding the compound all had iron gates, but he saw no guards or dogs at those.

"Looks like a regular fortress," Cat said. "Let's go around again."

Bill shook his head. "I don't think that's such a good idea. A friend of mine, another cab driver, got interested in it once, and they took his number. The cops called on him and gave him a hard time."

"Local pull, huh?"

"You know it. You got the kind of money those guys got, you can buy just about anybody you want in this city."

"You know the name of the guy who owns the house?"

"Nope, and it's not the sort of thing I'd like to ask too many questions about. I need to stop for some gas. You mind?"

"Go ahead."

Bill pulled into a service station a few blocks down the hill from the big house. As he stopped at the pumps, a large man got into a black Cadillac stretch limousine and drove away.

"Are there a lot of those in Cali?" Cat asked.

"Oh, yeah, a lot of Caddies; Rollses, too, but that's something new, the first stretch job in town. That belongs to the house up the hill."

Quickly, Cat memorized the tag number of the limousine and wrote it down in his pocket notebook, next to the tail number of the Gulfstream jet. He didn't pay a lot of attention to the rest of the tour — the stadium where the Pan-American games were held during the early seventies, the cathedral, the shopping district.

When he got back to the hotel, Meg was sunning herself on the terrace of their suite. "You're back early. Any luck?" he asked her.

"Yeah, they let me into their library, and I

talked with the guy on the business desk, too. The Anaconda Company came to Colombia about four years ago and started buying up agribusinesses. They've got half a dozen offices around the country. In Cali, they're big in sugar; in Medellín, they're into coffee; other places, they've got holdings in cattle, bananas and flowers."

"Flowers?"

"Big Colombian export to the States."

"Who owns the company?"

"This guy I talked to looked into it once. There's no one big name on the corporate roster. Each office has its own manager. Whenever he asked too many questions of the company P.R. guy, he got a runaround. They've become a local power in Cali very quickly. Sugar is the big crop here, and they've bought a lot of holdings. Been pretty ruthless about it, too. They're well plugged in with the local politicos, and the guy's boss at the paper won't have a bad word written about them."

"Well, I find it hard to believe that the local manager has a Gulfstream at his disposal. Only a chief executive officer rates that kind of transportation. Maybe the big man is in town at the moment."

He told her about his tour of the city and about the house and limousine he'd seen.

"Anaconda has a big office building here, too. The cab driver says there's a good restaurant on top of it. Why don't we try it tonight?"

"Sounds good to me."

He called the concierge and asked him to make reservations.

Bill drove them to the Anaconda building and agreed to pick them up in a couple of hours. There were four elevators in the marble lobby, but three of them were roped off, and a sign indicated the fourth was to be used to reach Le Caprice, as the restaurant was called. At the top of the building they entered a plush vestibule and walked to an equally plush dining room. They were shown to a small table by a large window and given menus. Cat ordered drinks for them and turned his attention to the view. Cali was spread out beneath them, a carpet of lights, and above them, the Belalcázar statue, spotlighted, gazed down. The menu was in French, and there seemed to be few Colombian favorites among the dishes. The wine list was outstanding, Cat thought, if extremely expensive. Most of the wines were French, and he ordered a good claret with their dinner.

They were on their first course when a

large party entered the restaurant and were shown to a huge round table in a nearby corner. Cat counted twelve, and two of them were Anglo-looking women, elegantly dressed. The men seemed a mixture of Anglo and Latino, and all wore sober business suits. One of them interested Cat more than the others. He seemed to be in his mid-thirties, and, in spite of his conservative suit, his hair was long, worn in a ponytail.

Cat nodded toward the table. "I have the oddest feeling that the man with the ponytail is the woman I saw playing tennis at the drug dealer's house this afternoon."

"Are you sure?" Meg asked.

"No, but I remember she ran in a masculine way. I think the hairdo may have clouded my judgment."

Cat glanced frequently at the table. No menus were offered, but food and wine appeared as if the host had ordered everything in advance. As Cat and Meg were finishing, and as waiters were clearing away the dishes from the first course at the large table, the man with the ponytail rose and walked in the direction of the men's room. Cat got up and followed him for a better look.

The man was smaller than Cat, and his pin-striped suit was closely cut, with double vents, a full skirt, and pinched at the waist.

Cat had been buying clothes in London long enough to know a Savile Row suit when he saw one. He was about to follow the man into the rest room, when another, larger man stepped in front of him and said something in Spanish.

Cat shrugged. "I just want the men's room," he said.

"One moment, please," the man said in heavily accented English.

Cat waited a couple of minutes, then the ponytailed man came out and walked past him back to his table, without so much as a glance at Cat. The larger man indicated that Cat could now enter the men's room. He did so, etching into his mind the memory of the ponytailed man. He was small, five-seven or so, well-built, athletic-looking, fair skin, light brown hair, an intelligent face, with a wide, vaguely cruel mouth. Cat had never seen him before, but he would never forget him, he was sure of that.

Back at the table, Cat lingered over coffee and dessert, trying vainly to pick up snatches of conversation from the larger table. At one point the two women went to the ladies' room and the bodyguard, who had been hovering nearby, followed them there and back.

Cat and Meg finished their dinner and left

the restaurant. As they came out of the building, Cat saw the stretch Cadillac limousine waiting at the curb, and a few yards away, Bill's taxi.

"Bill," Cat said, as they got into the cab, "drive around the block and park where we can see the building entrance." Bill did as he was told.

"What are you going to do?" Meg asked.

"I'm not really sure," Cat answered. "I just want to see where they go. As he spoke two other, shorter, limousines drove up and parked at the building's entrance. A few minutes later the party of twelve came down from the restaurant and spent a moment saying goodbyes out front. Two men got out of either side of the stretch limousine and waited as the ponytailed man got into the back seat. The others entered the smaller cars, and all three drove away in tandem.

"Bill, follow them at a discreet distance. If they split up, follow the big car."

"Mister, you been seeing too many movies," Bill said, but he followed his instructions.

After a few blocks, the big car turned left, while the other two continued. Bill obediently turned after it. It soon became obvious that they were headed toward the airport. The short road to the Aeroservice hangar turned off the main airport road and was darker.

"Turn off your lights and stop here," Cat said as they came to the turnoff.

They could see the limousine as it continued toward the hangar. The big Gulfstream was sitting on the apron outside the hangar with its engines running. They could hear the noise over the two hundred yards of distance between them and the airplane. As they watched the two men in the front seat of the car jumped out and opened the rear doors, then two people got out of the car and boarded the airplane. Immediately, the door closed, and the jet started to move, its landing lights flashing over the taxi as the jet turned onto the main runway. A moment later the craft was airborne.

"Drive to the hangar," Cat said, his voice tense.

When the cab pulled up, Cat got out and motioned for Meg to remain in the car. His heart thumping, he went to the office in the hangar and found the same young man who had showed them the jet that afternoon.

"Hi," he said, "I just want to get something out of my airplane."

"Of course, señor," the young man said.

"I see the Gulfstream is gone," Cat said. "Was that it I saw taking off as I drove up?"

"Yes, señor. She is off to Bogotá," he replied. "She will be the last plane to take off tonight. Takeoffs are prohibited after midnight. Noise abatement."

Cat made a show of unlocking the Cessna and rummaging inside it for a moment, then he went back to the cab.

"Bogotá," he said to Meg. "We can't take off until morning."

"Right," she said. "Cat, do you remember when the group came out of the office building and then got into their cars?"

"Yes."

"Well, I thought the man with the ponytail got into the stretch limo alone. But at the airport, two people got out of the back seat."

"I know," Cat said. "One of them was a woman."

19

The mountains surrounding Cali fell away to the broad, green valley of the Rio Magdalena as the airplane droned its way northeastward toward Bogotá. Then the valley ended and the mountains rose again. Worriedly, Cat rechecked the elevations on his charts. The Anaconda Gulfstream had, undoubtedly, gone to the international airport of Bogotá, Eldorado, with its long runway and concentrations of police and security systems. He had two pistols and a shotgun aboard, and he didn't want to be looked at too closely. Accordingly, he had filed for the smaller general aviation airport on the other side of the city. The elevation of the field was nearly nine thousand feet, and it was surrounded by mountains that rose even higher.

"I've been into this little airport," Meg said. "I don't remember it being much of a problem."

"It probably isn't for a turbocharged airplane," Cat replied, "but a normally aspirated engine like ours loses manifold pressure as altitude increases and the air gets thinner. I just don't want to have to try and gain altitude in a hurry under those conditions."

The weather was in their favor, though, and as the airport hove into view, the terrain around it was clearly visible. Cat set the airplane down on the short runway and taxied to a low cluster of buildings, which turned out to be the local flying school, Aeroandes. He arranged for fuel and tie-down and ordered a taxi.

"What's your plan here?" Meg asked.

"Plan? Jesus, I haven't had a plan since I got to this country. I guess we'd better start at the airport and see what we can learn there."

"We'll do better without all this gear. Why don't we drop it at a hotel. The Tequendama is good."

Driving into Bogotá in the taxi, Cat was, first, charmed by the flower sellers on either side of the highway, their stalls crammed with colorful blossoms, then appalled by the amount of security equipment on the local houses as they entered the city. The ground floor of every house was festooned with bars on every window and door. It didn't seem a pleasant place to live.

Downtown Bogotá was mostly modern and high-rise, with a scattering of older and more colorful buildings. Green mountains, ringed with clouds, hovered over everything. The Tequendama Hotel was one of Bogotá's older modern buildings and seemed to offer everything one could want. They spent half an hour getting settled into a suite, then Cat slipped into his shoulder holster again and checked that the automatic pistol was loaded. He felt he was getting close to something, and he wanted to be prepared. He checked the aluminum case into the hotel's safe.

Meg looked at the case curiously. "You a camera buff?" she asked. "I haven't seen you take a photograph yet."

"Nah, just some personal valuables. All you hear about is how good the thieves and pickpockets are in this country."

"Yes, and it's both true and a shame. It's a lovely country with wonderful people that's being eaten alive by drugs, poverty, and, nibbling at the edges, political terrorism."

They moved through the cavernous lobby toward the taxi entrance. "I wish I could feel more concern about Colombia," Cat said, "but all I want to do is find Jinx and get out of here as quickly as possible."

A modern, four-lane highway took them quickly to Eldorado Airport.

"I hate to keep harping on this," Meg said, "but what's your plan? What do you hope to learn at the airport?"

"Well, the Gulfstream got in late last night, which indicates to me that our man with the ponytail intended to sleep in Bogotá. First, let's find the airplane, then let's see if we can find out where in the city the guy is staying. If we can find him, we might find Jinx. That just might have been her getting on the airplane with him last night."

"Okay, that seems reasonable."

"I just hope to hell he doesn't have another fortress in Bogotá like the one in Cali. We wouldn't have much of a chance of getting inside a place like that, what with all the guards and dogs."

"If last night was any example, he's not going to be without a lot of heavy help wherever he is," Meg said.

"I'll cross that bridge when I come to it," Cat said, not at all certain how he would cross it.

At Eldorado Airport, Meg pointed at a group of hangars. "That's where the business aircraft get serviced."

A policeman looked briefly inside the cab, then waved them through the gate. Meg asked the taxi to wait. They entered a lounge area, obviously intended for passengers on private aircraft.

"What's our excuse for being here?" Meg whispered to Cat.

"We're looking for a business associate."

Meg pointed to a business office. "Let's try there."

At the counter a young woman came to help them.

"I'm looking for a friend who's supposed to be landing in a business jet. They may even have landed last night."

"Do you have the registration number, señor?"

Cat flipped open his notebook and gave it to her. "It's a Gulfstream."

"No," she replied, pointing to a wall chart of arriving aircraft. "We haven't had a Gulfstream in here recently, and I've no way of knowing when to expect your friend's plane. We don't know who's coming until they call us on the Unicom."

"Is there anyplace else on the field where the airplane might be serviced?" he asked.

"Well, sometimes the larger planes are serviced by the airlines, Avianca or Eastern,

at the main terminal. They have a full catering service there. Both the Avianca and
Eastern hangars are on the other side of the
main terminal, and you might have difficulty
getting through the gate without a pass."

"How can we get a pass?" Cat asked.

"The easiest thing would be to go into the
main terminal. If there is a Gulfstream
either at a service hangar or at a gate, you
should be able to see it through the windows
of the lounge. If your friend's plane is there,
you can apply at the airport manager's office for a pass."

"Thank you very much."

They left the office and the taxi took them
to the main terminal entrance. The airport
was mobbed. Well-dressed businessmen
stood, cheek by jowl, with peasants from
the countryside, all squirming to get
through security to their respective departure gates.

"Is it always like this?" Cat asked as they
picked their way slowly through the crowds.

"Usually. The road system is not very
extensive, and not as many Colombians own
cars as Americans. They take Avianca, instead."

With some difficulty they made their way,
foot by foot, to the windows overlooking
the apron, where jets were embarking and

disembarking passengers. They looked carefully up and down the row of Avianca and Eastern aircraft and those of half a dozen South American countries, then at the airplanes parked in and around the service hangars across the apron. None of the jets was a Gulfstream.

Cat stood, looking, willing the airplane to be there. If it wasn't, he was at a dead end; he had nowhere else to go.

"Look," Meg said, pointing down the apron.

Cat looked and saw, being towed down the ramp toward them by a small tractor, the Anaconda Gulfstream.

"It looks as though it's being towed to a gate," Meg said. "Maybe it's picking up the owner and his party."

As they watched, the airplane was towed into an empty gate, about a hundred yards down the terminal from where they were standing. A hatch opened at the rear of the airplane, and a catering truck began passing provisions through it.

"I've got to figure a way to get onto that airplane," Cat said. "If it's just arrived at the gate, chances are the passengers aren't on it yet, and I want to be there when they come aboard."

"What will you do then?" Meg asked.

Cat patted his shoulder "I'm armed. If Jinx is with them, I'll take her off the plane, one way or another. If she's not, I'll just have to talk my way off."

"We can try the airport manager's office for a pass, like the lady suggested," Meg said.

"No, that will take too long."

"Look who's here," Meg said, pointing out the window. A stretch limousine had driven up to the aircraft. A chauffeur was unloading the trunk, but the doors to the car remained closed.

But Cat's attention seemed to be elsewhere. "Cat, look out here a . . ." Meg stopped when she saw the look on Cat's face.

He had turned away from the windows and was staring into the crowd.

"What is it, Cat?" she asked.

Cat watched silently as the young man picked his way through the mob. "There, the young guy in the light blue, three-piece suit, no necktie."

"Dark hair?"

"No, ahead of that one. He's blond, has a moustache."

"Got him. What about him?"

Cat had started to move through the crowd. The moustache had made him wonder for a moment, but suddenly he had no doubt.

"Hang on, Cat!" Meg said, struggling to keep up with him through the mass of bodies. "Who is he?"

"It's Denny!" Cat called over his shoulder. "Our volunteer crewman on *Catbird*! The one who shot me!"

Cat pressed harder through the crowd. There were twenty people between him and Denny, but he kept the back of the blond head in sight. "Excuse me . . . pardon me," he was saying to ruffled people as he pushed past them. Now there were a dozen people between them. Meg had fallen hopelessly behind, trapped by a fat peasant woman with two large baskets. The crowd was thickening as it approached the bottleneck of a security checkpoint. Cat forgot courtesy and began fighting his way through the throng, closing inch by inch on the pale blue suit and blond hair. There, just ahead of him, was the one man in the world who certainly knew what had happened to Jinx, and Cat was not going to let go of his throat until he knew, maybe not even then. Denny passed the checkpoint and now, on the other side of the bottleneck, began to move faster.

"Get out of my way!" Cat was yelling,

yanking himself past startled and angry travellers. He, too, would be at the check-point in a moment and free to move. He forcibly drove his shoulder into a large man and pushed ahead of him past the security men. As he did the world seemed to explode. A loud bell began to ring, a red strobe light started flashing, and a tan-uniformed figure lunged at him and got hold of an arm.

"Let go!" Cat was shouting at the man, trying to free himself. Ahead of him, he saw Denny glance unconcernedly over his shoulder at the disturbance, then continue walking on toward a gate. Another policeman came at him from the other side now, shouting in Spanish.

"I've got to get to that man," Cat was trying to explain to the policeman, but the man on the left was tugging at Cat's clothing and shouting, too. Finally, Cat gave up any hope of convincing the policemen and began to fight with the desperation of a drowning man. Thirty yards ahead of him, he could see Denny turning into a boarding gate.

Cat, with an enormous effort, got swinging room and brought an elbow into the midsection of the officer on his left. Half free, and fighting as hard as he could, he was about to break free of the cop on his left.

Then something hard and heavy came down on his neck where it joined the shoulder, knocking him to one knee. He struggled to regain his feet under the weight of what now seemed like half a dozen policemen, and the club struck him again. His limbs seemed to melt, and he pitched forward toward the floor. His head struck a black shoe, then came to rest with his cheek against the cool marble floor. As he faded into unconsciousness, he felt, as if from a great distance, a boot making repeated contact with his back, accompanied, in Spanish, by what seemed a great deal of swearing.

20

At first there was just the pain. Then the cold crept in, and the cold became more pain. Then, before he was fully conscious, the shivering started, which increased the pain, which finally jolted him awake. He opened his eyes, then quickly closed them again. The light was too harsh. With some difficulty, he got to one elbow, opening his eyes for brief moments, allowing his pupils to close down to where he could bear the light.

He was lying on a rough concrete floor, entirely naked, in a small space enclosed by two walls of concrete and two of chain-link fencing. There was no furniture of any kind. He sat up and started rubbing his upper arms rapidly, trying to dispel the chill. The door must be behind him, he reckoned, but when he tried to turn and look at it, he got a thunderbolt of pain in his neck and left shoulder.

Down the hall a door opened and foot-steps rang on the concrete, accompanied by a low conversation in Spanish. The door behind him rattled open, but he still could not turn to see who was entering. A bald-headed man in a blue suit appeared in his vision and spoke some words to someone behind Cat. A blanket was thrown over his shoulders, and hands pressed him to lie down on the floor. The man in the blue suit produced a small flashlight and shone it into Cat's eyes, one at a time. He felt Cat's limbs and turned his head gently. Cat coughed out a yell.

"What is your name?" the man said in heavily accented English.

"My name is Ca . . . ah, Robert Ellis," Cat managed to croak.

The man spoke rapidly to the people behind Cat, and someone responded in what seemed to him slower and more awkward Spanish. He found himself being expertly lifted, laid on a stretcher, and covered with another blanket. He was wheeled rapidly down a hallway, through another door, and through a larger room. Another door opened, they were brief-ly outside, then the stretcher was put into an ambulance and an attendant climbed in beside it. Shortly, the ambulance began to move.

Cat closed his eyes and tried to relax, hugging the blanket to him. Eventually, the chills stopped and, in spite of his overall soreness, he fell into a light doze. He was aware of fast driving, of traffic, and of the silence of the man who sat next to him. He wondered if the man spoke English, but he didn't feel like conversation, himself, so he said nothing. He reckoned that wherever he was going was better than the place he had just left.

He woke as the ambulance stopped, then started again. Through a crack in a curtain he saw the top of a heavy iron fence as the ambulance drove through. The doors to the rear of the vehicle opened, and two men, one of them in a suit, rolled the stretcher out and through a door. They were in another hallway for a moment, then in an elevator, going down.

Another man shone another flashlight into his eyes and probed his body. Cat answered with loud grunts when the probing became painful, as it rather frequently did. Then the stretcher was wheeled into what Cat recognized as an X-ray room, and he was lifted onto a cold table where pictures were made. He felt relieved to know that he was in a hospital instead of a jail. The doctor and nurse, both Latino, sat him up and got him into a hospital gown, then he was placed back on the stretcher and wheeled down a hallway to a room and lifted onto a bed. The nurse tucked him in, but nobody said a word, and as soon as he had been made comfortable, he was left alone.

Cat lifted his head and tried to look around the room, but the effort defeated him. The room was small, but though sparsely furnished, it seemed to be in a real hospital and not in the medical ward of a prison. He closed his eyes and tried to rest without thinking. He was not ready to confront his situation, to try and figure out what to do next. He was aware of a murmured conversation outside the door.

A few moments later someone entered the room. Cat was too weary to raise his head, but there was a clanking noise, and the bed lifted him into more of a sitting position. A man in a gray, pin-striped suit stood at the end of the bed, looking at him with an expression of distaste, even disgust. He had closely cropped crew-cut hair, thick eyebrows, a square jaw, and a nose that had once been broken and had healed badly.

It had been twenty-five years, but Cat knew him. "Jesus, Hedger," he said, managing a small laugh, "you still getting your haircuts at Quantico?"

"Catledge," Barry Hedger said. He managed to make it both a greeting and an accusation.

"Am I in a hospital?" Cat asked.

"You're in the staff infirmary of the American Embassy, and damned lucky to be. You're lucky to be alive, too. You don't wear a pistol through a metal detector in any airport in the world, don't you know that? The cops down here would just as soon shoot you for that sort of thing."

"Thanks for bringing me here," Cat said with feeling. "How did you know?"

"Your friend *Señorita Greville,*" he nearly spat the name, "called me from the airport. I was in a meeting with the Ambassador, but she was insistent."

"Is she here?"

"No. I don't know where she is."

"We're both at the Tequendama. Can I call her?"

"There's no phone in this room, and you probably don't feel like moving around. I'll have my secretary call her. What should she say?"

"Just that I'm okay, and I'll call her there as soon as possible. Oh, ask her to try and find out where the airplane went."

"Airplane?"

"She'll know what I'm talking about."

"I expect she will, but I don't. What the hell are you doing, anyway?"

"It's a long story."

"I don't doubt it. A short story wouldn't cover somebody who's travelling, armed, in a South American country, with a false passport and seventy-one thousand dollars in hundred-dollar bills in his pocket."

Cat winced. "You're right, that wasn't very smart. I was trying to catch up to somebody; I didn't think."

The doctor walked into the room carrying an X-ray film. "Nothing broken," he said to Hedger, "but a hell of a lot of bruising. They worked him over pretty good."

"No more than he deserved," Hedger replied.

"When can I get out of here?" Cat asked.

"We'll keep you overnight, I think," the doctor replied. "Let's be sure there's no concussion. You can go tomorrow, if you feel up to it."

"He's not going anywhere until I say so," Hedger snapped. "Thanks, Doc, that's all."

"I'll send you a painkiller and something to help you sleep," the doctor said to Cat, then left.

Hedger turned back to Cat. "You're still under arrest," he said, "but I managed to get you released to my custody. You're not to leave the embassy compound without the permission of the Chief of Police of Bogotá."

"What's going to happen? Will I be prosecuted?"

"Probably." Hedger turned and walked to the door. "I've got some phone calls to make. I'll find you a lawyer, who will probably want you to cop a plea and take a shorter sentence. There's not much question of your guilt. You'll have the weapons charge, of course, at least one on resisting arrest, and one on violation of customs regulations — failure to declare all that money. You didn't declare it, did you?" He didn't wait for an answer. "I didn't think so. Get some rest; you're going to need it. I'll talk to you later." He left the room.

Cat closed his eyes. Christ, he had really blown it. He wasn't going to be any help to Jinx in jail. Maybe Meg would keep working on it. He needed her now more than ever. She might be his last chance. He closed his eyes and tried to stop thinking.

21

When Cat woke the next morning, there was a brown paper package on his bed. His clothes had been laundered and pressed. Getting out of bed was not as easy as he would have liked, but after twenty minutes under a hot shower, he found he could move about quite well as long as he did not take too deep a breath or try to turn his head too far to the left. He was shocked, though, by the bruises on his shoulders and back. He decided to stay away from mirrors until they went away.

Someone brought him bacon and eggs, and as he was finishing his second cup of coffee and starting to feel truly human again, a young American woman appeared in the doorway.

"I'm Candis Leigh, Mr. Catledge," she said. "I work for Barry Hedger. How are you feeling this morning?"

"Much better, thanks."

"Barry would like you to come up to his office, if you're feeling up to it."

Cat laughed. "If he's the same Hedger I used to know, he'd like me to come to his office whether I feel like it or not."

She laughed back. "You know him better than I thought." She clipped a plastic visitor's pass onto the pocket of his bush jacket. "Follow me."

She led him down the hall to an elevator and pressed the button for the fourth floor. She leaned against the paneling and sighed. "Don't mention I told you this, but he was on the phone to Washington yesterday afternoon and again this morning, and he didn't like it very much. My guess is, he's been told to give you whatever assistance you need, so don't take too much crap from him."

"Thanks, I appreciate your telling me."

"Seems you've got some juice at headquarters."

Cat shrugged. "What does Hedger do here, anyway?"

"He's Deputy Cultural Affairs Officer." She paused and looked at the ceiling. "Sort of."

Cat was about to ask more, but the elevator doors opened. He followed her down the hallway and was ushered into a medium-size office, panelled in a pale wood. Barry Hedger was sitting behind the desk, talking on the telephone. He pointed at a chair, and Cat sat down.

"Yeah, yeah, well, tell him that's all I can do for him at the moment. If I get any further word, I'll let him know. But tell him if he expects to keep getting paid, I want better stuff than that." He hung up without saying goodbye and stared at Cat. "You're ambulatory, are you?"

"Yep. Listen, thanks for getting me out of that cell yesterday. I'm really very grateful, and I didn't thank you properly."

Hedger nodded wearily. "Yeah, yeah, well, I know a little more about your situation now. I read the stuff about the boat and all, of course; sorry about that; it was tough."

"Thanks."

"Now you think the girl's alive, right?"

"I'm sure of it."

Hedger picked up the telephone and tapped in a number. "Well, I still don't understand your stupidity, but I guess I understand your motivation. Hello, Marge? Hedger. We're on our way up." He hung up the phone. "Let's go."

Cat followed Hedger to the elevator, up a couple of floors to a much-better-decorated hallway, through a small reception area to a

287

large door. Hedger rapped on it.

"Come in!" a voice shouted from the other side.

The two men walked into a large, handsomely furnished office.

"This is Wendell Catledge, sir," Hedger said. "Catledge, the Ambassador."

Cat shook the man's hand and accepted a chair.

The Ambassador looked at Cat silently for a moment. "Have you recovered from your little wrestling match with the police yesterday?" he asked finally.

"Yes, thank you. I'm a little stiff, but all right. Thank you for the use of embassy facilities last night. Everyone has been very kind."

The Ambassador turned to Hedger. "He's one of yours, then?"

Hedger looked uncomfortable. "Yes, sir, more or less." He started to continue, but the Ambassador held up a hand.

"More or less is good enough, thank you. I don't want to know any more." He turned back to Cat. "Mr. Catledge, first of all, I want to say how sorry I am about what happened to your family."

"Thank you," Cat replied.

"I understand your daughter may be alive and in this country."

"Yes, sir, almost certainly so."

"Of course I was aware of the tragedy when it occurred, and various requests came across my desk more than once. I want you to know that they received the very best attention this embassy could afford them."

"I appreciate that."

"You can understand how, in the circumstances, after the reports we had of the incident, we did not have the slightest indication that your daughter might still be alive."

He wants off the hook, Cat thought; that's why I'm here. He wants me to absolve him. "Of course, I understand. I thought she was dead myself until not very long ago."

The Ambassador nodded. "Now that there is reason to believe she might be alive, I am perfectly willing to call the Minister of Justice and ask that the police investigation be reopened. Is that what you want?"

Cat froze. He hadn't counted on this; he had become so accustomed to pursuing Jinx and her kidnappers on his own that the thought of the police coming into it shocked him.

Hedger spoke before Cat could. "If I may suggest, sir, I'd like to take a look at this situation with Mr. Catledge before we bring the police back into it."

"If that's what you think best," the Ambassador replied. "Mr. Catledge, is that your wish?"

Cat nodded. "Yes, it is. For the moment, anyway."

"Fine. Just remember that I am happy to relaunch official inquiries whenever you wish, and should Senator Carr's office inquire about our conversation, I hope you will tell them I told you that."

"Thank you. Yes, of course."

The Ambassador leaned forward and folded his hands on his chest. "Now, about the difficulties arising from your little indiscretion of yesterday."

Cat's stomach tightened. He didn't look forward to being returned to the Colombian police.

"I've had a word with the Minister of Justice, who has spoken with the Chief of Police. It is the consensus that all parties will best be served if the events of yesterday are deemed not to have occurred."

Cat was nearly faint with relief. "Thank you, Mr. Ambassador; I'm very grateful."

The Ambassador responded with a benevolent nod. "I need hardly say that all parties, especially you, will be happiest if further incidents of this or any other kind are avoided. There is only so much I can do, you understand."

Cat had the momentary feeling of being a schoolboy in the principal's office. "Yes, sir, I understand completely, and again, let me say how grateful I am for your help."

The Ambassador stood up and offered his hand. "Then I will return you to the tender mercies of Mr. Hedger and his colleagues."

Cat shook the man's hand and followed Hedger back to his office.

Hedger waved Cat to a chair, sank into his own, and opened a desk drawer. He tossed Cat a heavy manila envelope. "That's everything the police took off you yesterday except the piece. I'll hang on to that. Count the money."

Cat slipped on his Rolex and riffled through the bills. "It's all here. Thanks." He stuffed the money into the shoulder wallet and put it back into the envelope. "Where's my passport and ID?"

"You mean the Ellis junk? I'll hang on to that, too." He took out a telephone, somewhat larger than the one on his desk, and tapped in a number. "This is Hedger in Bogotá. Give me Drummond." He paused. "Good morning, sir, this is Hedger. Yes, sir." He pushed the telephone across the desk and handed the receiver to Cat.

Puzzled, Cat took the instrument. He

didn't know anybody named Drummond. "Hello?"

"Hi, this is Jim. You okay?"

"Oh, hello. Yes, I'm fine. The people here have been very helpful."

"You making any progress?"

"Yes, a lot."

"Good. Keep at it. They'll do what they can there, but it may not be a hell of a lot."

"Thanks, I appreciate that. And listen, I can't tell you how grateful I am to you for confirming the phone call from Jinx. Without that I would have given up."

"Glad to do it. Has Bluey been a help?"

Cat shrank inside. "I'm sorry, but Bluey was killed in Santa Marta." He explained what had happened. "I've already made some provision for his child."

"That was good of you," Jim said, "but you shouldn't feel too badly about Bluey. He used up all nine lives a long time ago. He had all these pipe dreams about retiring and going into some sort of legitimate business, but believe me, he wouldn't have. It just wasn't in him to lead a quiet life. If he hadn't caught it in Santa Marta, he'd have caught it somewhere else next week or next month. He was a pro, and he knew the risks better than you."

"Well, thanks for that, anyway."

"I gotta run. Keep Hedger posted; he'll keep me posted. Anything else?"

"I'd still like to keep the stuff you gave me."

"Sure. From what I hear, that hasn't been compromised. Give me Hedger. Take care."

Cat handed the telephone back to Hedger.

"Yes, sir?" He listened for a moment, then hung up, put the instrument back into the drawer, and tossed Cat his Ellis wallet and passport. "How'd you and Drummond get hooked up?" Hedger asked.

"Mutual acquaintance," Cat replied.

"You know why he's doing this."

Cat looked at Hedger, puzzled.

"You don't know. His daughter."

"What about his daughter?"

"He was station head in Paris four years ago. The girl, she was sixteen, was kidnapped on the way to school. They shot the officer who was driving her. Drummond got a note. One of the terrorist organizations."

"What did they want? Ransom?"

Hedger shook his head. "They wanted Drummond. Said they'd exchange the girl for him. Our people and the French laid on a big operation. It went wrong. They cut four Arabs in a car to pieces. The girl wasn't with them. After that, there was no more communication with the kidnappers. No demands, I mean."

"What happened to the girl?"

"They mailed her to Drummond in pieces. First, her fingers; then, her ears. It got worse. Went on for days. The police finally found what was left of her body in a raid on a safe house. She'd been alive when they were mutilating her."

Cat rubbed his forehead. "Jesus Christ."

"A few days later, the French caught one of the kidnappers. They left Drummond alone with the man, and, eventually, he gave up the three who were still alive. There was a police raid on a Paris apartment. None of the three survived. The French are more efficient about these things than we are."

Cat couldn't think of anything else to say.

"There's a little more. As a result of all this, Drummond's wife is permanently institutionalized. The girl was their only child. All Drummond does is work and visit her."

"That's the worst story I ever heard," Cat said.

"Yours is almost as bad, and it could get worse."

Cat looked at him. "Is that why you're telling me all this? To prepare me for the worst?"

"Yeah. I think you ought to know that

your chances of finding the girl alive are almost nil. You're looking for a miracle, and it probably isn't going to happen."

"The miracle has already happened," Cat said. "When I heard her voice on the telephone, when I knew she was alive, that was the miracle."

"I hope your luck holds," Hedger said. "You're not improving the odds by running around with that Communist, either."

Cat sat up. "Communist?"

"Your Señorita Greville. Don't you know who she is?"

"What the hell are you talking about?"

"Remember Charles Adam Greville?"

The name sounded familiar, but Cat couldn't place it.

"The House Un-American Activities Committee hearings, in the fifties?"

It was coming back to him. "You mean the guy who was hounded out of the State Department?"

"Hounded, my ass. The guy was a Russian agent."

"Come on, Hedger, that was never proved."

"He did time for it."

"No, I remember, he was jailed for contempt of Congress. He was a hero to a lot of people. Still is."

Hedger snorted. "Hero! He was booted out of State, never held a job again, died in disgrace. Of course the girl was just a kid at the time, but she followed in his footsteps. Half the reporting she's done has been inside stuff on Communist insurgents around the world. In Vietnam, she took the Vietcong side of things, went to Hanoi with Jane Fonda for Christ's sake. Since then she's been in Nicaragua, the Philippines, Cuba, and right here, in Colombia. She's plugged into the M 19 guerrilla organization, a very bad bunch."

"I don't believe that for a moment."

"No? We damn near got her citizenship revoked last year. Her old man married her mother, a Bolivian woman, when he was serving in the embassy in La Paz, and Immigration and Naturalization grabbed the girl's passport until she could prove her father had registered her as a citizen at birth, which he had, the crafty old bastard. She's managed to maintain dual citizenship and travel on a Bolivian passport when it suited her, using her mother's maiden name, Garcia. We didn't know about that for a long time. That's how she got into the Philippines. Marcos's people would have greased her if they'd caught her. After her stuff on the Communist guerrillas there ran on American TV, Imelda took to calling her the Red Reporter, the correspondent from *Pravda*."

Cat said nothing.

Hedger looked at his wristwatch. "I've got a series of meetings that are going to run until four o'clock. Go back to your hotel and get some rest, then meet me back here. I want to hear everything, and then we'll see what we can put together."

Cat rose. "All right." He turned for the door, then stopped. "Listen, there's one thing I hope you can check on right away. A Gulfstream jet left Eldorado Airport yesterday, probably right after I was arrested. Can you find out where it went?"

He led Cat into an adjoining office, where Candis Leigh was working at a desk. "Get hold of the Air Attaché and see if he has a source in the air traffic system who can tell us where a Gulfstream jet went from Bogotá yesterday. I want to know where it filed for and if it landed there."

Cat wrote down the airplane's tail number and gave it to the woman.

Hedger showed him to the elevator. "When you come back, don't bring Garcia-Greville with you. I don't want her on the premises."

"Whatever you say, Hedger," Cat said,

wearily, punching the elevator button. Downstairs, he turned in his visitor's pass and was let through the embassy gate by a Marine guard. A long line of Latinos stretched from the gate to the front door of the building, waiting to apply for visas, Cat supposed. He found a taxi, and on the ride to the hotel, took time to look at Bogotá. He had been too preoccupied to notice much of it yesterday. He tried to put Hedger's ranting about Meg out of his mind.

The city was a jumble of the modern and the decrepit. Traffic was heavy and noisy, with gaily painted schoolbuses, like those in Santa Marta, jammed with passengers. Green mountaintops hung about the city, occasionally obscured by clouds. The day was gray and cool, and there was a feeling of rain in the air.

At the Tequendama, he asked for his key. There were no messages. He let himself into the suite. "Meg?" he called out. He was greeted with silence. He went into the bedroom. His bags lay open on the bed, just as he had left them the day before. Meg's bags were gone; nothing of hers was in the room.

He looked around for a note, but there was none. He called the hotel operator and asked her to double-check for messages.

There were none.

He sat down wearily on the bed and tried to think where she might be. Had she gone back to her house near Cartagena? He suddenly missed her terribly, wanted her. Why would she simply walk out, leaving no message? Was what Hedger had said about her true? Did it matter? Not to him, not really. She must have known that Hedger would tell him about her father. He wanted to hear her side of it.

He lay back on the bed and gave way to soreness and fatigue. He thought about Drummond and what had happened to his family. They had a lot in common, the Drummonds and the Catledges.

22

At four o'clock Cat presented himself at the embassy gates, identified himself with his passport, and was searched and admitted.

A few minutes later Hedger showed him to a chair and picked up a telephone. "Both of you come in here when you're finished with your meeting." He hung up and was silent, apparently waiting for some others to join them.

"How'd you get into this line of work?" Cat asked, curious about Hedger's career since Quantico.

"I worked with these people a lot in Vietnam. When I got back, I had an invitation. It was a good offer."

Cat still didn't know exactly who Hedger worked for, but it wasn't hard to guess. He looked for confirmation. "You were working with the CIA in Vietnam? I'd have thought you'd have had a battalion by then." He couldn't help needling.

Hedger shook his head. "I only made light colonel. They found other uses for me."

He hadn't denied the CIA, and it seemed obvious that he had been passed over for promotion. If an Academy man couldn't make bird colonel in a war, he was going nowhere. Cat let it pass. He was going to need Hedger's help.

"I hear you did okay for yourself," Hedger said, sourly.

"Yeah, not bad. I had a good idea and a brother-in-law who was a good business-man."

Hedger nodded as if he had known all along that Cat's success was the result of somebody else's work. "We've got a bunch of your printers around the embassy. Pretty slick."

"Thanks." Cat wished that whoever was joining them would do so. Hedger had always been difficult to make small talk with.

As if in answer to his prayer, the office door opened and Candis Leigh and a young man came in.

"You've met Leigh," Hedger said. He nodded at the young man. "This is Sawyer."

Cat shook the man's hand.

"Okay, bring us up to date," Hedger said.

Cat hesitated. He didn't trust Hedger, and he wasn't sure whether it was simply a hangover from their old relationship or something more. "As Drummond may have told you, my daughter's telephone call was confirmed as having been dialled from a hotel in Cartagena. I went there and traced her to Cali, and maybe to Bogotá. I think she may have been on the Gulfstream jet I mentioned to you."

Candis Leigh spoke up. "We checked on the airplane. The pilot filed for Cali, then, as soon as he took off, refiled for Leticia. The airplane has an American registration number; Langley is checking ownership now."

Hedger looked annoyed at her for having spoken up. "Who does the airplane belong to?" he asked Cat. "Or do you know?"

"A drug dealer, I think. A big one."

"No shortage of those down here," Hedger snorted. "What else can you tell us?"

"That's about it," Cat replied.

"Well, guys," Hedger said to his two colleagues, "I think Mr. Catledge had better meet Buzz Bergman." He turned back to Cat. "My people don't get all that involved in the drug stuff," he said. "Our mission here is the political side, the guerrillas. That keeps us pretty busy." He picked up the phone and tapped in an extension number. "Buzz? Barry. There's somebody I'd like you

to talk to. Got a minute? Yeah, right now."
He hung up the phone and started for the
door. "Come on, I'll introduce you to the
head of the Narcotics Assistance Unit."

Cat followed him out of the office and
down the hallway. Candis Leigh and Sawyer
hung back. Hedger led the way through
another reception area into a large office.
The walls were covered with maps and
photographs. A short, thick man walked
from behind his desk.

"This is Buzz Bergman; Buzz, Wendell
Catledge. I expect you've read about what
happened to Catledge and his family, Buzz."

Bergman offered a hand. "Yeah, I'm sorry,
Mr. Catledge."

Cat shook the man's hand. "Thanks." He
liked Bergman immediately, he wasn't sure
why.

Bergman showed them to a sofa, but
Hedger hung back. "Buzz, my headquarters
and the Ambassador have offered Catledge
any assistance we can muster in finding his
daughter, who may still be alive. He thinks
her disappearance has something to do with
drugs, so I'll let him brief you, and you can
tell him what you're doing down here and
see if you can be of any help to him. Call
me when you're through." He left them and
closed the door behind him.

"I'm confused," Bergman said as they sat down. "I thought your daughter had been killed."

"It seemed that way at first, but a lot has happened since." Cat went through his story yet again.

Bergman looked at him silently for a moment when he had finished. "And the Gulfstream headed for Leticia?"

"That's what Candis Leigh said she learned. Where is Leticia?"

Bergman stood up and led him to a large map of Colombia on the wall. The country narrowed as it went south from Bogotá. Bergman's finger went to the southernmost tip of the country. "Here," he said, "on the Amazon."

"I never knew the country reached as far south as the Amazon," Cat said, studying the map.

"Yes, Leticia is at the very point where Colombia, Peru, and Brazil meet. The Amazon turns southeast where it meets the Colombian border. As you can see, Leticia is also at the southernmost tip of a trapezoidal area of Colombia bordered on the east and west by straight borders, on the north by the Putumayo River, and on the south by the Amazon. That area, the Trapezoid, is a hotbed of cocaine-making activity. The coca leaves are grown in Peru and Bolivia, then flown or shipped down the Amazon to Leticia and transported to factories in the Trapezoid, where cocaine is made." He led Cat to a bulletin board pasted with photographs of shacks and equipment, some of it on fire.

"From there it goes all sorts of places, but mostly north to the Guajira Peninsula, in the northeastern part of the country, from where it is smuggled into the United States."

"Yeah, I've been to the Guajira."

"No kidding? It's pretty rough up there."

"Tell me again — what is it you're the head of?" Cat asked.

"NAU, the Narcotics Assistance Unit. We were formed to help drug-producing countries cut off the supplies of narcotics at their source, before they can be shipped to the U.S.A."

"That's a new one on me," Cat said. "Are you something to do with the Drug Enforcement Agency?"

"No, the DEA is a law enforcement agency of the Justice Department that operates both in the United States and abroad. We're part of the State Department; we have no specific enforcement role. Our job is to motivate and materially assist the governments of narcotics-producing and trafficking countries."

"What sort of luck are you having?"

"Better and better, but it's a huge problem. These people are working in very remote areas under cover of jungle. They're hard to find, and when we do find them and wreck their facilities, they start rebuilding right away. We're dealing with a criminal group that has resources that are greater than those of a lot of countries. A concrete airstrip? Means nothing in terms of money. The Colombians bomb it one day and the next, these guys are repaving."

"With all that money around, there must be a big problem with corruption, too."

"Huge. If you're a police captain out in the sticks somewhere, and you're offered the choice between a couple of hundred thousand bucks in cash or being shotgunned in your bed, it's tough to say no. These people operate at a very high level of violence. The problem reaches higher, too, but for the most part, we think we're working with a group of clean government officials. Of course, it's tough to maintain security on an operation when some clerk or secretary may be getting thousands of dollars for just making a phone call to tip off somebody."

"Are you getting all the resources

you need?"

"We've got a decent budget, but we could be doing better if we could reach across agency boundaries and get help. For instance, there's a sort of airplane graveyard in Texas, with all sorts of military aircraft in mothballs — everything from Huey helicopters to C-130 transports. I can put a big aircraft back in shape for less than a hundred thousand bucks, and the Colombians could put it to good use, but I can't get the airplane. Red tape and interdepartmental rivalries screw it up every time."

"There's no cooperation between federal agencies?"

"Oh, sure, there is. I mean, the DEA guys and I are working together with the Colombians right now on something really big, but when you try to reach across from the State Department to the Air Force — well, sometimes I think that dealing with the Soviets would be easier."

"What is it you're working on right now?"

"I can't go into that, but I'll tell you, in strict confidence, it's the biggest thing we've ever gotten together, and it's in jeopardy because of just the sort of thing I've been telling you about." He collapsed back onto the sofa. "But enough of my problems; it's your problem we're supposed to be talking about."

Cat sank into a chair. "Yeah, and it looks like I'm going to have to go to Leticia."

Bergman shook his head emphatically. "Stay out of there. You'll be mistaken either for a dealer or a narc. If the cops think you're a dealer, they won't be nice to you, and if the dealers think you're a narc — well, the DEA is losing guys in fairly horrible ways. Anyway, you wouldn't have a chance of learning anything on your own down there."

"Well, what am I supposed to do? It's the only lead I've got."

"The airplane interests me. I mean, I've never heard of a Gulfstream down here. No Colombian business could afford it. That's a fifteen-million-dollar aircraft; it's got drugs written all over it. What else do you know about it?"

Cat leaned forward. "Do you think it might have something to do with this big operation you're working on?"

"Maybe. It's certainly a new wrinkle."

"It went to Leticia. Is that where your operation is going to be?"

"I can't discuss that," Bergman said, firmly. "Listen, you've told me you followed the airplane from Cartagena to here, but you haven't told me why. I get the feeling you know more about it than you're telling me."

Cat leaned back in his chair. He had always had a poker face, and he needed it now. "Maybe. You show me yours, and I'll show you mine."

Bergman had a pretty good poker face, too. He stared silently at Cat for about a minute, then he got up and started for the door. "I'll be back in a minute," he said.

He was gone for a lot longer than a minute. Cat walked around the room, looking at the material on the walls. There were charts showing tons of drugs captured and destroyed, photographs of crude living quarters attached to the factories, pictures of airstrips, rough and smooth.

Bergman came back into the room followed by Barry Hedger and another man, a Latino. "Mr. Catledge, this is Juan Gomez, agent in charge for the DEA in Colombia."

Cat shook his hand. "Are you Colombian, Mr. Gomez?"

Gomez was big for a Latino, athletic-looking. "Californian," he said. "Call me Johnny."

"I'm Cat." They all sat down.

"Okay, Cat," Bergman said, "I'll tell you what's on, but you can't go back to your hotel and chat with the bartender about it, understood?"

"Understood."

"For the last year and a half — especially for the last six months — we've been getting reports of a new drug organization, something bigger than anything we've ever dealt with before. Rumor has it that this outfit controls huge chunks of coca production in Peru, cocaine manufacture in Colombia, smuggling in the Guajira, and distribution in the United States."

"Mafia?" Cat asked.

"No, not in the conventional sense, at least. These people may be dealing with Mafia figures at some level, but it seems to be something separate and apart, something newer. It's said that they put their early profits into corrupting officials, and that's the reason we know so little about it. It has been operating, virtually unmolested, for an undetermined length of time, but probably not more than four years. What is so threatening about the group is that it is being run with very advanced business techniques. Most of its members are said not to have criminal backgrounds, which makes it very hard to get a handle on them. Someone has apparently recruited otherwise legitimate business people around the United States and has used them to establish a distribution network. Officials of reputable banks have been corrupted and are laundering money; well-placed executives of major international companies are employing their import facilities to smuggle drugs; small retailers are being recruited as a sales force — shopkeepers, hairdressers, salesmen — people who used to be straight are now dealing."

"All this in four years?" Cat asked.

"Our guess is that if this were a legitimate business, it would be in the top fifty of the Fortune 500. In a couple of years, if it continues to expand, it could be in the top ten, and it's their expansion that may give us a shot at them. We've heard that they're about to go multinational, that they're about to open up distribution in Europe and Asia, while doubling their volume in the United States. All at once, within a single year."

"Jesus," Cat said. "I know something about manufacturing and distribution, and that sounds impossible. Nobody could do it, not IBM, even."

"Suppose IBM could pay distributors a million dollars a month for the first six months and a million dollars a week after that," Bergman said. "Think that might speed up the process?"

"I suppose so," Cat admitted. "Is there really that kind of money available?"

"You better believe it," Bergman replied, "and when an organization is being run as ingeniously as this one, it can be put to very effective use."

"What about product? Can they get enough raw material and increase their production enough to keep up with all this new demand?"

"We hear there's a gigantic new factory in the Trapezoid that's already in production. At the moment, they're said to be producing an extremely pure product and stockpiling it."

"Do you know who runs the organization?" Cat asked.

"No," Bergman said. "We don't. We've heard all sorts of things — a Colombian, an Englishman, a consortium of Frenchmen. We just don't know. But he wouldn't have any trouble affording a Gulfstream jet for his personal use."

"By the way," Hedger interrupted, "we got a report. The jet landed at Leticia, then took off again last night; filed for Bogotá."

"Then it's here now?" Gomez asked.

Hedger shook his head. "No. It never arrived. It simply vanished. From Leticia, it has the range to fly anywhere in South America. We checked the tail number;

it's bogus."

"Shit," Bergman said.

There was a long silence; Cat finally broke it. "Gentlemen, I can tell you that the jet is registered to the Empire Corporation of Los Angeles. The number on its tail doesn't match the one on its registration certificate."

"How the hell did you know that?" Hedger demanded.

"Something else," Cat said. "I don't know who the head of this outfit is, but I think I can give you his description. He's American, about five feet seven or eight, a hundred and fifty pounds, fair complexion, light brown hair worn long, in a ponytail. He dresses in fine London tailoring and keeps a suite in the Caribé Hotel in Cartagena; he has a house up in the hills above Cali, and he has something to do with an agricultural conglomerate called the Anaconda Company."

The others stared at Cat. Bergman spoke up.

"I've heard of Anaconda; they're in fruit, or something. They're reputable."

Cat looked at Bergman. "I can introduce you to a drug dealer in Riohacha, a hotel manager in Cartagena, and a cab driver in Cali who will disabuse you of that notion."

23

Cat's information set off a flurry of activity, but as soon as he had told them what he knew, they had dismissed him like a child, told him to go back to his hotel and wait for them to call. Cat did as they asked, but he didn't like it.

He ordered dinner from room service and ate it while absently watching a soccer match on television. When that was over, the *Cosby Show* came on, but in Spanish.

He cursed himself for telling them what he knew before he had extracted more in return. In bed, he thought about Meg and wondered where she was, what had happened to her. There had still been no word whatever from her. He thought about Jinx, too. The story of what had happened to Drummond's daughter tore at him. He felt he had gotten close to Jinx, but now she might be in Leticia, or she might have disappeared with the jet and would now be in some other country, even farther from his reach. He phoned Meg's house. No answer. He did not sleep much that night.

The next morning he dressed and waited for Bergman to call. By noon he had read all the English-language newspapers available in the hotel, and he was beginning to pace. At two o'clock he started to telephone Bergman but decided the hell with it. He caught a cab to the embassy.

He got through the gates with his passport, but the receptionist insisted on calling Bergman to confirm his appointment. Then, frowning, she passed the telephone to Cat.

Bergman was on the line. "What are you doing here? I said I'd call you."

"I can't just sit in a hotel room and wait," Cat said, not without heat. "What's going on?"

"Look, all hell has broken loose around here. I just can't talk to you right now."

"I want to know what's happening," Cat demanded. "Now send somebody down here to get me, or I'll call the Ambassador."

Bergman put his hand over the phone for a moment, and Cat could hear a muffled exchange with someone else. He came back on the line. "All right, I'll send someone down."

Cat waited impatiently, and ten minutes later Candis Leigh appeared, smiling. In the elevator, she said, "I like the way you don't take any crap from these people."

"What's going on?" Cat asked.

"There isn't time to tell you," she said as the elevator doors opened. "Just keep it up, and you'll be all right. Don't let them push you around."

She led the way to Bergman's office. There were a half dozen people in the room, most of them on telephones. Bergman of NAU, Gomez of DEA, and Barry Hedger were sitting on the sofa, huddled over what seemed to be several departmental telephone books.

Bergman waved him to a chair, then ignored him. "What about Marv Hindelman?" Bergman was saying to Hedger. "Assistant Attorney General."

"It would never work," Gomez replied. "He's too far down the totem pole, and anyway, I hardly know him."

"Why don't we see the Ambassador?" Hedger asked. "Get him to call the Secretary of State."

Bergman shook his head. "He wouldn't do it, not on a funding request. Even if he did, not even the Secretary could get it moving in time."

"It looks like we're fucked," Gomez said.

"I've got my guy stashed at the Hilton, but I can't let him walk into that meet empty-handed."

The three men fell silent. There was only the low hum of other men speaking Spanish into telephones.

"What's going on?" Cat asked.

Bergman sighed. "We checked out Empire Holdings, the company you told us the Gulfstream is registered to, and ran the description you gave us against the board of directors." He shuffled through the papers on the coffee table and came up with a photograph.

Cat looked at the familiar figure in tennis clothes, posing with a group of men and women similarly dressed. He recognized three or four well-known movie actors.

"The FBI ran this down overnight and faxed it to us. It was taken at a celebrity tennis tournament in Los Angeles five years ago. His name is Stanton Michael Prince. He ran a chain of fancy car washes around L.A. called Stan's Detailers that were a front for cocaine dealing. The DEA busted him about a month after the photograph was taken; he jumped a two-million-dollar bail and hasn't been seen since, not in the States, anyway. He just walked away from a very successful legitimate business, which the government took. He could afford to. Apparently, he was a wholesaler as well as a retailer. He must have been raking it in for a long time. He had no previous record and wasn't openly consorting with any dirty people; it made him hard to nail."

Bergman shuffled through the papers again and came up with a sheet. "The guy has an MBA from Harvard Business School. He is some piece of work. We're still checking on the Anaconda Company, but so far it stands up as legit. Still, if this guy has anything to do with it, it ain't legit."

"Well, great," Cat said, "you know who he is. Now what?"

Bergman sighed again. "We're working on it."

Cat gestured around the office. "I can see that, but I can also see from the way you're all behaving that something is wrong. What is it?"

Hedger broke in. "What we've got here is a great big bureaucratic fuck-up."

"What sort of fuck-up?"

Hedger looked wearily at Bergman and nodded. "You may as well tell him. Maybe it'll get him off our backs."

Cat looked at Bergman expectantly. "Well?"

"All right," Bergman said, throwing up his

hands, "but, again, this is strictly confidential."

"Of course."

"I told you we'd had reports of this big new factory in the Trapezoid."

"Yeah, I remember that as if it were yesterday."

"Well, it was more than just reports; we're sure of it."

"I figured you were."

"The outfit — and your friend Prince may very well be the head guy — is holding a sort of international sales conference. Apparently fifty or so people have been invited from the States, Europe, and the Far East who are to be new distributors of cocaine, or maybe franchisees is a better word. They're setting up franchises, just like McDonald's."

"And you know when this is?"

"Yes, it's day after tomorrow."

"You're going to go in there and arrest them all, then?"

Bergman smiled sadly. "We'd like nothing better."

"You mean that, for some reason, you can't?"

"A couple of reasons, actually. First of all, we don't know where the factory is located."

"But you said —"

"Yeah, it's in the Trapezoid. I don't think you realize from the map just how big that is. We're talking about thousands of square miles of jungle. It's concealed from aerial observation by a canopy of trees and, of course, camouflage, and it would take an army years to cover it all on the ground. There's nothing down there but a few Indians."

"Where did you get the information you have?" Cat asked.

"From several sources, but mainly from one middle-level government official who got bought by the outfit, but didn't stay bought."

"Doesn't he know where the place is?"

"No, he's never been there. Neither has any other of our informants. However, we had worked out a way to find out where it is."

"*Had* worked out?"

"Yeah. By starting at the end of the cocaine chain, in the States. The DEA busted a lawyer in Miami who'd been instrumental in laundering money and couldn't stand the thought of going to jail, so he spilled a few beans. By keeping him on a short string, we've managed to get one of our people, well, sort of . . . accredited to this conference." Bergman stopped and laughed.

"Jesus, it sounds like we're talking about the United Nations instead of a drug operation, doesn't it?"

Cat brightened. "You mean you're going to have a man on the spot, undercover?"

Gomez spoke up. "The DEA has sent us a guy — somebody who's unknown in the drug trade, a fresh face. We couldn't send any of the people who are stationed here; there was too great a chance of their being recognized. But this new guy is perfect, and we've even managed to build him a cover that should hold, if they don't look at him too hard. You understand, this has all happened in just the past three or four days. We're playing catch-up just as fast as we can."

"And that's our problem," Bergman said. "It takes time to mount an operation like this, to get the paperwork done, to get it funded. Johnny Gomez and his people really came through for us, getting this guy down here on such short notice, and Hedger's people managed the cover, but funding is another matter."

"Funding?" Cat was puzzled. "You said you have a budget."

"Well, sure, we do. But remember, the Narcotics Assistance Unit isn't an operational outfit. The Colombians are meant to do all the work, and they've been moving very quickly to get a military operation mounted against this new factory, when we find it. But the American end of it, the undercover man, doesn't come out of Colombian funds, and, strictly speaking, this isn't a DEA operation, either, so their budget can't cover it. Neither can Hedger's."

"I'm beginning to see your problem with the bureaucracy," Cat said, "but just how expensive can bringing in one man be?"

Bergman was beginning to look embarrassed. "Well, it's not exactly bringing him in that we can't fund — I mean, the guy's a DEA agent, and he's on salary. It's the franchise fee."

"The what?"

"Remember, this outfit is, in effect, selling franchises."

"Like McDonald's."

"Right. And when you want to open a McDonald's restaurant, you have to buy in; you have to pay the company a franchise fee."

"Okay, so how much is the franchise fee?"

"A million dollars."

Cat stared at Bergman. "Let me get this straight," he said. "You have an opportunity to break up what sounds like the biggest drug operation in the entire universe, you've got an undercover agent in Bogotá, ready and waiting to go in, and you can't do it because all of you together — the combined State Department, Drug Enforcement Agency, and Central Intelligence Agency can't come up with a million bucks?"

Bergman, Hedger, and Gomez all looked sheepish. "That's essentially it," Bergman said. "I know it sounds crazy, when you hear about the billions in the federal budget, but it takes a great deal of doing to get any government agency to part with that much actual cash for any operation, especially if they don't know they'll get it back. If we were the DEA in Miami, we could use confiscated drug money, just turn it around and feed it back into an operation. But we're not, and the notion of a million bucks in hundred-dollar bills scares the shit out of any federal employee. Nobody is going to sign for it; nobody wants to be held accountable."

For a moment Cat stared at the wall in bemused silence, trying not to laugh at the absurdity of the situation. Then he turned back to Bergman. "Let me ask you something," he said. "You say this DEA undercover agent is a fresh face. Does that mean he's new on the job?"

Gomez nodded. "Yeah, he's only been with the agency for a couple of weeks, but he has a military background." Then he added defensively, "Look, the guy doesn't have to be James Bond; he just goes in there with the money, buys his franchise, lets us know where the factory is, then gets the hell out."

Cat leaned forward and looked at the three men. "Listen to me," he said. "I want to do it. I want to go to this 'conference.' "

Everybody was silent for a moment, then Bergman spoke up. "Mr. Catledge," he said, "I know how concerned you are about your daughter, and I agree that she might, indeed, be at the factory with this guy Prince, but you must understand that you are not the person to go in there and try to get her out. You are completely unqualified for such an operation."

"Am I?" Cat asked. "I think I'm as qualified as the guy you want to send in there. I have a military background — I was an officer in the United States Marines."

"It's not as simple as that, Mr. Catledge; there's the matter of cover. We couldn't get that together in time."

"I already have a very good cover, thank you, prepared by Hedger's people — passport, credit cards, a business identity, and backup. And I am, as you put it, a fresh face. Has Gomez's man had any special training for the job?"

"Well, no, except for a small-arms refresher."

"I'm pretty handy with small arms," Cat said. "Ask Hedger."

Hedger rolled his eyes. "That's true. I made Marksman, in the Corps, but he fired Expert." He smiled a little smile. "Of course he tried to carry a small arm through an airport metal detector, too."

"So, I made a mistake," Cat said. "I have a history of learning from my mistakes."

"Mr. Catledge —"

Cat would not be interrupted. "In addition, I am one hell of a lot more motivated than your DEA man — my daughter is being used by these people for a purpose I'd rather not, but can't help, think about."

"That's the problem," Hedger said. "You're liable to be more interested in her than calling in the troops."

"For Christ's sake!" Cat said, exasperated, "we'll be in the middle of a goddamned jungle! I'll *need* the troops!"

"Mr. Catledge," Bergman broke in, "this is an impossible notion. We —"

"And finally," Cat continued, "I have one qualification that neither your man nor any of you has."

Bergman looked at Cat, betraying amusement, but his interest was piqued. "And what would that be, Mr. Catledge?" he asked.

Cat permitted himself a small smile. "I have a million dollars in cash," he said.

Hedger leaned forward. "In cash, you say?"

"In hundred-dollar bills."

Bergman tried to interrupt, but Hedger waved him down.

"How long would it take for you to lay your hands on it?"

"Half an hour."

Hedger looked at Bergman. "We need a million bucks, he's got a million bucks."

Bergman nodded. "Listen, Mr. Catledge, you loan us that money, and I promise you, our man will do everything in his power to get your daughter out."

"Not a chance," Cat said. "Your guy isn't going to want a strange woman on his hands. He's going to want to get his ass out of there alive when the balloon goes up, and I won't give you a goddamned nickel to put him in there."

"Mr. Catledge, be reasonable," Bergman said plaintively. "I am a federal official. I do not have the authority to send a private citizen into a dangerous situation on a government mission."

"What government mission?" Cat demanded. "It's the fucking Colombians who are going in there, and do you think they give a shit who tells them where it is? You don't have to send me, just tell me how to get there, and I'll go of my own volition. I'll sign a release, if it'll make you feel better — take full responsibility for myself and my daughter."

Cat stood up. "I'll tell you something else. If you people have anything to do with sending the Colombian military into that place before I have an opportunity to get my daughter out, and she is harmed as a result, I'll hold each of the agencies you represent and each of you personally responsible. You've already seen the press on what happened to me and my family — just imagine the coverage I'm going to generate if you get Jinx killed."

The three men sat, speechless, staring at him. The other men on the telephones had stopped talking and were listening now.

"This is your situation, gentlemen," Cat said finally. "Without my money, you've got no operation — or, if you do find a way to get it together, you've got me, in Lyndon Johnson's memorable phrase, outside the tent, pissing in. On the other hand, use my money, let me go instead of your man, and you've got what you want — a crack at a gigantic narcotics operation and a chance to be heroes. You'll all be having lunch at the White House with Nancy Reagan." Cat sat down again. "And if it goes wrong, I won't be around to tell the tale."

Bergman, Hedger, and Gomez stared at him, still saying nothing. Finally, Bergman turned to Hedger. "You've known this guy longer than I have. Does he have what it takes to pull this thing off?"

Cat looked at Hedger, whose eyes had never left him. He waited nervously for an answer. Now it all turned on the word of the man Cat reckoned hated him more than anybody else in the world.

"I don't know," Hedger said, finally, "but I'll tell you this much — he's the most ruthless sonofabitch I ever knew."

24

Waiting again. Cat stood at the window of his room and watched clouds float past the green mountains that hung over the city. He had been back at the hotel for an hour. The phone rang.

"Hello?"

"This is Buzz Bergman. You're on. We'll get together tomorrow to talk more, but tonight you have to be vetted by these people. Here's Johnny Gomez to explain."

Cat waited silently. It surprised him that the hand holding the telephone was trembling slightly.

"It's Johnny Gomez, Cat. Now listen carefully. There's a nightclub on the top floor of the Tequendama — that's where you're staying, right?"

"Right."

"There's a Cuban review playing up there — the famous one from the Tropicana Hotel in Havana; it comes to Bogotá every year.

Call the club for a reservation. Say your name is Ellis, you're a friend of Mr. Vargas, you want a table for one. Got that?"

"Yes. I'm Ellis, friend of Vargas."

"Right. You're to take a hundred thousand dollars in hundreds, okay?"

"Yes. What happens after I get there?"

"Relax and enjoy the show; I hear it's terrific. Somebody will introduce himself as Vargas and ask for the money. He'll give you instructions on what to do next. He may ask you some questions. The guy who has introduced you to these people is a lawyer in Miami named Walter L. Jasper, called Walt. He does some work for your company in Florida, you got to know him over the last six months or so, and he invited you into this deal. Jasper is five-ten, weighs a hundred and fifty pounds, blond hair going gray, has a one-inch, crescent-shaped scar at the outer corner of his left eye, prominent. He has described you to them, said he knows you well enough. That's all he's told them, so if they ask a lot of questions, fake it. We'll get your answers back to Jasper, so you won't be crossed up, okay?"

"Okay. What else do I need to know?"

"Well, just to make you feel a little better, my guy from the States, the guy you're replacing, will be there somewhere. He's six feet, a hundred and eighty pounds, sandy hair cut short, badly pockmarked skin. He'll keep an eye on you, but don't speak to him or pay him any attention; it's important that you not seem connected with *anybody,* understand? You're down here on your own."

"I understand."

"When the meet is over, finish your drink, wait until the show is over, go back to your room, and call me at home." He gave Cat the number. "Any other questions?"

"I don't think so."

"Good luck."

"Thanks." Cat hung up, called the roof nightclub, and made the reservation. He went to the front desk and asked for his case from the safe. An assistant manager led him into the vault and turned his back while Cat took two banded packs of one hundred hundred-dollar bills from the briefcase and relocked it. He returned to his suite and tried to get in a nap. It didn't work.

At nine o'clock he took the elevator to the top floor and gave his name to the head-waiter. "A friend of Mr. Vargas," he reminded the man.

"Of course, señor," the headwaiter replied, "I understand."

Cat was led to a table in a corner of the

room, far from the stage. A small musical group was listlessly playing rather old-fashioned American dance music, and one or two couples were dancing. The room was filling rapidly. A waiter took his drink order and left a menu. He might as well eat, he thought, and ordered a steak and half a bottle of the Chilean wine he liked so much. He glanced idly around the room and immediately spotted Gomez's man at a table alone, near the stage. The pockmarked skin stood out even from across the room.

The music stopped and the musicians were replaced by a more gaily dressed group, who launched into a spirited Latin number. Immediately, the atmosphere of the room changed; the dance floor was suddenly packed with swaying couples, women in low-cut dresses and men in tightly tailored suits, dancing with a combination of aplomb and abandon. Cat smiled in spite of himself. It had been more than twenty years since he had seen a group of adults having so much fun on a dance floor, doing the mambo.

His steak came, and it was excellent. By the time he had finished it, the musicians had stopped and were being replaced by an even more gaudily dressed group. A moment later the music had started again, and the stage was filled with the Cuban troupe, dancing wildly and singing at the tops of their lungs. They finished their number and one of the girls, the most beautiful one, stepped to the center of the stage and began a steamy ballad. She was a knockout, Cat thought, and he felt a stirring and a longing for Meg. *Where the hell was she?* The show went on for an hour, and Cat became gradually absorbed by it, forgetting why he was there.

Then, suddenly, it was over, and people were leaving. The waiter came and placed a check on the table. Cat ordered a brandy, and the waiter went, reluctantly, to get it. It was obvious that he wanted Cat's table. People were beginning to arrive for the midnight show. Cat suddenly wondered if he should have come later. He had booked for the earlier show without thinking. His brandy came. Gomez's man, he noticed, had ordered another drink, too.

Abruptly, two men, Latinos, sat down at Cat's table. They were both dressed in business suits, conservative, for Bogotá. One was in his early thirties, hefty, blunt-looking; the other was closer to Cat's age, with sharp features and small eyes.

The older man placed a small, leather wallet on the table and opened it, revealing a badge.

Cat's insides froze. "Yes?" he managed to say.

"May I see your passport, please," the man said in accented English. It was not a request.

Cat produced his passport and passed it to the man, looking quickly around the room. Gomez's man was gone. Nobody who seemed to be Vargas was in sight. His heart was slamming against his chest.

"What is the purpose of your visit to Bogotá, Mr. Ellis?" the policeman asked, placing Cat's passport on the table and covering it with his hand.

"I am here on business," Cat said. His meet was blown, he knew. Nobody would approach him now. He resisted the urge to swear and pound on the table.

"And just what is your business?"

"I sell computer equipment. I'm hoping to open a new market in Colombia for our products."

"Let me see some other identification," the man said.

Cat gave the man his wallet, containing his Ellis driver's license and credit cards. What was he going to do now? Would Vargas arrange another meet after he had seen Cat rousted by the police? Surely, he was watching all this.

"Have you a business card?"

Cat gave the man a card.

The man looked at it closely. "Are you armed?" he asked.

"Of course not."

"Open your jacket, please."

Cat unbuttoned his jacket and held it open.

"What is in the left inside pocket of your jacket, Mr. Ellis?"

Cat flinched, involuntarily. If these policemen saw the money, he was bound to be arrested. Nobody would carry that much cash but a drug dealer. "An envelope," Cat replied.

"What does it contain?"

He looked around for help, but there was no one to help him. "My travelling expenses."

"Place it on the table, please."

Cat took out the fat envelope and put it before him. The man ripped it open, raised his eyebrows, and thumbed the money. He put the envelope in his own coat pocket, then shoved Cat's passport and wallet back across the table.

"Is this a robbery?" Cat asked. "Is that what the police do in this country?"

The man smiled thinly. "I am Vargas," he

said. "Be at the bar at Parador Ticuña, in Leticia, the day after tomorrow, at five in the afternoon. Bring nine hundred thousand dollars with you." Without another word, the two men got up and left.

Cat finished his drink and tried to calm his nerves. It had not been what he had expected. He signed the check and went back to his suite. He closed the door and dialled Gomez's number. "It's Catledge," he said.

"Are you all right?" Gomez asked, worriedly. "My guy said you were rousted by the cops."

"It was Vargas," Cat said. "I'm to be at a place called Parador Ticuña, in Leticia, the day after tomorrow, at five p.m., with the rest of the million."

"What questions did he ask you?"

"Just to identify myself and my business here. He looked at my ID pretty closely. Nothing else." Cat glanced across the room at the bedroom door. It had been open when he left, and the maid had already been in to turn down the bed. Now it was closed.

"Good," Gomez said. "Get a good night's sleep and come to the embassy tomorrow morning at nine. Ask for Bergman. We'll do some planning then." He hung up before Cat could say anything else.

Cat stared at the bedroom door. No light came from beneath it. He had left the bedside lamp on earlier. His small canvas bag lay on the living-room desk. He went to it and found Bluey's .357 magnum, checked to see it was loaded. He went back to the phone and, without lifting the receiver, dialled 0. "Hello, operator? I want to place a call to the United States." He spoke a number. "Yes, I'll hold on." He slipped out of his shoes and walked quickly to the bedroom door, his breathing rapid. Knowing that if he hesitated, he wouldn't be able to do it, he shoved open the door, the gun held out in front of him.

There was someone sitting on the bed in the darkened room, a woman. Cat found the light switch and turned it on, pointing the gun at her. The overhead light illuminated the room, and he found himself pointing the pistol at the head of the lead singer/dancer of the Tropicana review. He froze, too astonished to speak.

"For Christ's sake," a voice to his left said.

Cat spun left, the pistol still held out before him. Standing in the door of the bathroom, a towel in her hands, was Meg.

He let the pistol fall to his side. "What is going on?" he asked. "Where have you been?" His happiness at seeing her was overwhelmed by his anger at her for disappearing.

"Busy," she said. She walked to him, took the pistol, and laid it on a chest of drawers. "Didn't Barry Hedger give you my message?"

"What message?" He was still breathing hard.

"Oh, I see what's happened," she said. She walked to the bed and sat down. "When you got jumped by the cops at the airport, I called Hedger."

"I know about that," he said, sitting down on the opposite bed. "Thanks; it would have been even more unpleasant otherwise."

"There wasn't anything I could do myself, so I waited outside the jail until Hedger came with the ambulance and took you away. The next morning I called to see how you were. Hedger said you had been pretty badly beaten up, and you would be in the embassy infirmary for a few days."

"He never told me you had called the second time. Why didn't you leave me a note, or something?"

"I thought I'd be back here before you got out of the infirmary. I'm sorry, you must have been worried about me."

"Yes, I damn well was."

"Oh, forgive me," Meg said. "Cat, this is

my friend, Maribel Innocento."

Cat turned to the woman sitting on the other bed. "How do you do? I saw your performance this evening," he said. "You were wonderful." She smiled at him blankly. *"Qué?"*

Meg translated, and she smiled again. "Thank you very much," she said in heavily accented English.

Meg introduced Cat in Spanish to Maribel.

"Where did the two of you meet?" Cat asked Meg.

"I was in Havana three years ago for an interview with Fidel Castro. I stayed at the Tropicana, and Castro kept postponing the interview, so I was there for a couple of weeks, and we met on the beach. We became close."

"So you're having a little reunion, then?"

"Not exactly," Meg replied. "Not just a reunion, that is. Maribel is defecting from Cuba."

"Defecting to Colombia?"

"No, to the United States."

Maribel smiled brilliantly at Cat.

She really was gorgeous, he thought. Coal-black hair, lovely skin, and startlingly white teeth. For the first time, he noticed she was wearing a dressing gown. It was tied loosely, and a lot of her breasts were showing. "I don't understand," he said to Meg. "How can she defect to the United States in Bogotá?"

"I'm working on that," Meg said. "Her father is in Miami. He got out of Cuba years ago and has been trying ever since to get Maribel out, too. I've been in touch with the American Consul at the embassy. He wouldn't make any promises in advance, but he hinted heavily that, if she did actually leave the company and officially express a desire to go to the United States, that something might be arranged. She's a very big star in Cuba. The Reagan administration would make quite a show of her defection, I think."

"What's the next step, then?"

"We have to get her out of the hotel and into the embassy."

"You make it sound as if she has to be smuggled out in a laundry basket. Can't she just go downstairs and take a cab?"

Meg sucked her teeth and looked at the ceiling.

Cat had a sinking feeling. "Well?" he demanded.

"It's a little more complicated than that. You see, there are four Cuban secret policemen travelling with the troupe, just to prevent this sort of thing."

Oh, shit, he thought. "How did you get her away from them?"

"That was fairly easy. The troupe is housed two floors down. I was visiting backstage, and when the show was over, and everybody was going downstairs, I managed to get her into an elevator alone, and we got off on this floor."

"Jesus, didn't the four policemen notice that?"

"They all got onto one elevator just ahead of us. We were only a few seconds behind them, so I don't think they could see which floor the elevator stopped on. They probably think we've left the hotel."

As she spoke there was a knock on the door of the suite.

Cat jumped. "Probably," he said.

Meg spoke rapidly in Spanish to Maribel, and they both headed for the bathroom. "Get rid of whoever that is," Meg said to Cat, and closed the bathroom door.

Cat picked up the .357 magnum and stuck it in his belt, in the small of his back. When he opened the door, a heavyset Latino spoke to him in Spanish.

"I'm sorry," he replied. "I don't speak Spanish."

"Hotel security," the man said in English.

"We are looking for two women who robbed a customer in the roof restaurant. I must search your room."

"I'm afraid . . ." Cat was saying, but the man had already shoved past him. He looked quickly around the sitting room, then in the kitchen, then headed for the bedroom. "Hey, wait," Cat shouted, following after him and trying to sound authoritative. "My wife's in there."

The man didn't even slow down. He walked to the bathroom door and snatched it open. Meg was standing before the mirror in Maribel's dressing gown, a towel wrapped around her head, and her face smeared with a white cream. She immediately launched into a tirade of irate Spanish.

Surprised, the man stepped back, and Cat got in front of him. "All right, out!" Cat shouted at him as Meg continued her abuse of the man. Cat kept his arms at his sides, but bumped the man, hard, with his chest. "Get out of my room now, or I'll call the police!"

The Cuban turned and fled. Cat double-locked and chained the door after him and leaned against the door, his face in his hands. What else could happen to him in one evening? He calmed himself and went back into the bedroom. "What's that on your face?" he asked Meg, following her back into the bathroom. "I've never seen you use that sort of stuff."

"Toothpaste," Meg said, splashing water on her face. "It was all that was handy." She said something in Spanish, the sliding glass door across the bathtub opened and Maribel stepped out, naked, and quite unselfconscious about it. The two women laughed and embraced.

Cat retreated to the living room, but he had a hard time taking his eyes off Maribel's astonishing body. The two women followed him. Maribel's robe had been restored to her, but she had tied it only loosely, and Cat still found her distracting.

Meg said soothingly, "Tomorrow morning we'll find a way to get her to the embassy. She can stay here tonight, can't she? There are two beds. You and I can have one, and she can have the other."

Cat was shaking his head. "All this is getting too crazy for me. It's all out of control."

"Look," Meg said, "I know you're worried about Jinx — I am, too. But this won't slow us down."

"You don't know what's happened since I saw you. I have a lot to bring you up to date on."

"Do we have to do anything about it tonight?"

"Well, no, but . . ."

Meg placed a hand on his cheek. "Cat, we've got to get Maribel back to her father. I think you can understand how important that is to both of them, can't you?"

Cat nodded wearily. "Yeah, sure, okay," he said. "Jesus, what a day!"

"So what's happened while I was gone?" Meg asked.

Cat poured them all a brandy and brought Meg up to date.

"So we're going to Leticia?" Meg asked.

"*I'm* going to Leticia," Cat replied.

"Listen, Cat," she said firmly, "get used to this, now. Where you go, I'm going, too. You go to Leticia, I go to Leticia. It's as simple as that. You don't speak the language, remember? You still need my help. Anyway, I'm not letting you out of my sight again."

Cat tossed off his brandy and poured them all another one. "God knows, I'd rather go with you than without you. I wouldn't have gotten this far on my own." He stood up. "Listen, I've got to get some sleep. I'm whipped." He went into the bedroom, undressed, and got into bed quickly, out of modesty. He always slept naked, didn't own a pair of pajamas.

344

He was dozing off in no time, and the whispers and giggles of the two women did not disturb him. He was too tired to think about Vargas, or Maribel, or Hedger, or Bergman, or Gomez. The hell with all of them. If he was going to hold together, he needed sleep.

25

Cat stood with his back against the elevator wall and looked at the two women opposite him. Maribel wore pale makeup and lipstick, and her hair had been drawn severely back into a knot, so tightly that Cat wondered how she could blink. She wore a heavily rimmed pair of tortoise-shell glasses, sensible shoes, and her spectacular figure was hidden under a demure raincoat. Meg had come up with enough accoutrements to transform her into a not-very-interesting-looking woman, no small feat, as far as Cat was concerned.

Meg, on the other hand, resembled Carmen Miranda, without the fruit. Her makeup was florid, her hair wild, her dress tight, and her sunglasses extravagant. She didn't really look like Maribel, but the effect was riveting.

The elevator reached the ground floor. Cat took a deep breath, and preceded the women out of the car. He walked quickly to the corner of the elevator bank and peered into the lobby. He picked out the three Cuban policemen quickly. While they were not actually standing in the main entrance of the hotel, they were positioned so that they could be in a flash. He found the fourth of the group lounging near the second entrance, near the airline office.

Cat turned and nodded to Meg, who took a deep breath and started across the lobby, toward the main entrance, hurrying, nearly at a trot. The effect on the Cubans was galvanizing. As Meg rushed toward the revolving door, they converged on her from all sides. Meg let out a shriek and hit one of them with her heavy purse, staggering him.

The fourth Cuban abandoned his post and rushed to the aid of his compatriots, no doubt fearful of missing out on the action and on the credit for recapturing a defector.

Cat, with Maribel on his arm, emerged from the hallway containing the elevators and walked casually, arm in arm, toward the second entrance. As they passed the middle of the lobby, both of them, as planned, gawked at the commotion made by Meg and the four policemen. They would have looked very odd, indeed, if they had not. In a moment they were out of the hotel, climbing into a taxicab.

"The American Embassy," Cat said to the driver, and Maribel immediately said the same in Spanish.

Maribel clutched Cat's arm, and laid her head on his shoulder. "Thank you, thank you," she kept repeating.

Cat patted her hand. "It's all right," he said, "we'll be at the embassy soon."

"Thank you, thank you," she said again, and before he could react, she threw an arm around his neck and planted an enormous kiss on his lips.

Cat did his best to calm her, wiping the lipstick on the back of his hand. Shortly, the taxi pulled up to the same rear gate through which Cat's ambulance had driven not long before. Candis Leigh, accompanied by a Marine guard and another man, was waiting to let them in. Cat gratefully turned over Maribel to Candis and the consular official and followed them into the embassy.

In Buzz Bergman's office, he immediately telephoned the Tequendama and asked for his suite. Meg, to his relief, answered. "Are you all right?" he asked.

"Oh, yes! I haven't had so much fun in years! We had the manager, the local police, the doorman — *everybody* got into it. You've never seen Latinos turn the shade of red those guys did! Is Maribel safe?"

"Yes, she's in the Consul's office now, getting some paperwork done. I think she has already talked to her father."

"Good. Now listen, when do we leave for Leticia?"

"I want to take off tomorrow morning at eight, sharp, okay?"

"Okay, but I may not see you until then. I've got some things to do, but I won't miss the plane, believe me."

"I'll see you then," Cat said, and hung up.

Barry Hedger swept into the office carrying a briefcase. "Morning," he said. "You ready for some cloak-and-dagger stuff?"

"Sure, why not?" said Cat.

Hedger opened the briefcase and took out a fairly large Sony portable radio. "Okay," he said, "what we got here is an ordinary, multiband radio, you see?" He switched it on and twiddled the tuning dial. A mixture of voices and static came out of the set. *But,*" Hedger said, raising a finger, "if, instead of turning the knob the usual way, you pull the knob *out* and turn it counterclockwise" — he demonstrated — "then you got a transmitter that puts out a signal that can be picked up on the automatic-direction-finding equipment on every airplane."

Cat tried turning the radio on as instructed. "That's it, just turn it on?"

"Not quite," Hedger said. "You want to be outdoors, away from any large structures that might interfere with the signal, and you want to extend the antenna to its maximum, got it?"

"Got it. What sort of range does it have?"

"About forty miles, to an aircraft at two thousand feet, more at a higher altitude."

"That doesn't sound like much."

"It's enough to do the trick. We'll be overflying the Trapezoid on a regular basis from the moment you leave Leticia for Prince's base. The Colombian force will be in place tonight at a Brazilian army base just across the border, on the Amazon, here." He pointed at a spot on the map, downstream from Leticia. "The radio's batteries are good for an hour's transmission, if you don't spend too much time listening to rock and roll." He paused and switched off the radio. "Take care of this thing; otherwise you'll just have to find a phone booth."

"Right," Cat said.

Johnny Gomez came into the room. "Hi, Cat. I wanted to tell you that you'll have a friendly face on the ground at Leticia. My man, the one with the pockmarks who was in the nightclub last night, is already on his way down there. He'll be staying at Parador Ticuña, playing the tourist, registered under the name of Conroy. He'll be in the bar when you have your meet. If you want to bail out of this thing, he'll help, and that'll be your last chance. You understand?"

"I understand, but I won't be bailing out."

Buzz Bergman spoke up. "Cat, your best chance is to find your daughter, get her away somewhere, then turn on the radio and hide. When these troops hit the ground, they're liable to shoot anything that moves. Don't come out until the shooting is over. Be very, very careful that you don't get waxed by one of the good guys, okay?"

"I'll do my best," Cat said.

Bergman and Gomez shook Cat's hand and wished him luck, then Hedger escorted him out of the room and down the hall to his own office.

"How long since you fired a handgun?" he asked, taking Cat's H&K automatic and its holster out of his desk drawer.

"Not since I got out of the Corps," Cat replied, a little sheepishly.

Hedger beckoned him down the hall to the elevators, then down to a subbasement. He opened a door and switched on a light.

Cat could immediately smell raw earth. He followed Hedger into a rough room, one wall of which was earthen. Hedger switched on another set of lights, revealing a long, tunnel-like extension. At the end was a target with a human figure drawn on it.

"The Marine guards use it," Hedger said. He handed Cat the pistol. "Be my guest."

Cat checked the clip, worked the action, switched off the safety, and assumed the stance. He fired five rounds, then Hedger stopped him and pulled the target toward them on a long cord. Cat had missed it twice, and the other three shots were all over the target.

"Forget the military stance," Hedger said, taking the weapon from Cat. He crouched and held the pistol out with both hands. "Do it the police way." He changed the target and pulled it back into place.

Cat crouched and fired five more rounds.

Hedger peered through binoculars. "Better. That's a fair grouping, but they're all in the upper right-hand corner of the target. Squeeze, don't pull, remember?"

Cat fired five more rounds and began reloading the clip from a box of cartridges furnished by Hedger from a cupboard while Hedger pulled the target back.

"Much better," Hedger said. "In the middle of the target. Now you have to get the grouping smaller."

Cat shot for nearly an hour, becoming more and more comfortable with the pistol, accepting Hedger's pointers.

Finally, Hedger seemed satisfied. He took a leather and canvas grip from the ammunition cupboard. "Here's something that will be of use," he said, opening the grip. Pressing at the sides of the bottom panel, he lifted the panel out and exposed a shallow compartment. "There's room here for your weapon and ammo. Don't carry it through airport security, though."

"Thanks," Cat said. "I'll try and remember that."

Hedger walked over to a counter and found some cleaning equipment behind it. As Cat watched he effortlessly fieldstripped the weapon and began carefully cleaning it.

"You know," Hedger said, looking only at the pistol, "I hated your guts for a long time."

Cat said nothing.

"You whipped my ass more ways than one at Quantico, and I didn't like it."

"I'm afraid I liked it more than I should have," Cat said, apologetically. "I'm sorry."

"No need to be," Hedger said. "It made me tougher, later, when I needed to be tougher." He went on cleaning the weapon in silence, then reassembled it and handed it to Cat. "I admire what you're doing down here, what you're about to do. I'd like to think if I were in your place, I'd do the same. I wish you luck, Cat."

It was the first time Hedger had ever called him by his first name, Cat reflected. He took the offered hand and shook it.

26

Cat opened the aluminum camera case and counted out ninety stacks of a hundred one-hundred-dollar bills — nine hundred thousand dollars. He set Barry Hedger's canvas-and-leather grip on the desk and opened it, then removed the false bottom. He loaded one of the three clips into the H&K automatic pistol, arranged it in the compartment with the other clips, the shoulder holster, and the silencer, then loaded Bluey's .357 Magnum and tried it for size. There was barely enough room in the compartment for the second pistol and no room for the box of cartridges. Cat found a roll of cellophane tape and managed to fit another dozen cartridges into odd spaces. He replaced the false bottom and stacked the money in the case. It was still only about half full, so he put some shirts on top of the money, and Barry Hedger's high-tech portable radio on top of those.

He still had another million dollars in the camera case, and he was beginning to feel a little foolish about it. It was fortunate that he had misunderstood Bluey about how much money to bring; at least he had had the "franchise fee" when he needed it. Still, the other million dollars was something of a burden. He had thought of it, so far, as only a lot of paper, but now he remembered that the extra million represented everything he owned, except the house and the company stock. He dismissed the thought from his mind. If it took that to get Jinx back, so be it. He was going to have enough to occupy him without worrying about the money. He thought of leaving it in the hotel safe and coming back for it, but there was always the chance, he reckoned, that it might come in handy. He closed the camera case and spun the combination lock. His wristwatch said seven o'clock.

Cat checked out of the hotel and got a taxi to the airfield. The flying school was deserted, and Meg was nowhere in sight. It was just as well, he decided. He wanted her with him, but now he was heading into a situation where he might be better off alone, without having to worry about her safety.

At the airfield, he threw his bags into the back seat of the airplane, then got out the

356

little stepladder and checked the wing tanks. They were full, and so was the auxiliary tank in the luggage compartment. He gave the airplane a thorough preflight inspection and added a quart of oil. Then he got into the airplane, pulled out his charts and flight plan, and rechecked all his figures — courses, distance, and fuel. Everything tallied with the flight planning he had done the night before. He had a weather forecast from Eldorado Flight Services, and with the help of an English-speaking staffer, he had filed an instrument flight plan, something he had never done before. What the hell, he thought, his bogus Ellis license said he was instrument-rated.

It was a little after eight o'clock now, and there was nothing else to do but leave. Suddenly, he felt terribly alone. There were eight hundred miles of mountains and jungle to cross, and nowhere to put the airplane down in an emergency. Up until now he had had the help of, first, Bluey, then Meg, then Hedger, Gomez, and Bergman, but now he was on his own. For a small moment, he wanted to run — abandon the airplane, leave Hedger, Bergman, and Prince to their own devices. But he couldn't forget Jinx. He had no way of being sure that she was where he was going, but if there was even a chance she was there, then he would be there, too. He took a couple of deep breaths. Meg was nowhere to be seen, and he had to take off on time or have his flight plan canceled.

Feeling hollow inside in spite of a good breakfast, he picked up his checklist and started to work through it: seat belt and shoulder harness fastened; doors closed; radios and navigation aids set to correct frequencies; cowl flaps open; avionics power switch off; circuit breakers in; mixture rich; propeller control in; carburetor heat off; prime engine; master switch on; area clear — he made a sweep of the area to make sure nobody was standing near the prop. As he turned to his right, he jumped: Meg's face was framed in the window. She rapped on the glass.

He opened the door; she tossed her bags into the back seat, climbed in, and kissed him on the neck. "Sorry I'm late; you weren't going to leave without me, were you?"

"I was," he said, "and I still think I should."

She looked hurt. "You don't want me along?"

He shook his head. "It isn't that. It's because of you I've gotten this far. I don't have time to explain the whole thing right now — I've got to make a time window or they'll cancel my flight plan. All I can tell you is that if you come with me, there's an awfully good chance that neither of us will get out of it alive, and I don't think I should ask you to take that risk. I hope you'll believe that I'm not exaggerating."

She cocked her head to one side. "Listen, sport," she said, "I expect I've been in more tight spots than you the past few years, and I'm still in one piece. I'll stay that way — don't worry about me."

"I'll explain on the way," he said. "We can always part company in Leticia." He looked around the airplane again, opened his window, and shouted, "CLEAR!" He turned the key, and the engine coughed, then came to life. They both slipped on their headsets, and he continued with his checklist. There was no control tower to call, so he taxied to the end of the runway and stopped. He throttled up to 1,700 rpms and did his run-up checks. Finally, all was ready. He craned his neck to see the skies around him — no incoming traffic — then taxied onto the runway. It was shorter than what he was accustomed to, but plenty long enough — 1,000 meters. Mixture — full rich. He announced his takeoff to any possible traffic in the area, then shoved in the throttle. The airplane began to roll. Cat watched the airspeed, waiting for sixty knots, when the airplane could be flown off. The needle rose to forty, then forty-five knots, but it seemed to be moving upward very slowly. The airplane had used up three-quarters of the runaway when Cat realized they were not going to make it.

He glanced at the instruments, ready to slam on brakes, but he knew they would never be able to stop. They would drive straight ahead into the low shrubs off the end of the runway. Then he noticed that the manifold pressure was low, and suddenly he realized what was wrong. "Oh, shit!" he yelled, startling Meg. Quickly, he put in twenty degrees of flaps, and as the runway came to an end, the heavily loaded airplane lifted sluggishly a few feet into the air. It seemed to take forever to get to two hundred feet, then he reduced the flaps to ten degrees, and the airplane began to climb faster.

"What was that?" Meg asked, a little breathless.

"My fault," Cat replied, mopping his brow. "I forgot we are at about nine thousand feet of elevation here. The air is thin and the engine won't develop full power this high up, so the airplane needs more runway to get off. If I had put in flaps at the beginning, it would have worked a lot better."

He took out the last ten degrees of flaps, started his turn toward the Eldorado VOR beacon, and called Bogotá departure. The accent was thick, but the controller gave him his departure instructions. Soon they were out of the mountains and over the Magdalena Valley. Cat switched on the autopilot and relaxed, checking his position with the distance-measuring equipment. They would soon be out of range for that, and there was no loran this far south. There were enough other navaids to get them to Leticia, though.

"Okay," he said finally, "what have you been doing for the last couple of days?"

"I had some people to see," she replied. "Once I knew you were all right, I had time on my hands, and I'm always looking for a story."

"I thought you *had* a story," he said, a little miffed.

"Now, now," she said, "don't get jealous of my time. I had nothing else to do. Could I have come to all those meetings with you if I had been around?"

"No," he said. "Barry Hedger thinks you're a Communist agent, or something."

She gave a short, derisive laugh. "Of course. He told you about my father, didn't he?"

"Yes. I remembered the incident."

"It was a hell of a lot more than an incident, let me tell you. Father never recovered. He was only fifty-one when he died. They broke his heart."

"Hedger says most of the reporting you've done is about various Communist revolutionary movements."

"A lot of it has been," she agreed. "My father's name got used by all sorts of left-wing groups; he was a real hero to them. I suppose it was a sort of entrée for me."

Cat was silent.

"Oh, I see, you want to know if I'm a Communist spy, right?"

"Well?" he asked. "I mean, I don't really give a damn, but I would like to know."

She unclipped her shoulder harness and turned to face him. "Yes you do care, bless your heart," she said. "You're afraid you've gotten involved with a regular Red Menace, aren't you?"

"Look . . ."

"Well, I suppose I'm glad you care. No, I'm not a Communist spy, or even a Communist. I despise what a lot of the guerrilla movements are doing — or at least the way they're doing it. On the other hand, I despise the way the United States does a lot of what it does, too. Politically, I suppose I'm a stateless person. I mean, I'm glad that part of me is an American, and I'm glad that the other part is a South American — I feel just as comfortable here as I do in the States. The United States has a right-wing administration that I abhor, and Colombia has a left-wing guerrilla movement that I hate, too. There's no political home for me unless it's a place like Sweden, and I couldn't live there, because I'm not a Socialist, and half of me is a hot-blooded Latin."

Cat laughed. "I'll vouch for that."

Now they were over jungle. There was nothing else as far as the eye could see. It was so thick, Cat thought he could land the airplane on the treetops. Every couple of minutes, he scanned the instrument panel, looking for reassurance. The needles held steady, and the engine drummed monotonously along. Fuel flow was a bit more than he had planned, but he had a much bigger reserve than he and Bluey had had on the flight from Florida.

Meg had cranked her seat back and was sound asleep. He looked at her face, innocent and childlike in repose. He knew there was nothing he could say to talk her out of going to the Trapezoid with him, and he was glad. He remembered the terrible moment that morning, when he had thought he was alone.

They had sandwiches a little later, then, early in the afternoon, Cat looked out ahead of them and saw a strip of brown cutting across the green of the jungle. Cat felt a thrill of anticipation and of fear. The Amazon — the biggest river in the world, dwarfing the Congo, the Nile, and the Mississippi. It was a good thirty miles away, but down here there was no air pollution, only a haze rising from the rain forest. As they flew closer the river widened, until it became apparent what a huge body of water they were approaching. It stretched, east and west, as far as the eye could see. Twenty miles out, when Leticia was a smudge beside the Amazon, Cat called the tower and was instructed to start his descent. A few minutes later they were entering the traffic pattern, and as Cat turned onto the base leg for landing, a large helicopter rose from the airport and headed away north at a low altitude.

The heat was apparent long before they

landed, and as soon as they were on the ground Cat and Meg opened the airplane's windows. They were waved into a tie-down area by a teenage boy, and Cat switched off all the electrics and the avionics power switch, then cut the engine. He was sweating already, and he wasn't sure it was the heat.

While the boy got their bags onto a hand trolley, Cat made arrangements for tie-down and refueling, then they got a taxi to Parador Ticuña. As the cab pulled up at the hotel, a crowd was gathered out front. Meg asked the driver what was happening, but the driver didn't know. He got out and went to the trunk for their bags, ignoring the commotion.

Cat and Meg got out of the cab and approached the edges of the crowd. As they did so a policeman pushed past them, shouting at the crowd. The group parted to let him through, and Cat was able to see what was at the crowd's center. A man, a gringo, dressed in an American seersucker suit, lay stretched out on the ground, faceup. His head lay in a pool of bright red blood, and his lips and teeth were a mess. He had been shot in the back of the head, and the bullet had exited through his mouth, but he was still recognizable. Cat's eyes remained locked on the sandy hair and badly pockmarked face until the crowd closed in again and blocked his view.

He turned away, feeling ill. The man had joined Bluey Holland as a casualty in the effort to protect Cat Catledge. Who else would Cat get killed before this was over?

27

Cat looked at his watch again. It was a little past six, and they had been sitting in the bar since midafternoon. He had not told Meg who the murdered man was. He didn't intend to. At first, they had had the place to themselves, then, around five, the bar had started to fill with people, locals and a group of German tourists. He had begun to worry.

A tall, blond man wearing bush clothes entered the bar, glanced at something in the palm of his hand, then approached Cat. "Mr. Ellis?"

Cat stood up. "That's right."

"My name is Hank. Will you come with me, please?"

Cat and Meg began gathering their bags.

"Excuse me," the man said, uncertainly, "I was under the impression you'd be alone."

"Wrong," Cat said, firmly. "Miss Garcia is my business partner. I don't go anywhere without her."

The man looked at them for a moment, then made a decision. "Okay, follow me," he said. "You're my last passengers for the day. Sorry I kept you waiting; I've been doing a lot of flying today."

He led them to a waiting taxi, which drove them back to the airport. The cab drew up next to the helicopter Cat had seen taking off earlier. The tall man put their luggage into a rear compartment, then settled them into the back seat, instructing them to buckle in. Moments later they lifted from the tarmac and headed north, flying at no more than about five hundred feet.

The helicopter was luxuriously appointed, with leather seats for four and deep carpeting. The noise of the engine and rotor were well suppressed, but Cat didn't really feel like talking. He was on his way to Jinx; he knew it. He was both excited and frightened. He squeezed Meg's hand, and she smiled and nodded.

Cat craned his neck to look over the pilot's shoulder at the airspeed indicator and found they were making a hundred and thirty knots. Their heading was a little east of north. At this low altitude, the trees below them were something less than the green carpet they had seemed from ten thousand feet, but there were precious few gaps among them, and the jungle floor was rarely visible. They crossed a large river, then a couple of small ones. They had been airborne for an hour and eight minutes by Cat's watch when the chopper suddenly began to slow. A couple of minutes more and they were hovering, then sinking below the treetops.

The helicopter came to rest on a large patch of ground that seemed newly cleared. As they climbed out of the machine, Cat saw a group of workmen less than a hundred yards away, and as the copter's engine died, he could hear the angry growls of chain saws. To Cat's surprise, there was a small, high-winged airplane parked a few yards away with a camouflage net thrown over it. He wondered how it could have flown into so small an area — he estimated the clearing was about fifty yards wide and eighty or ninety long. Then he saw the name "Maule" painted on the fuselage of the airplane, and he remembered seeing such an airplane back in Atlanta. It was a STOL — short takeoff and landing — aircraft.

A servant in a white jacket appeared with a hand trolley and loaded their luggage onto it, motioning for them to follow him. As they left the clearing, the helicopter pilot and a couple of workmen had begun to cover the machine with camouflage netting.

The servant led them down a broad dirt path for a hundred yards or so, then the way became paved with flat stones. Both sides of the walkway had been landscaped and planted with exotic flowers, and beyond those, the jungle appeared incredibly dense. Although the sun was still well above the horizon, they were in a sort of twilight made from the shelter of the tall, hardwood trees that rose into the sky. Soon the path broadened, and they came into a garden. Cat had been expecting a crude camp like the ones in the photographs on Buzz Bergman's office wall, and he was surprised to see ahead of them a large house of beige stucco topped with green roof tiles. They climbed a dozen steps from the garden to a broad, tiled veranda before the house, and Cat noticed other buildings of the same materials scattered under the trees surrounding the house.

The servant opened a door for them, and as they stepped into a large entrance hall, they were greeted by a wave of cool, dry air. The building was air-conditioned. "I will wait here for you," the man said. "Please go first to the office just there." He pointed to an open door off the entrance hall.

Cat and Meg walked into a large, well-appointed office. There was a lot of leather furniture and, on one wall, a bookcase containing what appeared to be a large stereo system, with many switches and knobs. There was also, apparently, a public address system, since there was a table microphone resting on a shelf. Sitting behind an imposing desk was the narrow-faced man, Vargas, who had received a hundred thousand dollars from Cat in the rooftop nightclub of the Tequendama Hotel in Bogotá.

Vargas looked up and recognized Cat, then he saw Meg and frowned. He stood up and looked angrily at Cat. "Who is this person?" he demanded.

"This is Maria Eugenia Garcia, my business partner," Cat replied. "Meg, this is Mr. Vargas, whom I met in Bogotá."

"You were expected to come alone," Vargas spat, furious. "You said nothing of this woman."

"You hardly gave me an opportunity," Cat said, taking care to sound annoyed. "You simply took my money and left in a hurry. Half that money was Miss Garcia's."

"Then why was she not at the meeting?" he insisted.

"She had not yet arrived in Bogotá," Cat replied.

"Wait outside," Vargas said, "and close the door."

Cat and Meg stepped back into the entrance hall, closing the door behind them. "What now?" she said.

"There was a telephone on the desk," Cat replied. "I expect he's reporting to his boss."

A minute or two passed, then Vargas opened the door and waved them inside. "Give me your passport," he said to Meg.

She gave him her Bolivian passport, and he took it to a Xerox machine and made a copy. He returned the document to her. "I require nine hundred thousand dollars in cash," Vargas said to Cat.

"It's in my luggage," Cat said, turning for the door. "I'll be right back." He left the office and went to the veranda, where the servant waited with the bags, retrieved the canvas-and-leather grip, and returned to the office. He opened the grip, removed the shirts and Hedger's radio, and began stacking bundles of bills on the desk.

Vargas picked up Hedger's radio and looked closely at it.

Cat tried not to notice, kept stacking money.

Vargas switched on the radio and twirled

the tuning dial. Nothing but static greeted him.

"I didn't know we'd be this far from a radio station," Cat said.

"Don't worry, Mr. Ellis," Vargas said. "We will keep you entertained while you are here." Vargas did a quick count of the bundles of bills and seemed satisfied. "The two of you will have to share quarters," he said. "Our facilities here are stretched to the limit." He turned to Cat. "You will be staying in cottage number twelve," he said. "The boy will take you there. Please come back here for cocktails at seven o'clock, to be followed by dinner."

They followed the servant down another paved path. They passed a large swimming pool and a pair of fenced-in tennis courts, all deserted. Shortly, the path opened into a wider grass path, almost a street, with small stucco cottages on either side. The servant rolled his trolley to the front door of number twelve and ushered them in. Cat found himself in a small but nicely furnished sitting room. The servant showed them a bedroom, bath, and kitchenette. It was like something one might rent at the beach, Cat thought, but with better-than-usual furnishings. The servant left them.

"Christ," Cat said. "I wasn't expecting

anything like this. I thought we'd be camped in some jungle hovel."

"Yeah," Meg replied. "I think I'll have a shower." She put a finger to her lips and beckoned him toward the bathroom. She turned on the shower, then put her lips close to his ear. "There was an awful lot of electronic equipment in Vargas's office," she said. "Before we do any more talking, I want to have a look for bugs."

Cat watched as she produced a small electrical meter and methodically went through the whole cottage, checking every nook and cranny for hidden microphones. She checked the telephone, as well, then placed it back on its cradle. "Looks clean to me," she said, "and I'm pretty good at this. I've been bugged by the best."

"I'm impressed," Cat said, "but you'd better either get into the shower or turn it off."

She showered, returned. "Now tell me," she said, "where the hell did you get nine hundred thousand dollars in cash?"

"At the bank," he replied, "where else?"

"In Bogotá?"

"In Atlanta."

"You mean you've been hauling nine hundred thousand dollars all over Colombia?"

"More than that," Cat said. "I gave Vargas

a hundred thousand in Bogotá."

"Jesus, I'm glad you didn't tell me. It would have made me nervous," she said. "What now? What do we do next?"

"I guess we show up for cocktails at seven," he said. "If Jinx is here, maybe she'll be at the party."

"And if she is?"

"Well, we've got to get the lay of the land before we can try to get her out of here — find out where she is."

Meg laughed. "While you're at it, how about finding out where *we* are."

"I can tell you that, roughly," Cat said. "We're about a hundred and forty-five nautical miles northeast of Leticia."

"Swell. What else is around here?"

"Not a goddamned thing," Cat said. "Maybe a few Indians. Otherwise, just jungle — in every direction."

"And if Jinx is here, and if you can get your hands on her, what then?"

"I'm still working on that," Cat said.

"You want to take a look around the place before cocktails?"

"No. I haven't seen a soul here since we landed, except for staff and Vargas. Let's not attract attention to ourselves by snooping around."

"Why do you think they didn't search us

when we arrived?"

"Why bother? They've got a million dollars of our money, so they know we're not going to steal anything. And considering where we are, even if we're armed, what could we possibly do to them in the middle of an armed camp?"

"Right," Meg said. "What *can* we do?"

Cat walked to his bag and took out Hedger's radio. "This is a directional beacon. When we've gotten hold of Jinx, we turn it on and hide until the cavalry arrives. Colombian army. They'll be on the lookout for us."

"Jesus," said Meg. "I hope so."

A little after seven o'clock, Cat and Meg left the cottage and started toward the main house. The sky above them was still bright, but in the shadows of the giant trees, it was nearly dark. They followed the path, and as they did a few others, all men, left the cottages and walked ahead of or behind them. The air was still hot and heavy, and Cat was perspiring, not entirely from the heat. He wanted to break out of the procession and start searching for his daughter. Meg took his arm, as if she knew what he was thinking.

They crossed the veranda and entered the house. The large entrance hall was now lit by an elaborate chandelier, and a group of twenty or thirty men were helping themselves at a bar and at a table filled with beautifully displayed food. Cat reckoned that their host had an ice house, because a large block held what he reckoned was a gallon of caviar nestled in the scooped-out block.

The crowd was well dressed and seemed a little subdued. As Cat and Meg approached the bar, a tall man, sweating in a finely tailored, heavy wool suit, was asking, in an upper-class British accent, for a gin and tonic with *lots* of ice. They got a drink and some food, then they stood to one side of the room and had a closer look at their new colleagues. Cat immediately began to see people he knew.

Across the room, at the center of a small knot of men, stood Stanton Michael Prince, all smiles and charm, the ponytail flicking as he turned from one member of the group to another. At the edge of the group, looking carefully not at Prince, but at the men around him, was Denny. Cat's stomach knotted as Denny's eyes fell on him. Never mind his loss of weight and absence of beard, Cat felt naked; now he would be recognized and the alarm raised. Then Denny's eyes moved on; there had been no reaction. Cat started breathing again.

He had once met a President of the United States and had noticed that the Secret Service men guarding the President never looked at him. Instead, they watched the crowd, as Denny was doing now. Cat knew that Denny must be armed.

Then a movement on the broad staircase to the upper floor caught Cat's eye. A group of eight or nine young women, all pretty, all beautifully dressed, descended the stairs. It was a moment before Cat realized that the last of them, a tall beauty in a tightly cut strapless dress, was Jinx.

He stood, transfixed, unable to take his eyes off her. Her hair had grown longer, and she was wearing much more sophisticated makeup than she usually did. Her appearance was not one she would have chosen for herself. Cat felt a peculiar combination of elation and illness. He had found her, but he could do nothing; she was still out of reach. There she was, thirty feet away, alive and, as far as he could tell, quite well, and he could do nothing.

Meg squeezed his arm. "Look at me," she whispered.

Cat tore his eyes from Jinx and turned to Meg.

"Is the tall girl Jinx?" she asked.

"Yes. Everything about her is different — makeup, hair, clothes — but that's Jinx."

"Then, for Christ's sake, stop staring at her," Meg said.

Cat tried looking around more, not looking directly at Jinx, always at someone near her. As he looked around, the group reached the bottom of the stairs and dispersed into the growing crowd of men, chatting amiably with them. Jinx continued through the crowd until she reached Prince's side. He put a proprietary hand on her bare shoulder and began to introduce her to the group.

Before Cat could think further about this, he was distracted by a shout and a movement at the front door. A group of men was entering the room, and one of them was greeting someone he knew. Cat glanced at the group, then froze. He turned slowly toward them and saw, staring at him from no more than ten feet away, his son, Dell.

28

Cat thought he had never seen such a look. Dell stood, his face contorted into a hatred of which Cat would never have thought him capable. Even before Dell moved, Cat knew it was over. Within seconds Prince would know who he was and why he was there. There would be no way to get to Jinx. His and Meg's only hope would be to run for the jungle. Cat didn't think they could even make the door.

A man standing next to Dell put a hand on his shoulder, obviously wondering what was wrong. Dell shook off the hand, turned, and started across the room toward where Prince stood. Cat took Meg's arm and began to move her toward the front door of the house.

"Keep moving, and listen to me," he said, steering her through the crowd. "Someone here knows me. We've got to run for it. As soon as we make the door, run for the airstrip, and don't slow down for anything. Go straight across into the jungle, and stay with me. It's the only chance we have." He wished he were armed; he wished he had a map, food and water; he wished he had as much as a pocket knife; he wished he had a five-minute head start. He had none of these things.

Cat glanced back toward Dell and stopped. Dell was standing stock still in the middle of the room, looking toward Prince's group, perhaps fifteen feet away from where he stood. Cat could not see his face, but he knew that Dell had seen Jinx, and for the first time. He could not have known his sister was here. Cat squeezed Meg's hand. "Wait near the door. If a commotion breaks out, run for it." He left her and started toward Dell, his eyes darting from him to Jinx and back. She had not yet seen him.

He picked his way through the crowd as quickly as he could without exciting attention, excusing himself as he pushed past people, fixing a smile on his face to hide his fear. Jinx seemed to be staring past Prince into the middle distance. Please, honey, don't see Dell, don't see me, he prayed to her.

He reached Dell and took his arm, turning him away from Jinx. "Don't say anything, just smile, and come with me."

"What . . ." Dell began.

"Be quiet, and smile." Cat began steering him through the crowd toward some French doors at the rear of the room. "Just keep moving, and don't say anything," he said again. Cat got the door open and pushed Dell ahead of him. They were in a courtyard with a fountain, surrounded on all four sides by the house.

"She's dead," Dell said. "Isn't she dead?"

"No, she's not dead. It's Jinx." Cat led him to the fountain and sat him down on the edge.

"What's happening?" Dell asked in a small, frightened voice. "Why are you here? Why is Jinx here?"

"Listen to me," Cat said. "Jinx didn't die on the boat; it was another girl. She was taken off the boat while I was unconscious. I didn't find out until a few weeks ago. I've been looking for her ever since. I didn't see her until about a minute before you did." He stopped and waited for a reaction.

There were tears on Dell's face, and he was taking deep breaths.

"Just take it easy and relax," Cat said. "Just get your breath."

"I don't understand any of this," Dell said. "I break my ass to get a million bucks

together, and I get down here to this unbe-
lievable fucking place, and I find my dead
sister and you, for Christ's sake!" He turned
and looked at Cat for the first time.
"Where's Mom?"

"She died on the boat," Cat said. "There
was no mistake about that." He looked at
Dell closely. The boy seemed to be rational,
now. "I'm going to get Jinx out of here, and
it's important that you don't do anything to
screw it up."

"Screw it up?" Dell almost shouted.
"*You're* the one who's screwing it up! I'm
not going to let you screw it up. I've paid a
million dollars and only two hundred thousand was mine, and I'm going to get what I
came for. I can't go back to Miami without
it. They'll cut me into tiny pieces."

"That's not important anymore," Cat
said. "All that's important is getting Jinx
out of here."

"Are you out of your fucking mind?" Dell
asked. "Do you know where the fuck you
are? You're in the middle of the jungle, and
the only way out of here is by the helicopter
that brought you in here!"

"You can't turn me in to Prince," Cat said.

"Who?"

"The man with the ponytail."

"The Anaconda? Sure, I can turn you in

to him. I would have a minute ago, but when I saw Jinx I got confused. What is she doing with the Anaconda?"

"His name is Prince. He kidnapped her, or had her kidnapped, or bought her, or something — I'm not sure. All I know is that she's here against her will."

"No, no, that can't be; she's standing in there talking to people like she owned the place. She's gotta be here because she wants to be. She'd be screaming her head off, otherwise."

"Screaming? She's in the middle of the jungle with a bunch of drug dealers. What's she supposed to do, call the police?"

"I don't understand how you could have known she was here."

"She was being held at a hotel in Cartagena, and she got to a telephone and called me. I got some help, and I finally tracked her down."

Dell stood up and started pacing back and forth by the fountain. "And I'm supposed to believe all that? I think you're here because *I'm* here. You found out I got this deal together, and you're trying to fuck me again."

"Dell, I promise you I hadn't the slightest idea you were here until I saw you walk into the room. I don't care what you're doing here, and I'm not trying to screw it up for you, I just want to get Jinx out of here, and to do that, I need your help."

Dell whirled on him. "You bastard, you've got a lot of balls asking for my help."

"It's Jinx who needs your help. Do you hate her, too?"

"Of course not!"

"Then just do this — stay out of my way, and keep your mouth shut. Can you do that much, at least?"

"What are you going to do?"

"I don't know, and I need time to figure it out. Prince — the Anaconda — thinks I'm here for the same reason you are. I had to come up with a million bucks, too." Cat took a deep breath. "Look, I've got to trust you with something. Can I do that?"

"Probably not."

"You're in almost as much danger as Jinx is."

"Yeah, how? It feels pretty safe to me around here."

"It's not. This place is going to be raided by the Colombian army shortly."

"Bullshit! You expect me to believe that?"

"You've got to believe it. I've been in on the planning. They're going to hit this place with everything they've got — helicopters, paratroopers, heavy weapons — the works.

They're going to come in here and turn this place into a war zone."

"How can they even know where it is?" Dell demanded. "We're completely lost out here."

"They already know exactly where it is," Cat lied. "There was an informer. They're grouping their forces less than two hundred miles from here, in a place just across the Brazilian border, and when they hit, they're going to shoot at anything that moves."

"I don't believe you. How can I believe you?"

"You don't have to take my word for all this. Think about what you already know to be true. One of Prince's right-hand men murdered your mother and kidnapped your sister. God only knows what they've been doing to her. Your sister's life depends on what you do next. If that's not important enough for you, *your* life depends on it."

Dell walked back and forth a few times without speaking. Then he turned to Cat. "What is it you want me to do?" he asked, warily.

"First, stay away from Jinx. Don't let her see you. We can't surprise her while she's in the middle of this crowd. If she does spot you, tell her to be quiet and stay away from her. I'll find a way to get word to her that we're here. There's a woman named Meg with me. She's helping."

"This is crazy," Dell said, shaking his head.

"I know it's crazy, but you're stuck with it — all of us are stuck with it. What I've got to do is to get Jinx away from these people and hide her until the raid is over. We'll probably have to take to the jungle until the shooting stops, and I'd like you to come with us. Your chances are not very good here."

Dell was standing still, glaring at him. "What I'm going to do is to go back in there and tell the Anaconda about this raid. He'll know what to do about it."

"What can he do?" Cat demanded. "As far as I can tell, everybody at this meeting was brought here in one six-passenger helicopter — there wasn't another one at the Leticia Airport. You tell the Anaconda about this, you know what he'll do? He'll climb aboard that chopper and get out of here, and the hell with anybody else. It'll be the Colombian troops or the jungle — take your pick."

Dell laughed. "You really think he'd just walk away from this place and leave it to be destroyed? Can't you see how much money and work have gone into it?"

"Dell, this place represents only a fraction

of the man's wealth. He's got an office building and a house in Cali that are worth more than this, and a network of businesses all over this country and God knows where else, and he didn't get them by being nice to people. He'll fly out of here and never look back."

"Fuck you," Dell said. He turned and strode back toward the French doors.

Cat moved to go after him, but he was already opening the door. By the time Cat reached the door, Dell was standing in the middle of the large hall, alone. Someone had opened a pair of large doors, and the crowd had moved into another room. Dell followed them, and Cat followed Dell. He had to try and talk to him again before he got to Prince.

But Dell had stopped again, distracted by something. Cat joined him at the edge of the group and followed his gaze. At the center of the room were two large, round tables. One of them was piled high with an enormous stack of money, bundles of one-hundred-dollar bills. The other was piled with an equally high stack of clear plastic bags, each filled with a white powder. Cat glanced at Dell. Dell seemed stunned.

There was a tug at Cat's sleeve, and Meg said, "What's happening? Are we all right?"

"I don't know," Cat replied, keeping his eyes on Dell. "We're —"

"Gentlemen!" The voice came from the other end of the room. "Gentlemen, may I have your attention!"

Cat followed the voice and came to Vargas.

"Gentlemen, it is now my pleasure to introduce you to the man who has brought you here, who has made all of this" — he spread his hands to indicate the money and the cocaine — "possible. Gentlemen — and ladies — the Anaconda!"

There was a round of enthusiastic applause, and Prince stepped between the tables. "Good evening, gentlemen," he said, smiling. He waved a hand at the table of money. "Here we have the fruits of your efforts," he said. "Fifty million dollars." Then he waved another hand at the table of cocaine. "And here we have the fruits of mine. Fifty million dollars' worth of the finest cocaine. We have come together here to combine our efforts, to our mutual profit."

It was the first time Cat had heard Prince speak, and he was impressed. His voice was rich and pleasant, his manner confident. He might have been the chairman of some Fortune 500 company addressing his sales force. In fact, Cat thought, he probably is.

Prince continued. "This merchandise is only a tiny fraction of what I will produce here, and this money is an even smaller fraction of what you and I, together, will generate. A few hundred yards from this spot, back in the jungle, is the largest and most modern cocaine factory ever built, nearing completion. Next week we will abandon the crude and cumbersome methods which produced the product you see before you, and we will move into a new era of production. Within a month, after we have gotten the bugs out of the system, we will have increased our output by a factor of eight, and that is why you are here.

"You gentlemen, most of you chosen carefully for your success in legitimate business, will form the basis of a new distribution and sales system that will, in very short order, cover the world. We will, of course, supply you with the finest, purest product available, but we will do much more than that. During the course of your week's stay here, my people and I will be instructing you in our proven methods — management; the hiring of salespeople; the security of your network; the buying of key law-enforcement officials; your own insulation from unlawful activity, and — when necessary — the protection and defense of your operations.

"We have a busy week planned for you, but half of each day and all of each evening will be set aside for leisure activities. We can offer you everything a good resort hotel can — and, perhaps, a bit more. There is a large library of books and videocassettes available; there are swimming and tennis; there is a small casino, and there is quite a good discotheque. There will also be female companionship, although I must apologize for the short supply. Our facilities here are in full use, and we could not import extra ladies for this occasion." He smiled. "But our ladies are *very* willing, and you may be sure that none of you will have to go the whole week without company."

Cat's insides twitched. The young women he had seen were here to entertain the visiting firemen, and Jinx was among them.

"Finally," Prince said, "before we go in to dinner, let me mention one or two rules we have here. You may have the run of the place, explore all you like, except for the factory and the jungle. You will see the factory on guided tours, but we do not wish the work disturbed by unscheduled visits. Do not go into the jungle, for you are unlikely to return. It is denser than you can imagine, and it is all too easy to lose your bearings and head away from our camp when you believe you are heading toward it. And there are, of course, beasts which enjoy human flesh. I must ask you, also, to be in your quarters by midnight and not to venture out until daylight. We double the guard here at night, and my people are instructed to shoot first and ask questions later.

"Finally, and most important, I must tell you that I do not tolerate the use of drugs here. I do not, in fact, tolerate the use of drugs by anyone associated with me, and you gentlemen were chosen, in part, because you are not users. Still, someone may have slipped through my net of inquiries, and I warn you now — and I am perfectly serious — I will unceremoniously shoot the first person who is caught using drugs.

"But now, ladies and gentlemen, dinner is served. You will find a place card at each seat." Prince waved an arm and yet another set of huge doors opened to reveal an enormous dining room with a single, long table.

Cat hung back with Meg and watched Dell shuffle into the dining room with the others. "That's my son, Dell," he told her. "We haven't gotten along for several years. He's here as a buyer, and I can't promise you he won't turn us in, but we've got to take the chance."

"Oh, swell," Meg said, quietly.

"Something else," he whispered. "Jinx doesn't know either of us is here, and I don't want her to see us without warning, if I can help it. I don't know if we'll be sitting together, but try to get near her and tell her both Dell and I are here, so she'll have some warning. If you can, find out where her room is and how we might meet."

"Right," Meg said.

They entered the dining room to discover that everyone had gathered along one wall, which was of glass, with a door at one end. Cat and Meg followed the crowd. Behind the plate glass was a patch of jungle, brought indoors. There was a lot of greenery, and a small stream ran through the scene. Then Cat saw what everyone was looking at. Resting on a limb of a tree, parts of its body dangling, was the largest snake he had ever seen. "Christ," he said, involuntarily.

"It's an anaconda," Meg said. "I've seen one before, a much smaller one."

The huge reptile seemed oblivious of its audience, and the crowd gradually drifted to the table, looking for place cards.

Meg found hers, then Cat found his, across the table and half a dozen places down, near the center of the table. Dell, he saw was on Meg's side, near the end. Dell's expression was vacant, but he seemed calm. Then he saw Jinx take her seat, two down from Meg. Good, he thought, Meg might be able to speak to her. Then Denny took the seat between them.

Cat was in clear view of Jinx, and that worried him. Still, his appearance had changed. When Jinx had last seen him, his hair had been longer, his beard full, and he had weighed an extra fifty pounds. But Jinx would remember when he was slimmer and clean-shaven, back when she was in her early teens. Then she looked directly at him.

He looked away, then stole another glance at her. She had not reacted. Denny said something to her, but she ignored him, and he looked annoyed. Pointedly, she turned away and took up a conversation with the man on her other side.

Someone sat down next to Cat. Absorbed with watching Jinx, he ignored the man, until he spoke.

"Lovely, isn't she?" the man asked.

Cat turned and found Prince sitting next to him. "Yes, she is," he said. Then, after a moment: "How do you persuade such a beautiful girl to come to the middle of a jungle?" Cat wanted to pick up his fork and plunge it into the man's face.

Prince smiled, revealing white, evenly spaced teeth. "Oh, there are all sorts of attractions. You're Southeast, aren't you?"

It took Cat a moment to figure out what he meant. "Oh, yes. I'm Bob Ellis." They shook hands.

"Well, Bob, we're going to make you rich."

"I'm already rich," Cat replied.

Prince laughed aloud. "Of course you are. After all, you've paid a million dollars for a week's stay at a jungle resort, haven't you?"

"That's right."

"Tell me, Bob, what is it you want that you don't already have?"

Cat smiled a little smile. "I want to be as rich as you are," he said.

Prince laughed again. "I like that," he said. "I like ambition. You'll do well, Bob, you'll do well."

Cat nodded toward the glass case across the room. "That's an anaconda, is it?"

"Indeed it is. The largest one ever captured. Some Indians who were working to clear the land here caught it. It seemed a pity to kill it, so we built it some accommodation."

"What do you feed it?"

"Small animals; the odd man."

Cat couldn't tell if Prince was serious.

Soup came, and they began to eat.

"Tell me," Cat said, "how did I happen to be seated next to the Anaconda?"

"Luck of the draw, I guess," Prince replied. "I didn't ask for anybody in particular."

"I'm hurt," Cat said. "I thought you'd chosen me."

"Well, you see, I don't know anybody here, except my staff, of course, so I wouldn't have had a preference. I understand, though, that you brought someone with you."

"Yes, my business partner."

"Well chosen," Prince said, gazing at Meg. "If she's as bright as she is attractive."

"She is." Cat had a sudden thought. "Do you play tennis?"

"I do," Prince replied.

"Well, Meg and I make quite a mean mixed doubles team," Cat replied. He nodded toward Jinx. "Perhaps you and your young lady will give us a match. Does she play?"

Prince nodded enthusiastically. "Yes, indeed, quite well. Tomorrow morning at eight? I like to rise early; the heat gets up later."

"Eight is fine. I have a feeling I'd better stay sober tonight."

Prince laughed again. The main course

arrived, and he turned to talk with the man on his other side.

Cat glanced toward Jinx and discovered that her chair was empty. So was Meg's. Cat had an almost overpowering urge to go and look for them, but he made himself concentrate on his food, which was excellent. Five minutes later Jinx returned to her seat. She did not look his way and immediately began talking to the man next to her. Soon Meg returned, and she didn't look at him, either. She looked preoccupied.

Prince stood. "Now, my friends, if you have finished your coffee, we will adjourn. For those of you who would like a little nightlife, the discotheque is only a two-minute walk, and we have a little floor show for you."

Cat met Meg at the end of the table, and they followed the flow of the crowd out of the room. "What happened?" he demanded. "Did you talk to her?"

"I don't understand," Meg said. "Are you really sure that's Jinx?"

"What are you talking about? Of course I'm sure!"

"Well, this is very odd."

"What?"

"We were alone together in the ladies' room upstairs. I began telling her about you and Dell, and she didn't understand a word, until I switched to Spanish. The girl is South American."

"That's impossible."

"I can't quite get a handle on her accent. It's odd. Does Jinx speak Spanish?"

"Well, she studied it in school, but I don't see how she could speak it very well."

Meg sighed. "Look, if you had been kidnapped by a drug baron, and suddenly somebody walked up to you and said your dad was downstairs, wouldn't you react? She said, in Spanish, she didn't know what I was talking about, then she walked away. Are you absolutely sure that is your daughter?"

"Meg, I'm telling you, that is Jinx. Don't you think I'd know her?"

Meg didn't look at him. "I'm beginning to wonder," she said.

29

Cat shook Meg awake.

"What time is it?" she mumbled.

"Seven-thirty; we've got a tennis date at eight."

"What?"

"Sorry, I forgot to tell you last night. We're playing with Prince. And Jinx."

She sat up and rubbed her eyes. "This is ridiculous, you know, all of it. We come down to this jungle camp, which turns out to be a sort of Amazonian Rockresort, to find your daughter, who suddenly speaks nothing but Spanish, who is being held by a drug lord, and we're playing tennis with them."

"Well, I've never bored you, have I?"

She threw an arm around him and kissed him. "God knows that's true. Listen, I'd throw you down and screw you right now, if I didn't have to play tennis."

Prince was waiting for them, warming up with Jinx. "Morning," he called out cheerfully.

"Morning," Cat called back. "Sorry we're late." He watched Jinx walk back to Prince's side of the net. A little heavier, maybe, but it had to be Jinx, he thought. Even her tennis swing fit.

Prince won the serve, lost the first set, six-three. He called Cat to the net. "Listen, you're stronger than we are. Why don't we trade partners? That might make for a better match."

"Okay," Cat replied. "Meg, you play with our host."

He watched Jinx closely as she came around the net. She didn't avoid his eyes, but she gave no sign of recognition. Cat took his time serving, trying to figure out what to do next. They won the game and changed ends. Cat took care to walk next to Jinx. "Listen to me, but don't react," he said quietly. "I've come to get you out of here, and I need to know where your room is."

"*Qué?*" she said, raising her eyebrows and smiling. "I do not speak English," she said with a heavy accent. "Do you speak

Spanish?"

"For Christ's sake, Jinx, what's the matter with you? It's Daddy, don't you know me?"

They had reached the baseline. She smiled and shrugged, then pointed to herself.

Cat glanced at Prince. He was talking with Meg. "Yes, I've come for you!" he said, trying to keep from shouting.

Now she was pointing at the ball. It was her serve; she wanted the ball.

Cat finished the match in a fog of frustration and bewilderment. Prince and Meg won the next two sets easily. Prince waved them to a little pavilion at courtside. "Have you had breakfast?" he asked. "Join us."

They served themselves eggs, sausages, and bacon from a nearby buffet, then sat down at a beautifully set table.

"Good match," Prince said, "but you were a little off your game the second two sets."

"I guess I'm not awake yet," Cat said lamely. "Say, how did you choose this site for your factory and . . . all this?" He waved a hand.

"The factory came first," Prince replied. "I chose the site purely for its remoteness. We got in a chopper one day and left Leticia, just looking. There was a small clearing here, and there's a river not far to the north. We get our water supply from there. We began simply enough, but business was so good, it made sense to build a more permanent setup. Here, we are, for all practical purposes, immune from any intrusion."

"But surely the place will become known to the authorities eventually."

"Eventually, yes, I suppose it will," Prince replied. "But you don't understand the extent to which we have infiltrated the authorities. There is virtually nothing that goes on in the police or the army that I don't know about, and having access to that information is remarkably inexpensive, considering its value."

"You don't worry about arrest, then?"

"Of course not, but even if any of my people were arrested, they would never come to trial, and if they did come to trial, they would not be convicted, and if they were convicted, they would serve no sentence. There is almost no one who cannot be bought, and the exceptions have a way of disappearing."

Cat could think of nothing to say. Prince was wrong about the army; he had to be. Cat concentrated on his eggs.

But Prince was not through impressing him. "Let me tell you, Bob, that in another couple of years, we are going to completely control this country." He sat back and sipped his orange juice. "No person will run for office without our approval; no official will be appointed, no policeman hired or promoted, no army officer given command, no judge will sit. Not unless I say so. Have you ever thought of what it would be like to have an entire nation at your disposal?"

"No, I haven't," Cat replied.

"Oh, I don't want to be another Adolf Hitler," Prince said, waving a hand, "don't get me wrong. I have no interest whatever in politics or the international situation, except as they apply to my business. I don't wish to rule this country, just to control the people who do. And believe me, the people will be much better off when I do."

"How?" Meg asked. "Are you going to do something for them?"

"Indeed I am," Prince replied. "This country has a foreign debt of thirteen billion dollars. Not as bad as Brazil or Argentina, but bad enough. We're going to pay that off in one fell swoop."

Cat gulped. "*Thirteen billion dollars?* How the hell can you pay that off?"

"Our consortium, along with a dozen others, has considerably more worth than that," Prince said. "And once that debt is paid, Colombian tax dollars can be spent on housing, job training, industrial development, and, above all, drug rehabilitation programs."

"I'm confused," Cat said. "Why would you want drug rehabilitation programs in this country?"

"It's very simple," Prince said, spreading his hands. "A drug problem is very expensive for a nation — it generates violent crime, which requires a large police force and prison system to control. We will eliminate the drug problem very quickly because we control the source of the drugs. Without drugs, there will be no drug problem. We see the cocaine trade as purely an export business. Five years from now, when you visit this country, there will be general prosperity, the tourist trade will have been revived, the beggars and thieves will be gone from the streets, the bars will have come down from the windows and doors of homes. Colombia will be the pearl of the Western Hemisphere. Believe me, I will make all of this happen."

"That is a breathtaking plan," Meg said. "How many people will you have to kill to accomplish this?"

Prince shrugged. "Does it matter? As many as necessary. Those addicts who do not respond to rehabilitation will certainly have to go; a certain element in the government, in the courts, and especially in journalism, will have to be dealt with. We must control the press, but only to the extent of what is written about us. All of this will be conducted in a very businesslike way, you see. That is the secret of my whole program — that it is run strictly by proven entrepreneurial business methods."

Cat looked at Jinx. She had been quietly concentrating on her food, oblivious of the conversation.

Prince stood up. "Would you like a little tour of the place?" he asked.

"Yes, thank you," Cat replied, "we would." Prince turned to say something to a servant in Spanish, and Cat whispered in Meg's ear, "Try and talk to Jinx. Find out where her room is, what her schedule is."

Prince led the way to the main house. Cat walked alongside him, and Meg fell back with Jinx.

"How long has it taken you to build all this?" Cat asked.

"Less than two years, from scratch," Prince replied. "When you bring in your labor force, pay them well, and keep them here until the job is done, things happen very quickly. Not everything is complete yet, but in another couple of months we'll be finished."

"I see you're building an airstrip," Cat said.

"Yes, we'll have a runway that can take a large jet transport, not to mention my own airplane."

They strolled along the path, Prince pointing out the water purification plant, the vegetable garden and fruit orchard.

"We're pretty much self-sufficient here," he said, "but when the runway is finished, we can fly in what we need directly from Bogotá."

"Aren't you a bit cut off from the outside world?" Cat asked.

"Come, I'll show you something," Prince said. He led them into the house and into Vargas's office. Vargas looked up from his desk. "Don't let us disturb you," Prince said to him. He continued into an adjoining room, which was filled with electronic equipment. "What we have here is a complete communications center. We keep in touch the way a ship at sea would." He pointed to a bank of radio equipment, then to another bank being installed by a technician. "But soon we'll have our own international telephone system. Down near the factory a couple of dish antennas are being installed that will keep us in touch with the world by satellite — we'll also be able to receive whatever television we wish. I'd hoped to have it all up and running in time for this convocation, but things got a little behind."

Prince walked over to a computer terminal and began explaining his computer installation.

But Cat was distracted. At Prince's elbow was a Cat One printer, and next to it was the operator's manual. It was lying face-down on a desk, and on the back of the manual was Cat's photograph, taken in his office after the incident on the yacht, after the beard had been shaven, the weight lost. It was an awfully good likeness, Cat thought. His name was printed boldly under the photograph.

"We are as well set up as any large corporation," Prince was saying. "Our normal operations are conducted from our Cali headquarters, but I have sufficient facilities here for issuing instructions."

Cat made a show of walking around the room, examining the installation. He finished at Prince's elbow and picked up the Cat One manual, flipping idly through it. "Do you have an office here?" he asked.

"I have a comfortable suite of rooms upstairs; my office is there," Prince replied. He did not offer to show it to them.

Cat closed the printer manual and placed it on a bookshelf over the printer, out of Prince's view.

"Well, I have some work to do," Prince said. "You may order lunch in your cottage, and you've been given your schedule of seminars, right?"

"Right," Cat replied.

They followed Prince back into the main entrance hall, where he excused himself and went upstairs. Jinx followed him like a puppy.

Cat took Meg's hand and led her outside. "Well? Did you find out anything?"

"She lives with Prince in his suite," Meg said. They moved down the path toward their cottage. "The other girls have a sort of dormitory at the back of the main house."

"That's bad. She's going to be tough to get at if she's with him all the time." Still, it made him want to get at her all the more, and get at Prince, too. "Did you find out anything else?"

"She says she was born and raised in Cartagena, but the accent is wrong. She could be American."

"This is insane. That girl is Jinx, I promise you."

"She said something else."

"What?"

"I asked her how she met the Anaconda."

"And?"

"She said, 'I've always known Stan.' "

"Jesus, he's done something to her, drugged her or something."

"She doesn't play tennis like somebody who's drugged, Cat. The girl seems perfectly normal to me — at least as perfectly normal as anybody can be in a place like this. She seems quite content to be with old Stan."

"He's done something to her," Cat said, doggedly. "I've got to find a way to get her out of here."

Meg stopped and turned to him. "Cat, listen to me for a moment."

He stopped. "Okay."

"Maybe you're not crazy; maybe that girl is your daughter."

"Well, thanks for that, anyway."

Meg went on. "But she's not your daughter anymore — that has to be clear to you."

"What are you talking about? You mean that because she's not her old self I should just forget about her?"

"No, that's not what I mean. I know you're going to try to get her out of here."

"You're right about that."

"But you have to realize something."

"What?" he demanded.

"She's not going to want to go."

30

Cat sat numbly through an afternoon of instruction in how to set up a cocaine sales network in his franchised area. He had been in this place for nearly twenty-four hours, and he was getting nowhere. Granted, he knew where Jinx lived, but it had turned out to be possibly the most secure area of the entire camp — in fact, almost the only secure area. Everything else, except the factory, was easy enough to see, and no one questioned where he went. Prince and his people seemed to think themselves invulnerable because of their remote location, and since they had screened everyone who was here, they were arrogant enough not to be suspicious of anyone.

The meeting broke up, and he went back to the cottage. Meg was not there, still in a meeting of her own. The temperature outside was amazing, and the humidity worse. Cat got into a swimsuit and headed for the pool. There were half a dozen men scattered at tables, sipping drinks, and Dell was among them. It was the first time Cat had seen him since the evening before. Cat swam a couple of laps, then sat on the edge of the pool and waited. Soon, Dell came over and sat beside him.

"I tried to talk to Jinx last night," he said. "She pretended not to recognize me, to not even understand me."

"I know, I'm having the same problem," Cat replied. "I don't know if she's pretending, or what."

"What do you mean?"

"She may be off her head. It may be that what she has been through has been so horrible that she's just blocked it out."

Dell clenched his jaw and said nothing for a moment. "Were you serious last night?" he asked finally. "About the raid and getting Jinx out?"

"Yes, perfectly."

"All right, I'll stay out of your way."

"What about your million bucks?" Cat asked.

"I've been thinking about that. I think I can get it back when the raid starts. Maybe even more."

"Dell, you're crazy to try that. It's going to be tough enough just keeping from getting shot by the troops without trying something stupid."

"I don't need you to tell me what's stupid," Dell said through clenched teeth. "I can take care of myself."

"Whatever you say," Cat replied. He had to try not to have any more confrontations with Dell. "Just remember to hide someplace until the shooting is over, then give yourself up. Tell them who you are and that you were here to help me. If I don't make it out of the raid, ask for a guy named Barry Hedger. He's an important person in the Bogotá embassy."

"When is it going to happen?"

"I'm not sure, but if you hear helicopters, it's on."

"Right." Dell made to get up, but Cat held him back.

"Listen, when this is over, if we get out of here alive, I want us to talk, to try and find some middle ground between us."

For a moment Dell looked uncertain, vulnerable. Then he got up and walked away.

Cat went back to the cottage and found Meg stretched out on a bed fanning herself.

"What's up?" she asked.

He sat down on the bed beside her. "We're getting nowhere fast here," he said.

She sat up on an elbow. "What do you mean? I thought we were doing okay. We've found Jinx, we know where she lives, and I've got some great videotape," she said, patting her big handbag containing the miniature camera, which rested on the bed beside her. "I got all of that conversation with Prince during our tennis breakfast this morning. It's going to be incredible on the air. All I want now is some shots of the helicopters coming in."

"Sorry, I didn't mean we had got nowhere; I meant there was nowhere else to go. We're not going to be able to spirit Jinx out of Prince's quarters. I think we're going to have to take more direct action."

"What do you mean?"

"I mean it's time to switch on that radio and call the troops in. Tommorrow at dawn, I'll go jogging. I'll run down to where they're building the airstrip and set up the radio there. Then we have to position ourselves near the main house. When we hear the first chopper, we run upstairs to Prince's quarters and lock ourselves in with Prince and Jinx until the shooting is over. What do you think?"

"His quarters will be guarded."

"We'll shoot our way in, if necessary, but I'm depending on you to talk us in."

"Well," she said, "I guess I'd have a pretty good view of things from Prince's windows, wouldn't I?"

He grinned. "I guess you would." He leaned over and kissed her. She pulled him down onto the bed and nestled her head on his shoulder. Soon, she was asleep. It was just as well, he thought. He had been about to tell her about the other thing he was going to do tonight, but perhaps it was better if she didn't know.

Cat dressed for dinner, and while Meg was in the bathroom, he removed the false bottom from the canvas-and-leather grip and took out the H&K automatic pistol. He slipped into the shoulder holster, screwed the silencer into the barrel, and tried to fit the gun into the holster. It wouldn't fit with the silencer on. He unscrewed the silencer and put it into his trousers pocket, then slipped the pistol into the holster.

There were no place cards at dinner that evening. Cat and Meg took seats near the door, at the opposite end of the table from Prince and Jinx. The dinner was somewhat more convivial than the evening before. People were getting to know each other. Cat found himself sitting next to the Englishman he had seen wearing the heavy suit the evening before. He was more comfortably dressed now.

The Englishman introduced himself. "Where are you from, old boy?" he drawled.

"Southeastern United States," Cat replied.

"I'm a Londoner, myself," he said. He had had a lot to drink. "I live in Berkshire at the moment, but I expect I'll be taking a place in town again before long." He winked broadly. "Once the stuff starts to come in, you know. Property's awfully good value in London these days. I'm thinking of Eaton Square."

"Nice neighborhood," Cat said.

"The bloody Duke of Westminster owns the whole fucking thing, you know."

"I'd heard."

"We were in the army together."

"Were you?"

"Yes, indeed. Not what you'd call close, but still, I expect he'd be glad to have me in Eaton Square. The old regiment, and all that."

"It helps to have connections, I guess."

The Englishman winked again. "You had one of these girls yet?"

"No."

"Bloody marvelous they are. Had one last night, an American."

Cat stiffened.

"The Anaconda must treat them bloody well. She was damned enthusiastic."

Cat said nothing.

"I understand there's a little show at the disco tonight. You going?"

"I hadn't thought about it."

"Oh, you must, old fellow. Everyone'll be there. Bloody good show, they say." He winked again, but then his eyes did something odd.

Cat turned and followed his gaze. The dining-room doors had opened, and an Indian dressed in a plain khaki uniform, carrying an automatic weapon, stood in the doorway. There was a girl with him. He was holding her by the hair.

"Good God!" the Englishman spat. "She's mine! I mean, the one I had last night!"

The girl was trembling violently and crying. There was a dust of white powder on her nose and upper lip. The room had gone very quiet.

From the other end of the room, Cat heard a chair scrape on the floor and footsteps walking the length of the table. Still, he could not take his eyes off the terrified girl. Prince walked into his vision, toward the girl. He moved calmly, deliberately. He approached the girl and stopped. The soldier said something Cat couldn't catch. Prince reached down to the holster on the soldier's belt, unsnapped it, and removed a .38-caliber pistol from it. The soldier yanked backward on the girl's hair, and when she began to cry out, Prince put the barrel of the pistol into her mouth and fired. A long spray of blood and gore spurted from the back of her head, and she went limp. Prince handed the pistol to the guard, then turned to face his audience.

"I'm terribly sorry to have interrupted your dinner, ladies and gentlemen, but my rule against the use of drugs has been violated, and it was necessary for me to take steps. Please go on with your meal." He motioned to a waiter, who produced a napkin and began mopping up the blood. The guard dragged the girl from the room by her hair. Prince returned to his seat.

Cat sat, frozen. Meg picked up a glass of water and sipped it. Her face was pale. The Englishman made an odd noise, then got up and stumbled from the room, a napkin pressed to his mouth. A murmur rose from the crowd again, this time subdued. Cat looked down the table to where Jinx was. She sat, staring vacantly ahead, her lower lip trembling.

Cat wished to God he did not have to wait until morning to confront the Anaconda. If he had had any doubts before about what he would do to him, he had none now.

31

They stopped at a fork in the path. "How are you feeling?" Cat asked.

"Ill," Meg replied. "You know, I've seen people killed before. I've even seen people executed. In the Philippines I saw half a dozen men made to kneel, then shot in the back of the head by Communist guerrillas. But I've never seen anything quite so deliberately . . . casual. I think Prince is insane — and I need hardly point out — very dangerous."

Cat nodded. "That could as easily have been Jinx."

"It will be, eventually, if you don't get her out of here."

"I know. I'm going to do it tomorrow. Right now, though, I think you should go back to the cottage and get some rest. I'm not ready for bed yet."

"Be careful," she said, kissing him lightly. She walked on toward the cottage.

Cat stood and watched her go for a moment, then he turned and walked toward the discotheque, a building tucked away behind some trees a hundred yards from the main house. He struggled to maintain his composure. The anger that he had so carefully kept under control since the act of piracy on the yacht now threatened to overwhelm him, and the wanton murder of the girl had increased the pressure. Some part of him had known all along that he would do what he was going to do this evening, but still the realization surprised him.

He opened the door to the building, and a wall of noise struck him. Perhaps it was music, he couldn't tell, but the volume was staggering. He put his hands to his ears and squinted. There was some sort of light show in progress, and it seemed to be coordinated with the music, but no one was dancing. People, mostly men, stood on tiers descending to the dance floor, watching something. Cat walked to the rear of the crowd and stood on tiptoes to see.

On a mat spread on the dance floor, two young Indian men, prodigiously built, were dancing with a very beautiful blonde girl. As Cat watched, one of the men stretched out on the floor, and the girl knelt between his legs. She bent over him and took his penis into her mouth, leaving her hips raised. The other man rubbed his huge, tumescent organ with a lubricant, then entered her from behind. The three of them moved, locked in their bizarre sexual dance.

Cat looked away, nearly ill. She was no older than Jinx, and she seemed both drugged and frightened. Some of the crowd were shouting encouragement over the hideous music.

Cat forced himself to look around the audience carefully, and he found who he was looking for, standing at the edge of the crowd, near the front. The show seemed to have just started, and Cat had the feeling it would go on for some time. He wanted to have a look around the place. He edged past the crowd, past a column into a dimly lit hallway, closed off by a door at the end. He walked quickly down the hall, passed a ladies' room, then came to a men's room. Inside, there were four urinals and two stalls. Along the opposite wall was a counter with four sinks. It was expensively decorated and as dimly lit as the hallway. Cat left the men's room and stepped back into the hall. At the end, to his left, was a pair of swinging doors leading to a kitchen. A couple of staff members in white uniforms were working there.

He opened the door at the end of the hall, looked into the darkened room, and found a light switch. It was a large pantry, well stocked with canned food and staples. He stepped into the room. Against the opposite wall, next to sacks of potatoes and onions, were two identical barrels, one newly opened and filled with dried beans, the other with only an inch or two of beans at the bottom. He switched off the light, left the pantry, and returned to the main room of the disco.

The show was continuing, but the participants had changed. Now there were two girls, both Anglo-looking, and one enormously built young Latino. The crowd had lost none of its interest. Cat looked and found his man standing as before, but now looking bored. Suddenly, he turned and picked his way through the cheering crowd, toward the hallway. Cat moved sideways to the column and watched as he walked toward the men's room. Cat glanced at the crowd again to make sure no one else had followed, but they were rapt. This is too lucky, Cat thought. Something has to go wrong. He found he was breathing rapidly.

He walked quickly down the hall toward the men's room, glancing over his shoulder, and went in. Denny was standing at a urinal. Cat went to a sink and began to wash his hands. The music was still loud, even in here. Trembling, he splashed some water on his face. This moment that he had been afraid to hope for had come.

"Quite a show, huh?" Denny said loudly.

Cat jumped. He hadn't expected him to speak. "Yeah."

Denny zipped up his trousers and came to the sink next to Cat. He turned on the water and began to wash his hands. "Yeah, I picked those girls out myself." He sounded drunk. "Every one of them. The Anaconda doesn't like Latino girls, you know. Just Anglos, and they've gotta be classy-looking and young. I keep him supplied." He bent low over the sink, splashed some water on his face, and rubbed vigorously.

Cat stepped back from the sink, turned toward Denny, and, with all the force he could muster, lifted a foot and drove his heel into the base of the younger man's spine. Denny's scream was partly muffled by his mouth hitting the faucet over the sink, but with the din in the disco, no one would ever have heard him. He collapsed onto his back, still screaming, spitting blood and teeth.

Cat pulled the H&K automatic from its

shoulder holster.

Denny's face had shaped itself into a mask of disbelief. He suddenly stopped screaming. "You motherfucker!" he spat at his tormentor. "I can't feel nothing in . . . shit, I can't move my legs!"

Cat made a show of removing the clip from the pistol, inspecting it, then shoving it back into the handle. "That's because you're a paraplegic now."

"Who the hell are you?" Denny gabbled. "Why are you doing this to me?"

Cat took the silencer from his pocket and began screwing it into the pistol's barrel. "You've got a short memory, Denny," he said. "We met a few months ago — back when I owned a little yacht called *Catbird,* back when I had a wife and a daughter. I gave you a lift to Panama, remember? Of course we never made it . . ."

Denny's face collapsed into a paradigm of fear, and he began trying to pull himself across the floor with his hands, dragging his useless legs behind him.

Cat grabbed him by the collar, dragged him back, and propped him up in a corner. "Don't leave me, Denny. You left me last time, when you thought you'd killed me with my own shotgun, after you'd murdered my wife and that girl. Who was she, anyway?

Why did you kill her and leave her there?"

Denny stared at him speechlessly.

Cat brought the silencer sharply aross the bridge of his nose, breaking it. Blood spurted over Denny's shirt. "Tell me about it, or I'll keep hurting you," Cat said.

"She was Pedro's old lady," Denny blubbered, now incredibly anxious to please. "He was sick of her, and he thought it seemed like a good time to unload her. She'd been threatening to go to the cops about the coke he'd been dealing."

"Well, that was real clear thinking, wasn't it? Just blow her head half off, and leave her to sink with me, my wife, and *Catbird*." Cat grabbed him by the hair and banged his head against the wall. "What did you do to Jinx? Why won't she speak anything but Spanish?"

Denny cried out and grabbed his head with both hands. "I didn't do anything to her, I swear to God. I didn't even screw her! The Anaconda wanted 'em fresh! But she wouldn't talk at all, wouldn't even answer to her name. Me and Pedro got her to Cartagena, and she was just curled up like a baby in the back of the boat all the way. She refused to speak for weeks. The Anaconda had this woman looking after her all the time; she just kept talking to her in

Spanish. And finally, when she started to come around, she wouldn't speak anything but Spanish. I swear to God, I didn't do nothing to her!"

"No," Cat said, pointing the pistol at Denny, "nothing but murder her parents and leave them on a sinking boat, and sell her to a sadistic maniac who —" Cat stopped himself from thinking what Prince could have done to Jinx that made her want to separate herself from her identity, to the point where she refused even to speak her own language. "You slimy little bastard," Cat said quietly to Denny. He worked the action of the pistol, pumping a round into the chamber.

"Oh, Jesus," Denny whimpered, "please don't . . . oh, Jesus."

"It's a little late for you and Jesus, Denny," Cat said quietly. "Tonight, you sleep in hell." Cat waited a moment for that to sink into Denny's brain, then he followed it with a single shot to the forehead. The pistol made a noise like a hand slapping the side of a leather suitcase. Denny made a little sighing sound, and his head slumped to the right. Cat shot him again in the temple.

Cat stared at the corpse for just a moment, then walked quickly to the door and looked up and down the hallway. The merriment was continuing in the disco, and the hall was empty. Cat went back and grabbed Denny's body by a wrist, pulled it away from the wall, and got it up and slung onto his hip. Walking in a half-crouch, he peered into the hallway, then carried the body quickly to the pantry. Inside, he got the light on, then carried Denny to the nearly empty bean barrel. With some effort, he got the body into the barrel, feet first, and forced it into something like the fetal position. Then he rolled the barrel out a few feet, rolled the full barrel into its place, then rolled Denny's barrel to where the full barrel had been. He took a large scoop from the shelf above the barrels and began shoveling dried beans from the full barrel into the barrel containing the corpse. Soon, Denny's barrel was full to the brim, and the corpse had disappeared under the beans.

Cat switched off the light and stepped back into the hallway. Nothing had changed. He went back to the men's room, took some paper towels, and wiped the blood from the tiled wall. Then he rolled a waste container from under the sink and placed it on the spot where the carpet was bloody.

He stood back and surveyed the scene. With a little luck, nobody would know for a while that a man had been murdered here.

Not, at least, until somebody ate a lot more beans. Cat walked past the cheering crowd and left the building, mopping the sweat from his face and neck. He loosened his collar and started toward the cottage. He had just killed a man, and he wondered why he didn't feel terrible about it. He didn't feel elated; he hadn't actually enjoyed shooting Denny, but still he had the feeling of satisfaction that comes when something important has been accomplished.

He didn't feel finished, though. There was another task to complete: Prince. Before dawn that morning, he would turn on Barry Hedger's marvelous little radio, and an hour or two later the skies would rain helicopters and troops. By that time, he would be barricaded into Prince's apartment with Jinx, Meg, and Dell. By that time, Prince would be dead. Cat wondered if he could find a slower way to accomplish that than he had with Denny.

He reached the cottage and went inside. To his surprise, Meg was not asleep; she was sitting in a chair in the living room, and every light in the place was on. She looked very odd. "What's wrong?" he asked.

"When I came home, the place had been ransacked," she said. "It doesn't look it, but it has been very carefully ransacked."

Cat looked around the room. It seemed perfectly normal to him. "Was anything taken?" he asked. "Did they take your camera or tapes?"

Meg shook her head. "I think I must have surprised him. The bedroom window was open. Only two things are missing, as far as I can tell."

"What two things?"

"Well, he found the false bottom in your bag; Bluey's pistol is gone."

"What else?"

Meg sighed. "Barry Hedger's radio," she said.

32

"The question is, who took it?" Meg said.

"It doesn't much matter who took it," Cat replied. "Without it, we're fucked. There's no way to call in the raid."

"Sure, that's plain enough, but it matters a hell of a lot who took it. I mean, if it was just a simple burglary, that's one thing. If Prince had the cottage searched, that's quite another."

She had a point. "You're right. If Prince finds out what that radio is, we're dead. We've got to report it stolen."

"Isn't that just going to attract a lot of attention?"

"Sure, but if we report it, and if it was a burglary, then we have some chance of getting it back without Prince's finding out what it is. On the other hand, if Prince had the place searched, then it can't hurt to report it, since he already knows. It might look bad if we didn't. There's always the chance that he's got it and doesn't know what it is."

"Okay," Meg said, "we report it and see what happens. Anyway, I think this is a straight burglary; one of the staff, maybe."

"I hope you're right, but even if it is, unless we can get the radio back —"

"It's not all that bad," Meg interrupted. "I mean, we don't *have* to get Jinx out of here *today.* We can just wait until the conference ends, fly out of here in their helicopter, and report everything when we get back. We can give Hedger and his people the whole layout here, and they can take particular care about Jinx's safety when they come in."

"I wish it were as easy as that," Cat said. "It might have been once, but not anymore."

Meg turned to face him. "Cat, what are you telling me? What did you do tonight?"

"I killed Denny. I followed him to the discotheque men's room, then shot him and hid his body in a pantry. They might not find him immediately, but we've got another five days to go on Prince's program, and they're bound to find him before then. He's bound to be missed."

"But even if they do find him, they have no way of knowing it was you." She paused. "Do they?"

"Not unless somebody noticed that we

431

both went to the men's room. I don't think anyone did — they were all distracted at the moment — but I can't be absolutely sure. Even if they can't connect me with the killing, when they find the body, things are going to get a lot tougher around here. Security has been pretty lax, but it'll get real tight. Even if we last the five days, Prince could leave first with Jinx, and we'd be right back where we started."

"So what's your plan?" Meg asked. She leaned forward. "You do have a plan, don't you?"

"No," Cat replied, "but I have an idea. I wish it were a better one. Tomorrow morning, early, I want you to go and find Prince — he'll probably be on the tennis courts — and make a tennis date with him the following morning at eight — no, at seven, if he'll sit still for it." He got up and started to change clothes. "Make sure it's mixed doubles with Jinx. And don't tell him about the burglary. Let me do it."

"Okay, I can handle that. What's the rest of your idea? Mixed doubles is not going to get us out of here."

"I'll tell you when I've figured it out."
"Swell."

At seven the next morning Cat jogged eas-

432

ily up the path past the main house, then turned for the airstrip. He hoped nobody would be there this early in the morning. All the way, he tried to remember exactly a conversation he'd had with his flying instructor a few months back. The man had been cautioning him never to hand-spin a propeller unless he was prepared for the engine to fire, whether the switch was on or not. "You could have a hot magneto," the man had said. "In fact," he had continued, "that's the way airplanes get stolen — the thief just bypasses the ignition system and hot-wires the engine directly to a mag." Cat wasn't sure he could hot-wire an airplane, but there was one sitting down there in a jungle clearing that might fly them out of this place, if he could hot-wire it.

The path turned and he came into the clearing. His heart sank. The pilot who had flown them in from Leticia was working on the helicopter, apparently changing the oil. Cat waved to him and kept running. He began to run around the clearing, then, at the point where the workers were still felling trees, he began to run directly toward where the helicopter and the Maule airplane were parked, counting his steps. He drew up next to the helicopter, multiplying in his head. The clearing was longer than he had thought, about two hundred yards.

"Morning, Hank," he said to the pilot, panting.

"Hi, how you doing?"

"I'm wearing myself out, I think," Cat laughed. "I'm not in as good shape as I thought."

"Never could see it, running," the pilot said, continuing to work.

"You're a smart guy," Cat replied. "It's never too late not to start." He took a deep breath. "You fly the Maule, too?"

The pilot nodded. "Yeah."

"Mind if I have a look at her?"

The pilot looked suspicious. "What for?"

"I fly a Cessna 182 RG. I've never flown a Maule, but I saw one demonstrated once. Pretty impressive. I've got some farmland back home that wouldn't work for a proper strip, but I might be able to get a Maule into it and out."

The pilot stood up and wiped his hands on a rag. "You don't need much room for a Maule," he said. "Come on." He beckoned Cat toward the airplane.

Together, they pulled back the camouflage netting to allow access to the cockpit. The man opened the door and waved Cat into the pilot's seat. "It'd be a nice airplane by any standard," he said, "even if it didn't do short-takeoff and landing stuff. It's got the same Lycoming two hundred and thirty-five horsepower engine as your 182 RG, but the airplane weighs about five hundred pounds less than yours."

"Variable pitch propeller," Cat said, fingering a knob. He pointed at a handle next to his seat that looked like an emergency brake lever on an old car. "What's this?"

"Manually operated flaps," the pilot said. "They work faster than electric ones. Try it."

Cat pulled on the handle and immediately, the flaps snapped down.

"That's twenty degrees," the pilot said. "There are two more notches — forty and fifty degrees."

Cat pulled the handle again, and the flaps dropped more. "How about a demonstration?" he asked.

The pilot laughed and shook his head. "No sireee, not until they clear at least another fifty feet of strip." He pointed to the other end of the clearing. "Those trees are sixty, seventy feet high. I got the thing in here by the seat of my pants — scared the living shit out of me — but I'm not flying it out until I've got some room for error."

"I don't blame you," Cat said. "Those

trees look pretty daunting." They did, too. "Talk me through the procedure. I'd like to have an idea how it works."

"Well," the pilot said, "you push the button on the flap control and hold it in so it doesn't grab a notch; you put in twenty degrees of flaps, and you sit there with the brakes on and rev the thing up to full power. Then, when you think the engine is going to leave without you, you let go the brakes. Ever flown a tail dragger?"

"No."

"It's not like the tricycle gear on your plane. Almost as soon as you're rolling you give 'er some forward stick to get the tail up. You watch your airspeed, and at forty knots you slam in all fifty degrees of flaps, then yank back on the yoke. She'll spring right off the ground and pick up airspeed real fast, go up to fifty, sixty knots all at once. You'll think you're on a ride at Disneyland. Then, at about a hundred feet, when you've cleared any obstacle, you start easing off the flaps until you're flying it just like a normal airplane."

"Sounds pretty straightforward," Cat said.

"Don't you believe it, buddy," the pilot snorted. "The manufacturers say you ought to have seventy-five or a hundred hours in the airplane before you try any radically short-field takeoffs. I've got about a hundred and ten right now, and it still scares the shit out of me."

Cat reached forward and flipped on the master switch. There was a whine as the gyros behind the instrument panel started to spin.

"Hey, don't do that!" the pilot said.

"Sorry," Cat said. He flipped off the switches, but not before he had glanced at the fuel gauges. "What's her range?" he asked.

" 'Bout four hundred and fifty miles," the pilot said. "Come on, we'd better get her covered up again. The Anaconda doesn't want to get spotted from the air."

Cat got down from the airplane and helped the pilot get the netting over it again. "Well thanks for the tour," he said. "I'd better get myself some breakfast. You'd better, too," he said to the pilot. "You down here every day this early?"

"Well if I've got something to do on the aircraft, I like to get it done before the heat gets up."

"I don't blame you," Cat said. "I can feel it coming on now." He gave a little wave and started jogging up the trail toward the main house. The takeoff sounded pretty hairy, but he was encouraged by one thing.

In the map pocket at his feet had been a clipboard with a log sheet attached. And stuck under the clip had been the ignition key. He would not have to hot-wire the airplane.

But that was a moot point. The fuel gauges had read less than a quarter full. He would have to think of something else.

33

Cat stood in Vargas's office. There was no chair in which to sit, so he stood like a recruit before his commander.

"Our cottage has been burgled," he said.

Vargas stood up. *"What?"*

Cat was relieved that Vargas looked astonished, and he seized the advantage. "I thought I would give you the opportunity to explain before I brought the matter to the attention of Mr. Prince."

"Who?"

"The Anaconda."

Vargas was squirming now, and Cat was rather enjoying it. "Mr. Ellis, it will not be necessary for you to speak with the Anaconda about this. Please tell me what was taken from your cottage."

"Only a rather expensive Sony portable radio and a pistol, a Smith & Wesson .357 magnum. I am not terribly concerned about the radio, but I would like to have the pistol returned."

"Mr. Ellis," Vargas said fervently, "I will conduct an investigation immediately. You may be sure your property will be returned to you."

Cat was about to thank him when an Indian in a servant's uniform rushed into the room and began babbling in Spanish, gesticulating wildly. Vargas was even more upset by this news than he had been by Cat's report.

"Mr. Ellis, if you will excuse me, I will begin my investigation."

"What's wrong?" Cat asked, nodding at the servant.

"There has been a murder," Vargas said.

Cat felt a stab of panic and hoped his expression passed for surprise. "Oh? Who?"

"One of the staff."

"Do you think this might be in some way connected with the burglary of our cottage?"

"I have not had time to form an opinion about that," Vargas said. "Please excuse me now. I have much to do."

Cat left him issuing orders to the servant. As he left the room he glanced into the adjacent communications center. All that equipment, he thought, and no way to use it. He didn't suppose the Anaconda would allow him to make a telephone call.

He went back to the cottage to shower and change. Meg was dressing.

"So, are we going to take our chances in the jungle?" she asked.

"I hope we won't have to. With a few breaks we may be able to fly out of here."

"I would prefer that to walking, if it is at all possible to arrange it."

"I reported the burglary to Vargas. He was shocked. I think that if Prince had wanted the place searched and robbed, he would have told Vargas to arrange it, and Vargas seemed genuinely surprised. I don't think he's that good an actor."

"Oh, yeah?" Meg came back. "I seem to remember that he persuaded you that he was a cop back in Bogotá."

"I don't think he was acting. I think he is a cop, a bent one. I wish he weren't."

"Why do you care?"

"Because they've already found Denny's body, and I'd just as soon not have an experienced policeman in charge of the investigation."

"I see your point," Meg said. "Still, if we're getting out of here tomorrow morning, he doesn't have much time to play policeman."

"Maybe not, but then he's not constrained

by police practice, is he? He's promised that the radio and the pistol will be returned. I wouldn't be surprised if he simply started beating up the staff until somebody confesses. This place is a sort of medieval barony, after all. What does it matter to Vargas and Prince if a few serfs get roughed up?"

Meg sighed. "You're depressing me."

Cat shook his head. "I'm sorry. I don't know why I have to add my speculation to the problems we already have. What we have to do is to get through today and tonight as normally as possible."

"Then what? You still haven't told me your plan."

"Well, the pilot who brought us here likes to work on his helicopter early in the morning. I had another idea, about the little Maule airplane, but there's not enough fuel in it, and I'd much rather old Hank flew us out of here in the chopper. How does that sound?"

"Sounds good to me."

"Did you arrange our tennis date?"

"Not yet; I thought it was too early."

"If we can get Prince and Jinx out to the courts early tomorrow morning, maybe we can force him down to the helicopter."

"Prince, too?"

"You, Jinx, Dell, and me. I'd thought of leaving Prince with a bullet in his head."

"Can you do that?"

"I did it to Denny last night. I don't think I'll have any trouble pulling the trigger on Prince." He shot her a sardonic grin. "It's a dirty job, but somebody's got to do it."

Cat arrived at his scheduled meeting in time to watch Prince approach the podium.

"Good morning, gentlemen," the Anaconda said. "I believe you have all been well instructed in the pricing structure of our product, and you have seen how, with our system of direct supply, both your profits and mine will be enhanced, since we have no middleman with whom to share. This morning we are going to talk about what to do with those profits. After you have reinvested in more product and in widening your distribution, you will still be left with considerable cash reserves. Today we have with us Mr. Wiener and Mr. Simpson, who are representatives, respectively, of Swiss and Cayman Island banking firms. They will be talking to you about various deposit and investment arrangements in Europe and South America, and when they are finished you will have an opportunity to open accounts with them, if you have not yourselves already made such arrangements. Mr. Wiener?" He waved a short, bald man in a three-piece suit onto the platform.

As Wiener approached the podium, Cat felt a tap on his shoulder and turned to find Vargas standing behind him.

"Will you come with me, please?" Vargas said.

Cat got up and followed the man outside, through the courtyard of the house, then back into the foyer and upstairs. Vargas opened a door and waited for Cat to precede him. Cat walked into a large, handsomely furnished sitting room and was surprised to find Prince waiting for him, sitting on one of a pair of facing sofas. Apparently, he had known a shorter route to the suite. Several yards behind Prince, sitting at an easel, painting in watercolors, was Jinx. Her attention was focused outside the window.

"Please sit down, Bob," the Anaconda said. His manner was courteous, but cool.

Cat sat down on the sofa facing Prince, and Vargas sat next to him. They were placed so that Cat could not look at both of them at the same time.

"What do you think of our conference so far?" Prince asked.

"I'm very impressed," Cat said. "You seem to have left nothing to chance."

Prince smiled slightly. "It is my way to leave nothing to chance," he said. "Isn't that right, Mr. Vargas?"

"That is most certainly correct," Vargas replied.

"Now," Prince said, "could you please tell me how you spent last evening?"

"I had dinner in the dining room, then I went to the discotheque."

"Alone?"

"Yes, Miss Garcia was tired and wanted to retire early."

"And what did you do at the discotheque?"

"I watched the . . . performance."

"Please tell me exactly what you did from the time you entered the discotheque until the time you returned to your cottage."

Cat took a deep breath. "Well, when I arrived, the show had already started. I stood and watched."

"Did you see Denny?"

"Who?"

"Denny, my, ah . . . associate."

"I don't believe I've had the pleasure," Cat replied.

"Of course not," Prince said, almost to himself.

"Did you do anything else while you were at the discotheque?"

Cat shrugged. It seemed best to stick as close to the truth as possible. "I went to the men's room."

"For how long?"

"A couple of minutes, I guess. As long as it took."

"Was anyone else in the men's room?"

"No . . . wait, a man came in as I was leaving."

"Describe him, please."

"Well, I didn't pay him much attention. I just brushed past him on the way out."

"Whatever you can remember."

"Youngish, shorter than I, sandy hair, moderately long. I'm afraid that's the best I can do."

"Did you speak to him, or he to you?"

"No."

"What did you do when you left the men's room?"

"I went back and watched the performance."

"At what point in the show was this?"

"Well, there were two men and a woman at first, then, shortly after I came back, it changed to two women and one man."

"Did you speak to anyone else while you were there?"

"No."

"Did you stand next to anyone you knew?"

"It was pretty dark, and there were flashing lights. Anyway, my attention was on the performance."

Prince smiled. "Yes, I can understand that. What did you do when the performance was over?"

"I didn't stay that long. The show made me want to return to my cottage." He managed a little smile. "I left shortly after the second group started."

"Do you possess a 9-millimeter automatic pistol?" Prince asked.

"I had a .357 magnum until last night."

Prince frowned. "Of course, the burglary at your cottage last night. What was taken?"

"Only the pistol and a portable radio."

"Were there other valuables present?"

"I suppose so. I thought perhaps the thief might have been interrupted when Miss Garcia returned to the cottage."

Prince turned to Vargas. "What steps have you taken?"

"The staff are being questioned," Vargas said, lamely.

Prince turned back to Cat. "I must apologize," he said, "but of course everyone who was at the discotheque has to be questioned."

Cat shrugged. "Of course. I would like to

have the pistol back if it's recovered," he said.

"Not the radio?"

"I can buy a radio anywhere," Cat responded, "but I don't like being in this country without a pistol."

"Of course." Prince turned, put his feet on the couch, and placed a pillow at his back. "I have something else to ask you," he said to Cat, "and I want a full and complete response."

"What would you like to know?" Cat asked.

"Why do you think that my name is Prince?"

Cat cocked his head. "I'm sorry, isn't that your name?" he asked, playing for time. He had blown it somewhere along the way, but where? Then he remembered. He had said it to Vargas when he reported the burglary.

"Where did you hear this?" Prince demanded.

"At the reception on the first night," Cat said. "Perhaps I misunderstood."

"From whom?"

Cat wrinkled his brow. "From nobody in particular — I mean, it didn't come from anyone I met. As I remember, I was standing, waiting for a drink at the bar, and someone behind me was talking. Someone said, 'Anaconda? Doesn't the man have a name?' And someone else said, 'Yes, it's Prince.' "

"Who was this person?" Prince wanted to know.

"I'm sorry, it was no one I knew. I didn't even turn around, so I never saw his face. He seemed pretty sure of himself, though. He was quite definite."

Prince stared at Cat for a long moment without speaking. Finally, he said, "I understand you were looking at airplanes this morning."

"Yes, I went jogging, and I ended up there."

"You were asking quite specific questions about an airplane."

"Yes, the Maule. I saw one demonstrated once, and I was curious to know the technique."

"You are a pilot?"

"Yes, a very new one. I only got my license recently. I was hoping your man would give me a demonstration, but he said he only barely made it into the clearing and that it wouldn't be possible to take off from there until more land had been cleared. Apparently, a short-field takeoff isn't as easy as it looks."

"So I'm told," Prince said. He stood up.

"Well, I won't keep you any longer," he said.

Cat stood. "Will you and your friend join us for some tennis again tomorrow morning?" He nodded at Jinx who was still absorbed in her painting.

"Fine, eight o'clock?" Prince replied.

"How about seven?" Cat said. "I find I wake up early in the jungle."

"Seven o'clock then," Prince said.

Cat followed Vargas to the door, then stopped and turned. "By the way, if my pistol shouldn't be recovered, do you think I might have a replacement? I've heard a lot of horror stories about the street crime in this country."

Prince walked toward him. "I think we can find you something to take away with you," he said. He looked down and brushed something off his trousers.

Something caused Cat to look at Jinx. She was no longer looking out the window, painting what she saw. She was looking directly at him. Suddenly, she did something that struck him speechless. She gave him a broad wink.

Cat followed Vargas back downstairs, breathing rapidly. Jinx was coming out of whatever prison she had built in her mind, he knew she was. He had a memory of her, a tiny thing, learning how to wink one eye and keep the other open. It had been one of their personal forms of communication ever since.

He tried to contain his exhilaration. She knew who he was, but did she understand what was going on? And if she did, could she keep her wits about her until tomorrow's tennis match? She could if she was the old Jinx, he knew. He wondered if, after all she had been through, she could ever be the old Jinx again.

34

"I'm supposed to have everything between St. Augustine and West Palm Beach." Dell smashed his fist down into the water.

"Easy," Cat said. "Don't call attention to yourself."

They were in the pool. Dell pushed off and swam a couple of fast laps, and when he stopped he was breathing hard. "In a couple of years I'd have had enough money to last me the rest of my life, anywhere in the world."

"If you'd lived long enough," Cat said. "Look, Dell, the way it's done is, you get some education, you find a kind of work you like, you get good at it. You rise in a company, or you go off on your own, the way your uncle and I did. First, you make a living. Later, if you're good enough and lucky enough, you make some money. It may sound dull, but it's very satisfying."

"It may be good enough for you, but it's

not good enough for me," Dell said. "I know you don't understand that, but it's just not fast enough. I don't want to wait until I'm your age. That's why I've got to do it. That and the fact that if I go back without at least the million I brought down here, I'll get blown away by my own partners."

"Look, Dell, I'll make up what your partners have lost. What is it, seven hundred thousand? I'll sell something — the house, if I have to."

"What about my three hundred grand? You think I didn't bust my hump for that? Risk a lot?"

Cat fought hard to keep his temper. "All right," he said finally, "I'll make that up, too. It may take some time; I can't sell company stock without Ben's agreement."

Dell whirled on him. "Listen, there's fifty million bucks in cash in that house, and I know where it is. It's in a big closet hidden behind a wall in the communications room. Straight ahead, as you walk in the door; a bookshelf pulls out. Not a vault, or anything, just a closet. I ought to be able to carry away four or five million."

"That place has got to be manned twenty-four hours a day, you know. What are you going to do about that?"

"Whatever I have to," Dell said. "I'd have

a better chance if you helped me."

"I've offered to help you, already," Cat insisted. "I've offered to get you out of here alive, for a start; I've offered to make good yours and your partners' losses. What else do you expect from me?"

"Help me get at that cash."

"No," Cat said quickly. "This is the way it's going to happen. Some time between seven and nine tomorrow morning, I force Prince down to the clearing, and I force the helicopter pilot to fly us all out of here. That's it. If you want to come, be there early, don't get seen going or arriving. Stay in the brush until we're all there." Cat hauled himself out of the pool, grabbed a towel, and walked briskly back to the cottage. He was sweating again by the time he got there, and he reveled in the cool of the air-conditioning on his skin.

Meg came out of the bedroom. "Did you find Dell?"

"Yes. He wants to try and steal some of the cash we saw the other night."

"Jesus! Is he nuts?"

"Yes, probably. I've told him the plan. We'll take him with us if he's there. It's all I can do."

"You're right, it is all you can do. I'm glad you're smart enough to know that."

"There's something else." He paused.

"Yes?"

"Well, I don't really know; it's just that Jinx winked at me when I was in Prince's suite today."

"Winked at you? What does that mean?"

"Well, it's something we used to do, since she was a little girl. It was sort of a private joke; we'd wink at each other when nobody was watching."

"You think she's coming out of it, then?"

"Maybe, and that worries me."

"Why does it worry you? Won't it be a lot easier to get her out of here if she knows who she is and what we're doing?"

"I hope so, but I don't know. I don't know what sort of mental shape she's going to be in, in the middle of all this. You said, yourself, that in her present state, she might resist coming with us."

Meg came and stood behind him and rubbed his shoulders. "Look, there's no use making yourself crazy about this. You know what you're going to do, and chances are, it'll work. Try and relax."

Cat sighed. "There's just so much that can go wrong — so many loose ends, so much I have no control over."

The telephone rang, and they both jumped. Cat answered it.

"Mr. Ellis, this is Vargas. Will you come to my office, please? We've found your burglar."

Cat hung up. "Vargas says they've found the burglar."

"Maybe you'll get the radio back."

"Christ, I hope so." He got into some clothes and walked quickly to the main house. Vargas's office was empty. He went into the communications room, where a lone man was on duty.

"You seen Vargas?"

"He was there a minute ago," the man said. "He's probably gone to the can or something."

Cat looked around the room at the equipment. The printer manual with his photograph was still on the shelf where he had put it. Then he saw something he hadn't seen before — a small radio with the name "King" on it, the same name as the radios in his Cessna. Cat pointed at the radio. "You talk with airplanes?"

"Just with the chopper you came in on, and we can only reach him a few miles out. We don't have much height on our antenna, and he always flies low."

"Who do you talk to on the high-frequency radio?" Cat asked.

"Whoever we want to," the man answered.

"We call a marine operator — which one depends on the time of day — atmospherics and all that. We give 'em an account number, and they call whatever number we want, just about anywhere in the world." He looked up at Cat. "You've got to have an approval, though, from the Anaconda or Vargas."

"Oh, I don't need to make a call," Cat said. "I just wondered how it all worked."

"Mr. Ellis?"

Cat jumped. Vargas had walked up behind him.

"I have something for you," Vargas said, walking back into his office.

Cat followed him. "You've caught the burglar?"

"Yes," Vargas replied, "a kitchen worker at the discotheque. He committed the murder, too. He has already been dealt with."

Cat didn't want to know what that meant. "Did you find my pistol?"

Vargas opened a desk drawer and placed the .357 magnum on the desk. "Yes, but I will keep it for the duration of the conference. It will be returned to you when you depart."

Cat nodded. "Okay." He turned to leave, hoping against hope.

"Oh," Vargas said.

Cat turned around. "Something else?"

Vargas placed the radio on the table. "We found this, too."

Cat smiled. "Oh, good." He picked up the radio. "Thanks a lot." He turned and left the room, feeling Vargas's eyes on his back, hoping he hadn't had the radio inspected by one of his communications specialists.

On the path back to the cottage, he made a point of not looking at the radio, but as soon as he was through the door, he went over it carefully. There was a large dent in the case. He turned the power knob. Nothing happened. It should be making static noises, but nothing happened.

"Does it work?" Meg asked.

"No. Do you have a small screwdriver, by any chance?"

"No."

Cat thought for a minute. "How about a manicure kit?"

"Sure." She went into the bedroom and came back with a small leather pouch.

Cat took one of the small tools and got the screws out of the back of the case. It was densely packed with electronic bits and pieces, most of which looked familiar.

"Can you fix it? You are some sort of engineer, aren't you?"

"That's right, but before I can fix it, I've

got to figure out what's wrong with it. So far, everything looks normal." He chose another tool, and with some difficulty, removed a circuit board to reveal another layer of electronics. "Oh, shit," he said.

"What is it?"

Cat picked up the tweezers and reached into the radio. He came out with some small pieces of material.

"What is that?"

"It's what's left of a printed circuit board. Whatever made the dent in the case smashed it into several pieces. It looks like custom work, nothing standard."

"Can you fix it?"

Cat shook his head. "If I had it in my shop, and most important, if I had a schematic of the board, maybe. Probably not even then. Certainly not here and with nothing."

"Well," Meg sighed, "at least we're no worse off than we were this morning."

"Maybe not," he said. "On the other hand . . ."

"What?"

"How did it get damaged? It looks as if someone stomped on it. Why?"

"It was probably an accident."

"I hope so. I hope nobody's had a look inside the thing. Anybody who knows anything about radios would know it's no ordinary Sony."

"Oh, come on. If Prince knew anything, he'd have been all over us by now."

"Maybe. But if he is onto us, he knows now that we can't hurt him. Maybe he's playing cat and mouse with us."

35

They sat at the long table at dinner. Cat refused wine; so did Meg. They didn't do much with the food either. Jinx was at the far end of the table, too far away for Cat to get any sort of reading on her state of mind.

"I'm scared," Meg said.

Cat laughed. "Isn't everybody?"

"I've never been in a spot quite like this," she said. "Being a journalist usually bought me protection, but I doubt it would be much help if I flashed my credentials here."

"I think you're right." Cat threw his napkin on the table. "Excuse me. I'll be back in a minute." He got up and asked a waiter for directions to the men's room, knowing quite well where it was, just across the foyer from Vargas's office. He had nothing specific in mind; he just wanted a few minutes in that communications room, and he was groping for a way to achieve that.

As he walked past Vargas's office, he could

hear the quiet whir of the Cat One printer coming from the radio room. He used the men's room, and as he was about to leave, a man in a uniform came into the men's room and went into a booth. Maybe, Cat thought, just maybe. He walked quickly across the hall into Vargas's office, then into the communications room. He wasn't sure what he would say if someone was in there. No one was. The duty man was across the foyer on the can. Cat went to the printer, switched it off, and lifted the cover. Using his ballpoint pen, he changed the settings on the dip switches, then closed the cover and switched the printer on again. Nothing happened. The printer was now useless. He started out of the office, but he heard an all too familiar sound from across the foyer — a flushing toilet. The noise disappeared as the men's-room door closed. The radioman was on his way back. He was trapped. Then he heard footsteps and the voices of two men. He had a moment.

Cat turned to the only refuge he knew about. Quickly, he followed Dell's instructions. The bookshelf, dead ahead as you walked into the room, opened. He began looking for the door handle, feeling behind the books. He heard footsteps on the marble floor again just as he found it. The shelf swung out silently, and Cat stepped inside the closet, pulling the shelf closed behind him. Standing in the dark, he heard the voices of two men as they entered the communications room.

"Oh, shit," one of them said. "The goddamned printer's down."

"You sure it's plugged in?" the other man asked.

"Of course — it was running just a minute ago. Vargas is really going to be pissed. He wanted this job done by morning, and it's a big one."

"Let me take a look at it," the other man said.

Cat heard a scraping noise as the cover was lifted.

"Jesus, that's Greek to me," the man said.

"You think there's a reset button or something? What's that, there?"

It was obvious to Cat that both men were looking into the printer. Their backs would be to the door. He felt under his arm, to be sure the pistol was still there, pushed open the door, carefully closed it behind him, and tiptoed into Vargas's office. There, he took a moment to catch his breath, then he walked back into the communications room. "Excuse me," he said. Both men turned around. "I was wondering if I could borrow a soldering iron. I've got a broken circuit board on a portable radio, and I think I can fix it."

"Sorry," the radioman said. "I haven't got one here. You'll have to see maintenance about that, and they won't be around until tomorrow morning."

"Okay, thanks anyway," Cat said, turning to go. "Got a problem there?"

"Yeah, the printer's down."

"That's a Cat One, isn't it? I used to sell them. Want me to have a look at it?"

"I'd really appreciate it," the man said.

Cat walked to the printer and removed the cover. "Have you got a small screw-driver?" he asked.

"Hang on," the radioman replied. He went and rummaged in a drawer. "How's this?" he said, holding up a screwdriver.

"Ideal," Cat said. "Just give me a minute." He wondered how the hell he could get rid of them for a few minutes.

"Listen, Tom," the radioman said to the other man, "you want to do double shifts? You do twelve to eight tonight, and I'll do tomorrow night. We'll both get more sleep."

"You think Vargas would mind?"

"What the hell? The room will be covered, and he never comes around here in the middle of the night, anyway. He's never set

464

foot in that office before nine, and you know it."

"Sure, okay. I'll relieve you at midnight. See you then." He left the room.

Cat reached down with the little screwdriver and reset the dip switches. He closed the cover. "Let's try it now," he said. He switched the machine off, then on again. It purred away, the print head moving fast, back and forth across the paper.

"Hey, that's fantastic," the radioman said. "My ass would have been in a wringer if I hadn't gotten this job done tonight."

"No problem," Cat said. "It was just a small adjustment. That rarely happens, and it'll probably never happen again."

"Listen," the man said. "I'm back on duty at eight tomorrow morning. I'll get you a soldering iron from maintenance, if you like."

"Thanks, I'd appreciate that. I'll stop in after breakfast to get it."

Cat left the communications room with even more information than he'd expected, walked through the foyer, and back to the dining room. Dessert was just being served.

"You okay?" Meg asked.

"Yeah, I'm fine, and I think I may have a shot at getting those troops in here."

"How?"

"I'll tell you later. Right now, I've got to talk to Dell."

Some of the diners were leaving the table, and Dell was among them.

"Come on, let's go," Cat said, rising. Followed by Meg, he made his way out of the room and managed to draw up alongside Dell. "All right," Cat said. "I'll help you get the money out."

"I can manage by myself," Dell said.

"Listen to me, dammit!" he whispered hoarsely. "There's one man on duty there all night, and by early in the morning, he's going to be pretty sleepy. I'm going in there at five a.m. to use the radios, and I'm going to have to disable the operator. Can you get there at that time?"

"Yeah, I can do it."

"All right, meet me in the men's room across the foyer from Vargas's office at five, and for God's sake be careful. There'll be guards out at that hour."

"Okay, you're on."

"Do you have a gun?"

"Yeah."

"Bring it. Plan on going straight from the radio room to the clearing where the helicopter is."

Dell nodded and drifted into the crowd.

36

Cat could not sleep. While Meg drew deep breaths beside him, he stared at the ceiling and gave in to memories he had fought off for months. He remembered Kate in the days when he had come home from twelve or fourteen hours of work, when she had rushed home from her own job to make his dinner and listen to him enthuse about his work. He remembered Jinx as a doll of a toddler and Dell as a silent, resentful six-year-old. He was still baffled by the contrast in the two children. Jinx had been such a joy, and Dell such a trial. Still, he wanted both of them back, and he thought that if he could only get them out of this place, there might be another chance with Dell. Surely being here had taught him what sort of people he was dealing with.

At four o'clock he got up and took a shower and shaved. He got into his tennis clothes, unable to shake the feeling that this was his last day on earth. There were so many things that could go wrong with what he was going to do today. Too much was improvised, too little certain. He made some instant coffee and drank it, sweating, in spite of the air-conditioning.

Meg came into the sitting room and startled him.

"Jumpy, huh?" she asked.

He nodded. "I may get you killed today, Meg."

"I've thought about it. I think you're doing the best you can under the circumstances."

"Under the circumstances, maybe."

She put her hand on his cheek. "Listen, I haven't told you what a great thing you've done. You started with nothing on this, and you found her."

"I'd have given up on finding Jinx in Santa Marta if it hadn't been for you. I'd have given up on everything else, too. But you made me realize that there was still something in me that could love somebody, something I thought had been wrung out of me. I do love you, you know."

She smiled. "I know. And I love you." She bent and kissed him.

"If we get out of here alive . . ." he started to say.

"Then we'll talk about it," she said. "Not much point right now. Let's concentrate on the matter at hand."

He stood up. "You're right." He took Hedger's canvas-and-leather grip and set it on the sofa, open. Then he worked the combination on the aluminum briefcase and started transferring the money into Hedger's bag.

"Jesus," she said, rolling her eyes.

He packed the money into the case, and put a towel on top of it. "Pack anything you can't bear to leave into one small bag and take it to the tennis court with you. Our date with Prince and Jinx is at seven, and I may not be able to come back here first. Will you take this bag for me, too?"

"Sure. All I really need to take of my own is my camera and tapes and my passport. The rest is expendable."

"Put some towels on top of the bag to make it look as much like a tennis bag as possible." Cat slipped the H&K automatic into the shoulder holster and put it on. He put on dark gray trousers and a blue blazer over his tennis clothes and slipped the silencer into his pocket. He took a deep breath. "Let's be at the court a little before seven."

"All right."

He didn't want to go. He kissed her and slipped out the door. He stood in the doorway for a few moments and let his eyes become accustomed to the dark. There was no moon, and he was grateful for that. Nothing was moving in the night. He stepped off the small porch. Would it be best to simply walk to the main house? Then, if he was stopped, he could plead insomnia and a walk. They might just send him back to the cottage. On the other hand, if they caught him sneaking around, he'd be up before Vargas or Prince very quickly. He decided to sneak. It seemed his best chance of making the house.

He kept off the main path and moved from tree to tree, looking as far as he could in every direction. Still nothing. Finally, he came to a place with little shelter. There were sixty or seventy yards of open ground to cover, and only low shrubs for cover. He took one more look around, then ran for it. It seemed to take forever, but he reached the side of the main house. He paused a moment to let his breathing return to normal. Then he stepped around the corner of the house to the front veranda. He nearly ran head-on into a khaki-clad guard carrying a machine gun. The man was standing, looking up at the sky, not three feet from the corner of the house. Cat ducked back around the corner, hoping he had not made a noise.

He stood, frozen, the gun in his hand, pressed against the side of the house. Then he realized the silencer had not been fitted to the barrel. He fumbled in his pocket for it, cursing his own stupidity. If he had to use the gun out here without the silencer, he'd bring the whole place down on him. He got the silencer screwed into the barrel; he heard the man yawn, then his footsteps recede. Cat peeped around the corner of the house and saw him walking down the veranda in the opposite direction. Cat waited a few seconds longer to be sure he was gone, then ran to the front door. Locked. Damn. He started back the way he had come, then stopped. There was a window in the men's room, he remembered. He went back past the front door, found the window, and tried it. Locked. He looked around once more, then with his elbow, smashed the glass. There wasn't much noise; most of the glass fell inside the house. He reached inside, unlocked the window, and stepped through. Quickly, he removed the fragments of glass from the window and put them into a wastebasket. Maybe no one would notice the empty pane. The room was dark, but the glow from his Rolex said ten to five. Dell was going to have trouble getting into the house, too. Cat eased open the men's-room door and looked around the large foyer. Empty. A light from the communications room cast a dim glow over Vargas's office. He could hear the sound of big-band jazz coming from a radio in the room. Cat slipped off his tennis shoes to keep the rubber soles from squeaking on the marble floor, then tiptoed to the front door, keeping his eyes on the door to Vargas's office. He reached the front door and started to turn the lock. As he turned his eyes back from the office door, he opened the front door an inch, then jerked back. A man was standing on the other side of the door. Too frightened to move, he stared at the shadowy figure on the veranda. The man motioned for him to open the door. Holding the pistol behind him, he did, and Dell stepped in. Cat motioned him toward the men's room.

"Christ, you scared me," Cat said when they were safely inside.

"Same here," Dell said, panting.

They stood there in the dark, composing themselves.

"What now?" Dell asked.

"I was afraid you were going to ask me that," Cat said, ruefully. "I guess we go in there and take that guy. Did you bring a gun?"

"Yeah." Dell held up a snub-nosed .38-caliber revolver.

"If there's any shooting to do, let me do it," Cat said. "I've got a silencer. You can point, but don't shoot; you'll bring the house down on us."

"Okay, who goes first?"

"I do, I think. The guy who's on duty saw me this afternoon. I fixed his printer. I'll be a familiar face." He took a deep breath. "Let's go."

Cat checked the foyer, then stepped through the door. He tiptoed across the floor toward Vargas's office. At the door he motioned for Dell to hang back, then walked into the communications room. He walked hard into the radio operator, who was coming out.

The man leapt back. "Who the hell are you?" he demanded. "What are you doing here?"

The music was coming from a big Zenith Transoceanic radio on the shelf above the other radio equipment.

"Easy," Cat said, holding the pistol behind him, "you scared me, too." He had forgotten how big the man was. "I was in here this afternoon. I fixed your printer, remember? I want to place a call to my bank in Switzerland."

The man relaxed a little but still seemed suspicious. "At five o'clock in the morning?"

"It's eleven o'clock in Switzerland," Cat said.

"You've got to have an authorization from the Anaconda or Vargas," the man said. "How the hell did you get into the house?"

"The front door was open," Cat said. "And I have the Anaconda's permission. I've got to transfer some money to his account in Cali."

"Nobody said anything to me," the man said.

"The Anaconda should have," Cat said. "And I've got to get the money wired before noon Swiss time, or it won't get to Cali today."

The man looked doubtful. "I don't know."

"Shall we wake up the Anaconda and ask him?" Cat asked.

"Jesus, no," the man replied.

"Look, you can place the call and listen in. All I have to do is give them my account number and the Cali account number and the amount, a million dollars."

"You didn't bring it with you, huh?"

"There was a misunderstanding."

The man scratched his head. "Well, okay.

Who do you want to call?" He turned toward the chair before the single side-band set.

"Credit Suisse, in Zurich. Ask the operator to get you the number. Which marine operator do you use this time of day?"

"New York," the man said, spinning a knob to set the frequency. "It'll go a lot faster if you can remember the number."

Cat took the pistol by the barrel, and swung it hard at the base of the man's skull. The man let out a grunt of pain and dropped from the chair to one knee, but he was still conscious. He made another noise, then turned and grabbed Cat's right arm, twisting. Cat, amazed that the man wasn't out, went down on one knee, too. He grabbed at the pistol with his left hand and tried to hit him again, but the man got an arm up and blocked it, then grabbed at the pistol. They were both on their knees now. It was a test of strength, and Cat was losing. Dell appeared in the door, saw what was happening. He ran up and put his pistol to the radio operator's head. The man ignored him.

"Hit him!" Cat grunted.

Dell drew back and brought his gun down on top of the man's head. He grunted again, but kept fighting. Dell put down the gun, clasped his hands together, and swung hard at the back of the man's neck. His grip on Cat slipped, then he fell forward onto his hands. Dell hit him again, and he collapsed onto the floor.

"Christ," Cat panted, "it's not like the movies, is it?"

"Let's tie him up or something before the bastard comes to."

Cat rummaged through the room, looking for something to tie him with. He opened a drawer and found a thick roll of duct tape. "This ought to do," he said.

Dell brought the man's hands behind him, and Cat bound them securely with the two-inch-wide, heavy tape. Then he bound the ankles and passed the roll twice around the man's head, taping his mouth shut and covering his eyes and ears. Dell took the roll and passed it completely around the radio operator's body, taping his hands to his back.

"I think that ought to do it," Dell said. "What do we do with him? He's going to wake up soon."

Cat went to the bookshelf and found the handle to the closet door. He opened the door, then went and helped Dell drag the man into the closet. The little room was filled with canvas bags, and they placed several on top of him. "By the time anybody starts looking for him, we'll be gone," Cat said.

"This is what I want," Dell said, opening one of the bags. "How much do you think is in here?"

"From the looks of it, I'd say four million, maybe five," Cat said. "I got two million into a large briefcase."

Dell slung the bag over his shoulder. "Okay, I'm happy," he said. "Where's Jinx?"

"Prince is bringing her to the tennis courts at seven, and Meg and I will bring her from there. You get out of here and down to where the helicopter is. I'm going to try and contact somebody on the radio."

"Can you handle it alone? Is there anything I can do?"

Cat laughed. "You know, this is the first time in a long time we've done anything together."

Dell laughed, too.

"Come on, I'll go to the door with you." He led the way out of the communications room, across the foyer to the front door. He opened it and peered out into the darkness, then turned to Dell. "Looks clear. Be careful, I saw a guard on the veranda earlier."

"Don't worry," Dell said.

Cat put his hands on the young man's

shoulders. "I will worry, until we're all out of here," he said. "The pilot should be down there by eight. I'll try to be there about then. Stay in the bush and keep a sharp eye out for us."

"Okay, Dad."

It had been a long time since Dell had called him that. Cat wanted to say more, but he pushed his son through the door and waved him off. Cat watched him disappear into the darkness, then turned and went back to the communications room. He switched off the music and picked up the microphone of the high-frequency set. The frequency had been tuned in, but the set was not on. He pushed the power button and waited impatiently for it to warm up. Soon there was a crackle of static. Cat turned down the volume and picked up a headset, switching off the speaker.

"Marine operator, marine operator, marine operator," he said into the microphone. A distant garble of voices reached his ears, but no one replied. Cat double-checked the frequency. He knew it by heart from calling from *Catbird.* "Marine operator, marine operator, marine operator," he said again. No voice came back.

Cat sat before the set for half an hour, sweating, calling and calling, with no response. He looked around the room for a list of other marine operators but found none. A hint of light began to show in the sky outside the window. He switched the frequency to 2182, the international emergency channel. "Mayday, Mayday, Mayday," he said into the microphone. "Does anybody read me?"

He released the key and waited. No response. The Atlantic must be full of merchant ships, who are supposed to monitor this frequency, he thought, but it's early morning, and nobody's listening. He tried again and again. Was the whole world asleep? It was getting to be daylight now.

Suddenly, someone walked past the window. Cat didn't see who; it had just been a shape. Then he heard the scrape of a key in a lock and a rattle as the front door of the building opened. There were footsteps on the marble floor of the foyer, then a voice caused Cat to jump. "Yo, there, you alive?"

"Yo," Cat called back. "All's well."

"I'll bring you some coffee as soon as it's made."

"Thanks," Cat replied.

The footsteps receded across the foyer and another door opened and closed. Cat knew he was all out of time. He had one other shot, he thought. He reached up and switched on the aircraft radio and tuned it to 121.5, the aircraft emergency frequency. "Mayday, Mayday, Mayday," he said into the microphone. He waited thirty seconds, then repeated the call. Suddenly, a voice, amazingly loud, leapt out at him.

"This is Avianca 401 to aircraft calling Mayday," a voice said in heavily accented English. "What is your position?"

Cat's heart leapt. "I am on the ground approximately one hundred and forty-five nautical miles northeast of Leticia VOR, on approximately the zero one zero radial. Do you read?"

"I read one four five nautical from Leticia, zero one zero radial. Is that correct?"

"Affirmative."

"What is your trouble? Have you crashed?"

"Yes, I have crashed, but I and my party of three are alive. Can you transmit a message to Bogotá for me?"

"Affirmative. We are en route from Buenos Aires to Bogotá, arriving in one hour fifty minutes." The voice was growing weaker. It was obviously a jet travelling fast.

"Can you transmit to Bogotá?"

"Affirmative. I will ask for a search."

"No, listen. I do not need a search. Instead, ask Bogotá to telephone the American

Embassy and ask for the duty officer. Do you read?"

"Your transmission is broken now. You say call the American Embassy?"

"Affirmative," Cat said, speaking as rapidly as he could. "Tell them to contact Barry Hedger, that's Hotel, Echo, Delta, Golf, Echo, Romeo. Do you read?"

"I didn't get that. Spell again, please."

Cat spelled again, desperate for the man to get it right. "Tell them to contact Hedger wherever he is — repeat, wherever he is, and give him that position. Extreme emergency. My name is Cat. Charlie, Alpha, Tango. Do you read?"

A garbled voice answered. Cat could only get about every fourth word.

"I will leave my key open on 121.5 and 2182," Cat said, praying the pilot could hear him. "Over and out."

Cat mopped his brow and looked for the duct tape. He taped down the microphone key on the aircraft radio, then did the same to the high-frequency set. He turned the volume all the way up on both sets, then switched on the Zenith again. An announcer was saying he was listening to the Voice of America. With another strip of tape, he fixed the two open microphones to the back of the Zenith, out of sight. Nobody would be able to use the emergency frequencies for a while, but anybody tuning them in would get a good Count Basie concert, and that would be enough for the Colombian troops to home in on, if they had the right equipment. God, there were so many ifs!

He went to the closet and checked on the radio operator. Still out, apparently. He arranged the bags better to hide him, then went into Vargas's office. He peeped into the foyer, then tiptoed across, his shoes in his hand. In the men's room, he went into the booth, sat down on the toilet lid, and wiped his face with a handkerchief. He checked his watch. Just after six. Less than an hour to wait.

37

"Hey!"

Cat jerked upright.

"You in there?"

Cat gulped. "Yeah. Gimme a few minutes."

"I put your coffee in there. Don't let it get cold. I gotta start breakfast for the morning shift."

"Thanks."

The man went away, but Cat was still nervous. He checked his watch: six-thirty. The sun was well up now; no one would question his being out. He slipped off his blazer and trousers and wrapped the shoulder pouch with his two passports and the holster and pistol in the jacket. He opened the door slightly to check the foyer. A man came in the front door and passed through, then all was quiet. Cat stepped into the foyer and walked to the front door. Then, dressed for tennis, with his other clothes bundled under an arm, he left the house and walked toward the tennis courts. Two guards in a golf cart drove past him and waved. He waved back, smiling.

Cat tried to think what might go wrong now. The radio operator's relief wouldn't arrive until eight. Even then, he might not be discovered, and the microphones might not be noticed, tucked behind the Zenith. Of course, all might be discovered any minute, but Cat had to base his judgments on what would most likely occur. Say eight. At eight the relief would probably, if not necessarily, discover the taped microphones and/or the operater and sound some sort of alarm. The pilot would be working on the helicopter by eight. All right, eight was the hour. Cat would have to be at the clearing with Jinx, Meg, and Prince before eight. He walked on.

No, why wait that long? When Prince and Jinx arrive, get them down to the clearing immediately. They'd be there when the pilot arrived. That was it; no waiting. He liked that better.

He arrived at the deserted tennis courts, found a racket and some balls, and started hitting against a backboard. Soon the sun was over the trees. It was going to be a hot day. He was already soaking wet by the time

Meg arrived, at ten minutes before seven. He joined her at the table in the little pavilion.

"What's happened?" she demanded.

"We're okay so far, I think," he replied. "Dell's got his money, and I managed to get a message off to a Colombian airliner. Trouble is, he was moving fast, and I'm not sure how much of it he got."

"Wasn't there somebody guarding the radio?"

"Yes, we . . . subdued him. I don't think he'll be discovered before eight. As soon as Prince and Jinx get here, I want to go straight to the helicopter and wait for the pilot."

"All right. I'm ready when you are."

There was the sound of a vehicle, and Cat looked up to see a jeep arriving with Prince at the wheel. He was alone.

"Uh-oh," Meg said.

"Easy, let's find out what's happening."

Prince swung down from the jeep and approached the court. "Good morning," he called out.

"Morning," Cat said. "Where's your partner?"

"She couldn't get herself out of bed. Too much to drink last night."

Cat shot a glance at Meg, who looked

worried.

"But that's okay. I wanted to play you some singles, anyway. We seem to be pretty evenly matched."

"I'm afraid you've disappointed my partner," Cat said.

"I do apologize," Prince said to Meg. "Maybe tomorrow. Lola doesn't usually drink so much. She's been upset about something, I think."

"I'm all warmed up," Cat said. "Why don't you hit a few against the backboard and let me catch my breath for a minute?"

"Okay." Prince took a racket and some balls and walked onto the court.

"Now what?" Meg asked.

"Let me think a minute," Cat said, flopping down in the chair beside her. He rubbed the towel through his hair, forcing himself to be calm. All hell was going to break loose around here in a little while, and he had to do something. "Go get her," he said quietly to Meg. "Their room is upstairs on the left. If there's a guard, say the Anaconda wants her right away. Get her into some tennis clothes and down here. Get in the jeep; I'll see you and bring Prince."

"Seems like the only thing to do," Meg replied.

"Ready when you are," Prince called from the court.

Cat got his racket and trotted out onto the court.

"Hey, you guys," Meg called from courtside, "if you're depriving me of a game, I'm depriving you of an audience. Get stuffed, both of you!" She got up and left the court.

Cat laughed and waved her off. He spun his racket, and Prince won the serve. "Want to hit a few first?" Cat asked.

"First serve in counts?"

"Fine. I'm ready."

Prince served a hot ace down the middle of the court.

"You're not kidding, today, huh?" Cat yelled.

Prince said nothing, but served another ace.

Cat took some deep breaths and tried to settle down. It was hard; he kept thinking of Meg and Jinx. Prince took the first game forty-love. They switched ends, and Cat served. Prince got a racket on it, but it went astray. Cat won the next game forty-fifteen.

The play got more and more serious, and Cat got more and more nervous. He began to get the feeling that there was more at stake for Prince than just the match. There certainly was for himself. He wanted to humiliate the man, but he was having trouble concentrating. Cat tried to empty his mind of everything but the tennis, but it didn't work. Meg had been gone how long — five minutes? Ten?

They played on for another ten minutes. Cat played for the corners, wanting to run Prince ragged, but the man was in good shape. Cat began to break up the play, hitting short chops when Prince expected line drives, even serving soft when Prince was laying back. Irritation began to show in Prince's face.

The set went to five-three, and Cat was at match point. He checked his watch: nearly seven-thirty. He looked up and saw Meg and Jinx coming, walking, still a couple of hundred yards away. They were in good time, Cat thought. We can still be at the helicopter well before eight in Prince's jeep. But he had another minute or so to play tennis.

Cat drew himself up and served a hot one straight at Prince. Prince got a racket on it, and the ball went high and short. Prince, stupidly, continued to the net. As Cat went for the ball, he knew what he was going to do. He got under the ball in mid-court and wound up for a slam as Prince waited, hapless and out of position, at the net. As the ball came down, Cat took a full backswing, and, ignoring the ball, threw his aluminum racket straight at Prince's head.

Prince caught it full in the face and went down with a short scream.

Cat jumped the net and walked toward him. Prince was on his knees, with his face in his hands, spitting blood and making angry noises. "I believe that's game, set, and match, you little bastard," Cat said. He kicked Prince hard in a kidney. Prince screamed again and rolled over. Cat kicked him again.

"I'll tell you something, Stan," Cat said, "this is the most fun I've ever had on a tennis court." Prince had struggled to one knee, and Cat hit him in the face as hard as he could. Prince went down like a sack of potatoes and lay, groaning, on the court.

"Easy, Cat," Meg called from the jeep. "We're going to need him."

Cat grabbed Prince by the ponytail and dragged him to the shelter of the pavilion. He got Prince to his feet and shoved him into a chair, struggling to control himself. All the anger and hatred of the man that he had suppressed was boiling up now, and he had to keep himself from killing him until he no longer needed him.

"Let's go, Cat!" Meg shouted.

Cat looked at his watch. The new man would be coming on duty in the radio room. Meg had taken a long time with Jinx. He threw a towel at the man. "Clean yourself up, Stan," he said, and reached for his clothes.

Prince dabbed at his ruined mouth with the towel. "I'm going to watch you die for this," he said. His anger was beginning to overwhelm his pain.

Cat slipped into the shoulder holster, got his jacket on, and drew the silenced pistol. "No, Stan," he said, "you're not going to get that chance. And before the day is over, you're going to wish you were back in the car-wash business." He drew the pistol and held it at his side.

"How do you know about that?" Prince demanded. "Who the hell are you?"

"My name is Catledge," Cat said. "Does that ring a bell?"

Prince looked bewildered for a moment. "But who . . ." he started to say, then stopped. The penny had dropped.

"That's right," Cat said, pointing at the jeep. "I'm her father."

Prince made to run, but Cat fired a shot into the court ahead of him, and he stopped. The pistol had made only a *pffft* noise.

"There are fourteen more in the clip," Cat

said. "I'd be happy to put them all into your head if you try that again. Do you believe me?"

Prince nodded.

"All right, let's get into the jeep," Cat said. "I'm right behind you."

Prince, still dabbing the towel at his face, walked to the jeep.

"Into the front passenger seat," Cat said. "Meg, you drive; Jinx, in the back with me."

Cat got into the back seat of the jeep, and Jinx climbed in beside him. She looked tired and out of sorts.

"Is it really you?" she asked, suspiciously.

"It's really me, kitten," Cat acknowledged. "Are you all right?" His voice was a little shaky.

Jinx drew back and slapped him hard across the face. "You sonofabitch!" she said. "Where the hell have you been?"

38

The windshield was down on the hood of the jeep, and the breeze felt good to Cat. "Just drive at a normal clip," he said to Meg. He had a tight grip on Prince's collar and he let it go. "If you move or say anything to anybody except what I tell you, I'll shoot you right through the back of the seat, do you understand?"

"Yes," Prince said, "but where the hell do you think you're going? There's nowhere to go but jungle."

"We're going out of here in your helicopter," Cat said. "Now shut up."

They drove up the path from the tennis courts toward the main house.

"Jinx, are you okay?" Cat asked again, uncertain, and not wanting to get slapped again.

"Oh, shut up," she said.

"Don't you know me?" he asked, bewildered.

"Of course I know you!" she said. "Where have you been all this time? Don't you know what's been going on?" She was clearly furious.

"Well, look, we had to find you first, you know —"

"Vargas!" Meg suddenly said.

Cat looked up, and as they approached the main house, he saw Vargas running out the door, waving them down. "Okay, Meg, stop, but be prepared to leave in a hurry." He yanked Prince's ponytail. "Handle him, or you'll die here and now." He lowered the gun between his legs.

They drew up next to Vargas, who was waving excitedly. "Anaconda," he said, breathlessly, "something is wrong. The duty operator has disappeared, and someone has been tampering with the radios."

"Not right now," Prince said to him. "We'll talk about it later."

Then Vargas noticed Prince's smashed mouth. "What has happened? What . . ." He was looking from Prince to Cat, then he was looking down between Cat's legs.

Cat raised the pistol and, keeping it low, pointed it at him. "Get in the jeep," he said to Vargas, sliding over and pulling Jinx with him to make room in the back seat.

Vargas stood frozen to the spot. He looked

at Prince.

"Do as he says," Prince said.

Vargas climbed into the back seat, and Meg drove on toward the clearing.

"What is happening?" Vargas wanted to know.

"Just shut up and sit still, Vargas," Cat said, looking around. There was no one else in sight. Meg drove the jeep down the jungle track toward the clearing. In the distance, Cat could see the helicopter. He began to feel something like hope.

As they made the clearing, Dell stumbled out of the bush, pushing a man ahead of him. "Our pilot came to work real early," he said, grinning and holding his pistol to the man's head.

"I'm glad to hear it," Cat said. "Prince, this is my son, Dell."

"Pleased to meet you," Dell grinned. He held up a canvas sack. "I hope you don't mind, but I've helped myself to five million bucks of yours. Actually, two million of it is mine and my dad's."

"Let's get out of here," Cat said.

Meg had stopped the jeep a dozen yards from the helicopter. As Cat started to get out, Vargas pushed him. Off balance, he fell sideways, landing on a shoulder and dropping the gun. He scrambled for the weapon, found it, then found Dell on the ground with him. As they both got to their feet, Cat saw the pilot running toward the helicopter, and Vargas with a hold on Jinx's wrist, dragging her away from the jeep, a gun in his other hand. The pilot reached the helicopter and grabbed something from inside. Cat had just recognized it as a gun when Dell fired three quick shots at the pilot.

One caught the pilot and spun him around, throwing him against the helicopter; another struck the door behind him, and another struck the fuel tank. The helicopter vanished in an orange bubble of flame, and the explosion knocked both Cat and Dell down again and sent all sorts of wreckage flying around them.

When Cat found his feet again, Prince had Vargas's gun and Jinx. "Get back to the house!" he shouted at Vargas. "Get some help down here!" Vargas began to run toward the house.

Cat shot him, catching him squarely between the shoulder blades. Vargas pitched forward onto the ground and did not move again.

"Hold it, goddamnit!" Prince screamed. "I'll blow her fucking head off unless you do as I say!"

Cat crouched behind the jeep trying to

get a grip on things. Meg crawled out from under the jeep, and he pushed her down, motioning her to stay there. Jinx started to struggle like a wildcat, clawing at Prince's arm, which was clamped around her neck, as he used her as a shield.

"No," Dell shouted, standing up and letting his pistol hang on his index finger. "Don't hurt her."

Jinx continued to struggle.

"Take me, instead," Dell said, stepping from behind the jeep and holding up the canvas bag. "I've got the money. I'll do what you say, just let her go."

Prince looked greedily at the bag. "Get over here!" he shouted at Dell. "Throw the gun away. Put the money on the jeep."

"No, don't do it, Dell!" Cat shouted. He stood with the gun held out before him, ready to shoot, if he got the chance. Jinx was still struggling to get free, and he thought Prince wanted to be rid of her. "He won't shoot Jinx; he knows I'll kill him."

But Dell tossed the canvas bag onto the hood of the jeep, threw the gun away, and walked toward Prince. When he drew near, Prince shoved the struggling Jinx aside and grabbed Dell, spinning him around. Dell stood perfectly still, his hands in the air.

"Get away from there, Jinx!" Cat shouted.

She ran around the jeep and threw herself down beside Meg.

"Throw your gun down and walk over here with your hands on your head, all of you, or I'll shoot the boy!" Prince shouted.

"Do it, Daddy!" Jinx cried. "He'll kill Dell!"

"No he won't!" Cat shot back.

"Looks like we've got a stand-off," Meg said quietly.

"Dad, listen to me," Dell said. "Take Jinx and get out of here! Please," he said, "do it!" Everyone stood still where he was for a moment. No one spoke.

Cat looked around him desperately. The helicopter was still burning, sending up a column of black smoke. That would guide the Colombian troops in, but it would bring guards down from the main house, too. He had to move. He made a decision, the hardest one he had ever been faced with. "Meg," he said, as firmly as he could, "you and Jinx run over to that airplane and get the camouflage net off it. Get it completely out of the way, then get into the airplane. Do it right now."

"No!" Jinx said. "Stan will shoot Dell!"

"No, he won't," Cat said. Not yet, anyway, he thought to himself. "Now get going, both of you!"

Meg grabbed Jinx and got her running toward the Maule. They had about thirty yards to cover. Cat crouched behind the jeep, and took careful aim at what he could see of Prince's head.

"Stop them, Catledge, or I'll shoot him!" Prince shouted.

"You do, and you're dead," Cat shouted back. He glanced over his shoulder. Meg and Jinx had reached the airplane and were tugging at the netting.

"Dell, break away from him and give me a shot!" Cat shouted. "He won't shoot you! Just drop!"

Dell shouted, "Run, Dad!" then threw his feet out and fell backward onto Prince.

Cat stood up, trying to get a shot, but Dell was on top of Prince, who had an arm around his neck and was trying to get the gun to Dell's head again.

"Get out of here, Dad! Get Jinx out!" Dell shouted again.

Cat stood frozen for a moment, his pistol pointed at the two struggling men, then he made his decision once again. He turned and ran toward the airplane.

When he got there Jinx was in the back seat, and Meg was in the right seat. He flung himself into the airplane, grabbed the key from the clipboard in the map pocket and, trembling, got it into the ignition switch. The same engine as his Cessna, the pilot had said. Cat shoved in the mixture, propeller, and carburetor controls and pulled on the primer. One, two, three, four strokes of the plunger. He flipped on the master switch, then looked back toward the jeep, where he had left Dell and Prince. They were both standing now, fighting over the gun.

Cat turned the ignition key. The propeller turned a few times, then the engine caught and roared to life. Cat throttled back and looked again toward the jeep. Dell had started running toward the airplane, zigzagging, and Prince was on the ground, scrambling toward the gun.

He's going to make it, Cat thought. "Run, Dell!" he shouted. He opened his door and waved at him. "Come on, Dell, come on!" Jinx was yelling from the back seat, too.

Dell was only twenty yards from the airplane when he went down. Prince had regained his feet and fired. Cat couldn't tell where Dell had been hit, but he was getting to his feet again. Cat struggled with his seat belt; he had to help Dell. But then, Prince squatted, took careful aim, and fired again. Cat saw a pink cloud explode from the back of Dell's head.

"Nooooo!" Jinx screamed. Cat froze, looking at his dead son's crumpled body. Then he jerked, as Prince put another bullet through the side window of the airplane. Prince kept pulling the trigger, but nothing was happening. He was out of ammunition.

Cat shoved in the throttle and started to taxi wildly to the other end of the clearing, the airplane bumping over the rough ground. He had to get as long a ground roll as he could manage.

Dell is dead, Cat said to himself. Dell is dead, but Jinx is alive. I have Jinx.

At the edge of the clearing, he slammed on the left brake, and the airplane spun around. He stopped and looked at the controls. Twenty degrees of flaps, he said to himself, taking hold of the handle and pulling. No time for a run-up. Mixture rich, brakes on, full power. The little airplane shuddered as the revolutions climbed. Cat looked up and saw Prince climbing into the jeep.

The engine roared to full pitch, and Cat released the brakes. The airplane shot forward.

Prince had gotten the jeep started and rolling.

Cat pushed on the yoke, and the tail came off the ground.

Prince whipped the jeep around and pointed it directly at the airplane. They were rushing toward each other now.

Cat tried to watch the airspeed and Prince at the same time. The canvas sack of money was still on the jeep's hood, on top of the folded windshield.

He'll pull out of the way, Cat said to himself. He won't drive the thing into us. Thirty knots was showing on the airspeed indicator. It wasn't enough to fly; he needed forty.

Suddenly, inexplicably, Prince looked straight up. He was no longer watching the Maule. He would drive straight into the airplane. At almost the same moment, the ground a few yards to the right of the jeep exploded. The jeep and the airplane were only yards apart.

Cat yanked instinctively back on the yoke. The little aircraft came off the ground. There were two quick, dull jerks, something struck the airplane's windshield — Prince's head, Cat realized — and the windshield suddenly turned red. Hundred-dollar bills were plastered over nearly the whole area. The whole airplane began to vibrate wildly.

Cat glanced at the airspeed indicator. Only thirty-five knots. He pushed forward on the yoke to level the airplane, looking out the side window to orient himself. He had no idea how far the trees were ahead of him. The airspeed indicator hit forty knots. Cat yanked back the yoke and simultaneously pulled the handle back for full flaps. The airplane turned its nose to the sky, and Cat felt as if he were in some sort of lunar rocket.

But before they could gain much altitude, there was a hard jolt, and the airplane's nose came down again. Cat looked out the side window and was stunned at what he saw. The landing gear had hit a tree, pulling the nose down, and they were now, literally, skimming the treetops. Cat pulled the nose up, but immediately the airplane was jolted again.

"Cat!" Meg yelled. "We're being fired on by a helicopter!"

That was crazy, Cat thought. Prince's helicopter had exploded. Then he saw a shadow on the trees in front of him, and a huge, olive-drab helicopter with two rotors rushed past them and banked hard to the left. They were turning for another pass. Cat banked into a hard right turn, pulling on the yoke to stay out of the trees. He reduced flaps to pick up speed. The throttle was still wide open, and the airplane was vibrating so much that he thought it would come apart. The propeller must have been bent when it decapitated Prince, he thought.

He stayed low and turned sharply to the left, glancing over his shoulder at where the helicopter had been. It was right behind him. He got a glimpse of other helicopters back toward the clearing, sinking below the trees. Cat cut back to the right, nearly standing the little airplane on its wing. The moment he could straighten up, he turned left again and looked for the helicopter. It was flying in the opposite direction, back toward Prince's camp. He could see columns of smoke rising from the camp.

"The Colombian troops!" he shouted at Meg. "They found the place!"

He turned back to the right and glanced at the compass, bringing the airplane on a heading of due south. The blood had blown away from much of the windshield now, and although there were still a lot of hundred-dollar bills stuck to it, he could see reasonably well.

Cat eased back on the throttle. He had to get rid of some of the vibration, or the airplane would break up. He came back from full power to twenty inches of manifold pressure. There was still vibration, but it was not nearly so bad.

"Where are we going?" Meg asked.

"We can't go back there," Cat said. "They don't know who's in the airplane. They'll blow us out of the sky. I'm going to make for the Amazon. It's the only place to go — there's nothing but jungle for hundreds of miles."

He got the airplane trimmed and as settled as he could, then looked at the fuel gauges: less than a quarter of each tank. How far was it to the Amazon? A hundred and forty-five nautical miles, he estimated. They were flying at about a hundred and ten knots. A little more than an hour. He eased back on the yoke and gained some altitude, taking the airplane up to a thousand feet or so. He didn't want to be high enough to attract the attention of another Colombian army helicopter, but he wanted some gliding room if the fuel ran out.

By simply flying south, he would come to the river, eventually. He thought that was better than trying to aim for Leticia, which lay south and slightly west — he might miss it. He would find the river, then turn right and fly along it until he came to the town. Simple enough, if the fuel held out. If it didn't, he was going to have to put this airplane down, and there didn't seem to be anyplace to put it except into the treetops.

"I managed this," Meg said, holding up

the canvas-and-leather grip.

Cat laughed aloud. "Terrific! We may need some travelling expenses!"

Jinx looked at them both as if they were crazy. "Daddy," she said, "when did you learn to fly an airplane?"

Cat looked back at her and laughed. "I'll tell you all about it later, kiddo! Right now, both of you get your seat belts on. We may not have enough fuel." They did as they were told.

Cat relaxed a little, but not much. He still couldn't believe they were alive, and they weren't out of it yet. He thought about Dell and a lump gathered in his throat. He wondered what it would have been like if he had made it out. Would it have been different? Better? He would never know. He thought about Bluey Holland. He would have to explain about Bluey and his daughter to Jinx. The man had died trying to find her. He thought about Meg, sitting beside him. He'd have to figure that out later.

Cat glanced at his watch. They had been flying an hour and seven minutes. He strained his eyes ahead and thought he saw a brown streak across the jungle. The engine coughed. Straight and level, he told himself, straight and level. Get the most out of the fuel. The engine coughed again. They were not going to make Leticia, but they might make the river. The brown streak was wider now. It was out there. Eight, nine miles, maybe? The engine stopped, then started again. He checked the altimeter: a thousand feet. What was the glide ratio? Two miles for every thousand feet of altitude? That was for the Cessna, but the Maule had fixed landing gear, creating more drag. Surely, it wouldn't glide as far.

He turned to the two women. "Listen, we're almost out of fuel. I'm going to try for the river, and if we make it, we'll have to ditch. The airplane will probably turn upside down when the landing gear hits, so tighten your seat belts. Since the tanks are about empty, the airplane should float, at least for a little while. Wait until we stop moving, then unbuckle and get the hell out, okay?"

Meg and Jinx nodded.

Cat looked at the river; it was only a couple of miles now. They might make it. As he thought that, the engine coughed and died. Cat held back the yoke and let the airspeed bleed away. Best glide speed for the Cessna was eighty knots, probably a little slower for the Maule. He looked at the river and saw what seemed to be a little passenger steamer headed upstream, toward

Leticia. He pointed the airplane at it.

When they crossed the riverbank, he still had a hundred feet of altitude. He made a right turn and aimed the gliding airplane upstream. They shot past the steamer, a couple of hundred yards to his left. The river seemed about five miles wide here. He glanced around at Meg and Jinx. Both were staring, wide-eyed, at the brown water ahead, rushing up to meet them.

Cat grabbed the handle and put in twenty degrees of flaps. The airplane floated a little and slowed down. When they were twenty feet off the water, he put in the full flaps, then put both hands on the yoke. The stall speed must be something like thirty-five or forty knots, he reckoned. He held the nose up, bleeding off speed; until the stall warning horn went off. He let the airplane down from there, keeping the horn going, right on the edge of a stall. When they were almost skimming the water, he brought the yoke back into his lap. The nose came up slightly, and he felt the airplane's tail bump the water.

A second later, the airplane's nose dropped, and the world turned upside down with a wrenching jolt. Suddenly, all Cat could hear was the sound of rushing water.

"Is everybody okay?"

He got two positive answers. Bracing a hand against the ceiling of the airplane, he got his seat belt undone, then helped Jinx with hers. Meg was already free and opening a door. The high-winged airplane was floating, high and dry. Cat helped Jinx out Meg's door, then grabbed the canvas-and-leather grip and went out his side.

They stood on the airplane's wings and looked around them. They were drifting with the current, the trees on shore a hundred yards away moving past them. Cat looked upstream and saw the steamer turning downstream toward them.

"Hey, Cat!" It was Jinx's voice. She sounded like her old self.

He looked across the inverted airplane's fuselage at her. They all looked ridiculous, he thought, standing on an upside-down airplane's wings in the middle of the Amazon river, dressed in tennis clothes. "What is it?" he called back to her.

"You could lose your license, you know, doing this to an airplane!"

Cat roared with laughter. "Are you kidding? *What license?*"

EPILOGUE

Cat was in the kitchen making a sandwich when the intercom rang. It was the security guard, down at the gate.

"There's a Mr. Drummond here, Mr. Catledge. Do you know him?"

"I know him," Cat said. "Send him up to the house."

He padded through the house in his bare feet, tossing his sweat socks at the washing machine along the way, and opened the front door.

It was Jim. He looked fresher than the last time Cat had seen him, in the hotel room in Washington. His suit was neatly pressed, and he was closely shaved. "Hi," he said.

"Come in, come in," Cat said, pumping the man's hand. "What a surprise! I'm delighted to see you!"

"I was changing planes at the airport," Jim said, "and I had a couple of hours layover. I just thought I'd look in on you.

I'm sorry I didn't call first."

"Don't worry about it, I'm glad you're here," Cat said, clapping him on the back. "Sorry about the guard — we've had a lot of press attention since Meg's piece ran on the *Today* show. Jinx and Meg are playing tennis. Let's go into the study and have a drink before we go down to them." He propelled Jim into the study and gave him a chair. "What'll you have?"

"I guess I've got time for a small scotch."

Cat made the drinks and flopped down onto the leather sofa. "You know," he said, "I thought I might never see you again, and I've got a lot to tell you."

"Your letter told me most of it, I guess. I just wanted to know how your girl is doing."

"Better and better," Cat said. "It was tough on her at first. I think I wrote you that when we found her, she was like another person — had, for all practical purposes, become another person, according to the shrink. She wouldn't speak English; she had just blocked out everything that had happened to her before she arrived in Cartagena."

"She's gotten past that, though?"

"Yeah, she started to come around when we still were in the jungle. After that, it was mostly a matter of time, I guess. She didn't want to leave the house, at first, after we got home. The shrink came here every day for nearly a month. She's a resilient girl, though, and she's pretty much her old self again. A bit more serious, maybe."

"I'm glad she's okay. Did you get your airplane back?"

"Yep, and my million bucks, too. We flew it back to Bogotá, and the air attaché at the embassy flew it home from there and got it through customs. I'm not quite sure what route the money took. It just arrived here one day in a registered package from Washington. I figured it was from you."

Jim laughed. "I only forwarded it. It was really from Barry Hedger. He said the Colombian chopper pilot who chased you was impressed with your flying."

Cat grinned. "I got my pilot's license, too. I'm working on my instrument rating now."

"Are you back at work yet?"

"I haven't figured out what I want to do about that. I'll probably just do some development work for the company as a consultant."

"Miss Greville is here, too, you say?"

"Yep, she's been here the whole time. She's been a big help to Jinx. They get along well."

"What's going to happen there?"

"I expect we'll probably get married before too long; we're just playing it by ear."

Jim shifted in his chair. "I had a look at her FBI file. There was a lot of Hoover-style garbage in it, nothing whatever of substance. It doesn't exist anymore; I shredded it myself. She's off the customs and immigration shit list, too. She won't get any more grief in airports."

"Thanks, Jim, I appreciate that — and everything else you've done. I never would have gotten to first base without you."

"Don't mention it. Glad to help."

"I haven't heard much about what happened in the jungle once we got out. We were in Bogotá only long enough to get a plane for the States."

"There was some shooting, but no organized resistance, since Prince and Vargas were dead. The Colombians shot the place up pretty good, killed a couple of dozen people. Most of the franchisees were rounded up. They're in Colombian prisons, now, and they won't see the light of day for a long time."

"Did they find the money?"

"In the nick of time. The soldiers were having a look around the place before putting the torch to it, and they heard somebody kicking on a wall in the radio room."

Cat laughed. "I know who that was. Dell and I put him there."

"There was more than seventy million dollars in that room," Drummond said. "That will fund a lot of drug busts in Colombia, and the Narcotics Assistance Unit won't have quite so many budgeting problems." He paused. "I'm sorry about your boy, Cat. If we'd known he was there, we'd have at least gotten his body out for you. I'm afraid he went into a mass grave with the others."

"It's all right," Cat said. "Katie's in the sea, Dell's in the jungle. Maybe it's better that Jinx and I don't have any graves to visit."

Drummond nodded and stood up. "Well, I'd better catch my plane."

"Can I drive you to the airport?"

"No, I rented a car."

Cat stood. "Well, before you go, you have to meet Jinx and Meg. Especially Jinx." He walked Drummond through the house and out onto the deck. They could see the two women playing on the court below.

Drummond stopped and put his hand on Cat's arm. "This is okay," he said.

"Don't you want to meet her?" Cat asked.

Drummond managed a smile. "If you

don't mind, I just wanted to have a look at her." He stood and watched Jinx for a moment, then turned and went into the house, rubbing his eyes.

Cat followed him to the door. "I'll never be able to thank you enough," he said.

Drummond's voice trembled. "The sight of her was enough," he said.

Cat watched from the door as Drummond went to his car and drove away. He went back into the house and walked out onto the deck, standing where Drummond had stood. The man had been right, he thought, watching Jinx serve the ball to Meg. The sight of her was enough.

ACKNOWLEDGMENTS

I had the help of many people in researching this book. Among them, I am particularly grateful to: Robert Coram, for sharing his knowledge of Colombia and his contacts with me; John Ford, for the same; Tom Susman, once again, for sharing his knowledge of Washington; Nancy Soververg, of Senator Edward Kennedy's office, for introductions to helpful people; Lee Peters, of the State Department, for his advice about Colombia and for introductions at the American Embassy in Bogotá; Dr. Jose M. Vergara-Castro, president of Asociación Colombiana de Aviación Civil General, for his kind assistance in finding and renting an airplane; Rodrigo V. Martinez Torres, for a superb tour of Cartegena, especially the Old City, and for sharing his knowledge, as a lawyer, of the Colombian drug trade; Maribel Porras Gil, for her services as copilot, radio operator, navigator, interpreter, liaison with the Colombian Police, and especially, for her good company; Candis Cunningham, Press Attaché at the American Embassy in Bogotá, for introductions, advice of all sorts, and for a lifetime supply of the best Colombian coffee; Morris Jacobs, Cultural Affairs Officer, and Teresa Bocanegra, adviser to the U.S. Ambassador on Colombian Law, for their advice; John Stallman, head of the Narcotics Assistance Unit in the Bogotá embassy, now in happy retirement in Florida, for a detailed look at the big picture of the Colombian drug trade; Maria Arango, for enlightening conversations about Colombian life; Lt. Col. David Mason, Air Attaché at the Bogotá embassy, for his advice about flying in Colombia; Bill, the Colombian-American taxi driver in Cali, for the grand tour and inside knowledge; Dan Spader, Sr., of Maule Air, Inc., for a hair-raising ride in a Maule Lunar Rocket; Gibson Amstutz, for his knowledge of drug-trade flying; and especially, Mark Sutherland, who was brave enough to fly all over Colombia with me, for his good company; and Agent Gregory Lee of the Drug Enforcement Agency, for information on how the Agency operates.

I am also most grateful to: my editor Laurie Lister, for her sharp eye and unerring ear, and her assistant, Scott Corngold, for keeping things moving; Michael Korda, for his enthusiasm; my agent, Mort Janklow, his associate, Anne Sibbald, and everyone at Morton Janklow Associates for their faith and hard work on my behalf.

While I received briefings and advice from many people in official positions, they cannot be held responsible for the accuracy of any statement in this novel, or for any view I may have formed and transmitted in the book. It is the responsibility of the novelist to be plausible, not accurate, and I have bent all sorts of information to my own uses in order to tell a story.

Finally, I must apologize to my friend Ben Fuller for borrowing his appearance for my most awful character.

AUTHOR'S NOTE

I am aware that *White Cargo* is also the name of a 1942 movie starring Hedy Lamarr and which seems to be chiefly remembered for her deathless line, "I am Tondelayo," which, as Pauline Kael says, "... served a generation of female impersonators." It was too good a title to pass up.

There has been a sad side to writing this book, in that things are as bad in Colombia as I have made them out to be — maybe worse — and they don't look like they're getting better. Colombia, a country of great natural beauty and kind and lovely people, is under a siege laid down by the drug dealers. One can only hope that the courage of the people and the government will endure until these vermin have been imprisoned or expelled, or until they have exterminated themselves.

I hope one day to return to a Colombia at peace with itself.

ABOUT THE AUTHOR

Stuart Woods is the New York Times bestselling author of twenty novels including *Worst Fears Realized*, *Orchid Beach*, *Swimming to Catalina*, and *Dead in the Water*. He lives on the Treasure Coast of Florida, on an island off the coast of Maine, and in Litchfield County, Connecticut.